Disney

Part of Your World

A *TWISTED TALE* GRAPHIC NOVEL

For everyone at the Mass Audubon Wellfleet Bay Wildlife Sanctuary—and all
who work to save our oceans —Liz

For Ezra, who recognizes (correctly) that Ursula is terrifying —Stephanie

Thanks to all our friends and family for their support;
we couldn't have done it without you! —Kelly and Nichole

Copyright © 2023 by Disney Enterprises, Inc.

All rights reserved. Published by Disney • Hyperion, an imprint of Buena Vista Books, Inc. No part of this
book may be reproduced or transmitted in any form or by any means, electronic or mechanical, including
photocopying, recording, or by any information storage and retrieval system, without written permission
from the publisher. For information address Disney • Hyperion, 77 West 66th Street, New York, New York
10023.

First Edition, June 2023
10 9 8 7 6 5 4 3 2 1
FAC-034274-23118
Printed in the United States of America

Designed by Marci Senders

Names: Strohm, Stephanie Kate, author. • Braswell, Liz. Part of your world. • Matthews, Kelly (Comic
book artist), illustrator. • Matthews, Nichole, illustrator. Title: Part of your world : a twisted tales graphic
novel / by Liz Braswell; adapted by Stephanie Kate Strohm ; illustrated by Kelly Matthews &
Nichole Matthews. Other titles: Little mermaid (Motion picture : 1989) Description: First edition. •
Los Angeles ; New York : Disney-Hyperion, 2022. • Series: A twisted tale • Audience: Ages 12–18. •
Audience: Grades 10–12. • Summary: Five years after the infamous sea witch defeated the little mermaid,
Ariel—now the voiceless queen of Atlantica—must confront Ursula to restore justice on both land and sea,
find her father, and reclaim Prince Eric's affections. Identifiers: LCCN 2021023467 • ISBN 9781368064095
(hardcover) • ISBN 9781368068185 (paperback) Subjects: CYAC: Graphic novels. • Kings, queens,
rulers, etc.—Fiction. • Mermaids—Fiction. • Witches—Fiction. • Adventure and adventurers—Fiction. •
Braswell, Liz. Part of your world—Adaptations.• LCGFT: Graphic novels.Classification: LCC PZ7.7.S788
Par 2022 • DDC 741.5/973—dc23 LC record available at https://lccn.loc.gov/2021023467

Reinforced binding
Visit www.DisneyBooks.com

Disney

Part of Your World

A *TWISTED TALE* GRAPHIC NOVEL

ADAPTED BY
STEPHANIE KATE
STROHM

ILLUSTRATED BY
KELLY MATTHEWS &
NICHOLE MATTHEWS

BASED ON THE *NEW YORK TIMES* BEST-SELLING NOVEL BY
LIZ BRASWELL

Disney • HYPERION
Los Angeles   New York

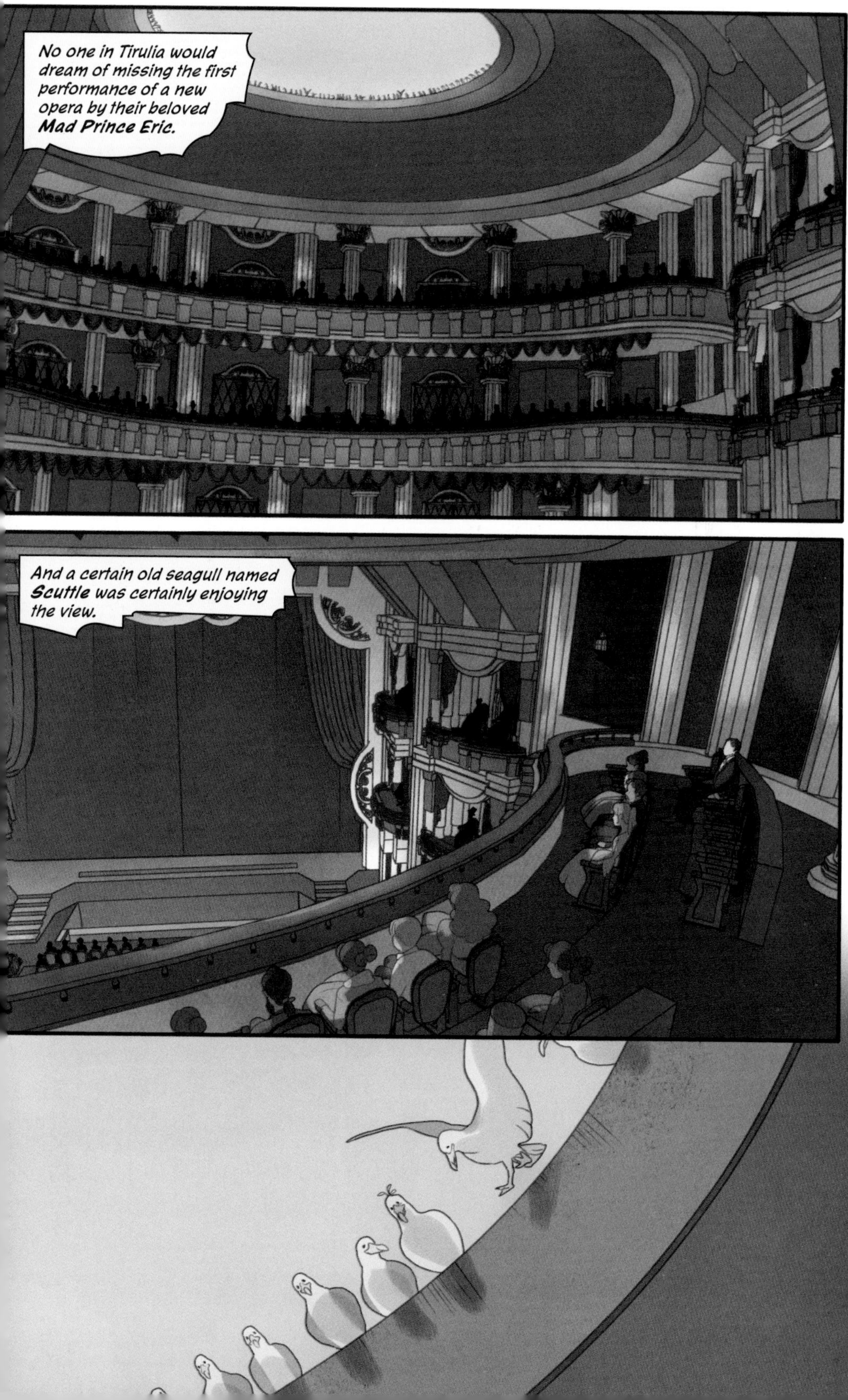
No one in Tirulia would dream of missing the first performance of a new opera by their beloved Mad Prince Eric.
And a certain old seagull named Scuttle was certainly enjoying the view.

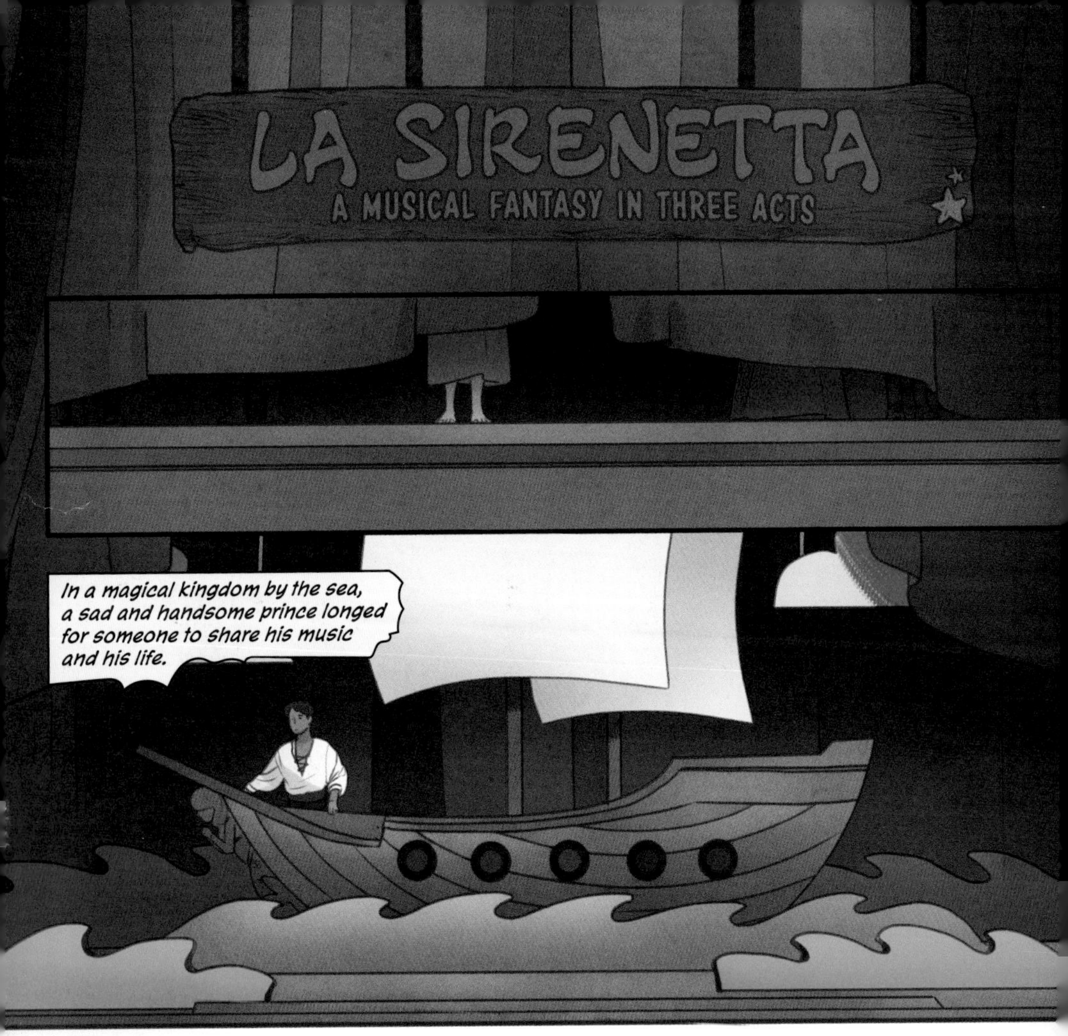
LA SIRENETTA
A MUSICAL FANTASY IN THREE ACTS
In a magical kingdom by the sea, a sad and handsome prince longed for someone to share his music and his life.

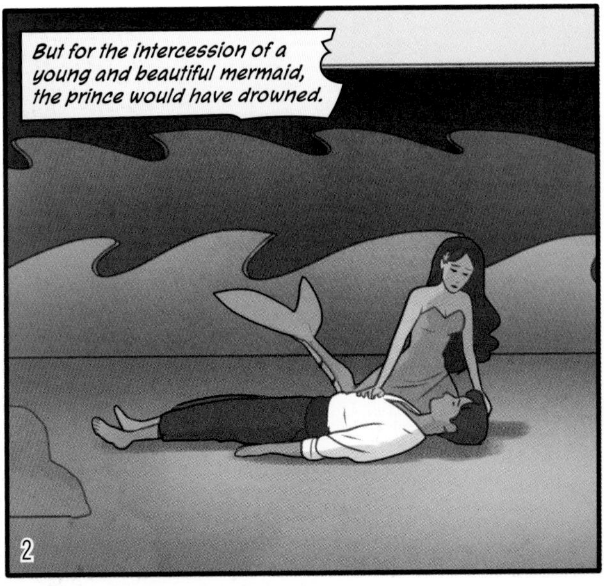
But for the intercession of a young and beautiful mermaid, the prince would have drowned.

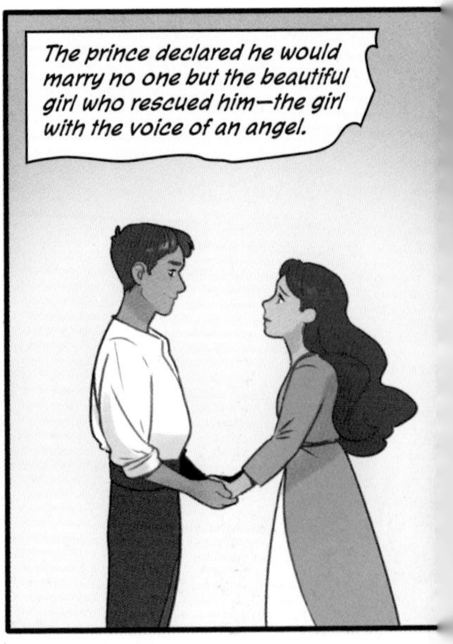
The prince declared he would marry no one but the beautiful girl who rescued him—the girl with the voice of an angel.

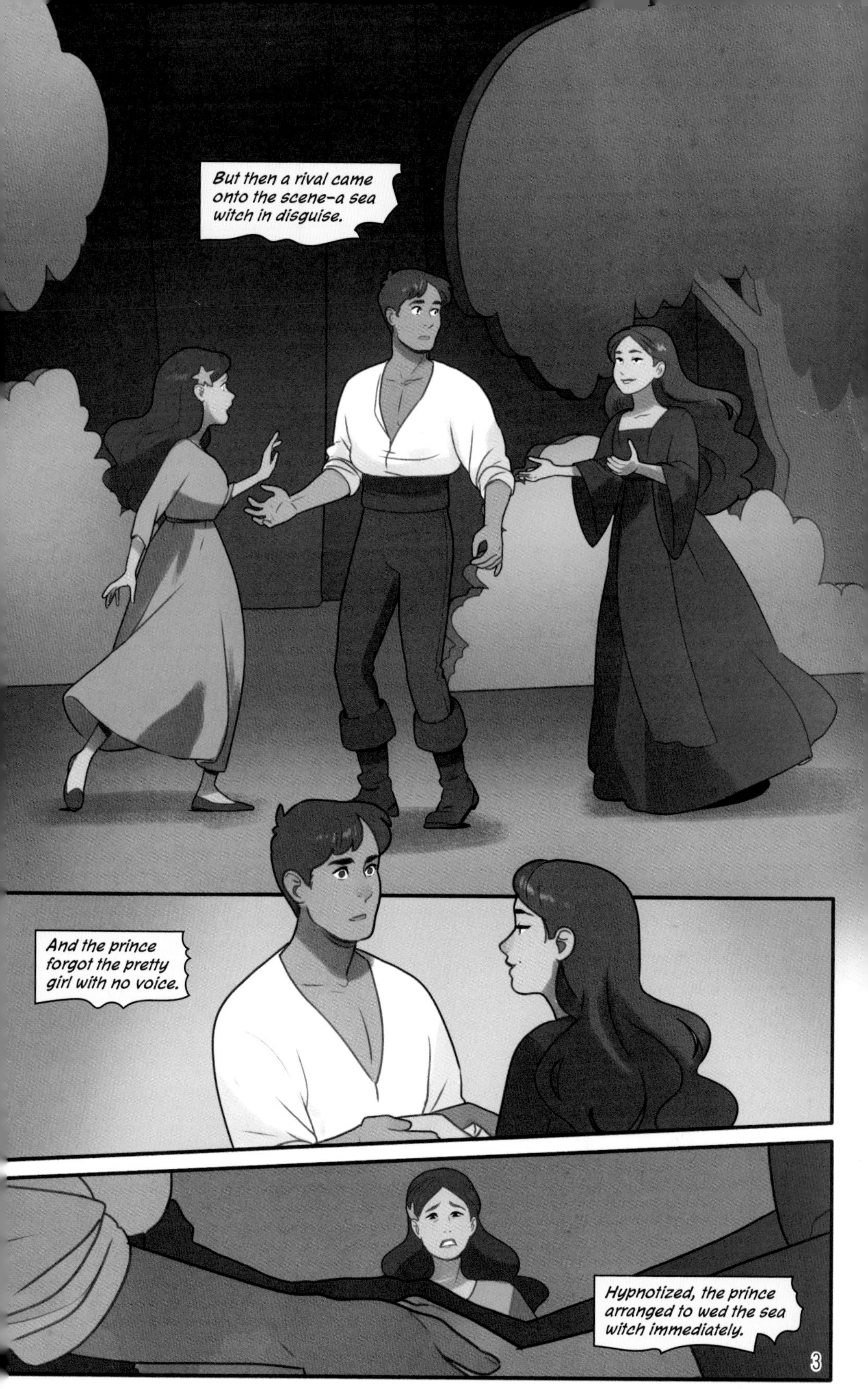
But then a rival came onto the scene–a sea witch in disguise.
And the prince forgot the pretty girl with no voice.
Hypnotized, the prince arranged to wed the sea witch immediately.

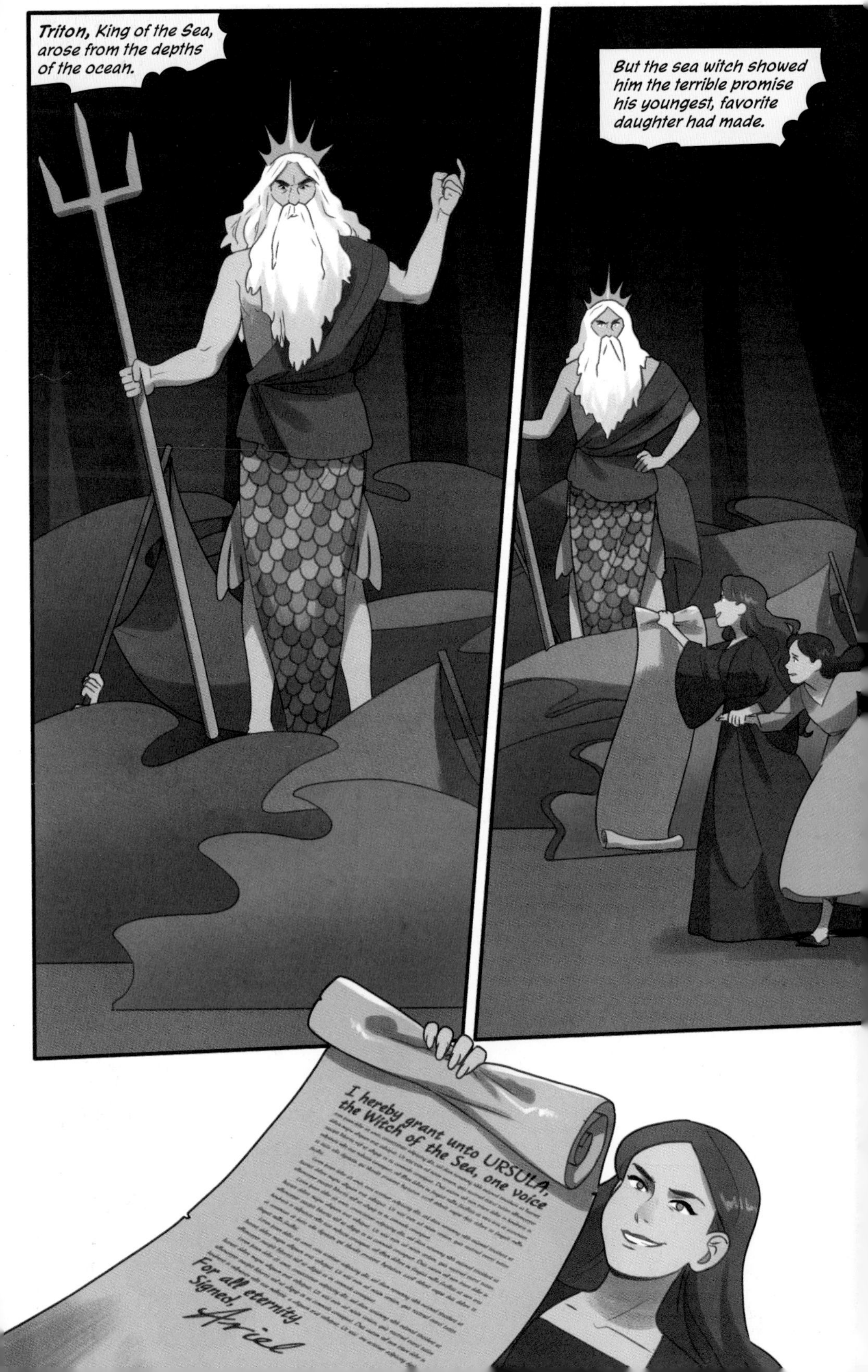
Triton, King of the Sea, arose from the depths of the ocean.
But the sea witch showed him the terrible promise his youngest, favorite daughter had made.
I hereby grant unto URSULA, the Witch of the Sea, one voice
For all eternity.
Signed,
Ariel

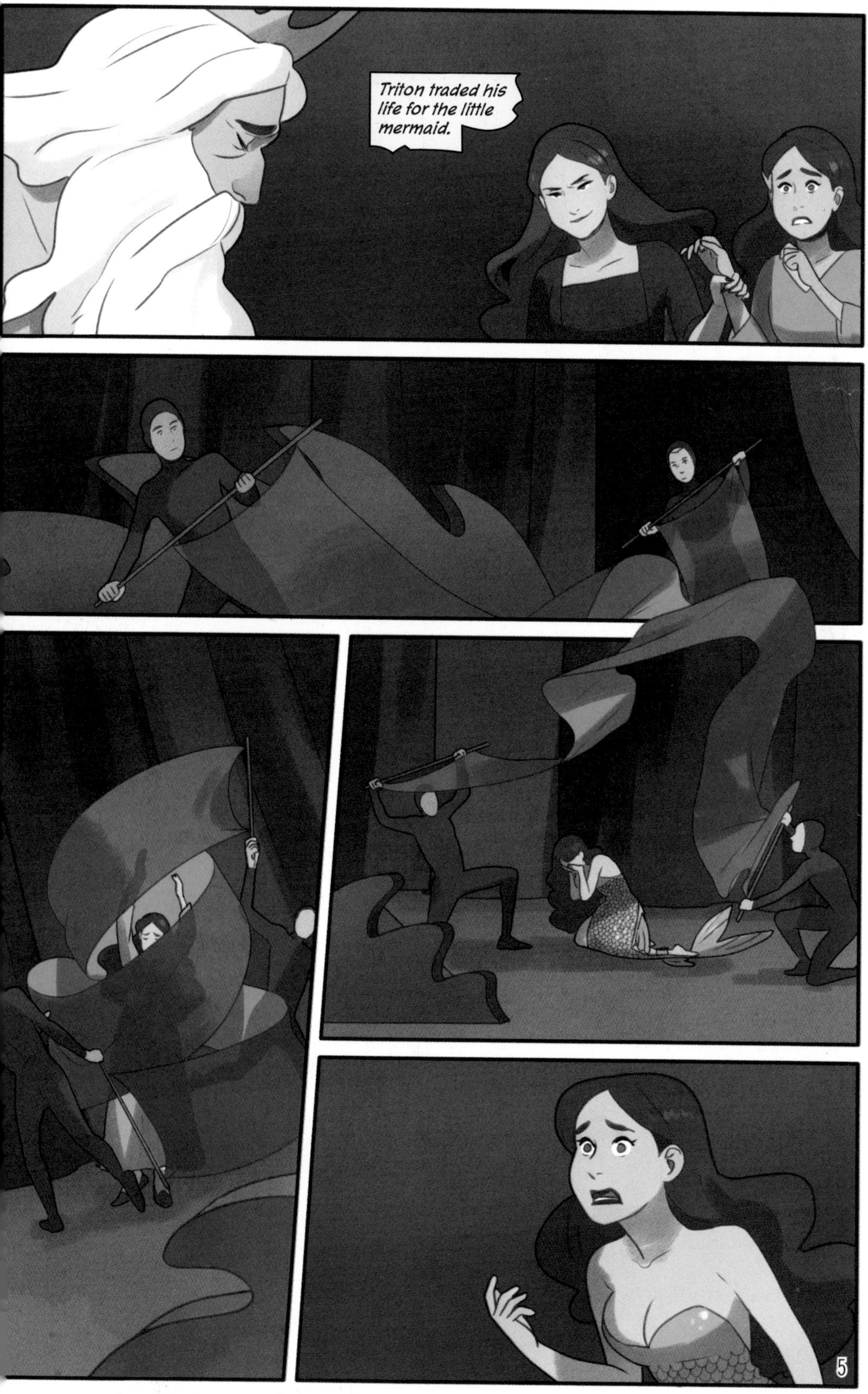
Triton traded his life for the little mermaid.

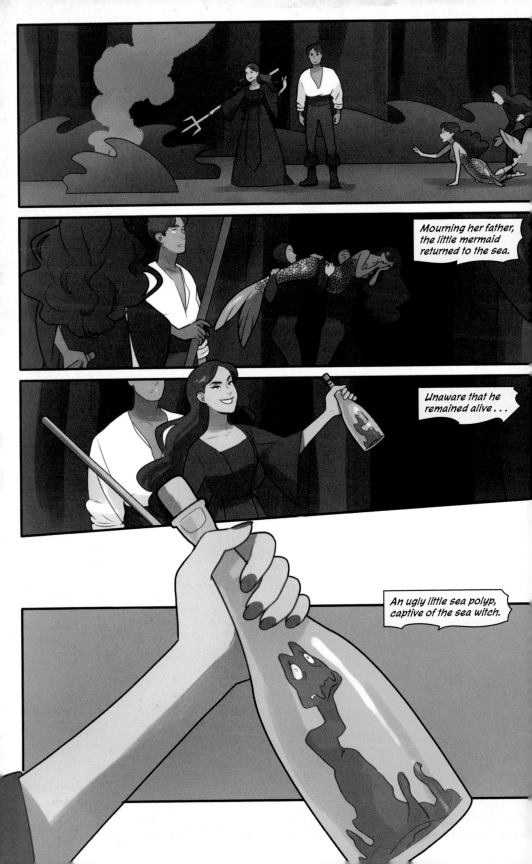

Mourning her father, the little mermaid returned to the sea.

Unaware that he remained alive...

An ugly little sea polyp, captive of the sea witch.

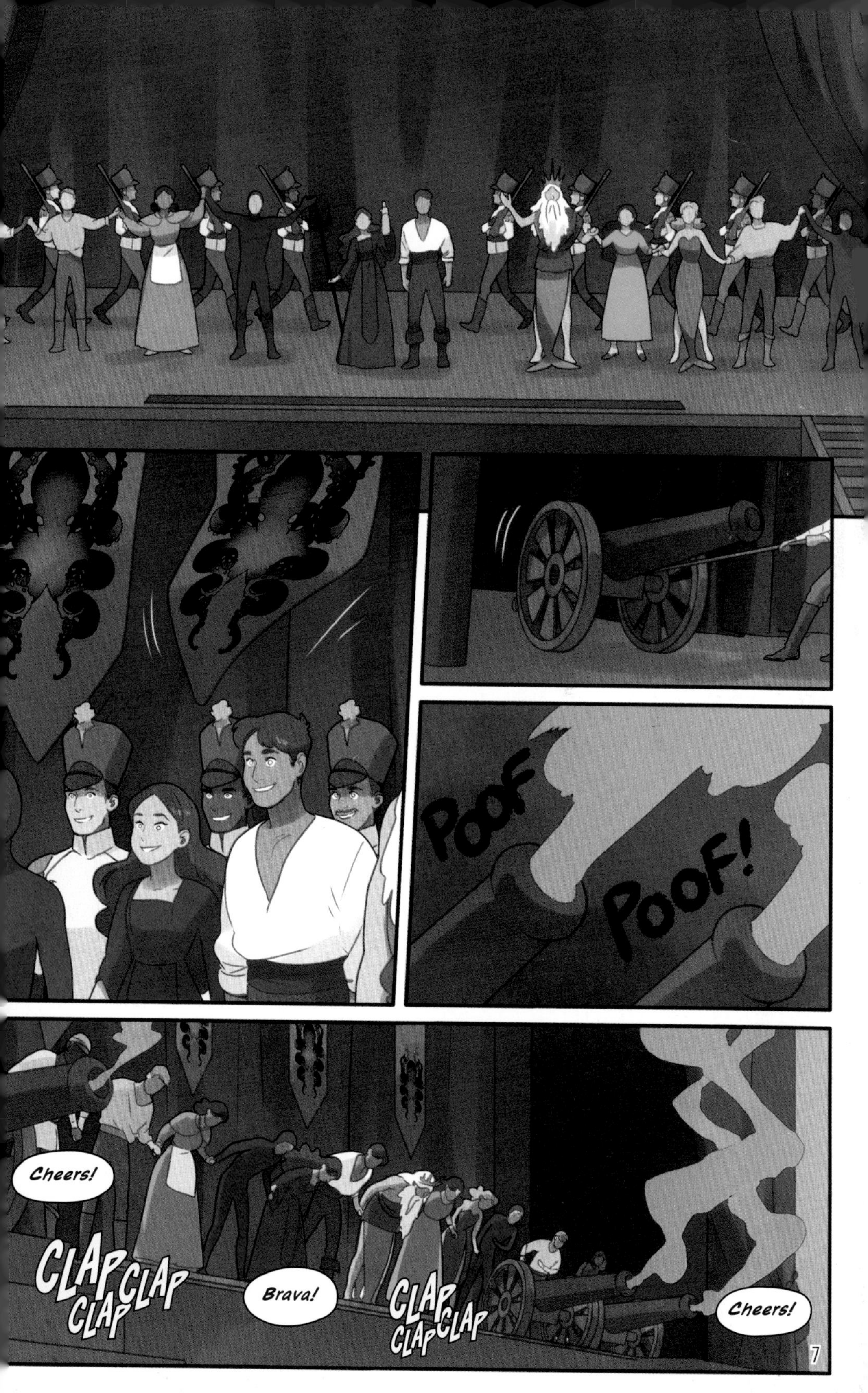

POOF
POOF!
Cheers!
CLAP CLAP CLAP
Brava!
CLAP CLAP CLAP
Cheers!

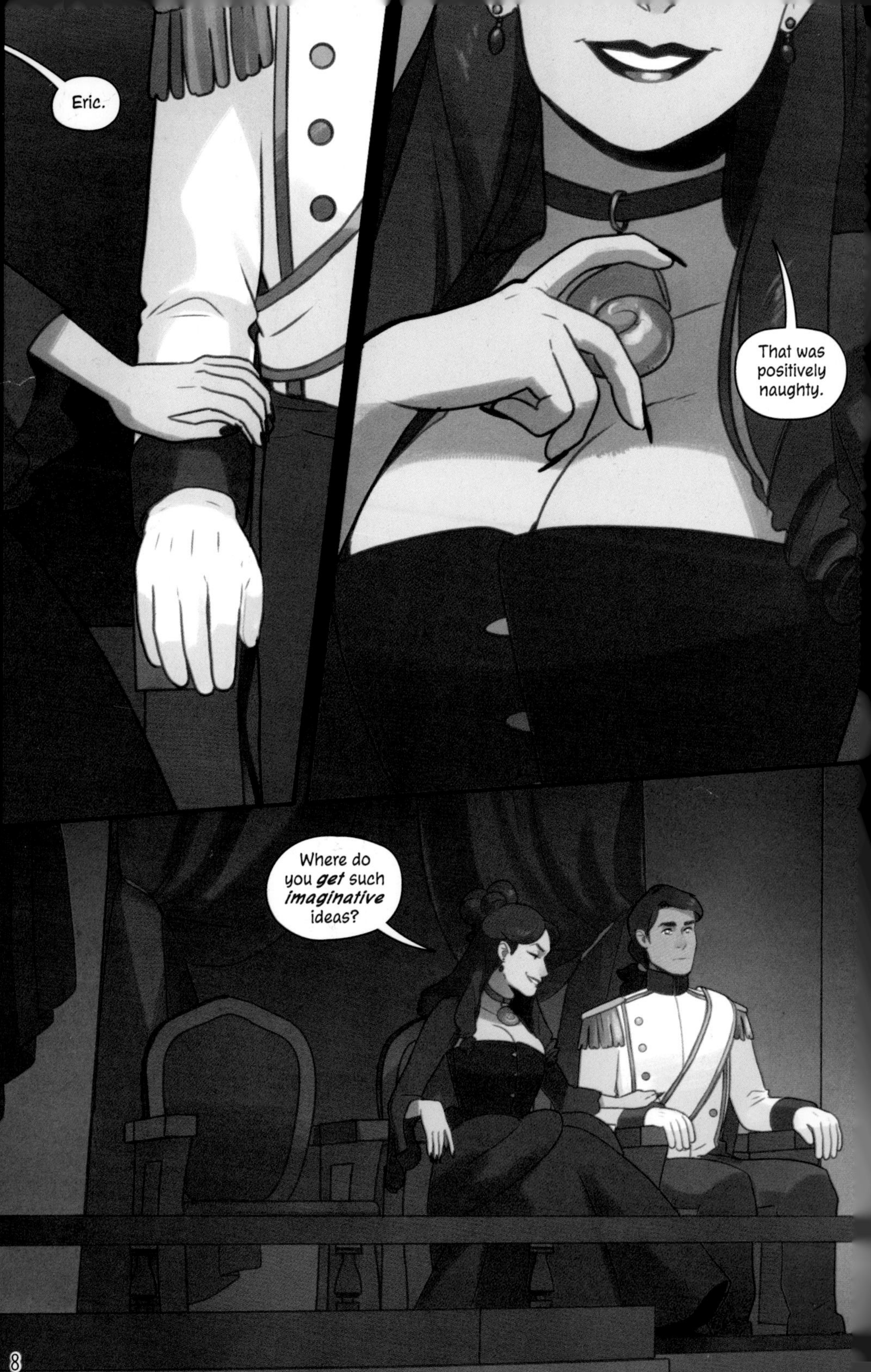
Eric.
That was positively naughty.
Where do you ***get*** such ***imaginative*** ideas?

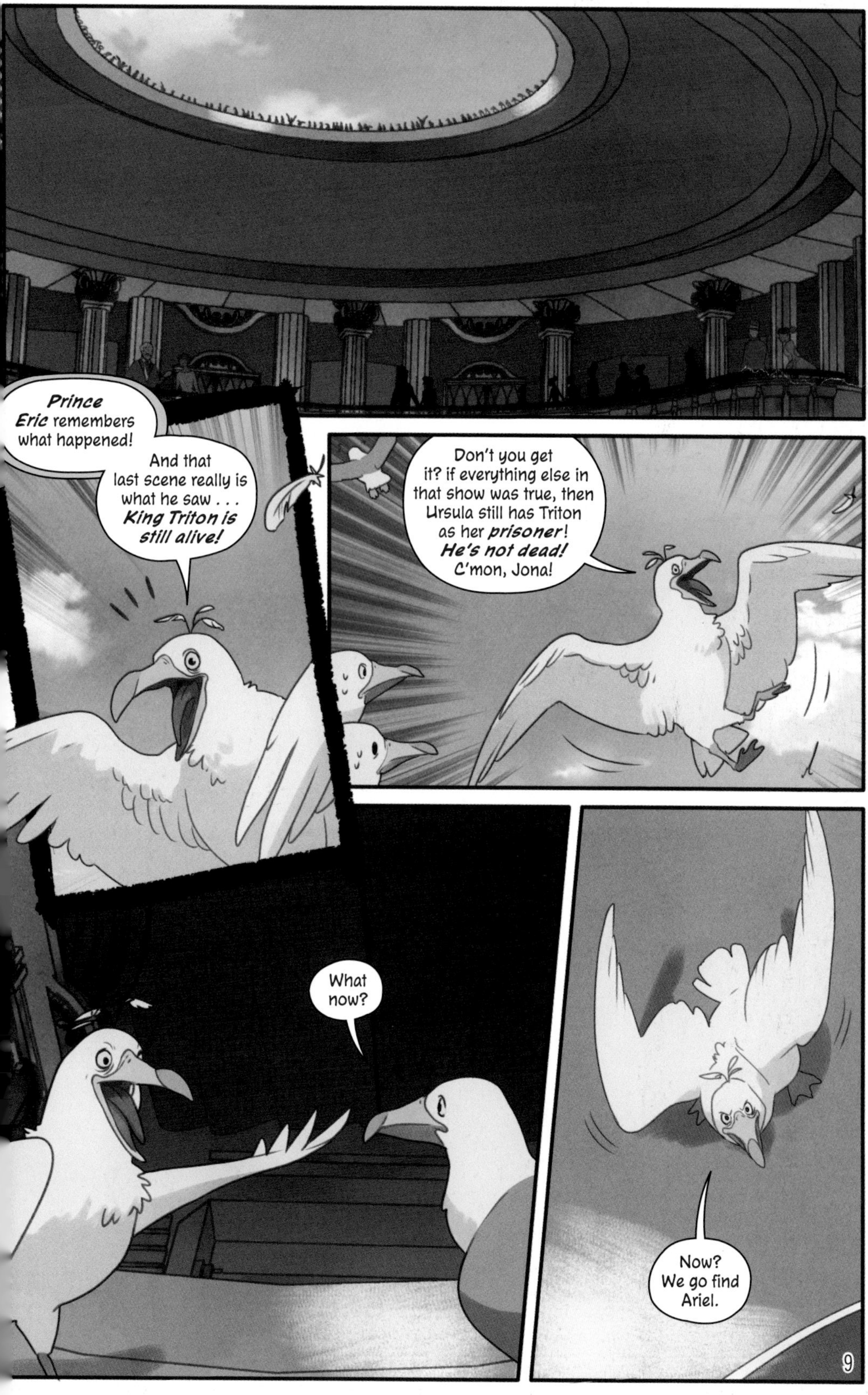

Prince Eric remembers what happened!
And that last scene really is what he saw . . . King Triton is still alive!
Don't you get it? if everything else in that show was true, then Ursula still has Triton as her prisoner! He's not dead! C'mon, Jona!
What now?
Now? We go find Ariel.

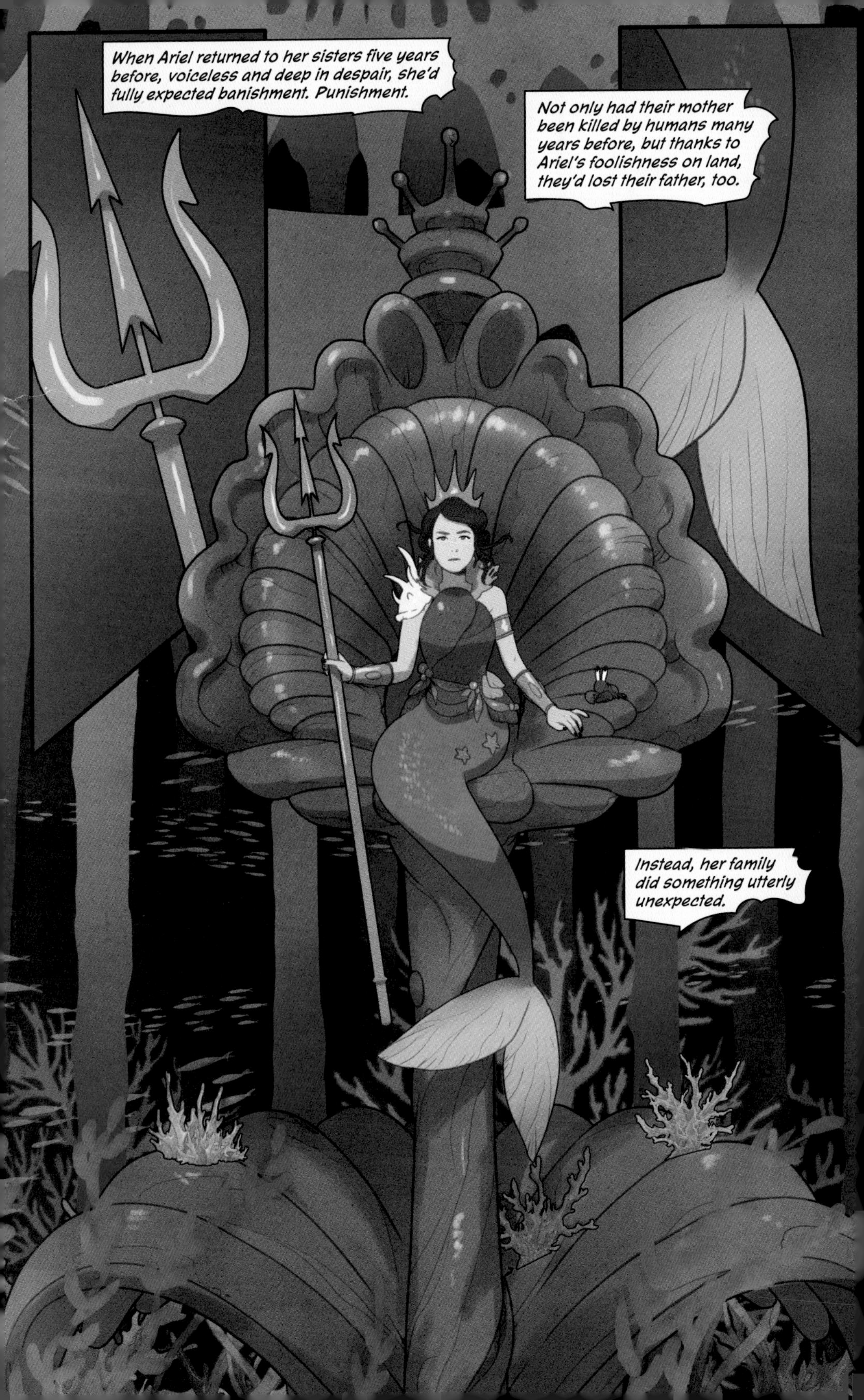
When Ariel returned to her sisters five years before, voiceless and deep in despair, she'd fully expected banishment. Punishment.
Not only had their mother been killed by humans many years before, but thanks to Ariel's foolishness on land, they'd lost their father, too.
Instead, her family did something utterly unexpected.

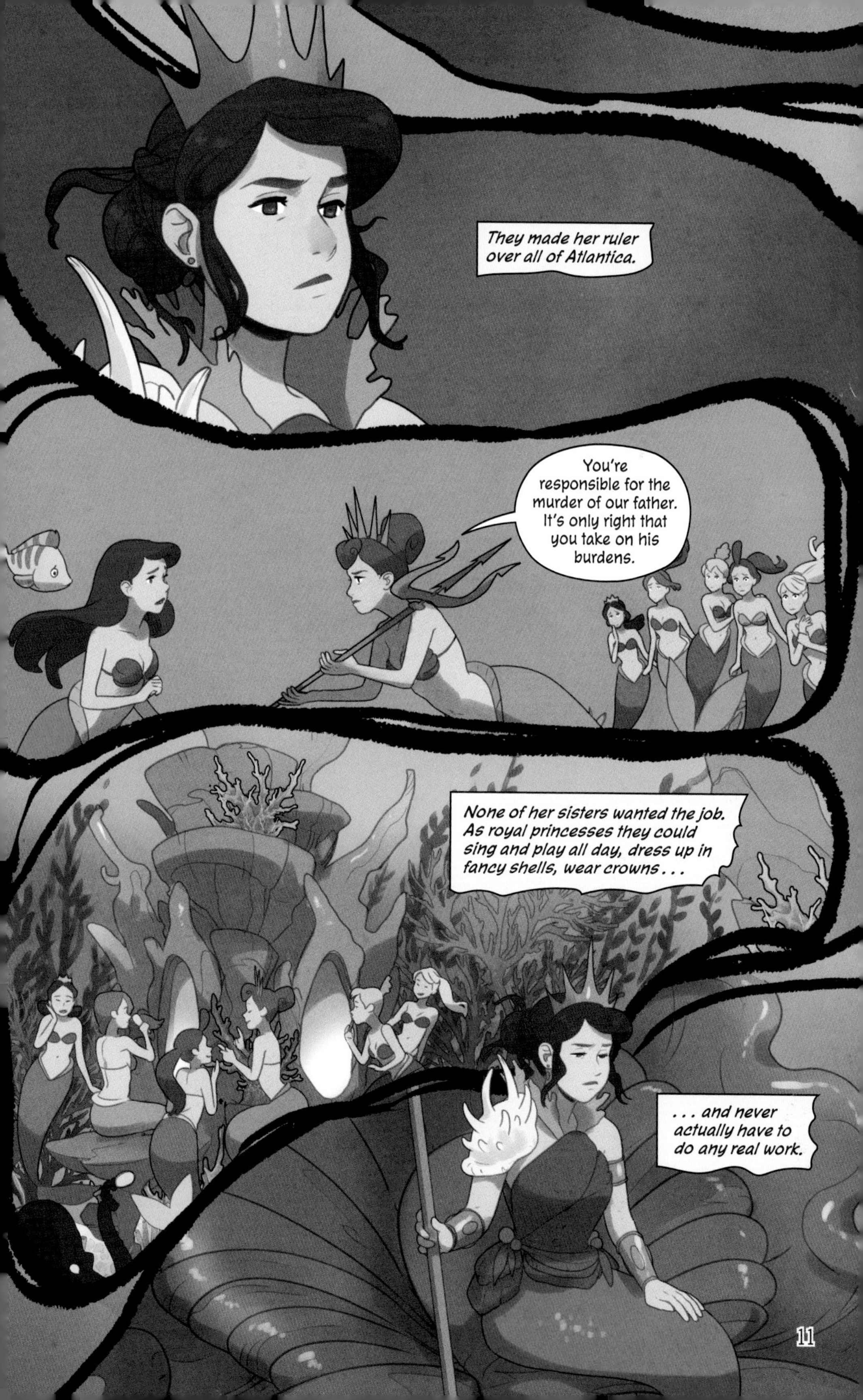
They made her ruler over all of Atlantica.
You're responsible for the murder of our father. It's only right that you take on his burdens.
None of her sisters wanted the job. As royal princesses they could sing and play all day, dress up in fancy shells, wear crowns . . .
. . . and never actually have to do any real work.

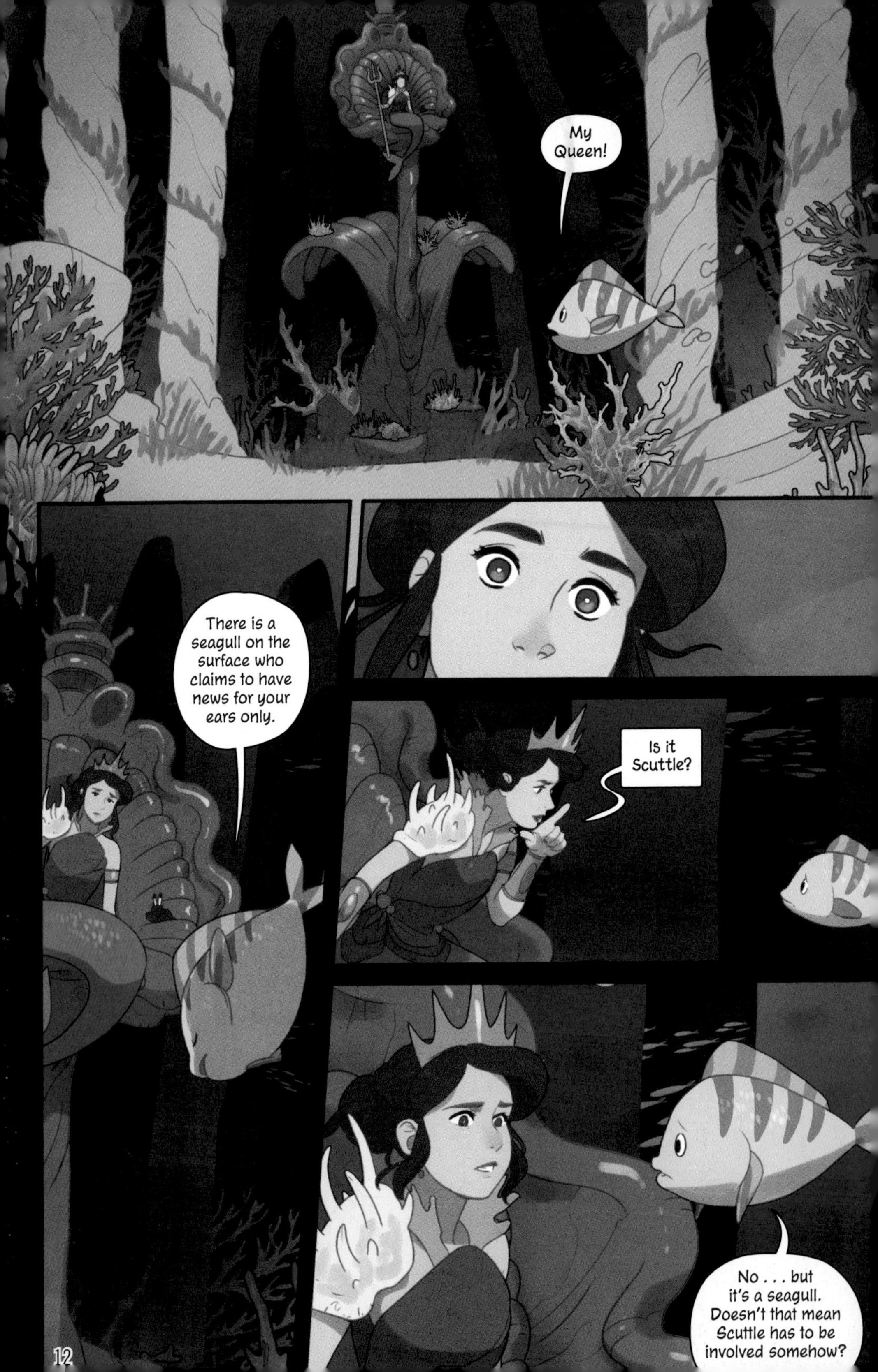
My Queen!
There is a seagull on the surface who claims to have news for your ears only.
Is it Scuttle?
No . . . but it's a seagull. Doesn't that mean Scuttle has to be involved somehow?

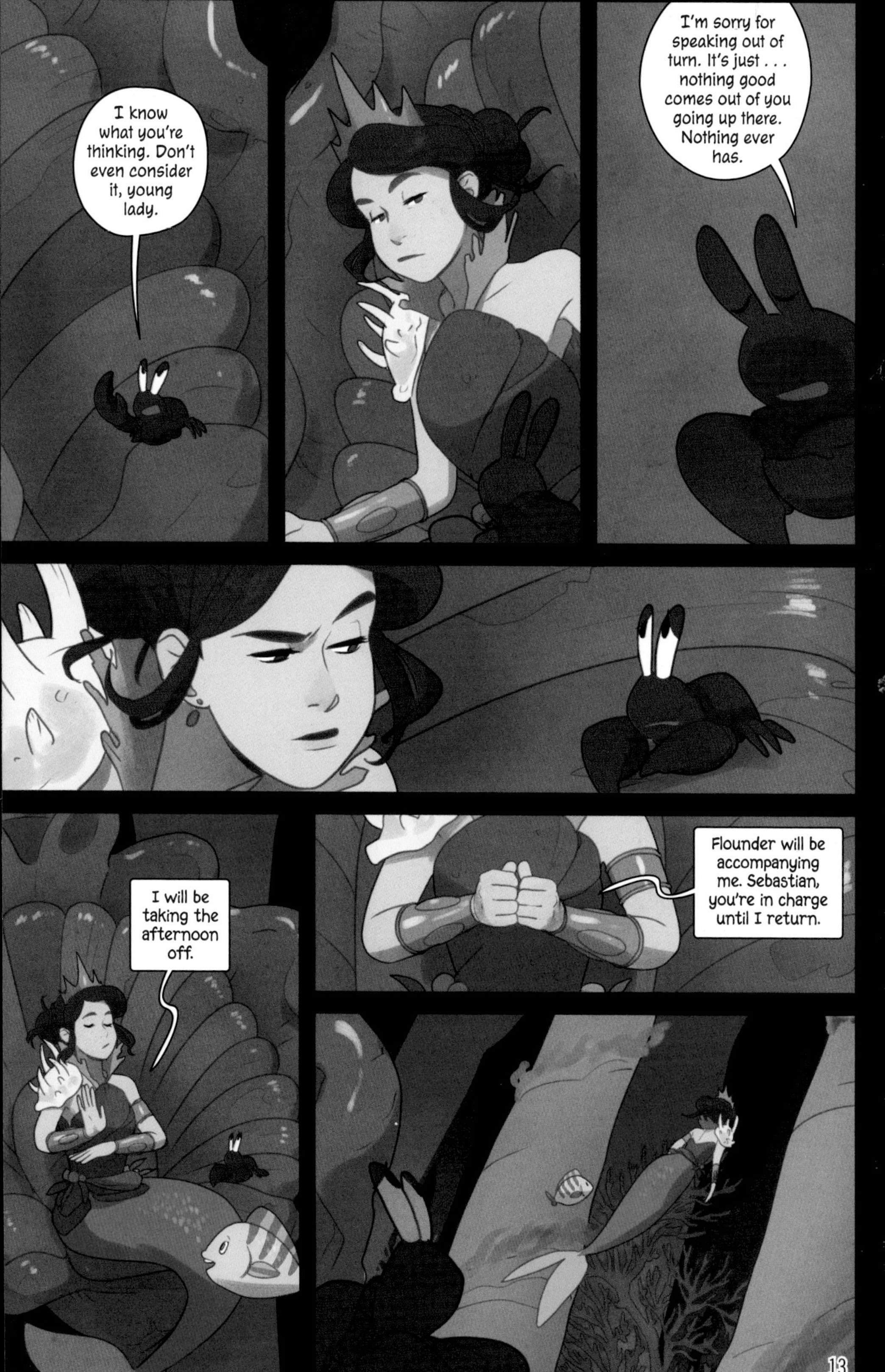

I know what you're thinking. Don't even consider it, young lady.
I'm sorry for speaking out of turn. It's just . . . nothing good comes out of you going up there. Nothing ever has.
I will be taking the afternoon off.
Flounder will be accompanying me. Sebastian, you're in charge until I return.

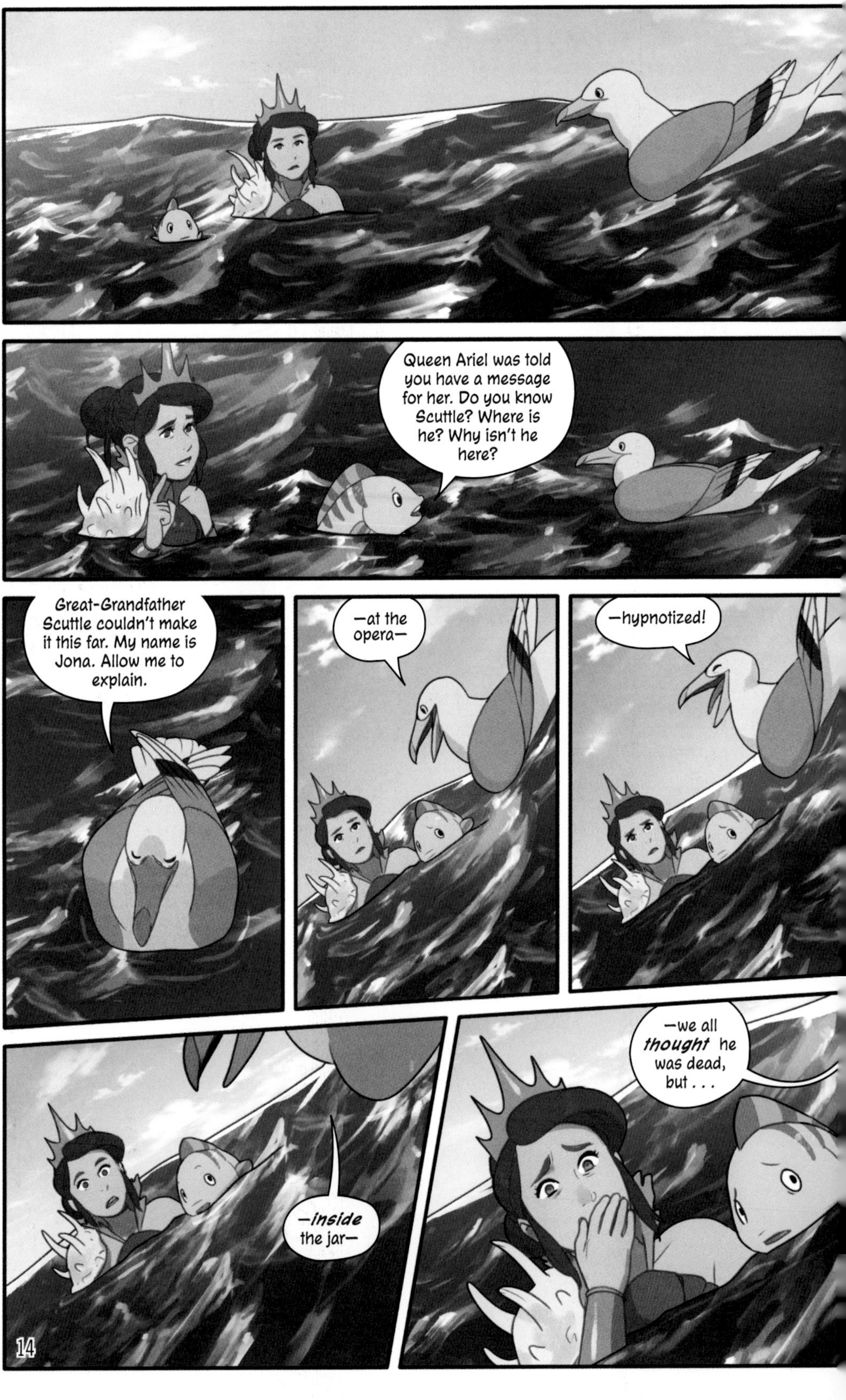
Queen Ariel was told you have a message for her. Do you know Scuttle? Where is he? Why isn't he here?
Great-Grandfather Scuttle couldn't make it this far. My name is Jona. Allow me to explain.
—at the opera—
—hypnotized!
—*inside* the jar—
—we all *thought* he was dead, but . . .

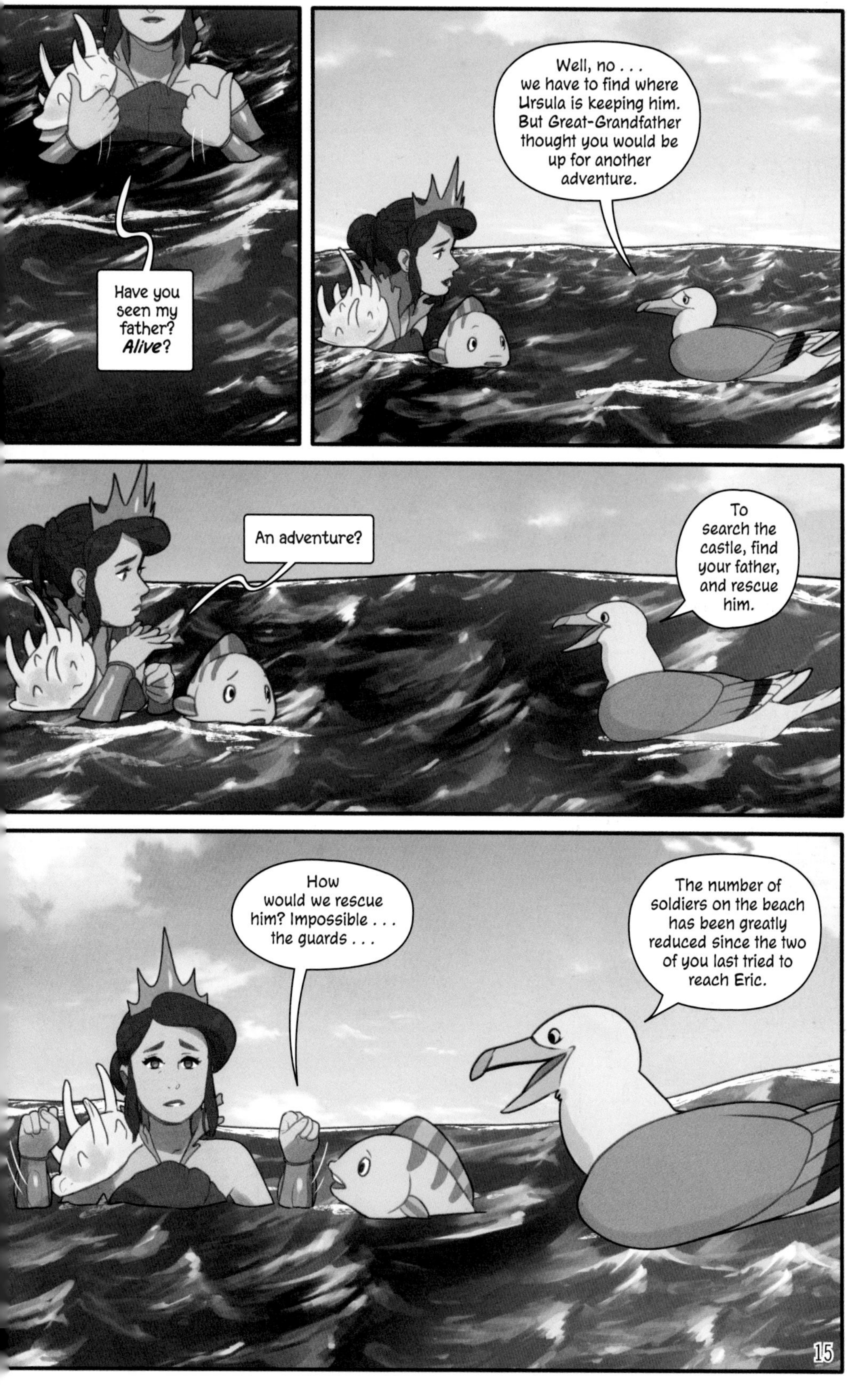
Have you seen my father? *Alive*?
Well, no . . . we have to find where Ursula is keeping him. But Great-Grandfather thought you would be up for another adventure.
An adventure?
To search the castle, find your father, and rescue him.
How would we rescue him? Impossible . . . the guards . . .
The number of soldiers on the beach has been greatly reduced since the two of you last tried to reach Eric.

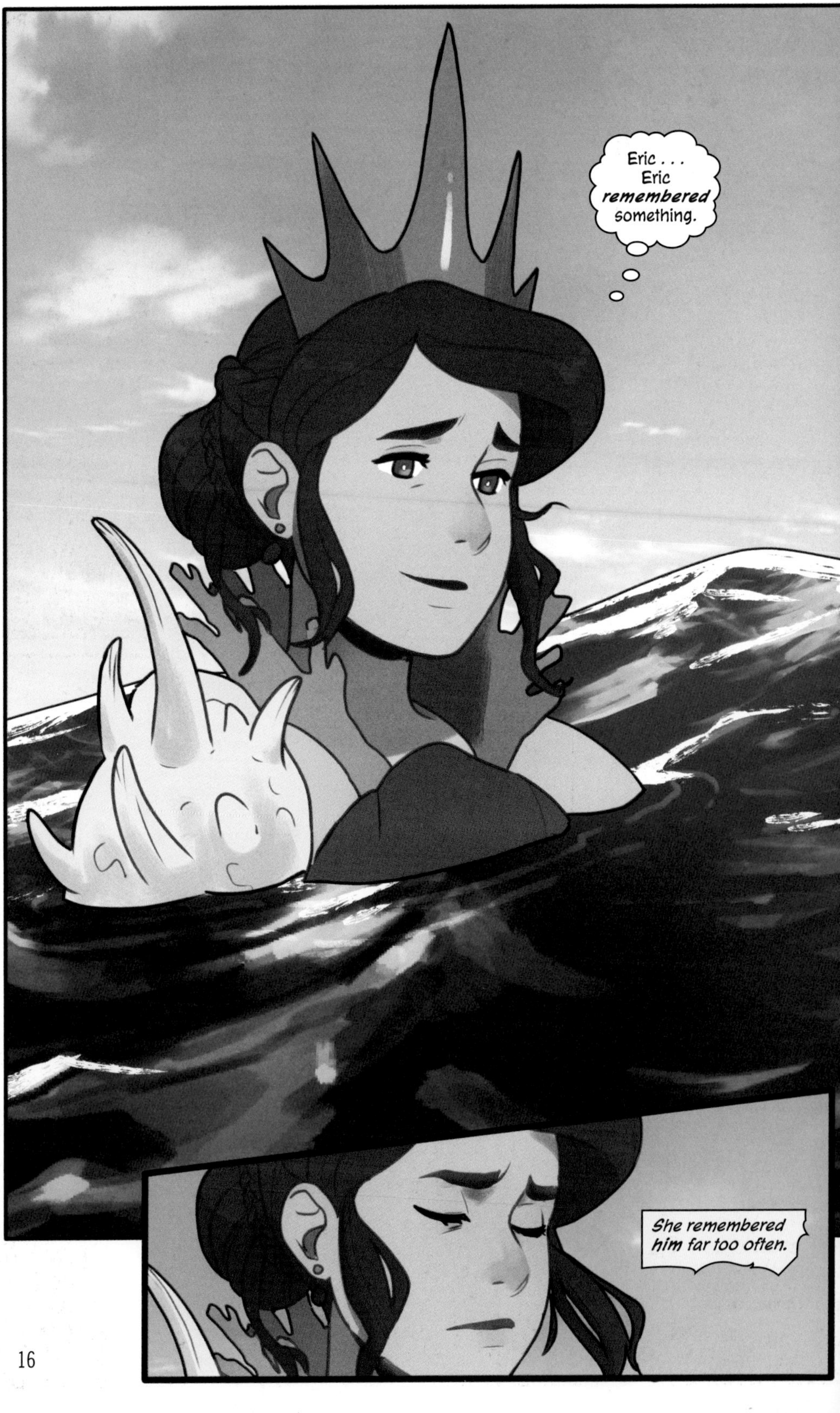

Eric . . . Eric *remembered* something.
She remembered him far too often.

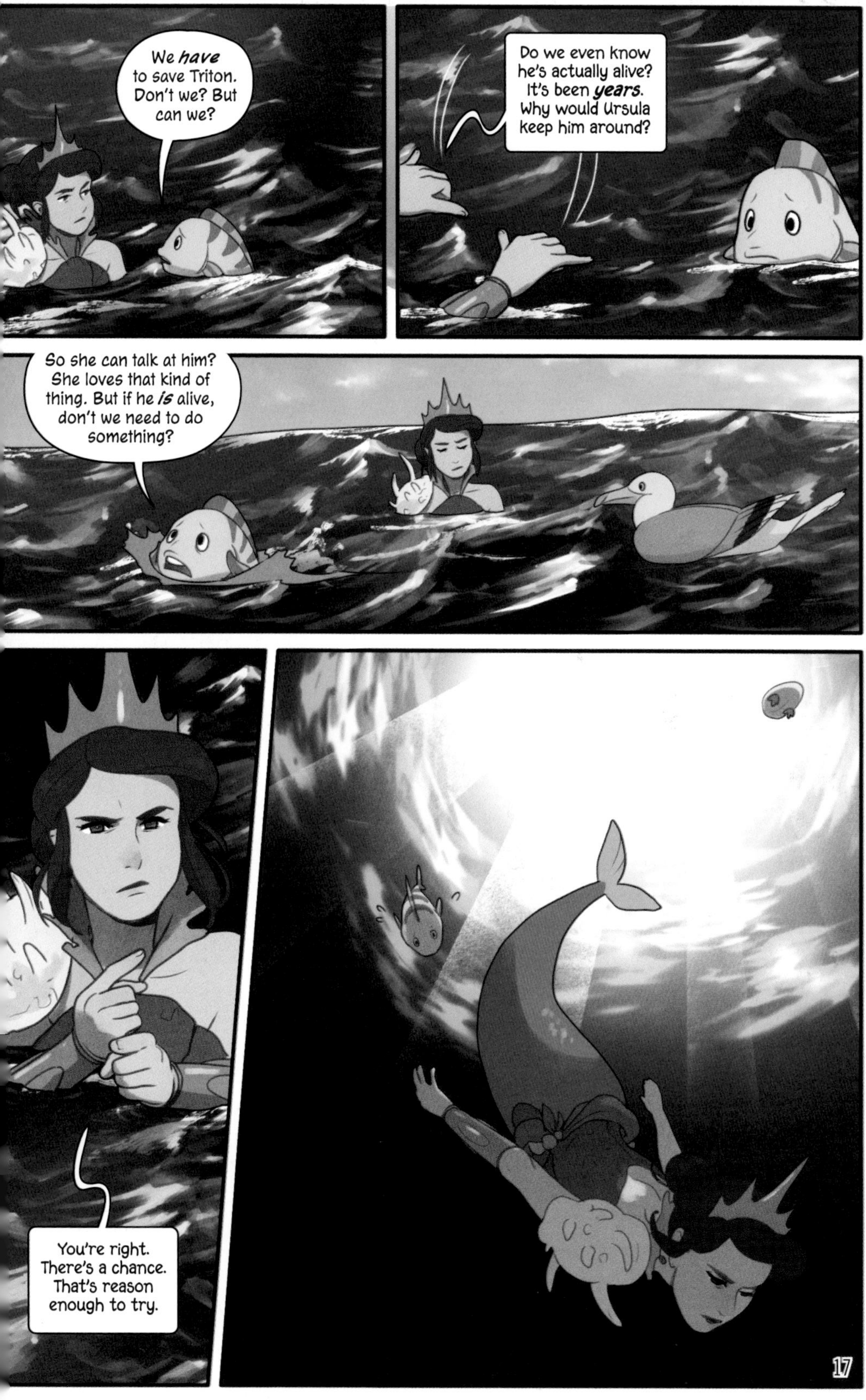
We *have* to save Triton. Don't we? But can we?
Do we even know he's actually alive? It's been *years*. Why would Ursula keep him around?
So she can talk at him? She loves that kind of thing. But if he *is* alive, don't we need to do something?
You're right. There's a chance. That's reason enough to try.

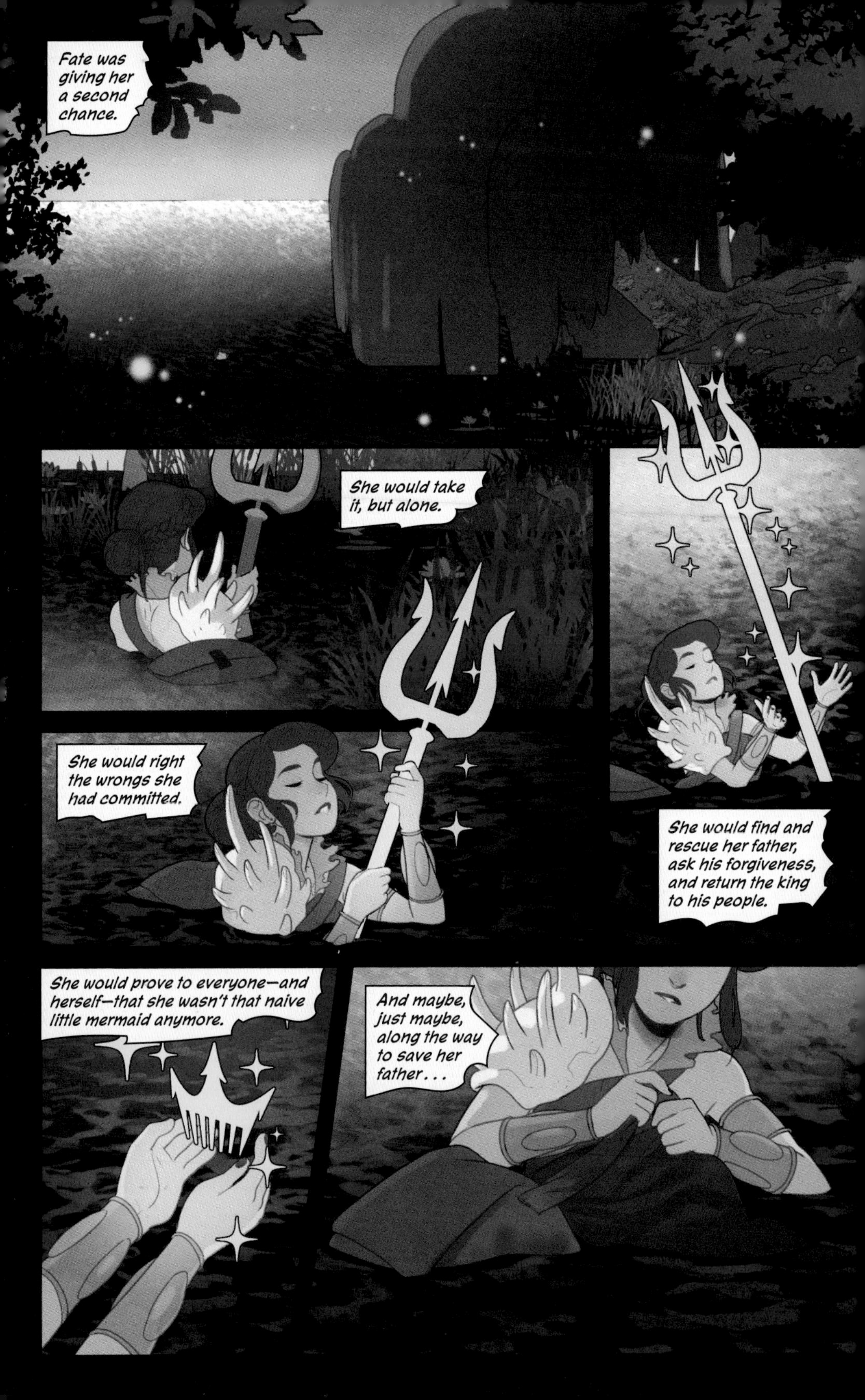
Fate was giving her a second chance.
She would take it, but alone.
She would right the wrongs she had committed.
She would find and rescue her father, ask his forgiveness, and return the king to his people.
She would prove to everyone—and herself—that she wasn't that naive little mermaid anymore.
And maybe, just maybe, along the way to save her father . . .

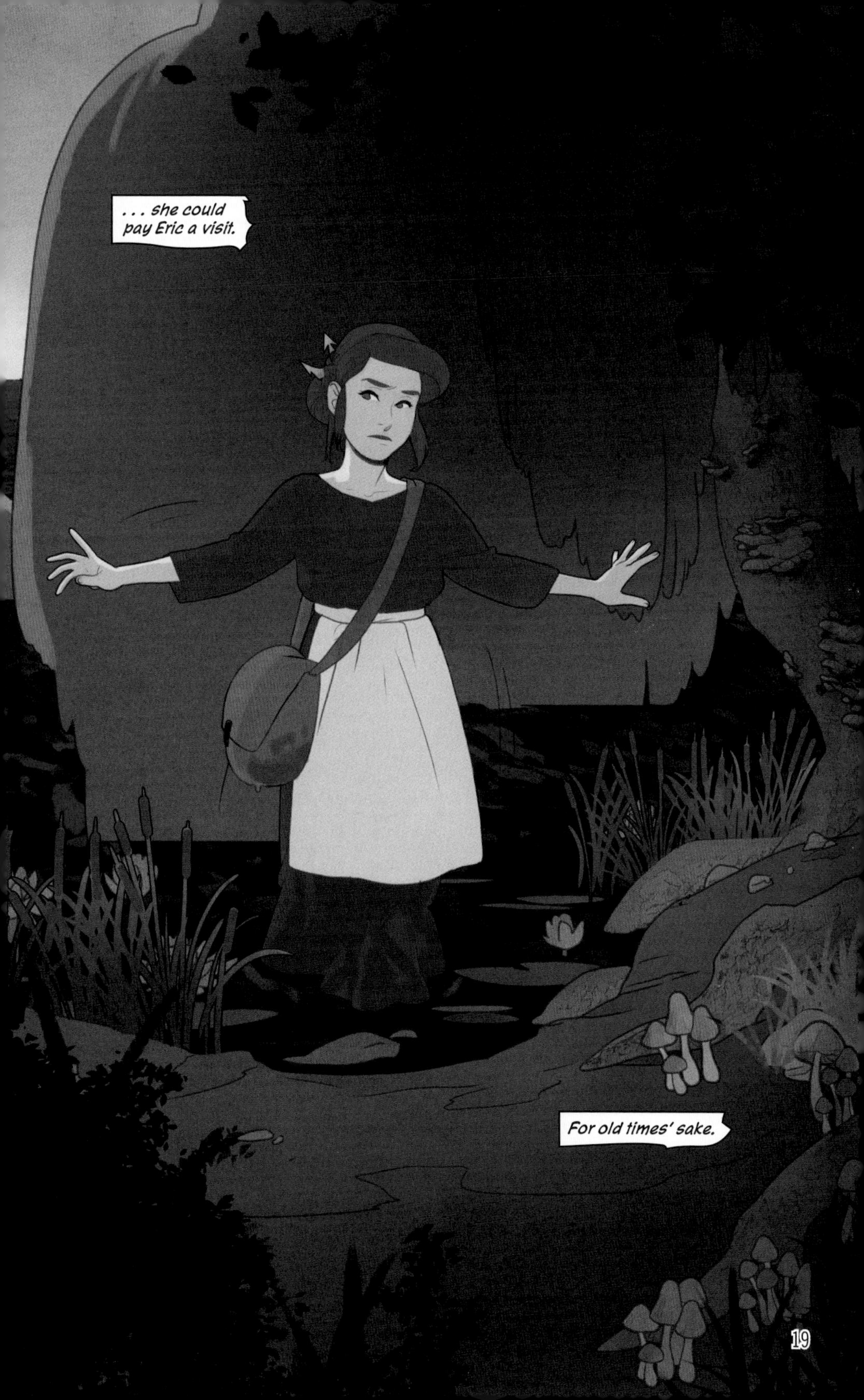
. . . she could pay Eric a visit.
For old times' sake.

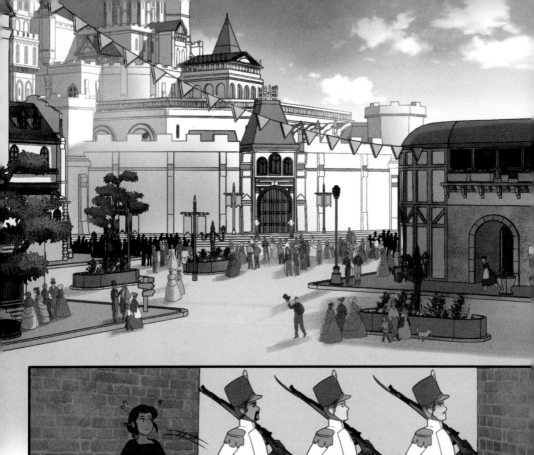

Things
look . . .
different . . .

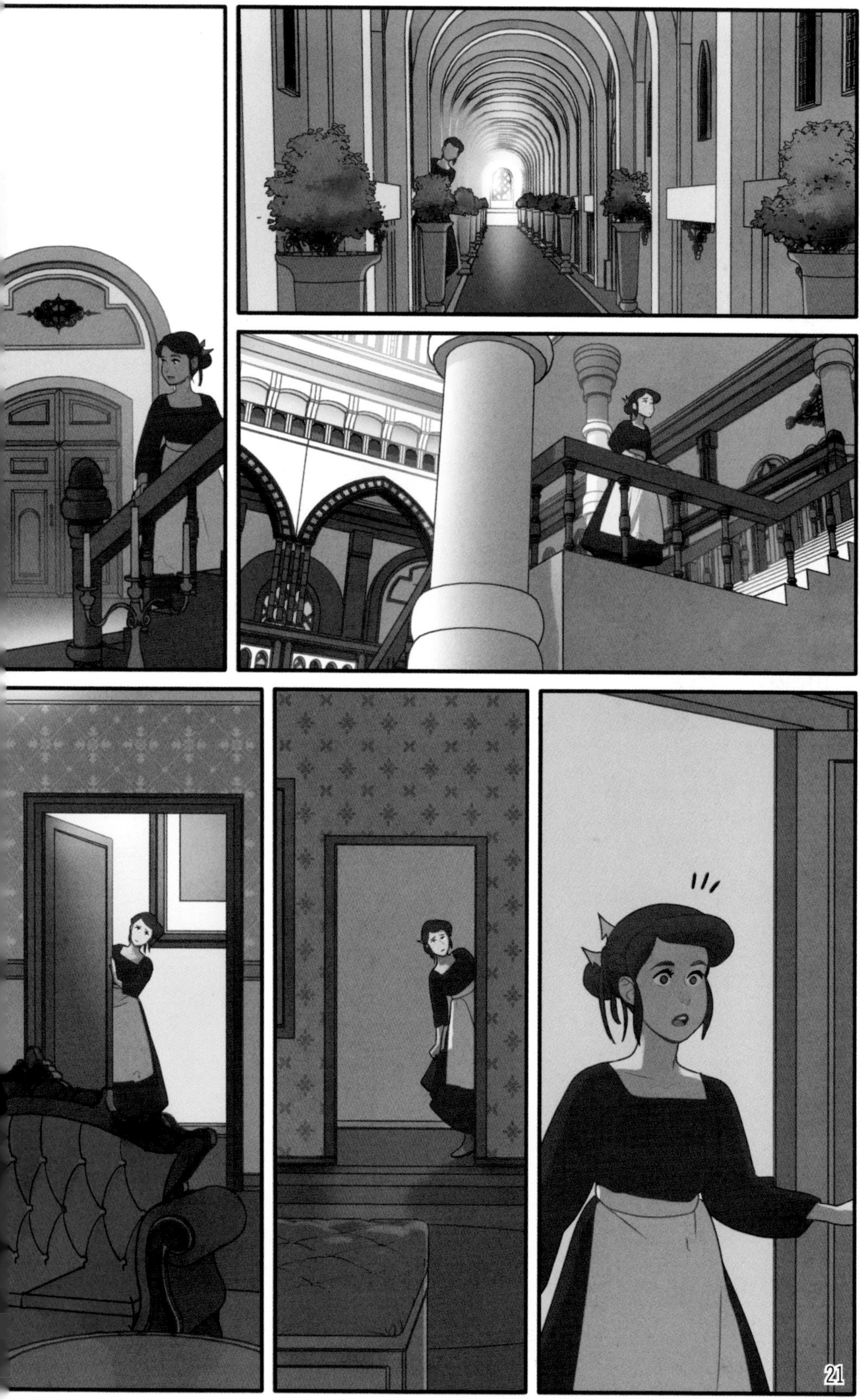

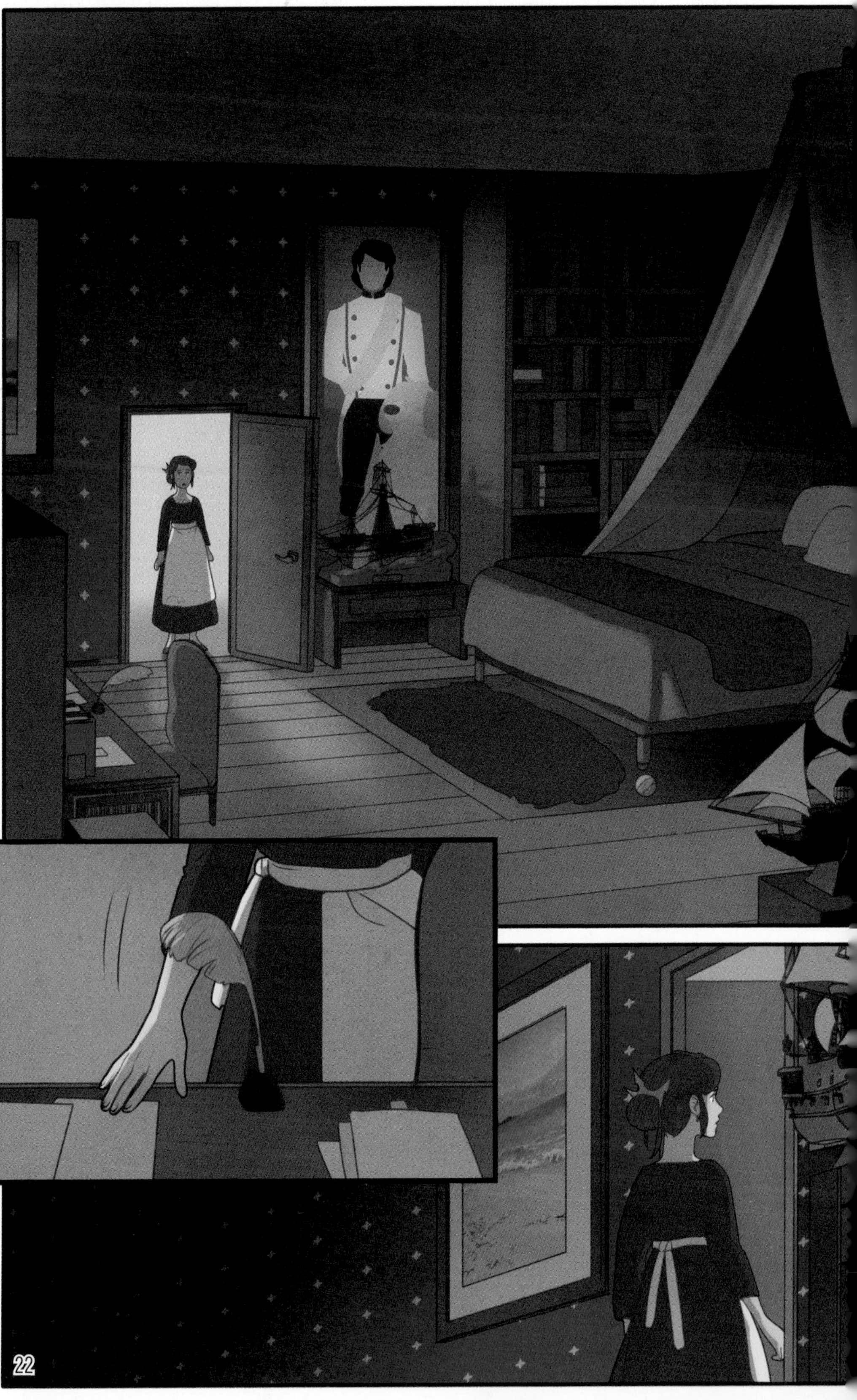

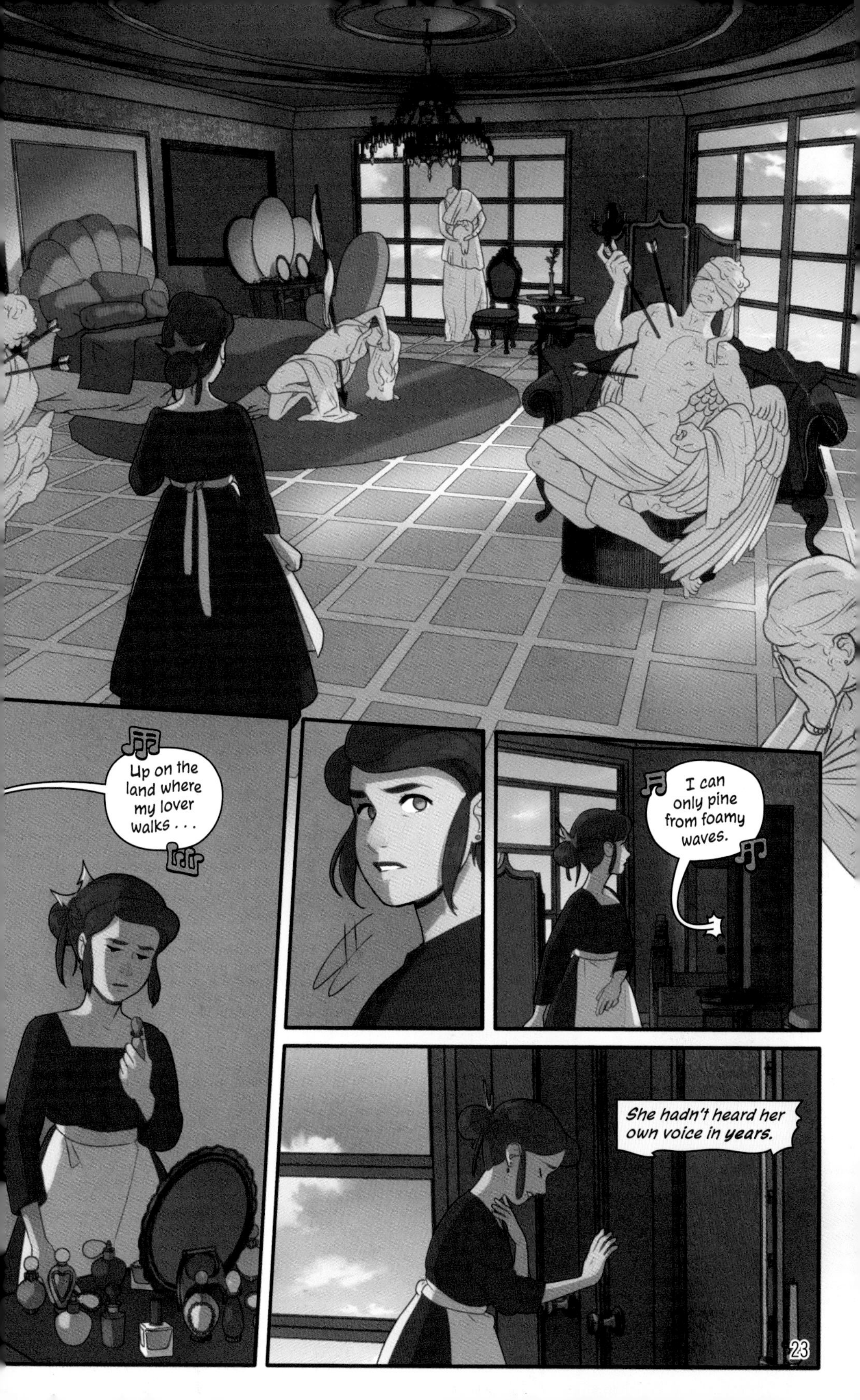
Up on the land where my lover walks . . .
I can only pine from foamy waves.
She hadn't heard her own voice in years.

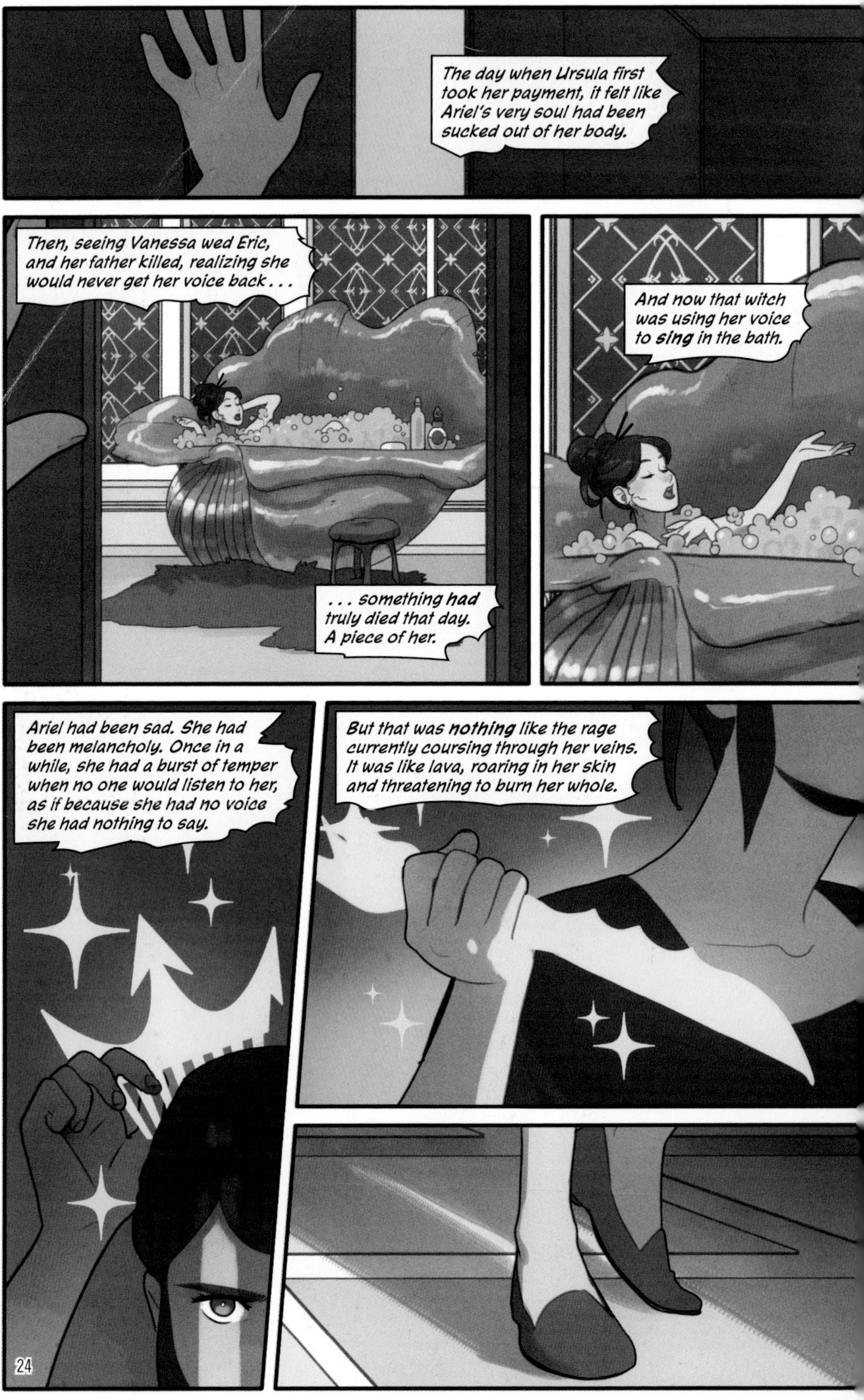
The day when Ursula first took her payment, it felt like Ariel's very soul had been sucked out of her body.
Then, seeing Vanessa wed Eric, and her father killed, realizing she would never get her voice back . . .
. . . something had truly died that day. A piece of her.
And now that witch was using her voice to sing in the bath.
Ariel had been sad. She had been melancholy. Once in a while, she had a burst of temper when no one would listen to her, as if because she had no voice she had nothing to say.
But that was nothing like the rage currently coursing through her veins. It was like lava, roaring in her skin and threatening to burn her whole.

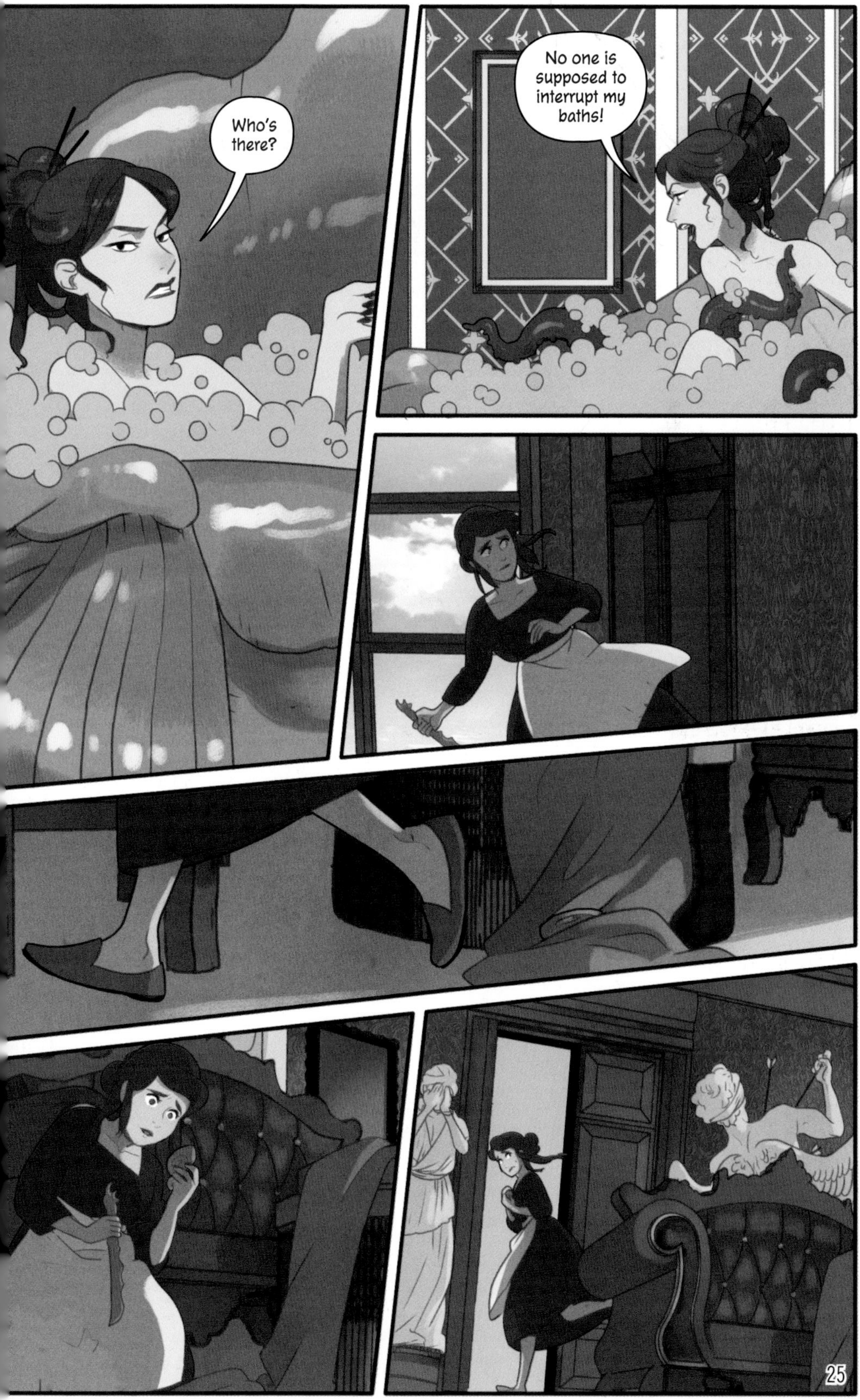
Who's there?
No one is supposed to interrupt my baths!

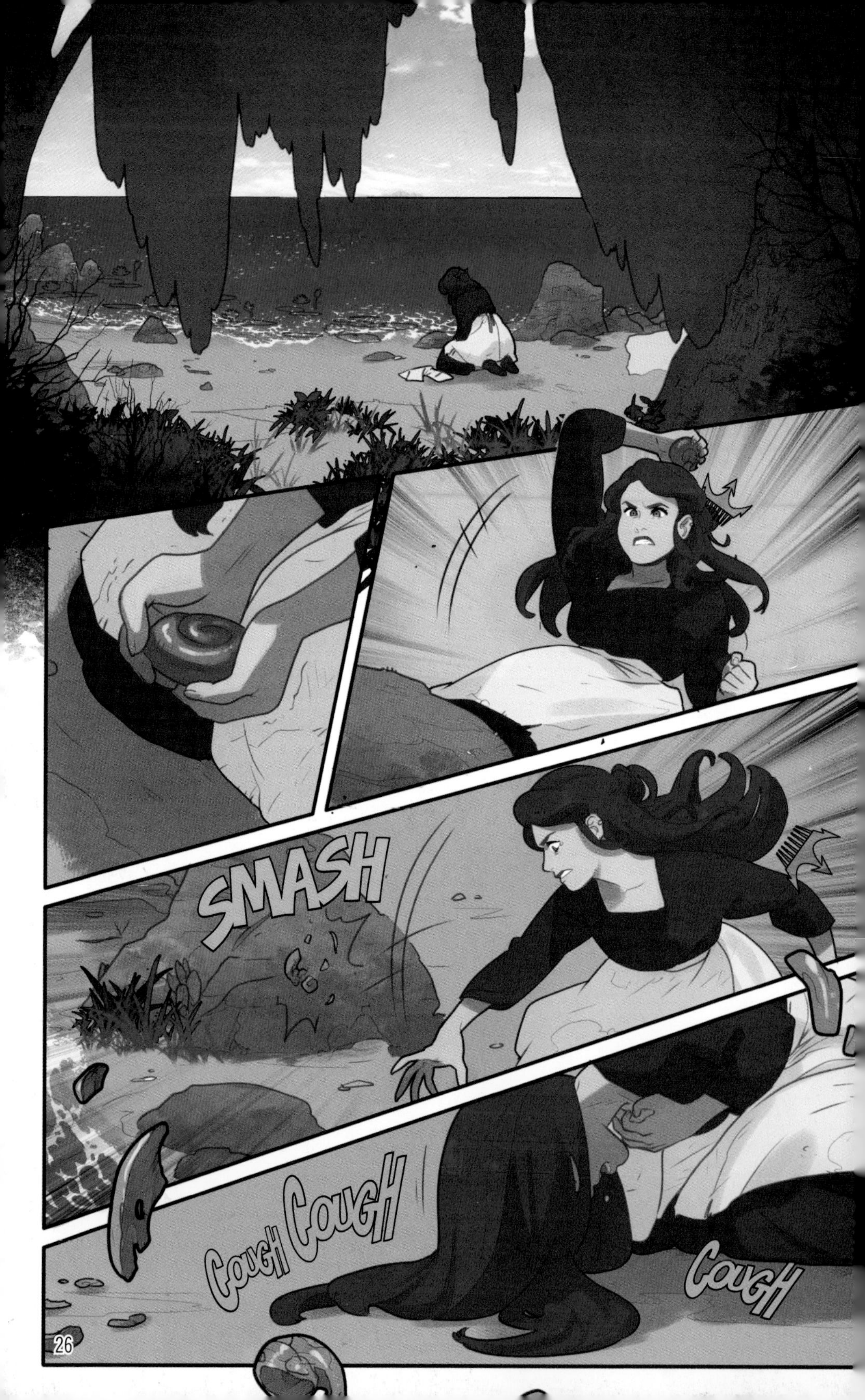
SMASH
COUGH COUGH
COUGH

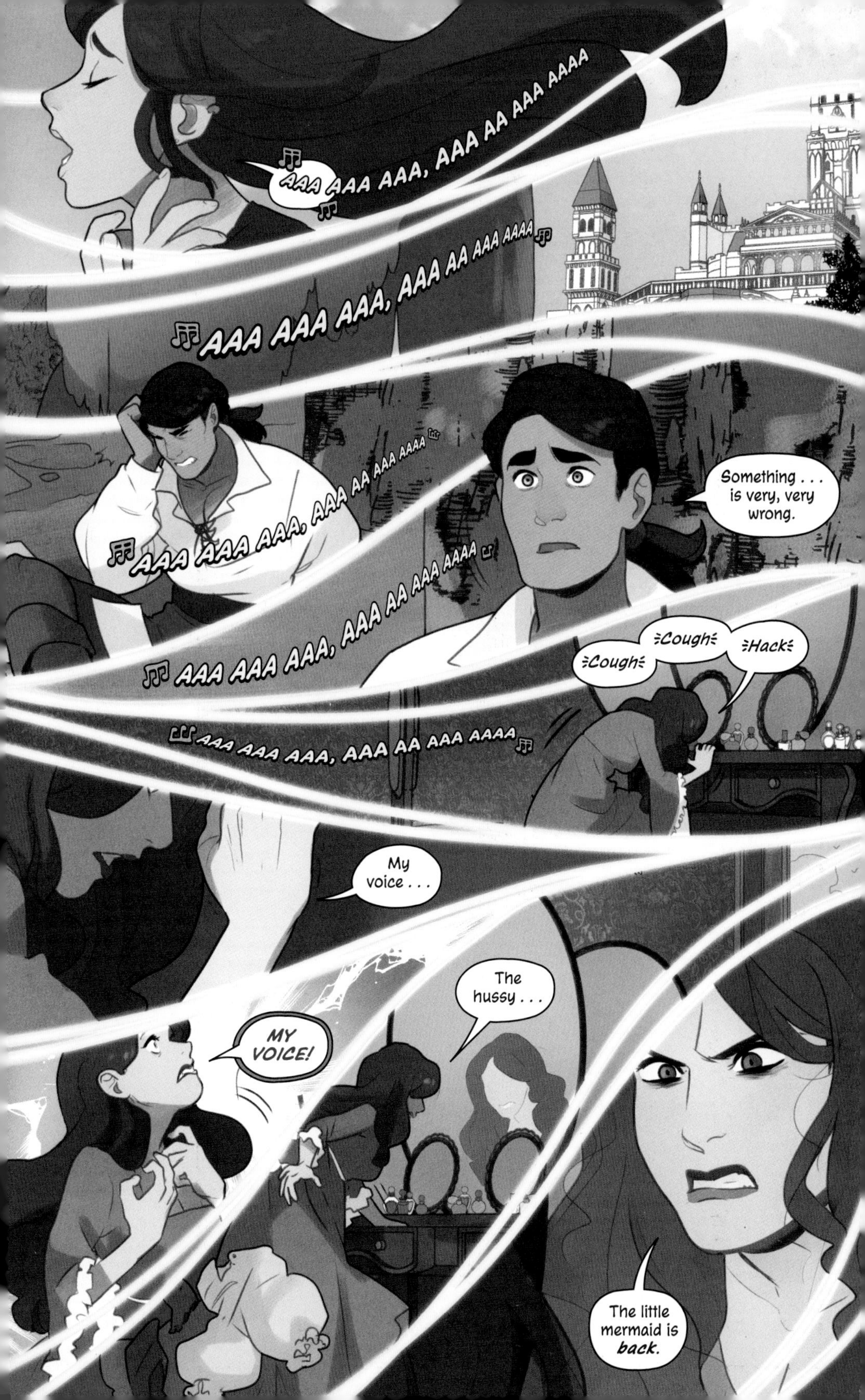
AAA AAA AAA, AAA AA AAA AAAA
AAA AAA AAA, AAA AA AAA AAAA
AAA AAA AAA, AAA AA AAA AAAA
AAA AAA AAA, AAA AA AAA AAAA
Something . . . is very, very wrong.
AAA AAA AAA, AAA AA AAA AAAA
Cough
Cough
Hack
My voice . . .
MY VOICE!
The hussy . . .
The little mermaid is *back*.

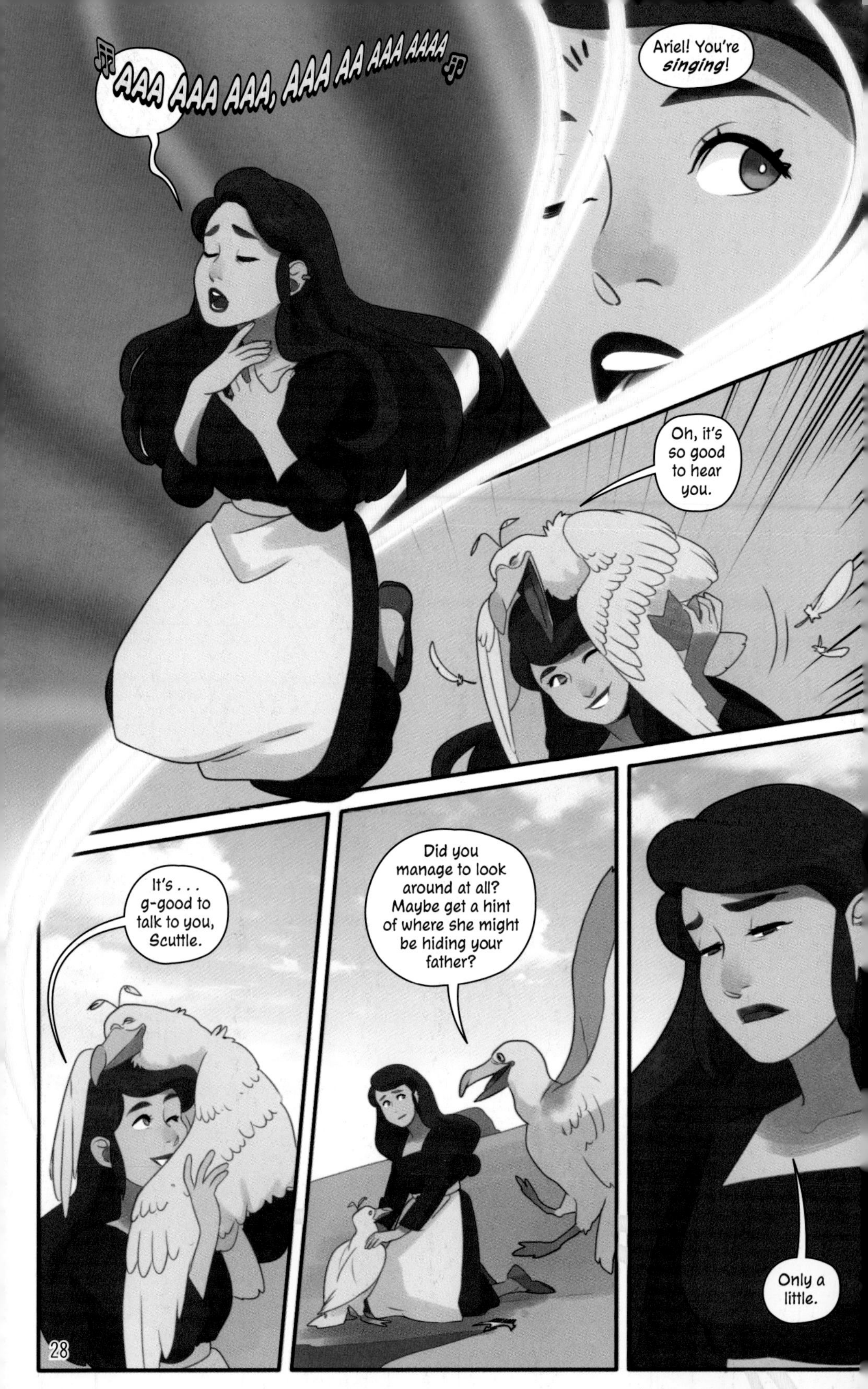
AAA AAA AAA, AAA AA AAA AAAA
Ariel! You're singing!
Oh, it's so good to hear you.
It's . . . g-good to talk to you, Scuttle.
Did you manage to look around at all? Maybe get a hint of where she might be hiding your father?
Only a little.

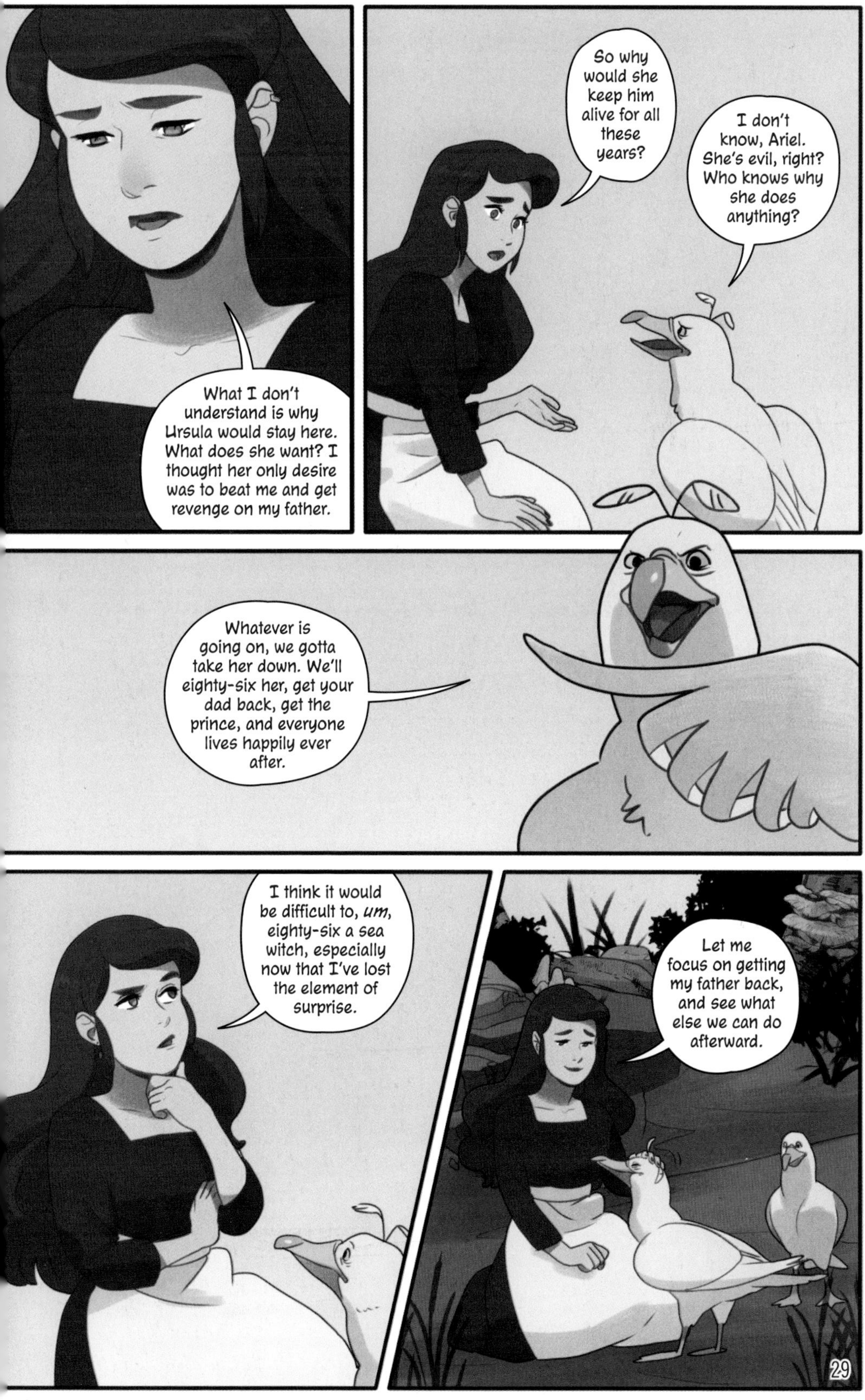
What I don't understand is why Ursula would stay here. What does she want? I thought her only desire was to beat me and get revenge on my father.
So why would she keep him alive for all these years?
I don't know, Ariel. She's evil, right? Who knows why she does anything?
Whatever is going on, we gotta take her down. We'll eighty-six her, get your dad back, get the prince, and everyone lives happily ever after.
I think it would be difficult to, *um*, eighty-six a sea witch, especially now that I've lost the element of surprise.
Let me focus on getting my father back, and see what else we can do afterward.

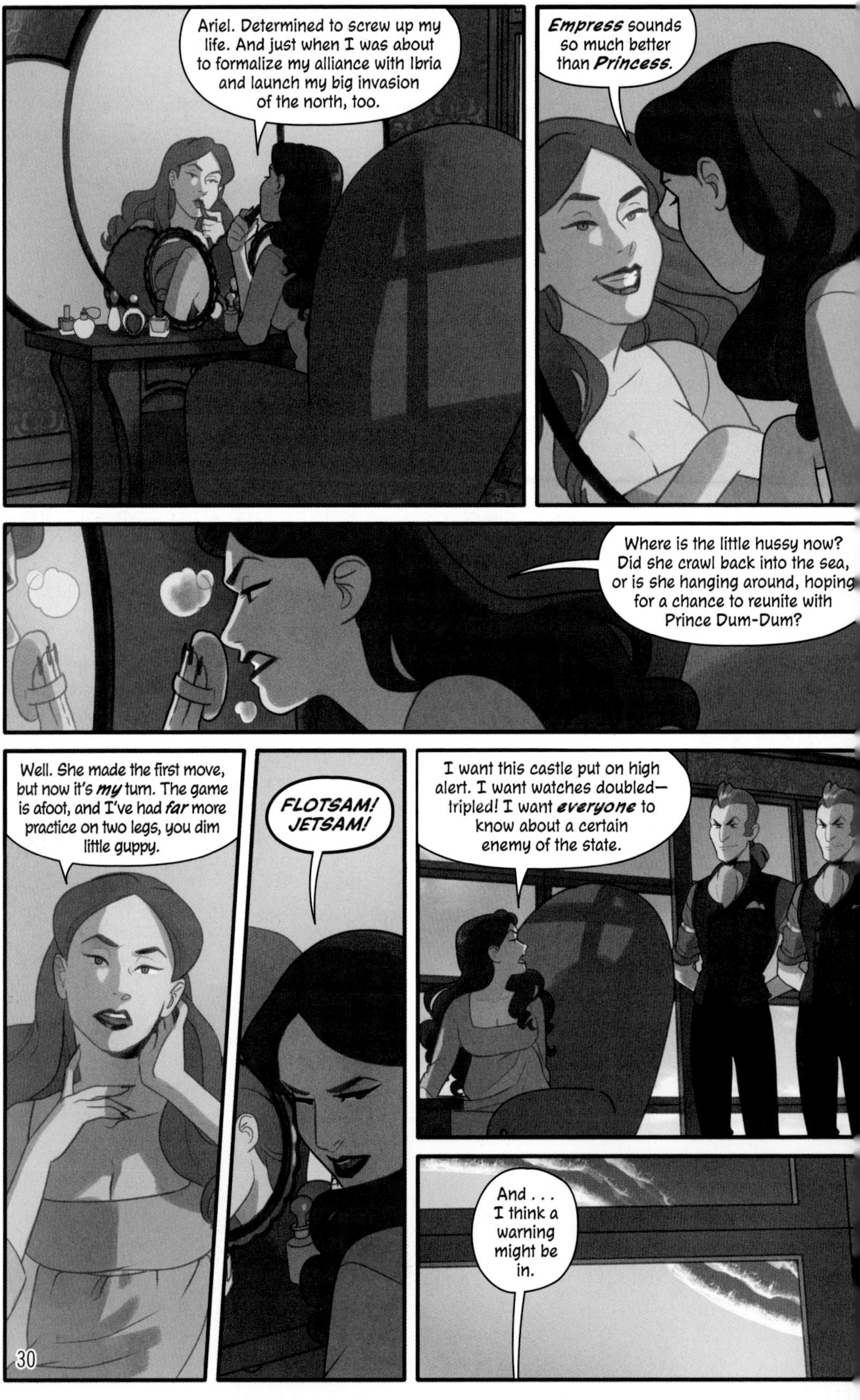
Ariel. Determined to screw up my life. And just when I was about to formalize my alliance with Ibria and launch my big invasion of the north, too.
Empress sounds so much better than *Princess.*
Where is the little hussy now? Did she crawl back into the sea, or is she hanging around, hoping for a chance to reunite with Prince Dum-Dum?
Well. She made the first move, but now it's *my* turn. The game is afoot, and I've had *far* more practice on two legs, you dim little guppy.
FLOTSAM! JETSAM!
I want this castle put on high alert. I want watches doubled—tripled! I want *everyone* to know about a certain enemy of the state.
And . . . I think a warning might be in.

They put up quite a fight . . .

But we torched the place good. Not a barn left standing.

See what I got? Pretty, ain't it? It was practically *begging* to be took.

This is not the same sleepy seaside town I knew.

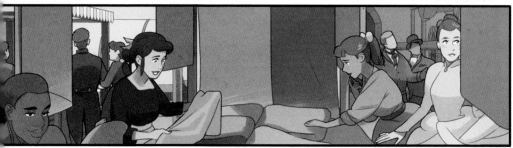

At least *some* things haven't changed.

Mmm . . . fresh-baked . . . *something*.

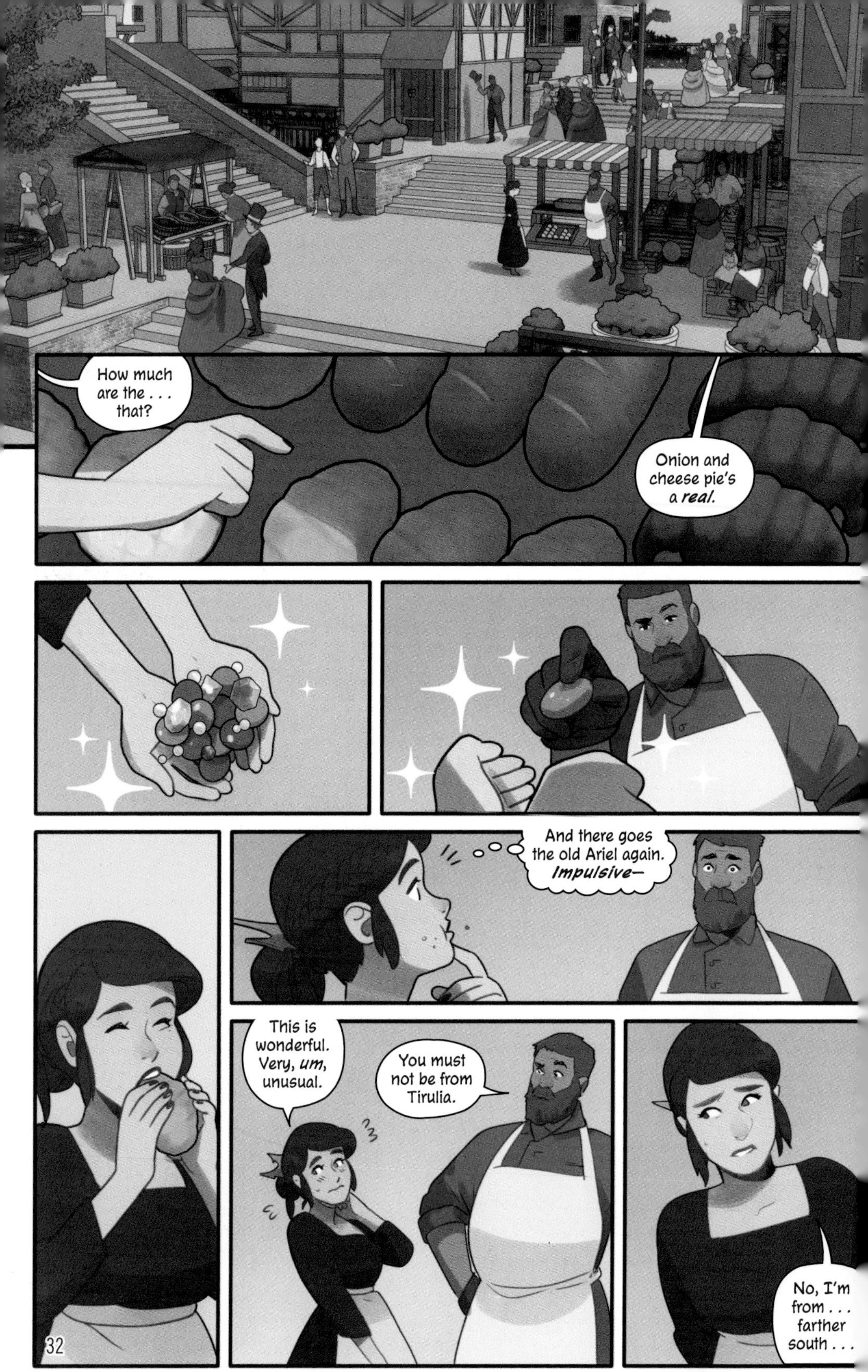
How much are the . . . that?
Onion and cheese pie's a *real*.
And there goes the old Ariel again. *Impulsive*—
This is wonderful. Very, *um*, unusual.
You must not be from Tirulia.
No, I'm from . . . farther south . . .

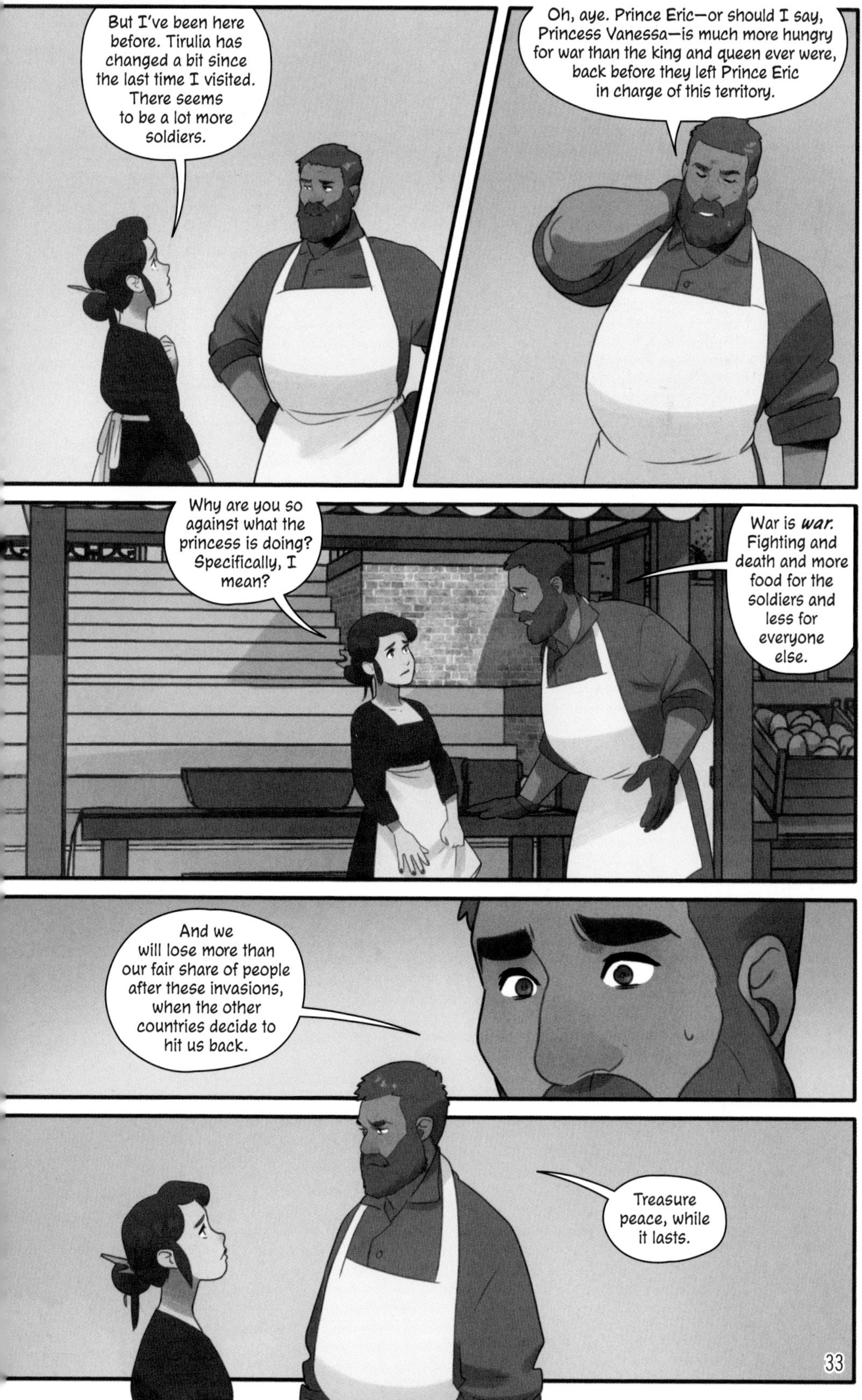
But I've been here before. Tirulia has changed a bit since the last time I visited. There seems to be a lot more soldiers.
Oh, aye. Prince Eric—or should I say, Princess Vanessa—is much more hungry for war than the king and queen ever were, back before they left Prince Eric in charge of this territory.
Why are you so against what the princess is doing? Specifically, I mean?
War is *war.* Fighting and death and more food for the soldiers and less for everyone else.
And we will lose more than our fair share of people after these invasions, when the other countries decide to hit us back.
Treasure peace, while it lasts.

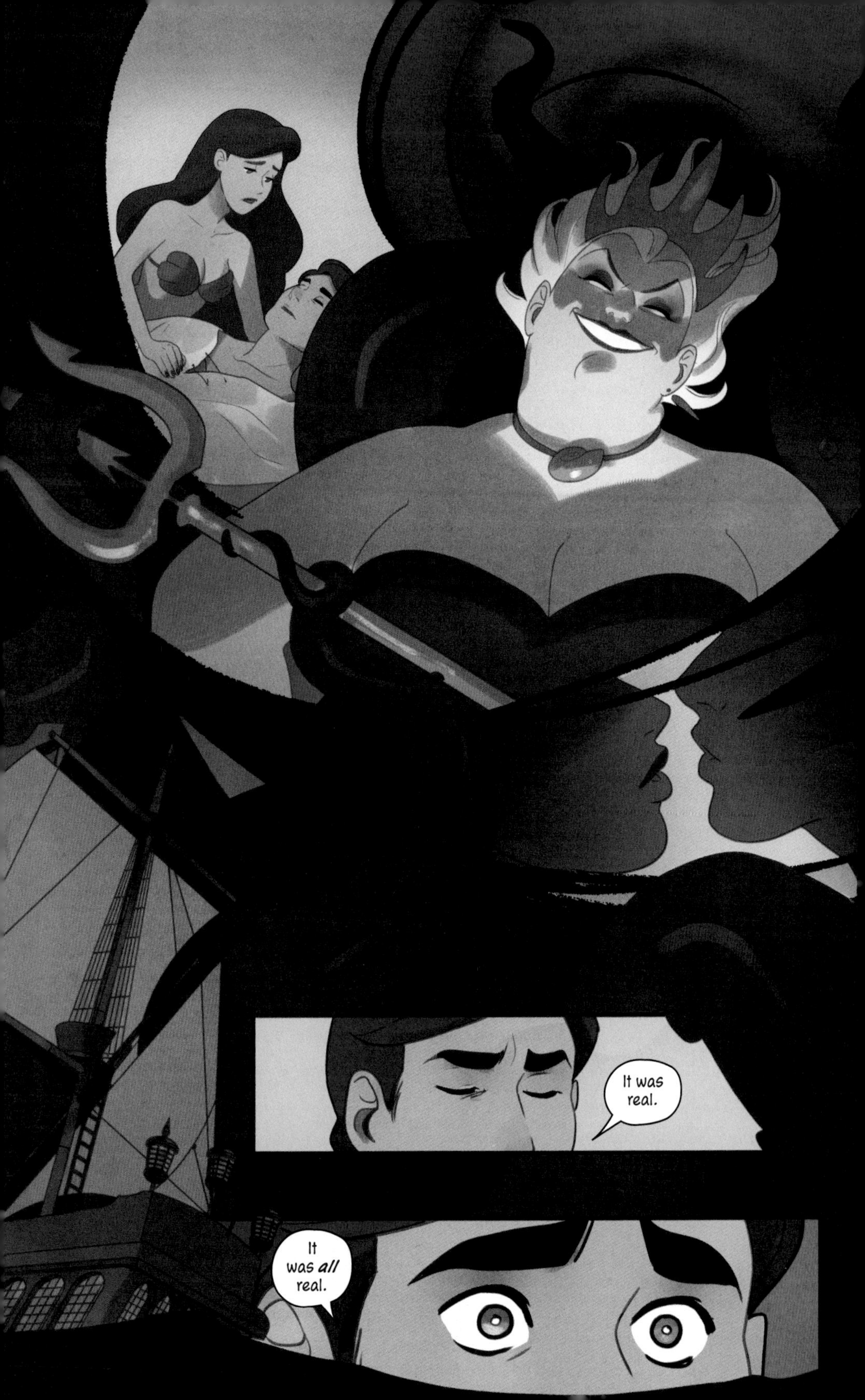
It was real.
It was *all* real.

Master Eric, are you feeling all right?

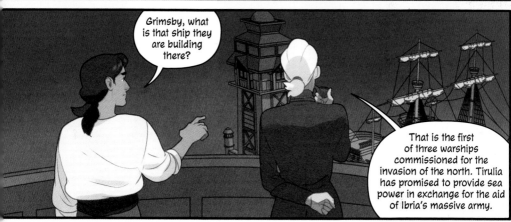

Grimsby, what is that ship they are building there?

That is the first of three warships commissioned for the invasion of the north. Tirulia has promised to provide sea power in exchange for the aid of Ibria's massive army.

Invasion? I approved this?

. . . but I believe it was Princess Vanessa who originated the plan and wrote up the decree.

You signed the order, Prince Eric . . .

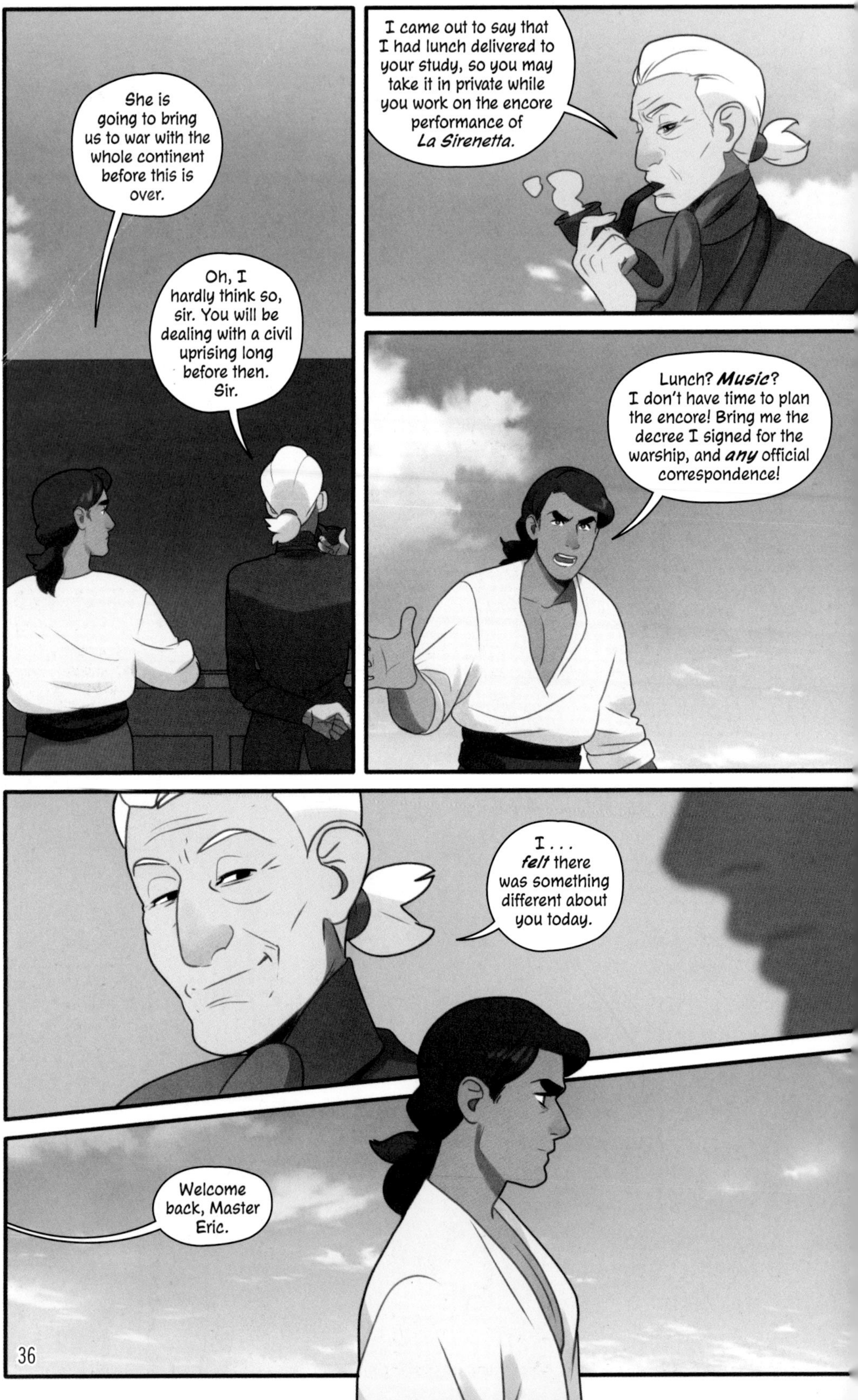
She is going to bring us to war with the whole continent before this is over.
Oh, I hardly think so, sir. You will be dealing with a civil uprising long before then. Sir.
I came out to say that I had lunch delivered to your study, so you may take it in private while you work on the encore performance of *La Sirenetta*.
Lunch? ***Music***? I don't have time to plan the encore! Bring me the decree I signed for the warship, and ***any*** official correspondence!
I . . . *felt* there was something different about you today.
Welcome back, Master Eric.

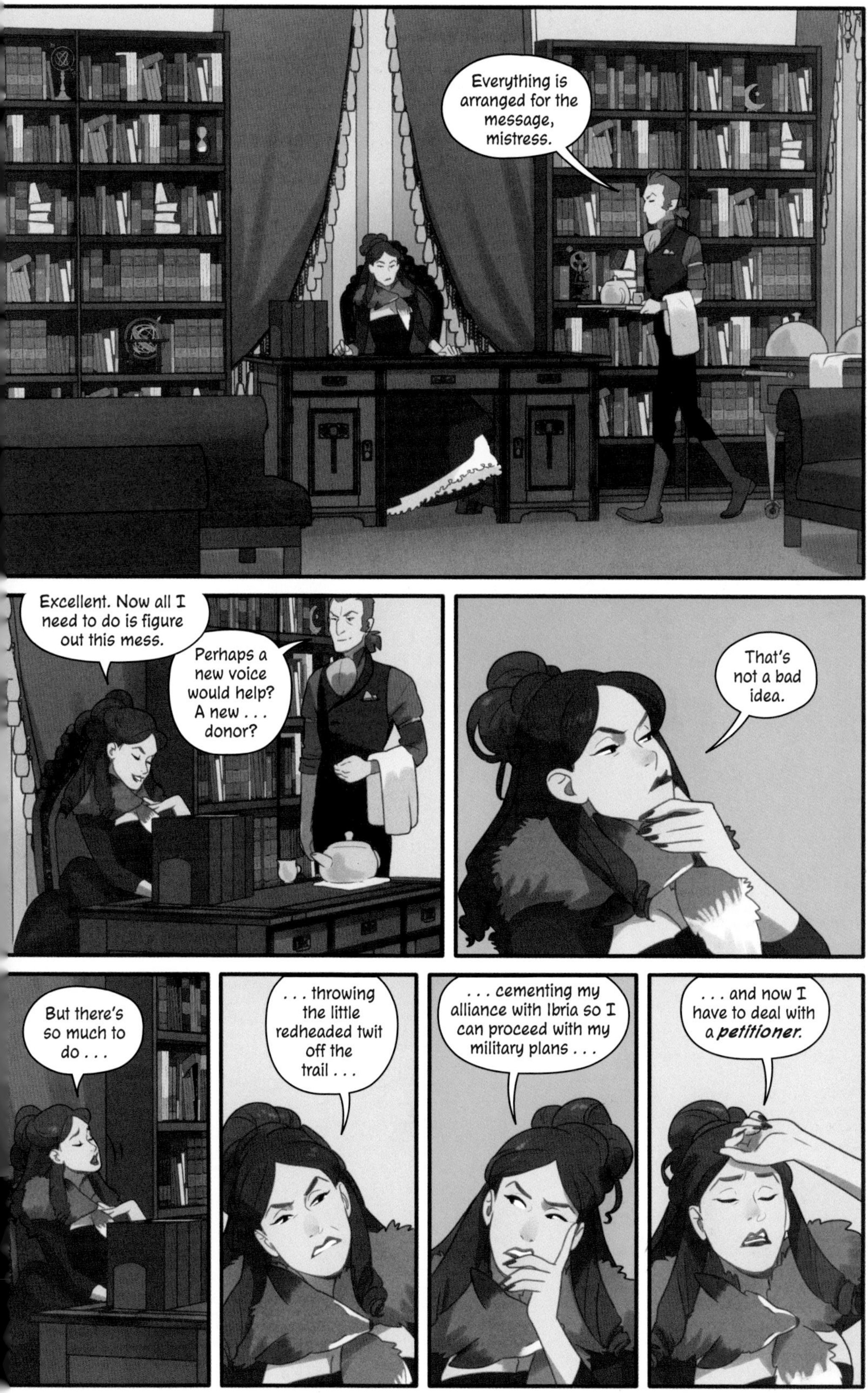
Everything is arranged for the message, mistress.
Excellent. Now all I need to do is figure out this mess.
Perhaps a new voice would help? A new . . . donor?
That's not a bad idea.
But there's so much to do . . .
. . . throwing the little redheaded twit off the trail . . .
. . . cementing my alliance with Ibria so I can proceed with my military plans . . .
. . . and now I have to deal with a *petitioner.*

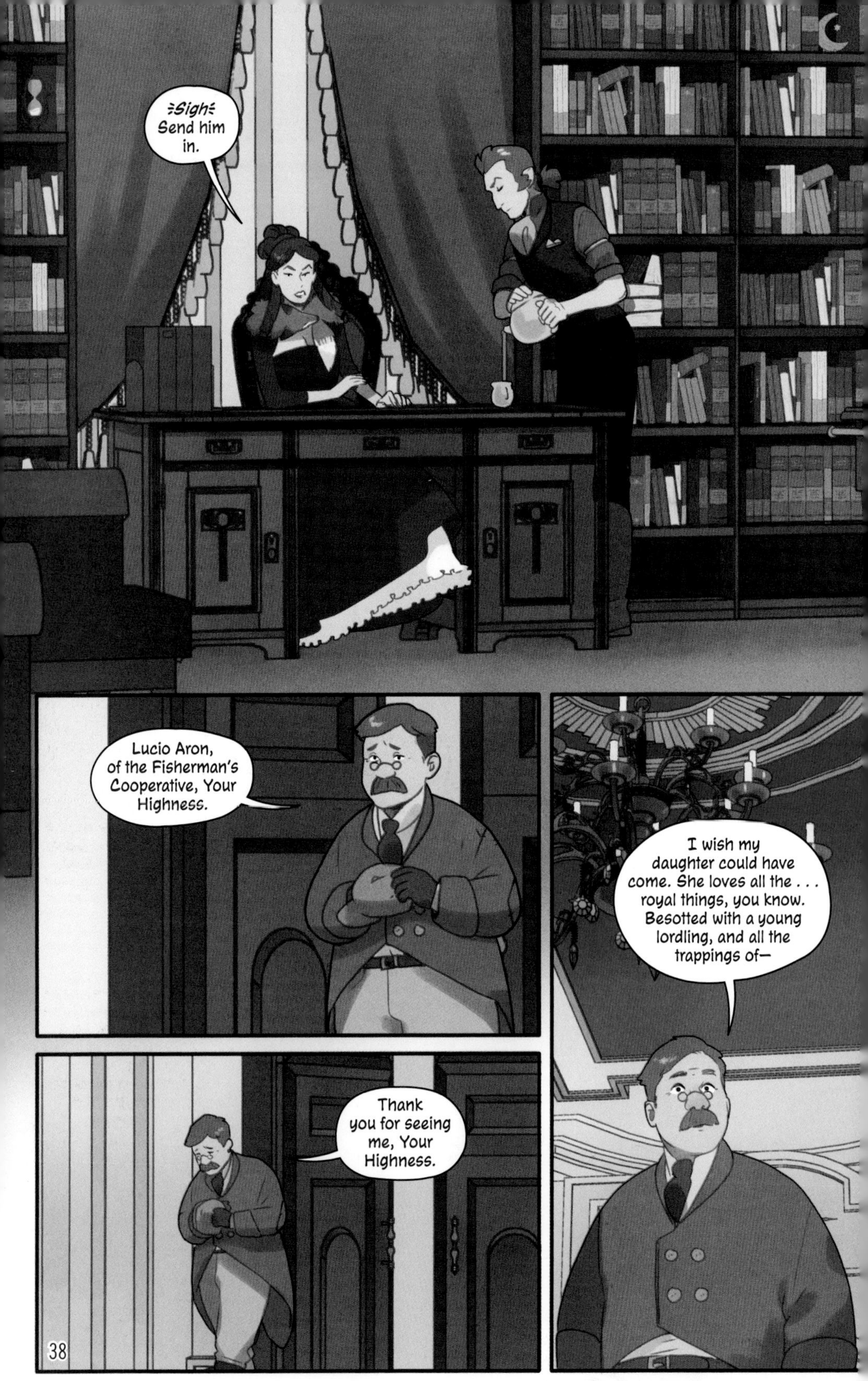

≈Sigh≈ Send him in.
Lucio Aron, of the Fisherman's Cooperative, Your Highness.
Thank you for seeing me, Your Highness.
I wish my daughter could have come. She loves all the . . . royal things, you know. Besotted with a young lordling, and all the trappings of—

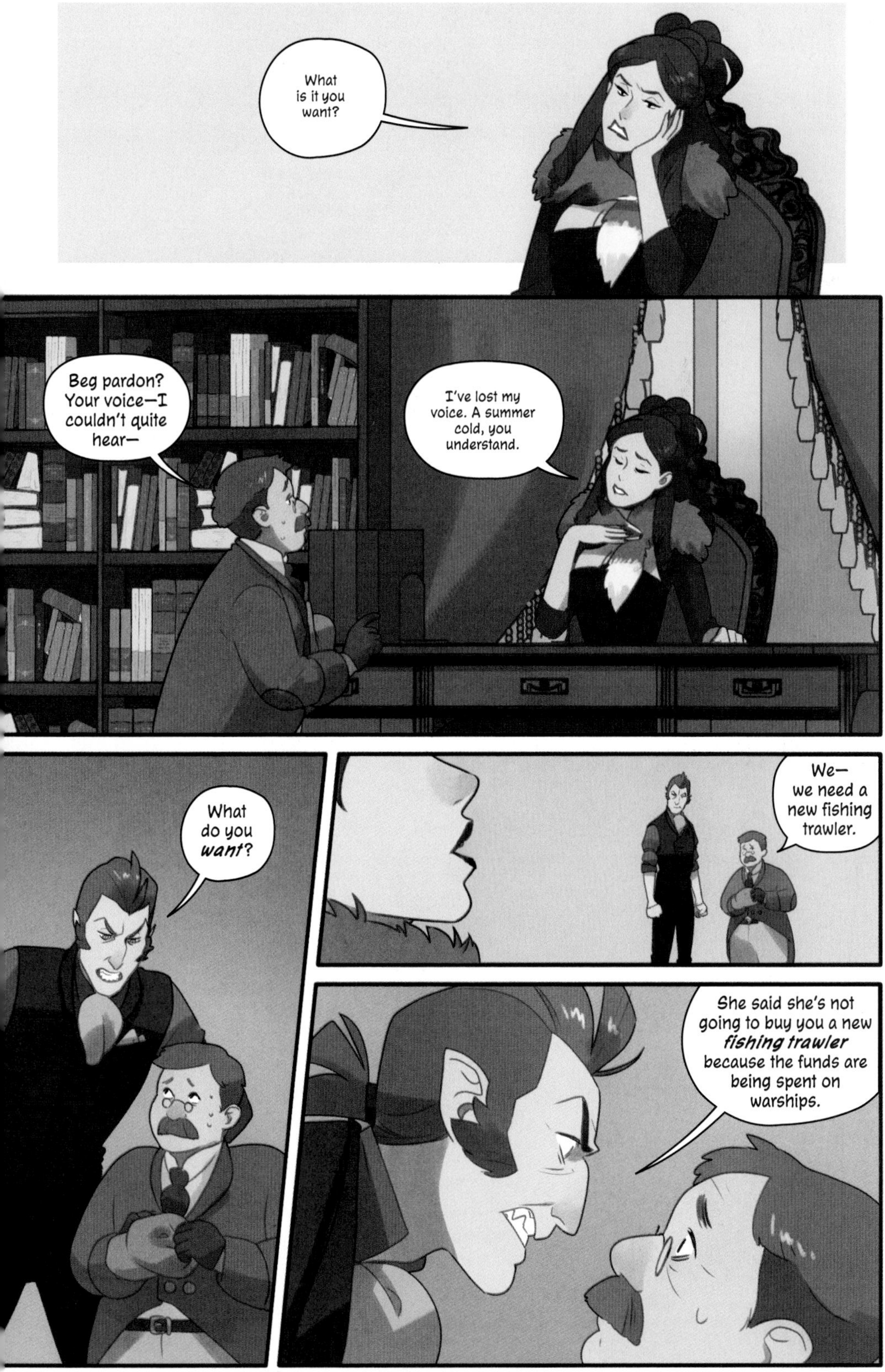
What is it you want?
Beg pardon? Your voice—I couldn't quite hear—
I've lost my voice. A summer cold, you understand.
What do you *want*?
We— we need a new fishing trawler.
She said she's not going to buy you a new *fishing trawler* because the funds are being spent on warships.

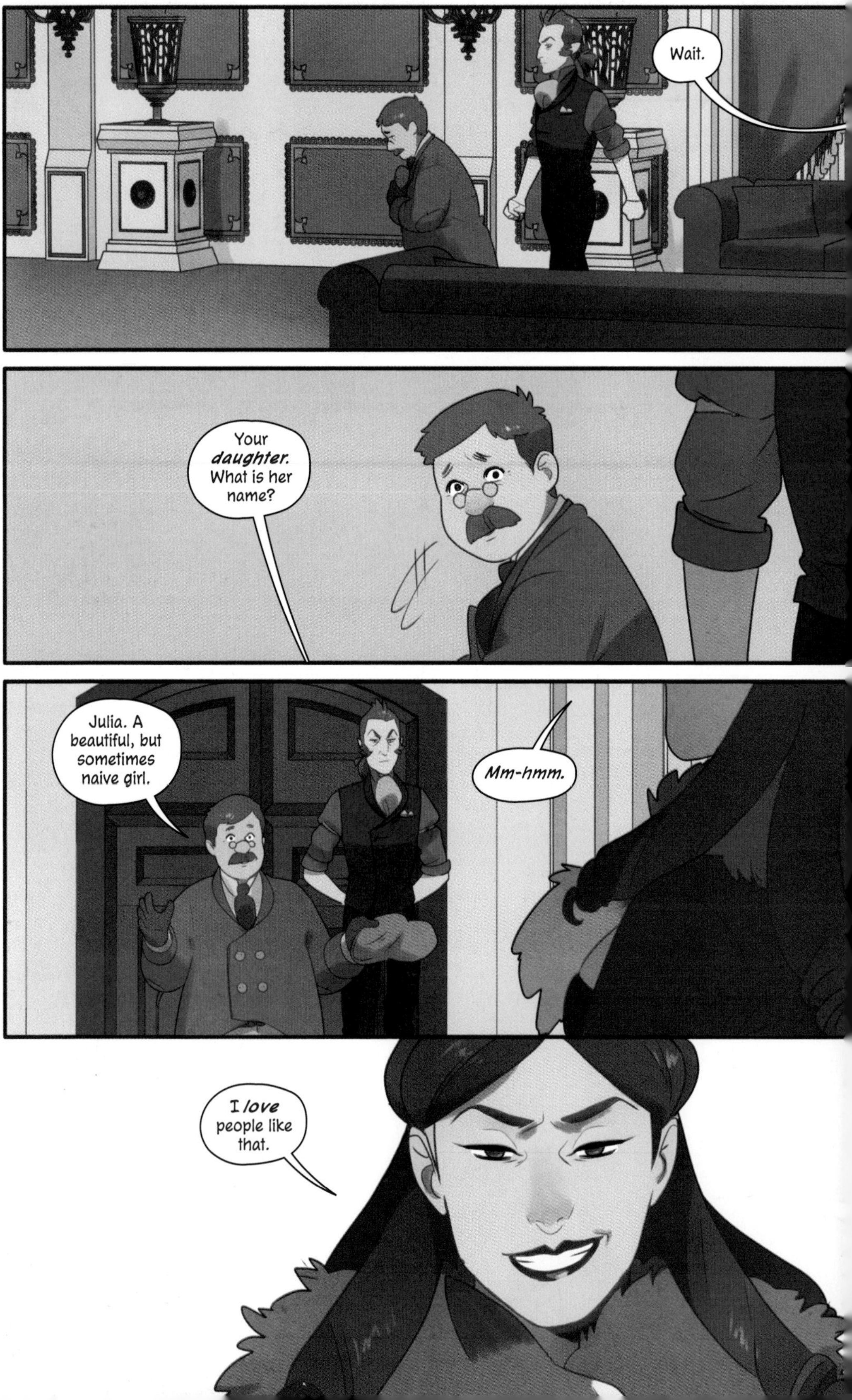
Wait.
Your *daughter.* What is her name?
Julia. A beautiful, but sometimes naive girl.
Mm-hmm.
I *love* people like that.

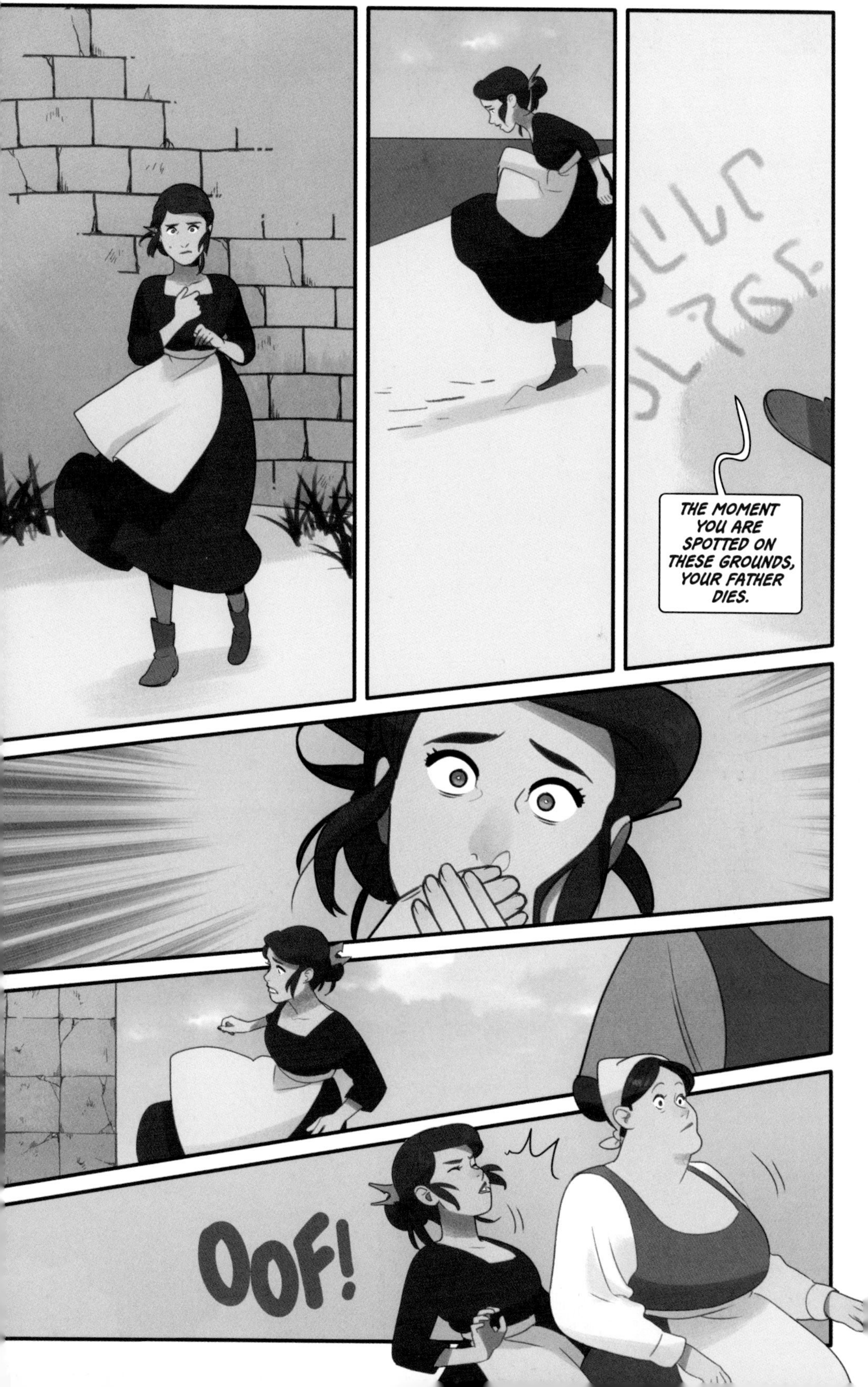
THE MOMENT YOU ARE SPOTTED ON THESE GROUNDS, YOUR FATHER DIES.
OOF!

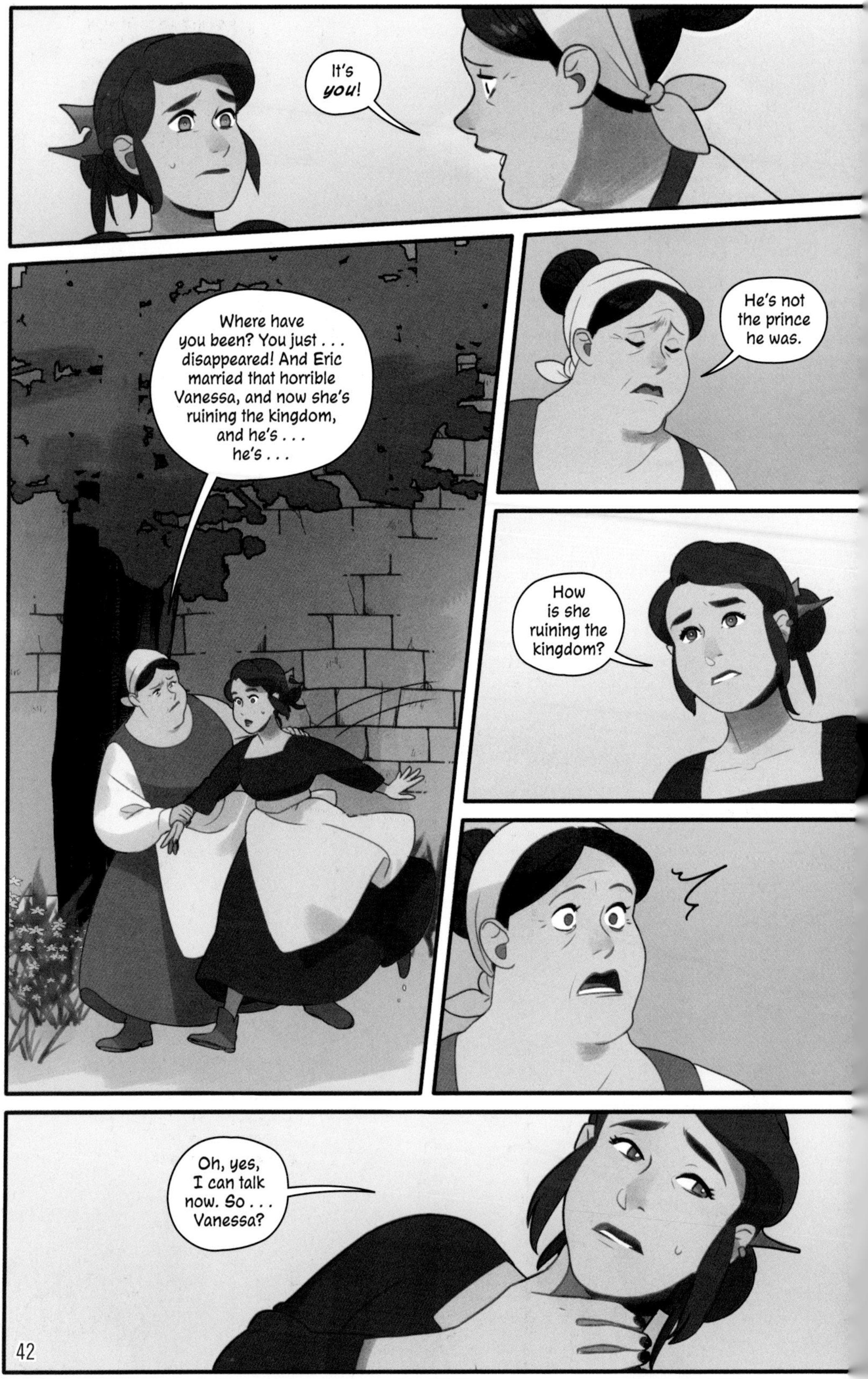
It's *you*!
Where have you been? You just . . . disappeared! And Eric married that horrible Vanessa, and now she's ruining the kingdom, and he's . . . he's . . .
He's not the prince he was.
How is she ruining the kingdom?
Oh, yes, I can talk now. So . . . Vanessa?

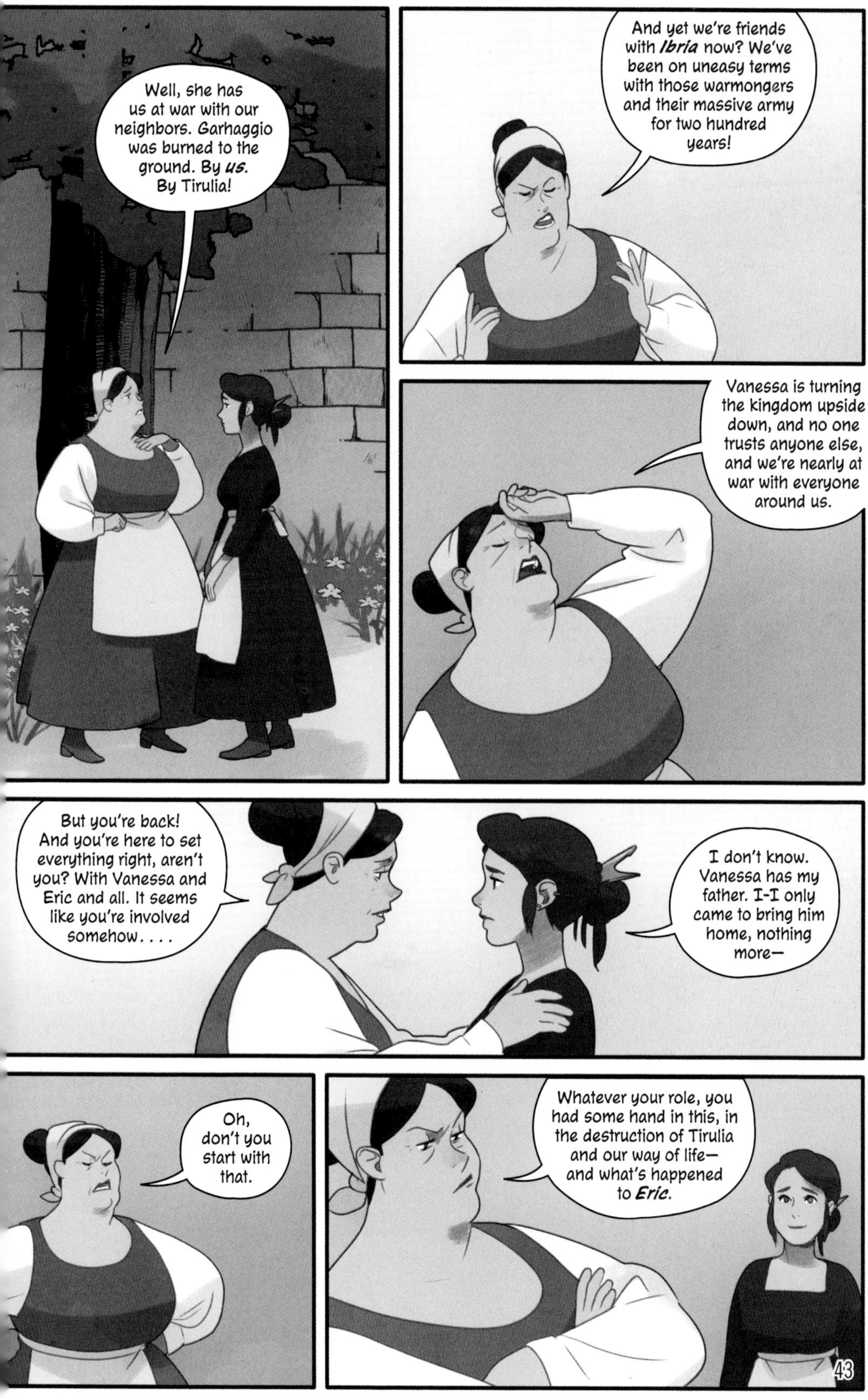
Well, she has us at war with our neighbors. Garhaggio was burned to the ground. By *us*. By Tirulia!
And yet we're friends with *Ibria* now? We've been on uneasy terms with those warmongers and their massive army for two hundred years!
Vanessa is turning the kingdom upside down, and no one trusts anyone else, and we're nearly at war with everyone around us.
But you're back! And you're here to set everything right, aren't you? With Vanessa and Eric and all. It seems like you're involved somehow. . . .
I don't know. Vanessa has my father. I-I only came to bring him home, nothing more—
Oh, don't you start with that.
Whatever your role, you had some hand in this, in the destruction of Tirulia and our way of life—and what's happened to *Eric*.
43

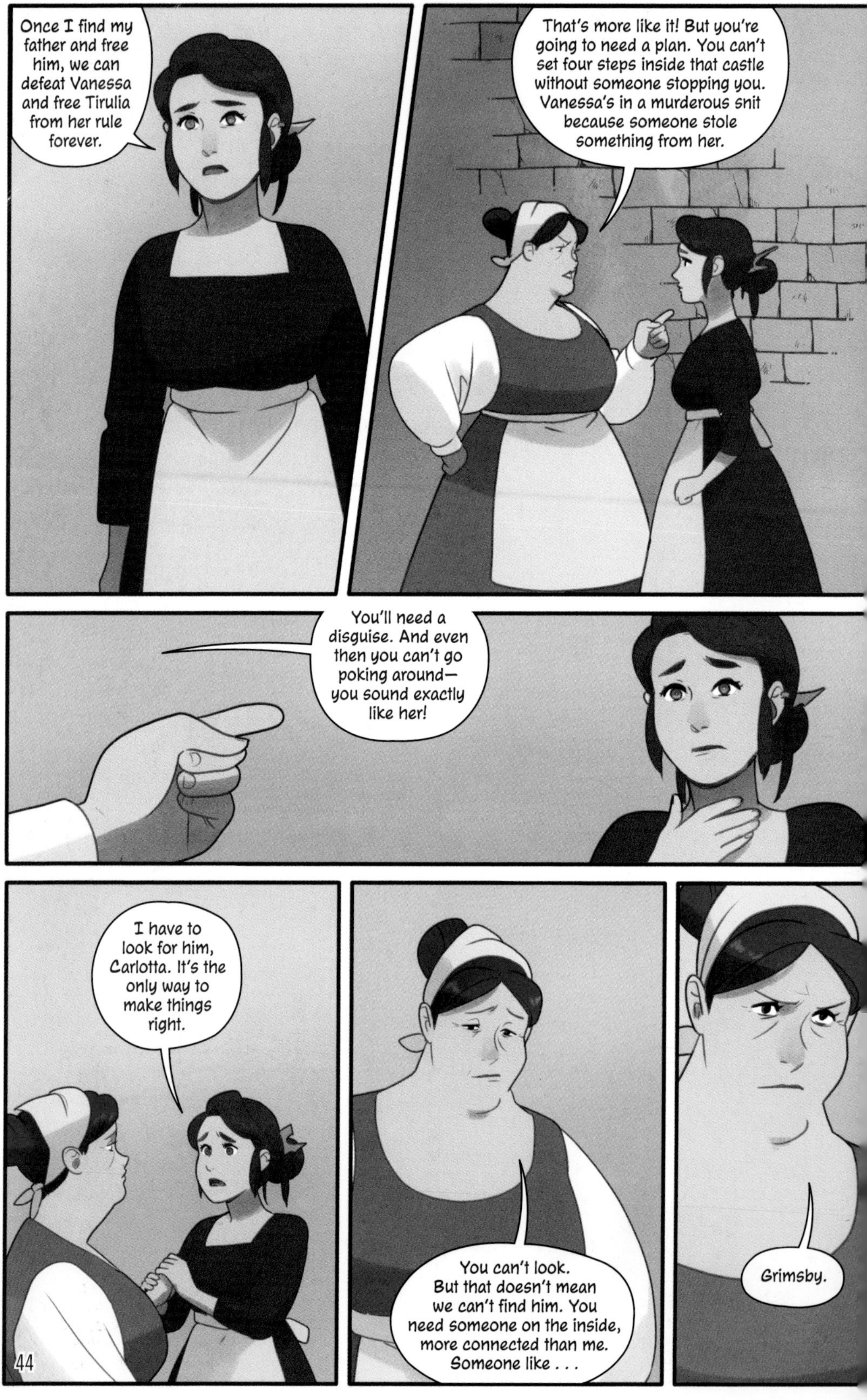
Once I find my father and free him, we can defeat Vanessa and free Tirulia from her rule forever.
That's more like it! But you're going to need a plan. You can't set four steps inside that castle without someone stopping you. Vanessa's in a murderous snit because someone stole something from her.
You'll need a disguise. And even then you can't go poking around—you sound exactly like her!
I have to look for him, Carlotta. It's the only way to make things right.
You can't look. But that doesn't mean we can't find him. You need someone on the inside, more connected than me. Someone like . . .
Grimsby.

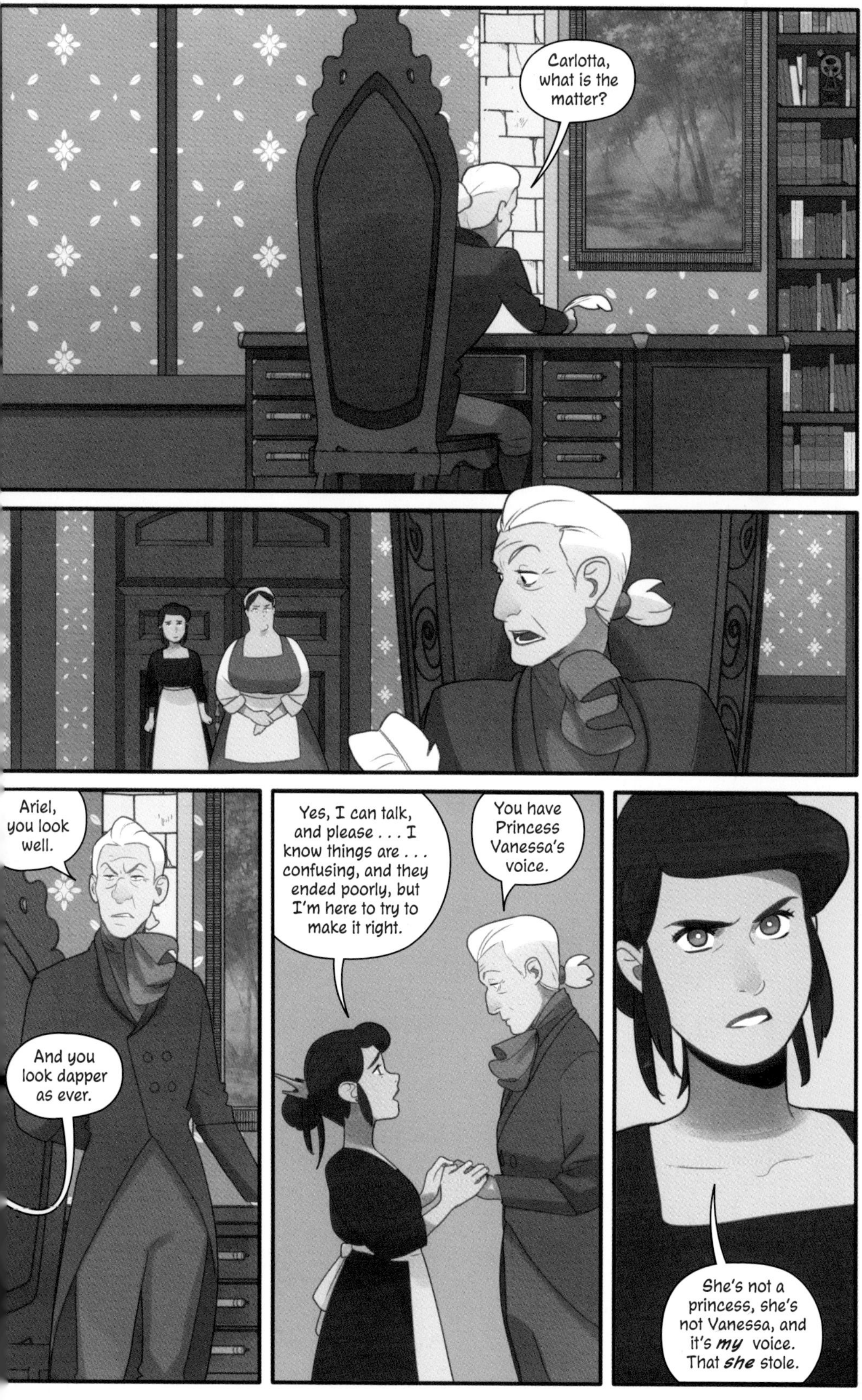
Carlotta, what is the matter?
Ariel, you look well.
And you look dapper as ever.
Yes, I can talk, and please . . . I know things are . . . confusing, and they ended poorly, but I'm here to try to make it right.
You have Princess Vanessa's voice.
She's not a princess, she's not Vanessa, and it's *my* voice. That *she* stole.

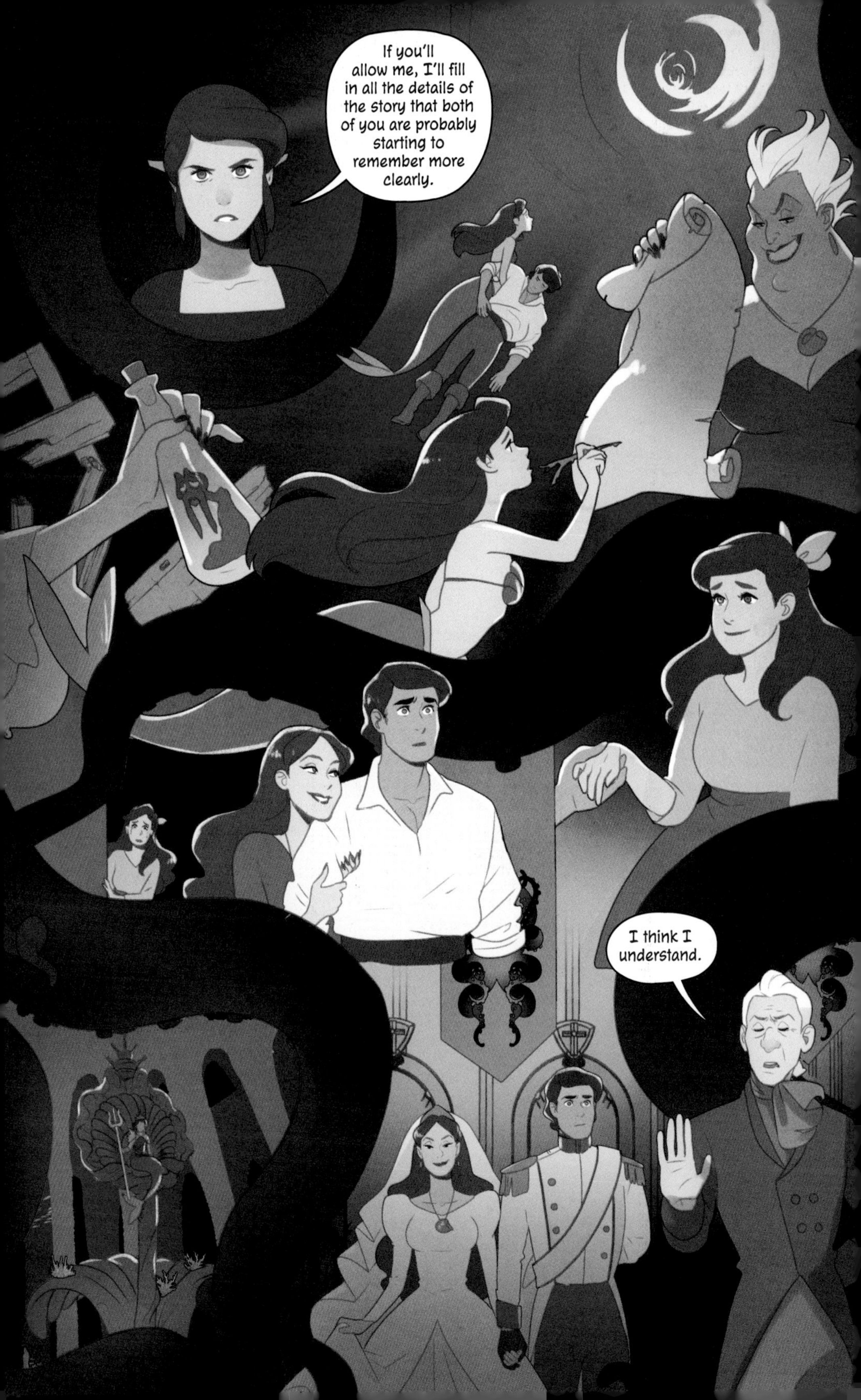
If you'll allow me, I'll fill in all the details of the story that both of you are probably starting to remember more clearly.
I think I understand.

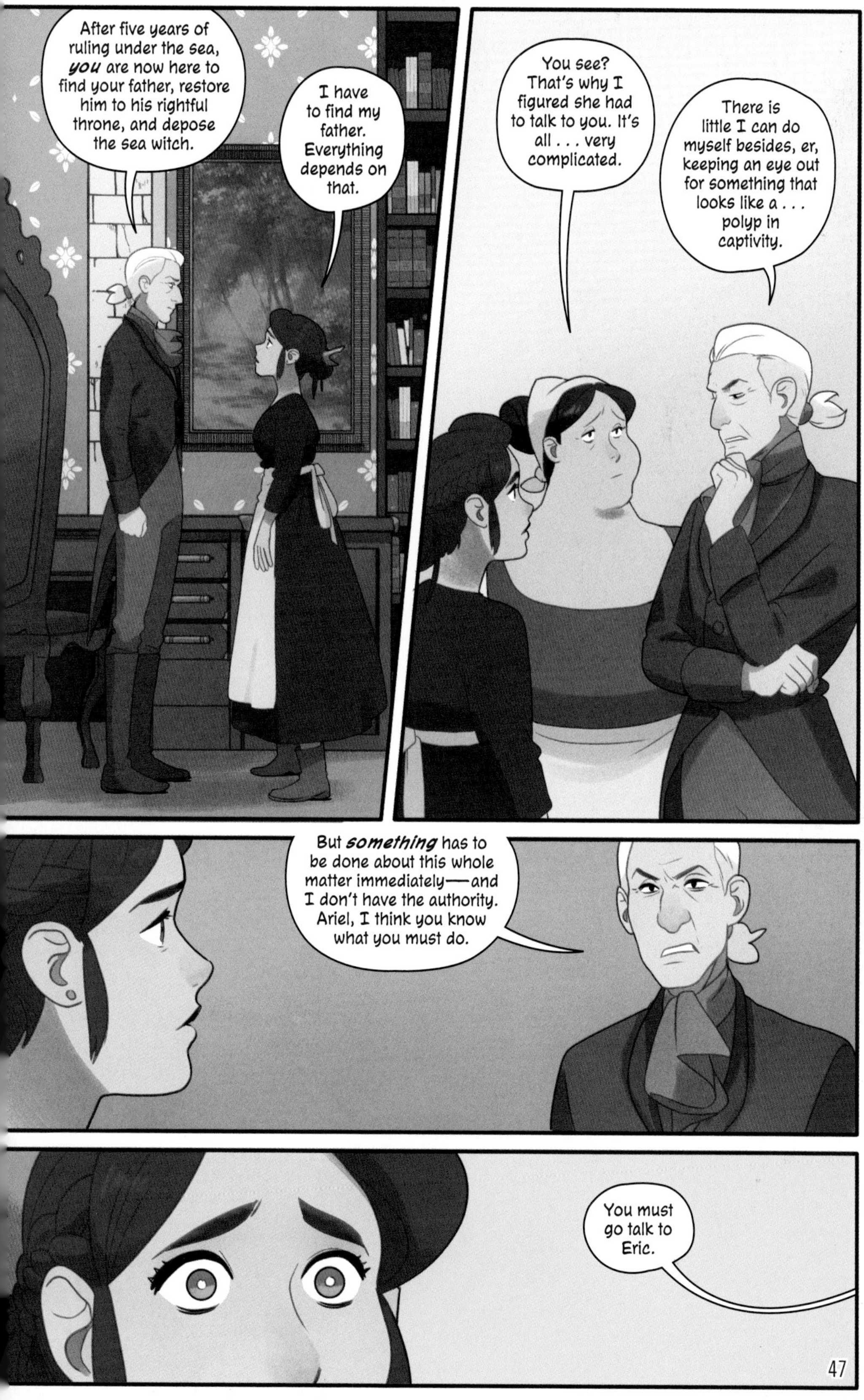
After five years of ruling under the sea, *you* are now here to find your father, restore him to his rightful throne, and depose the sea witch.
I have to find my father. Everything depends on that.
You see? That's why I figured she had to talk to you. It's all . . . very complicated.
There is little I can do myself besides, er, keeping an eye out for something that looks like a . . . polyp in captivity.
But *something* has to be done about this whole matter immediately—and I don't have the authority. Ariel, I think you know what you must do.
You must go talk to Eric.

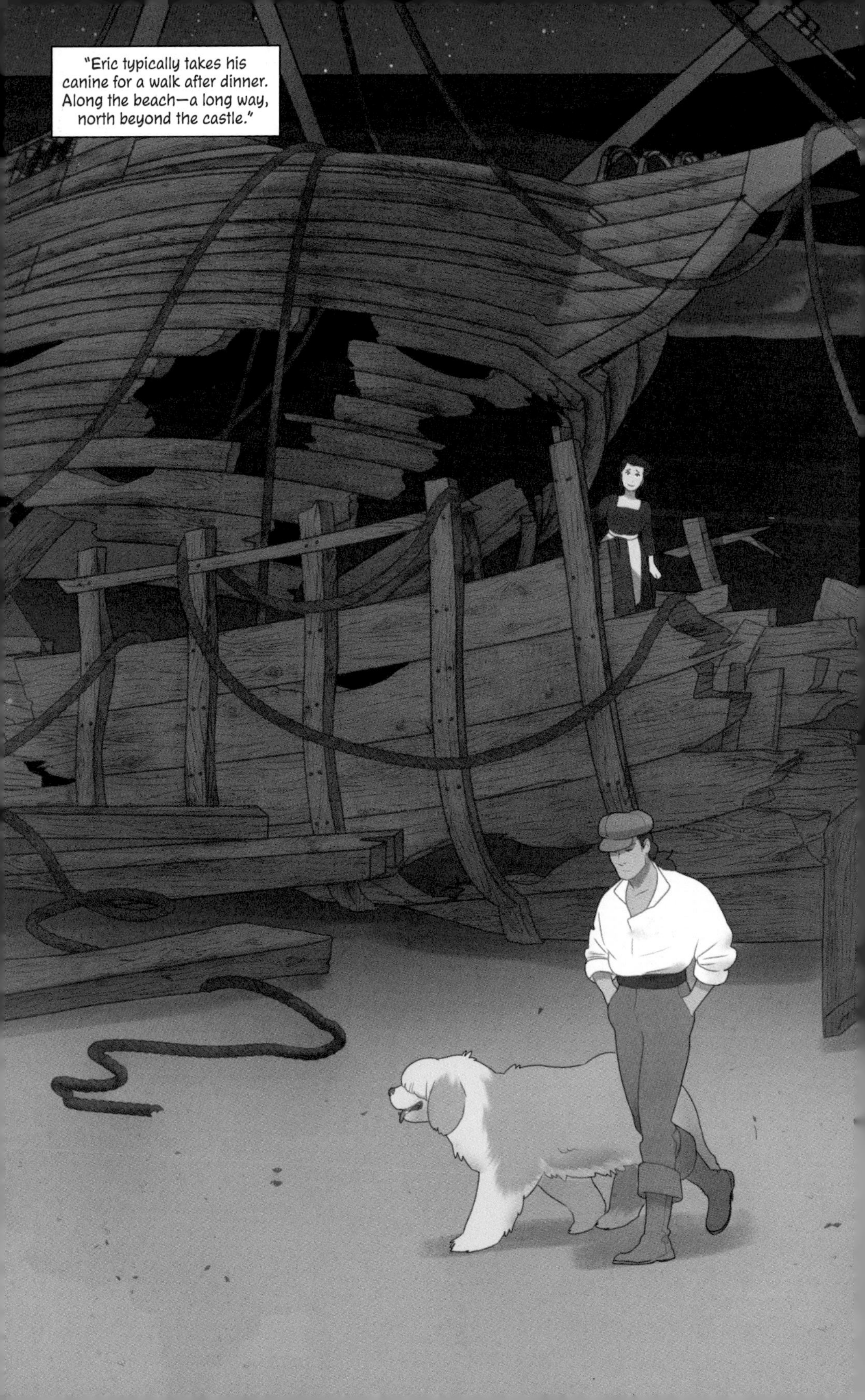
"Eric typically takes his canine for a walk after dinner. Along the beach—a long way, north beyond the castle."

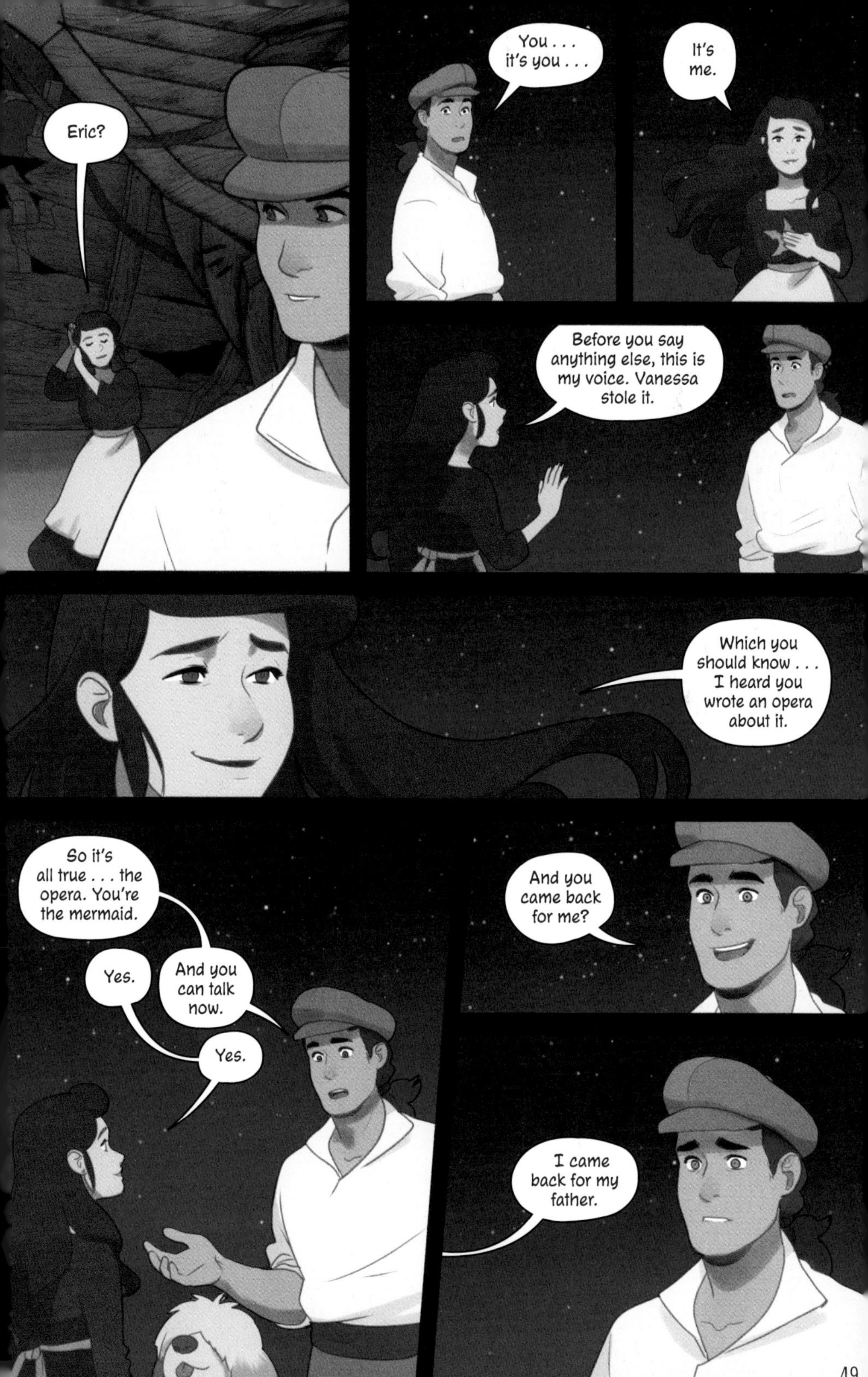
Eric?
You . . . it's you . . .
It's me.
Before you say anything else, this is my voice. Vanessa stole it.
Which you should know . . . I heard you wrote an opera about it.
So it's all true . . . the opera. You're the mermaid.
Yes.
And you can talk now.
Yes.
And you came back for me?
I came back for my father.

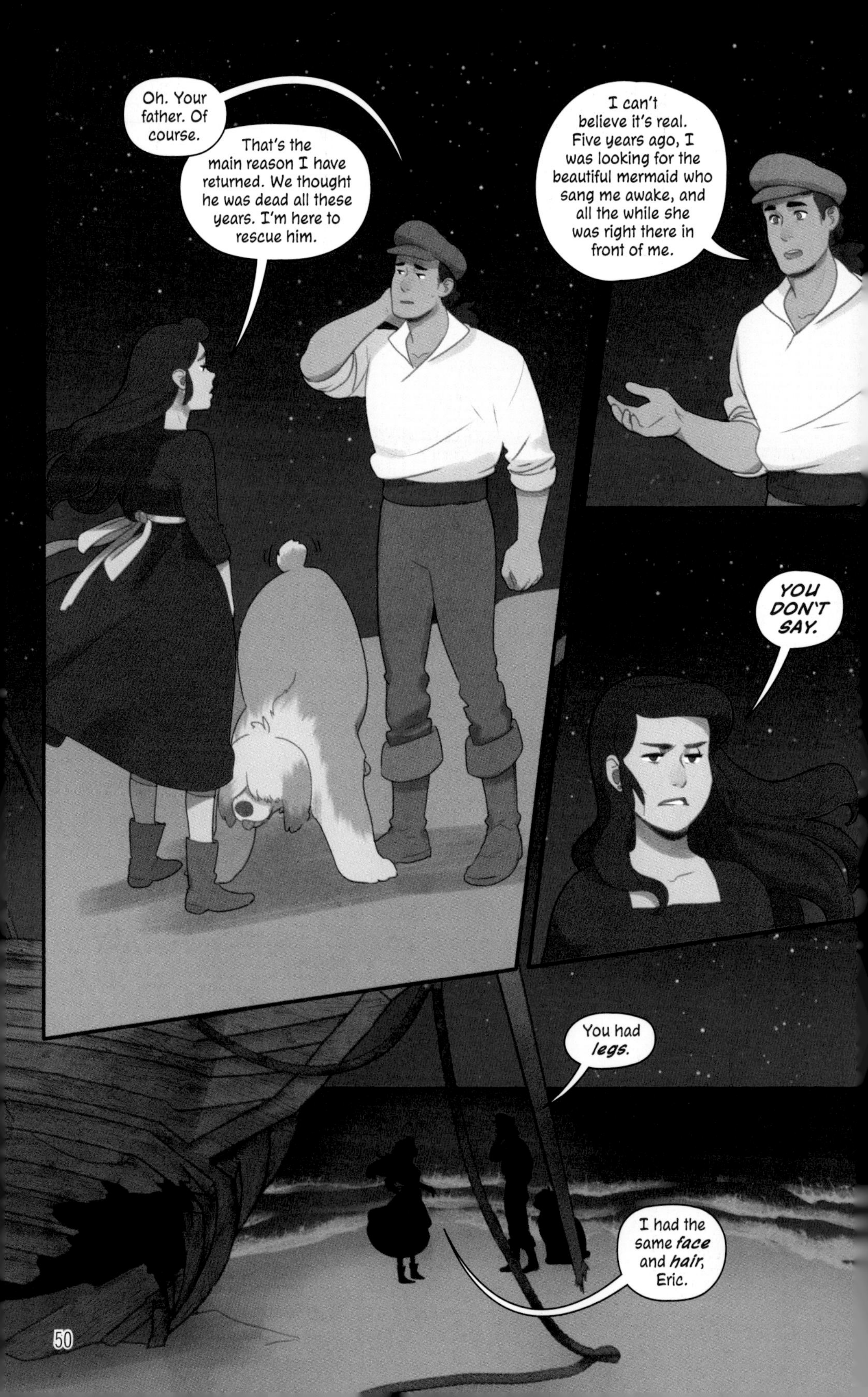
Oh. Your father. Of course.
That's the main reason I have returned. We thought he was dead all these years. I'm here to rescue him.
I can't believe it's real. Five years ago, I was looking for the beautiful mermaid who sang me awake, and all the while she was right there in front of me.
YOU DON'T SAY.
You had *legs*.
I had the same *face* and *hair*, Eric.

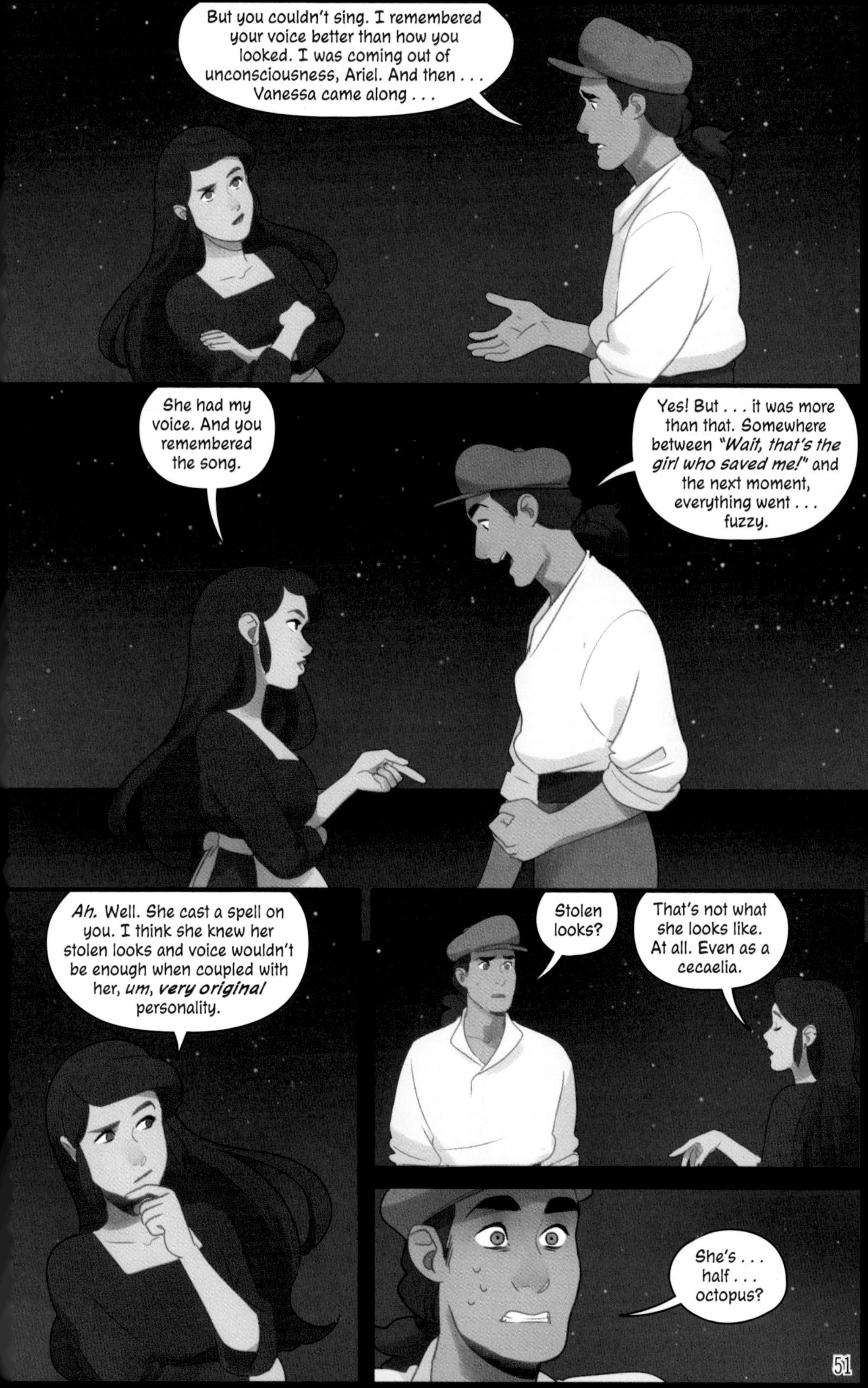
But you couldn't sing. I remembered your voice better than how you looked. I was coming out of unconsciousness, Ariel. And then . . . Vanessa came along . . .
She had my voice. And you remembered the song.
Yes! But . . . it was more than that. Somewhere between "*Wait, that's the girl who saved me!*" and the next moment, everything went . . . fuzzy.
Ah. Well. She cast a spell on you. I think she knew her stolen looks and voice wouldn't be enough when coupled with her, *um*, ***very original*** personality.
Stolen looks?
That's not what she looks like. At all. Even as a cecaelia.
She's . . . half . . . octopus?

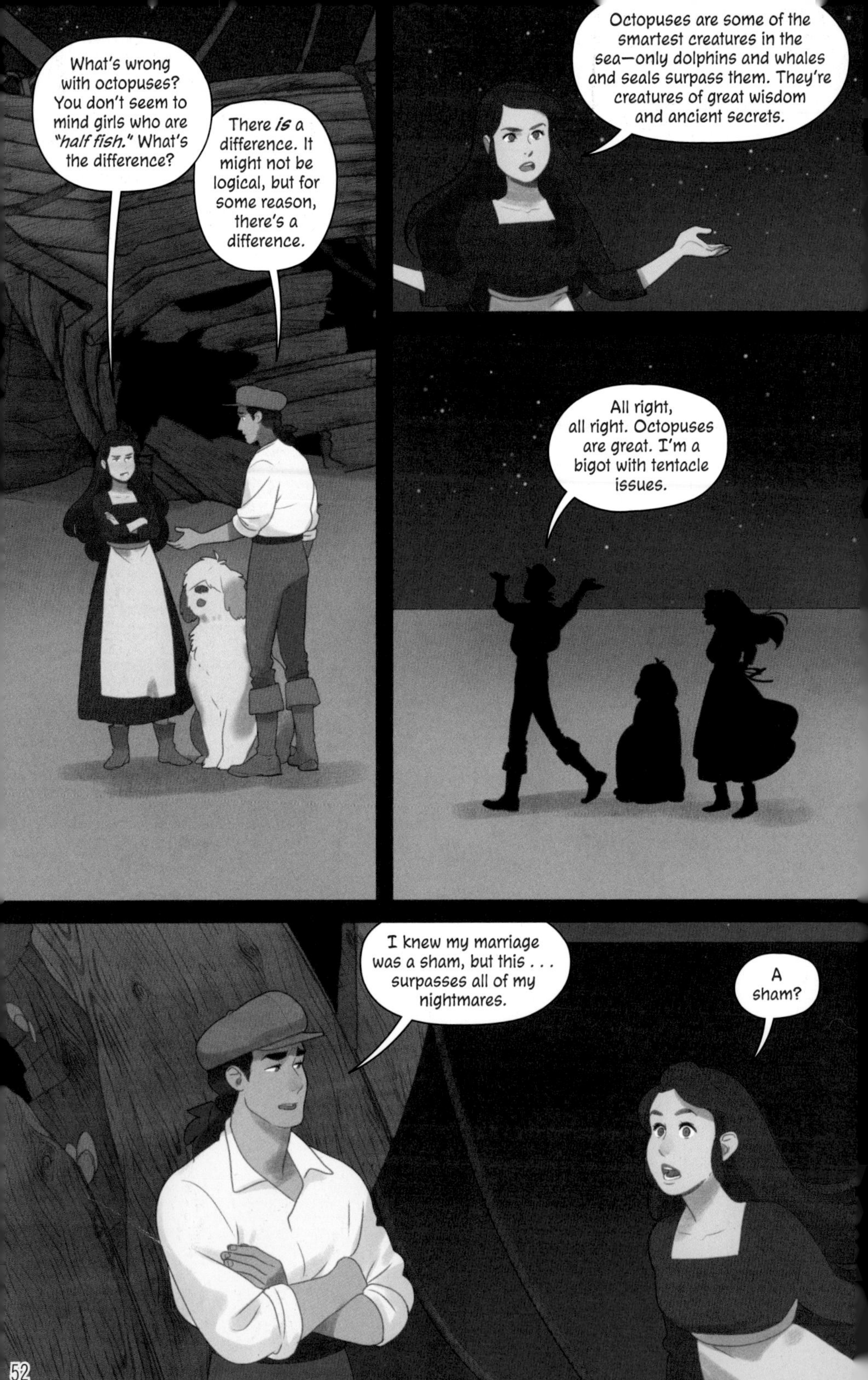
What's wrong with octopuses? You don't seem to mind girls who are *"half fish."* What's the difference?
There *is* a difference. It might not be logical, but for some reason, there's a difference.
Octopuses are some of the smartest creatures in the sea—only dolphins and whales and seals surpass them. They're creatures of great wisdom and ancient secrets.
All right, all right. Octopuses are great. I'm a bigot with tentacle issues.
I knew my marriage was a sham, but this . . . surpasses all of my nightmares.
A sham?

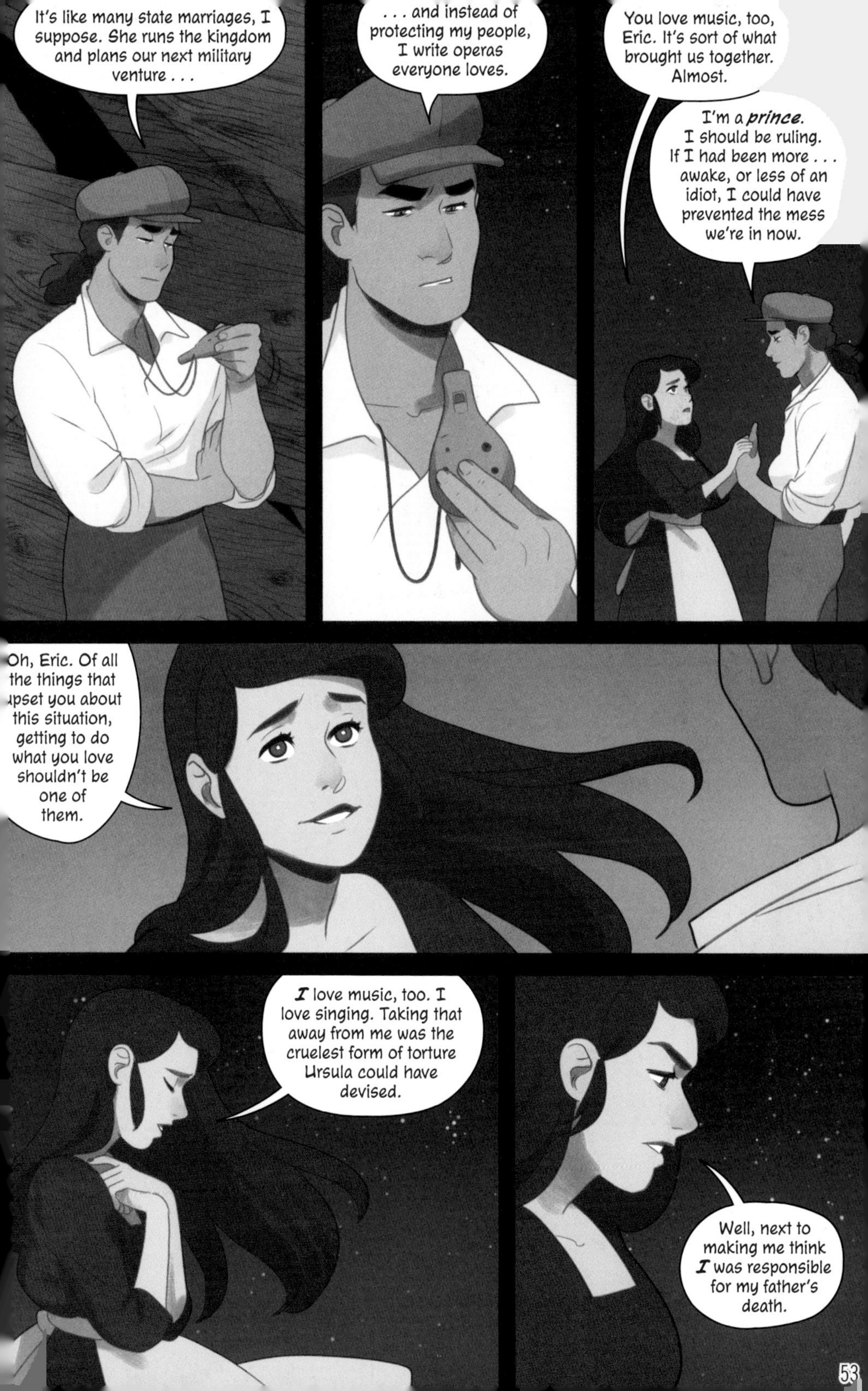
It's like many state marriages, I suppose. She runs the kingdom and plans our next military venture . . .
. . . and instead of protecting my people, I write operas everyone loves.
You love music, too, Eric. It's sort of what brought us together. Almost.
I'm a *prince.* I should be ruling. If I had been more . . . awake, or less of an idiot, I could have prevented the mess we're in now.
Oh, Eric. Of all the things that upset you about this situation, getting to do what you love shouldn't be one of them.
I love music, too. I love singing. Taking that away from me was the cruelest form of torture Ursula could have devised.
Well, next to making me think *I* was responsible for my father's death.

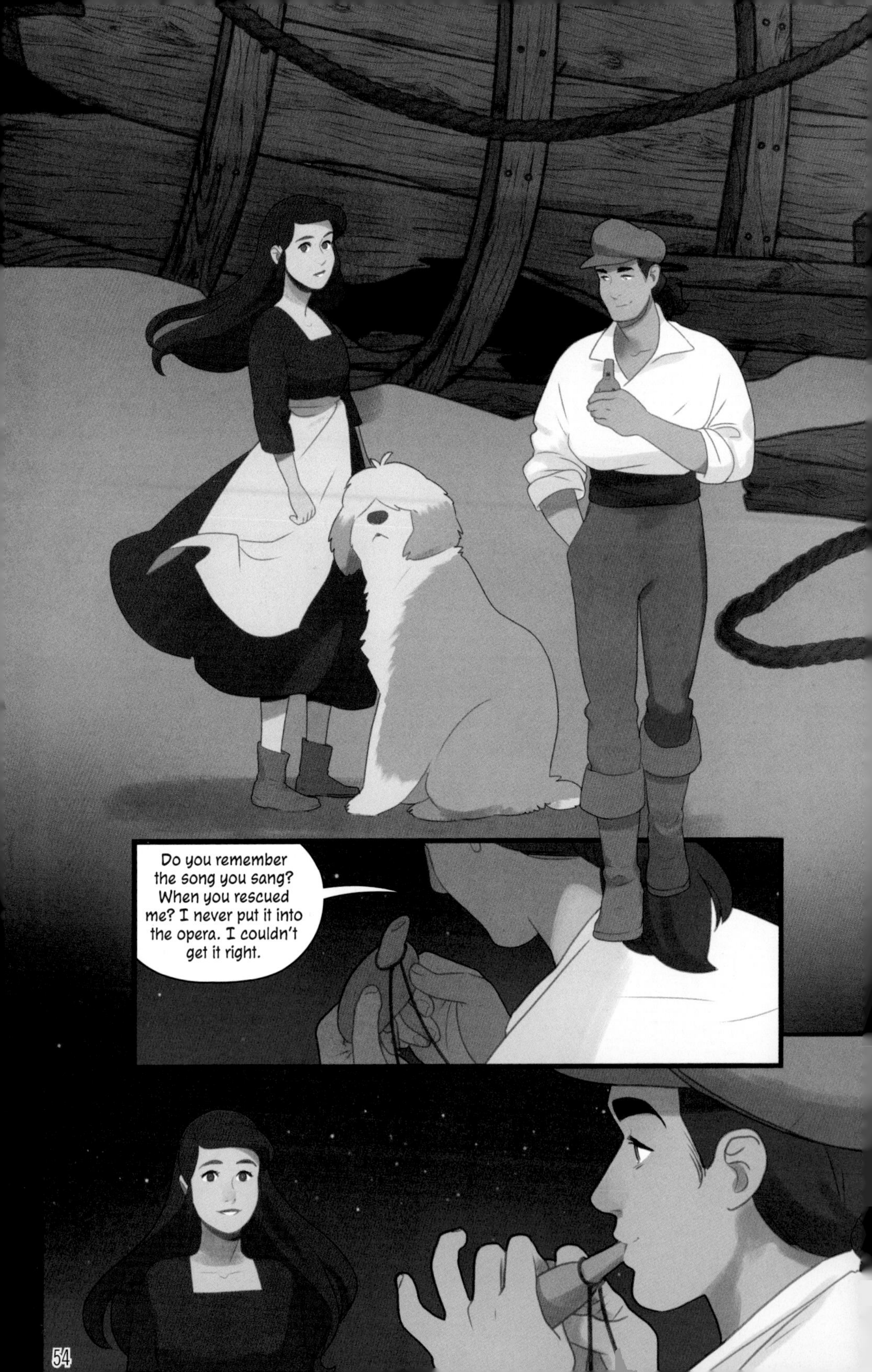
Do you remember the song you sang? When you rescued me? I never put it into the opera. I couldn't get it right.

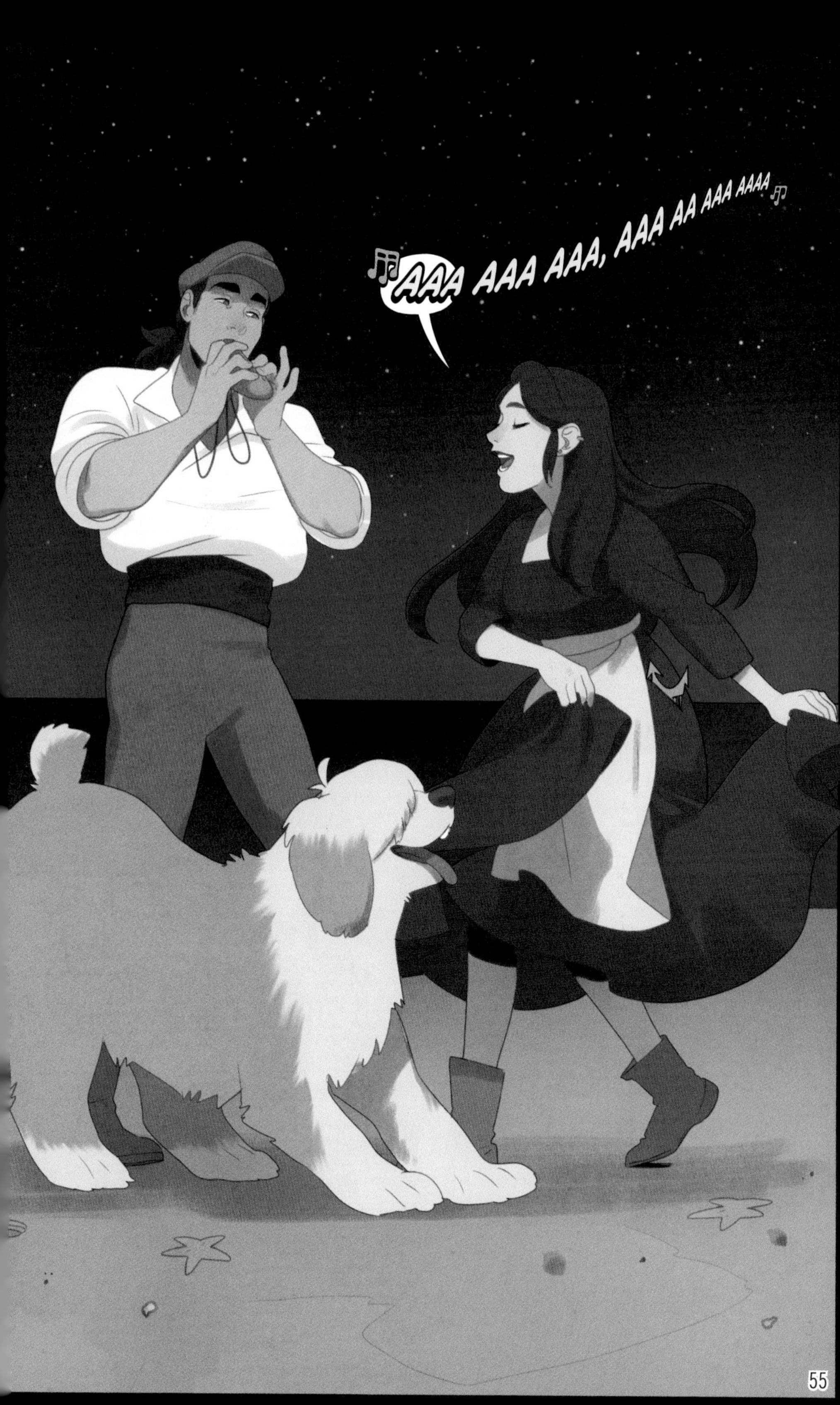
AAA AAA AAA, AAA AA AAA AAAA

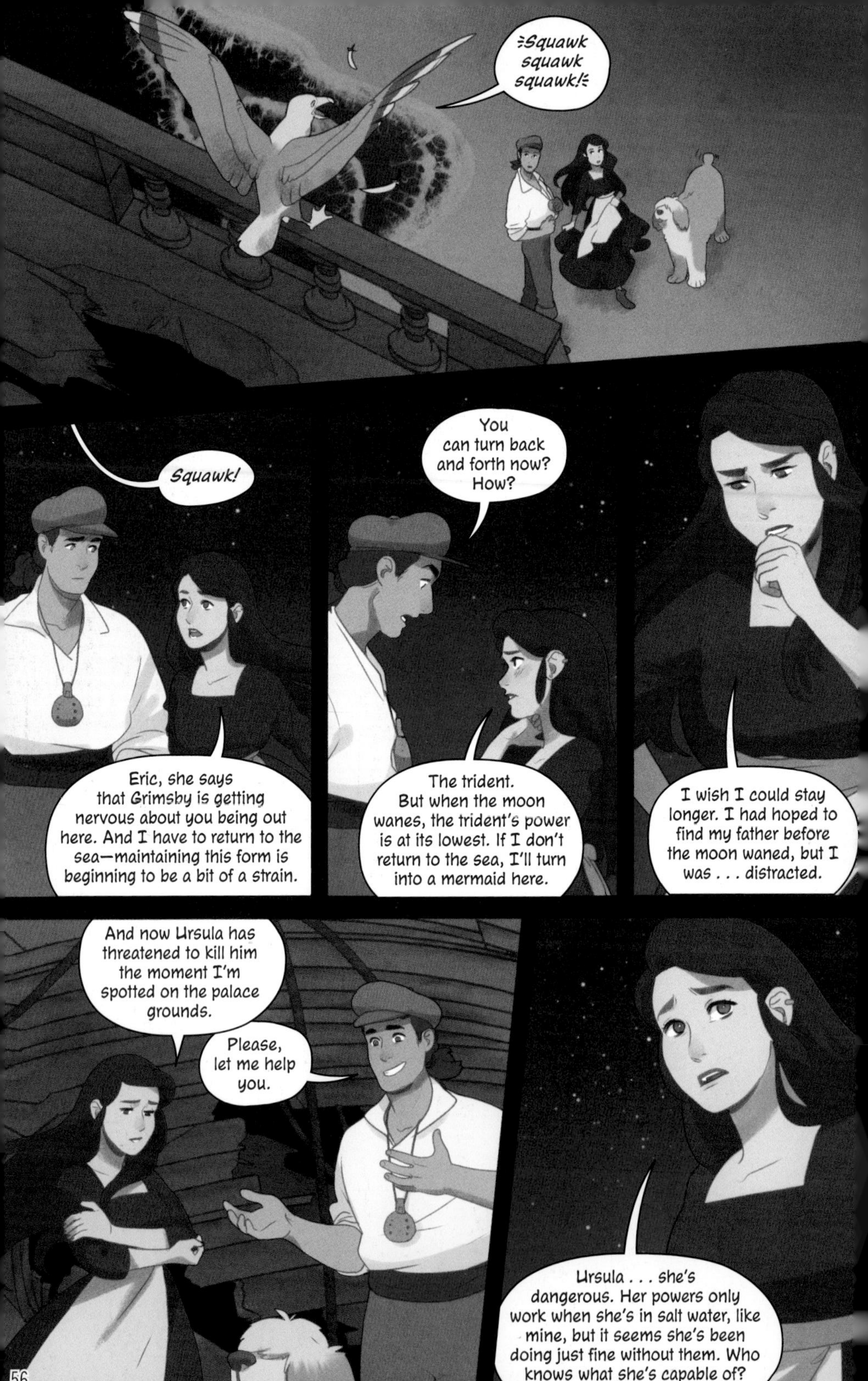
Squawk squawk squawk!
Squawk!
Eric, she says that Grimsby is getting nervous about you being out here. And I have to return to the sea—maintaining this form is beginning to be a bit of a strain.
You can turn back and forth now? How?
The trident. But when the moon wanes, the trident's power is at its lowest. If I don't return to the sea, I'll turn into a mermaid here.
I wish I could stay longer. I had hoped to find my father before the moon waned, but I was . . . distracted.
And now Ursula has threatened to kill him the moment I'm spotted on the palace grounds.
Please, let me help you.
Ursula . . . she's dangerous. Her powers only work when she's in salt water, like mine, but it seems she's been doing just fine without them. Who knows what she's capable of?

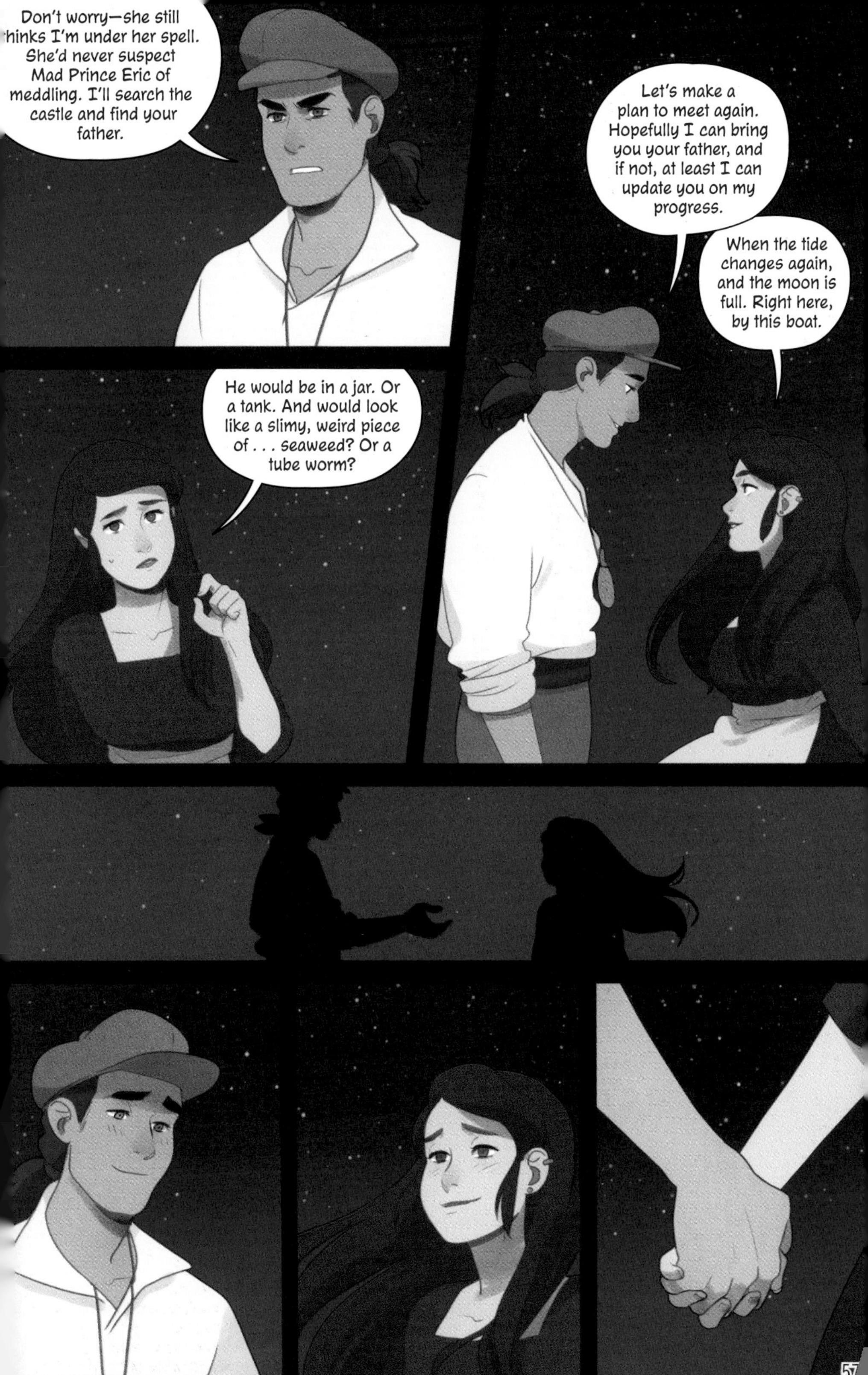
Don't worry—she still thinks I'm under her spell. She'd never suspect Mad Prince Eric of meddling. I'll search the castle and find your father.
Let's make a plan to meet again. Hopefully I can bring you your father, and if not, at least I can update you on my progress.
He would be in a jar. Or a tank. And would look like a slimy, weird piece of . . . seaweed? Or a tube worm?
When the tide changes again, and the moon is full. Right here, by this boat.

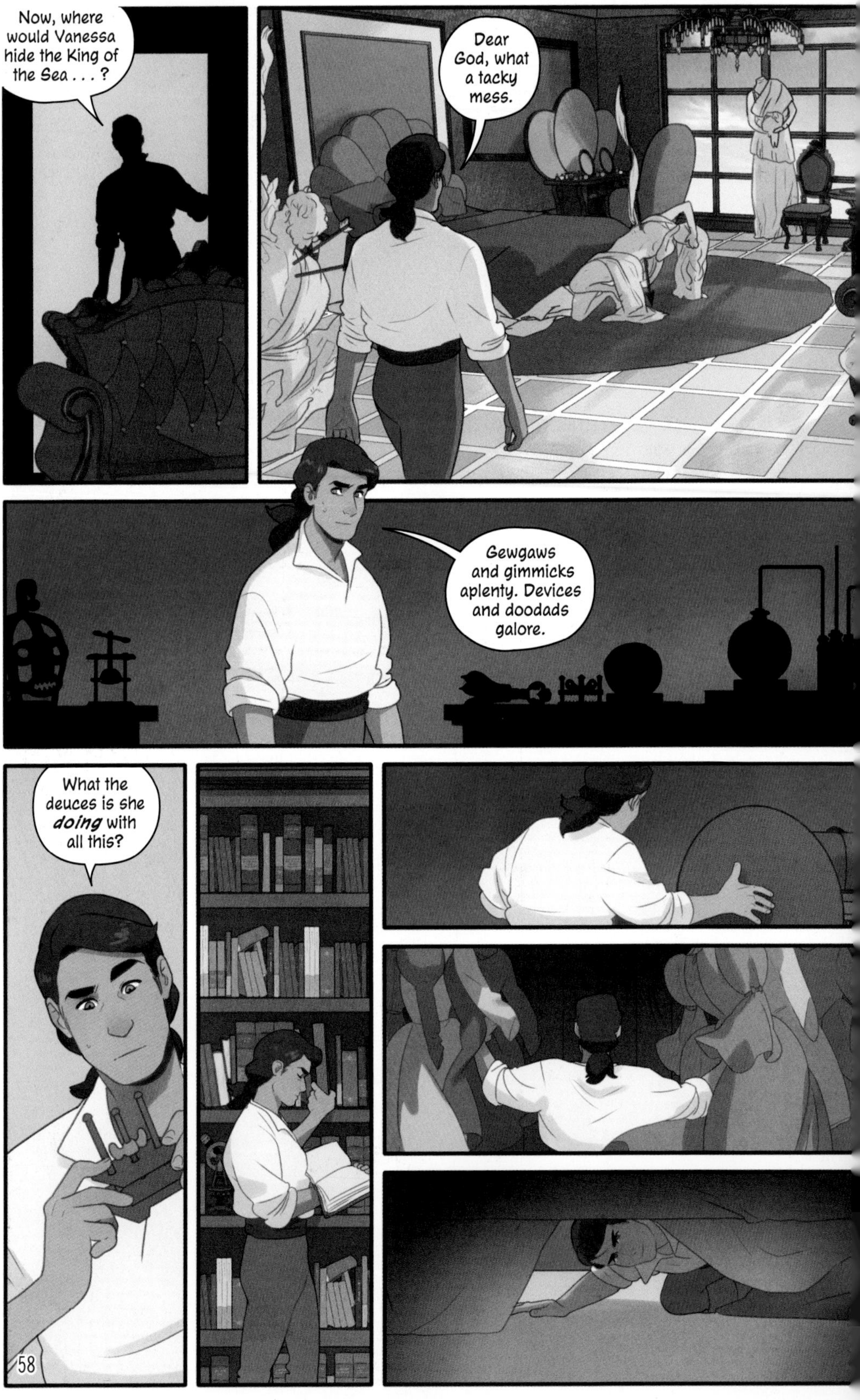
Now, where would Vanessa hide the King of the Sea . . . ?
Dear God, what a tacky mess.
Gewgaws and gimmicks aplenty. Devices and doodads galore.
What the deuces is she *doing* with all this?

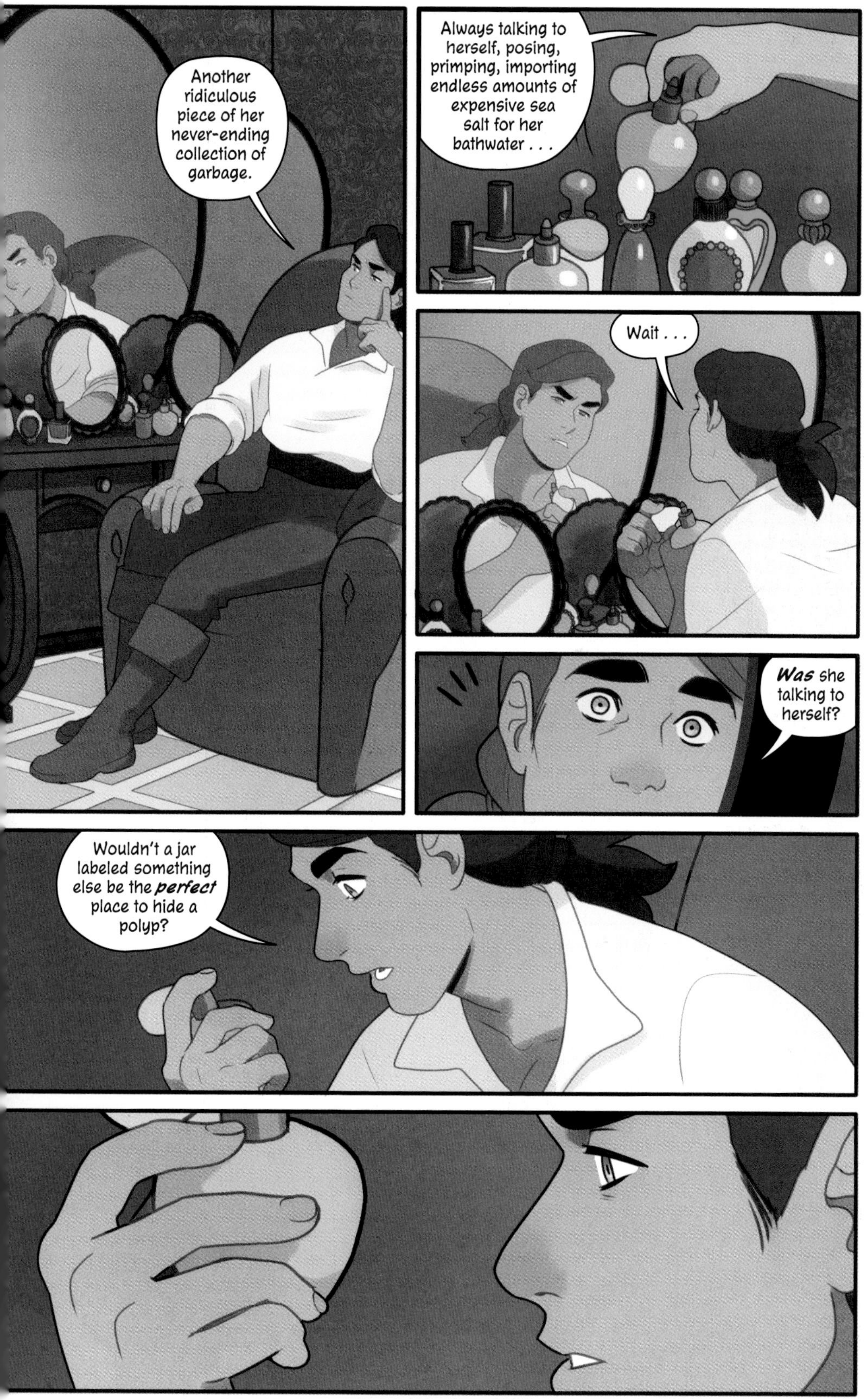
Another ridiculous piece of her never-ending collection of garbage.
Always talking to herself, posing, primping, importing endless amounts of expensive sea salt for her bathwater . . .
Wait . . .
Was she talking to herself?
Wouldn't a jar labeled something else be the *perfect* place to hide a polyp?

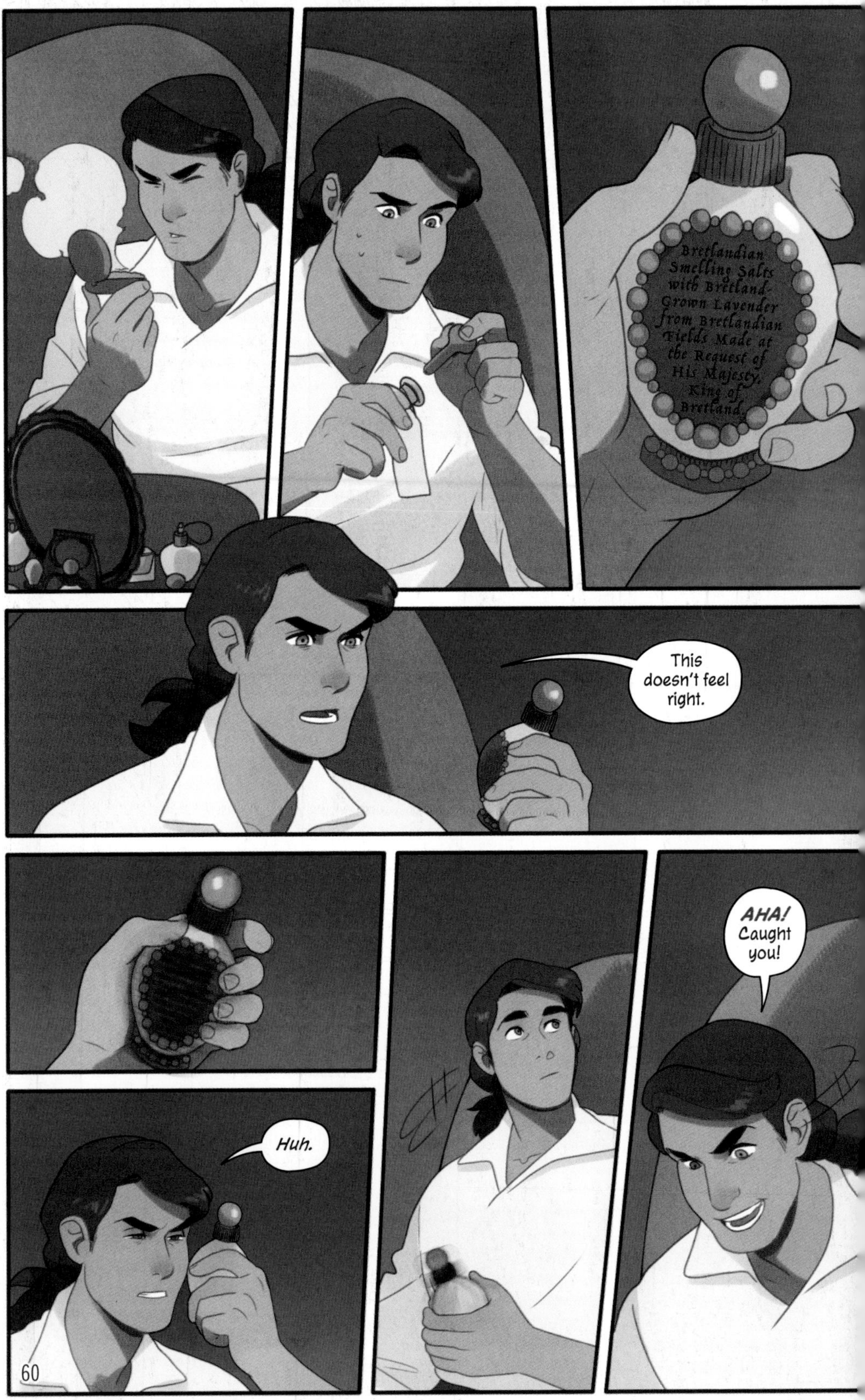
Bretlandian Smelling Salts with Bretland-Grown Lavender from Bretlandian Fields Made at the Request of His Majesty, King of Bretland.
This doesn't feel right.
Huh.
AHA! Caught you!

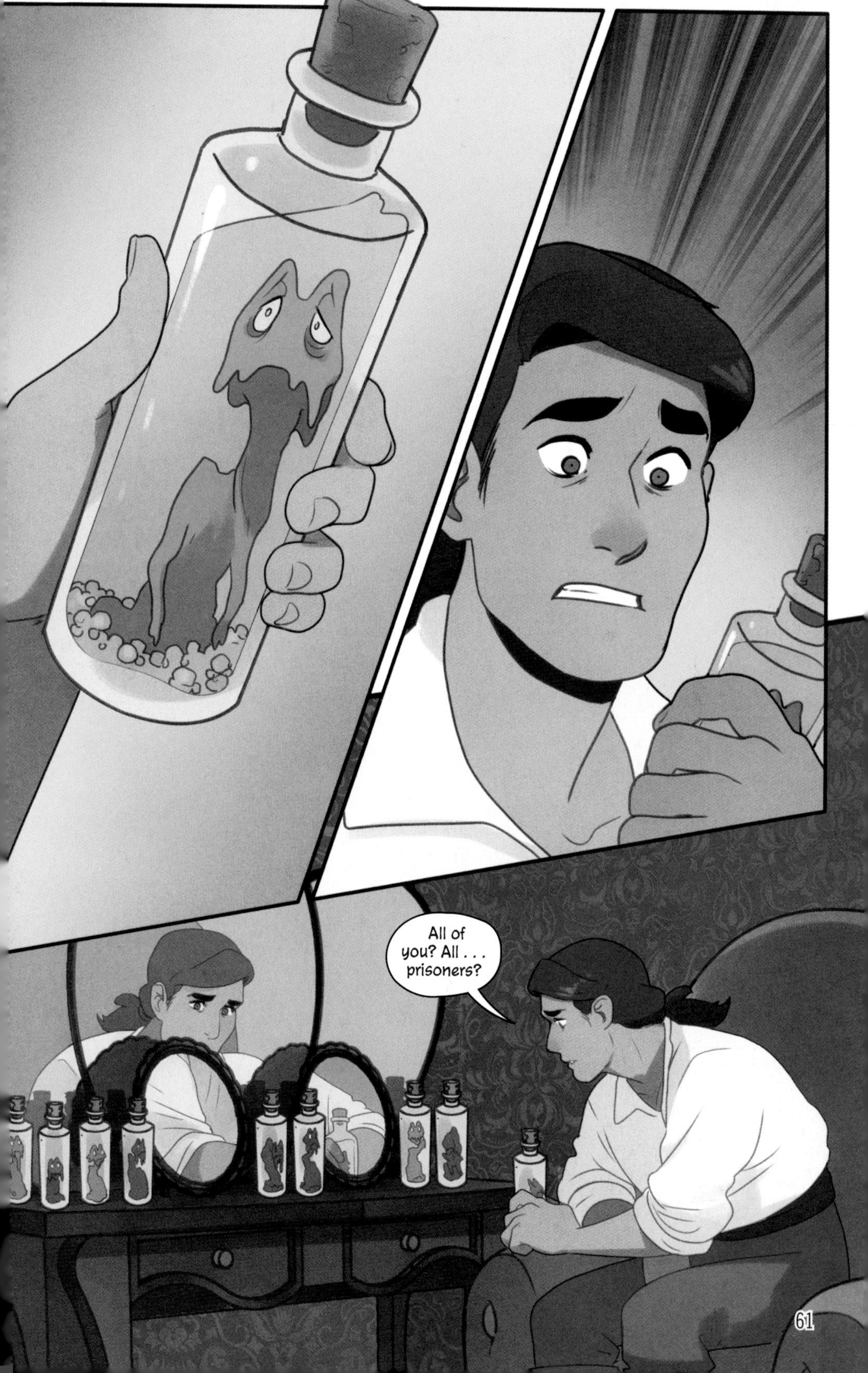
All of you? All . . . prisoners?

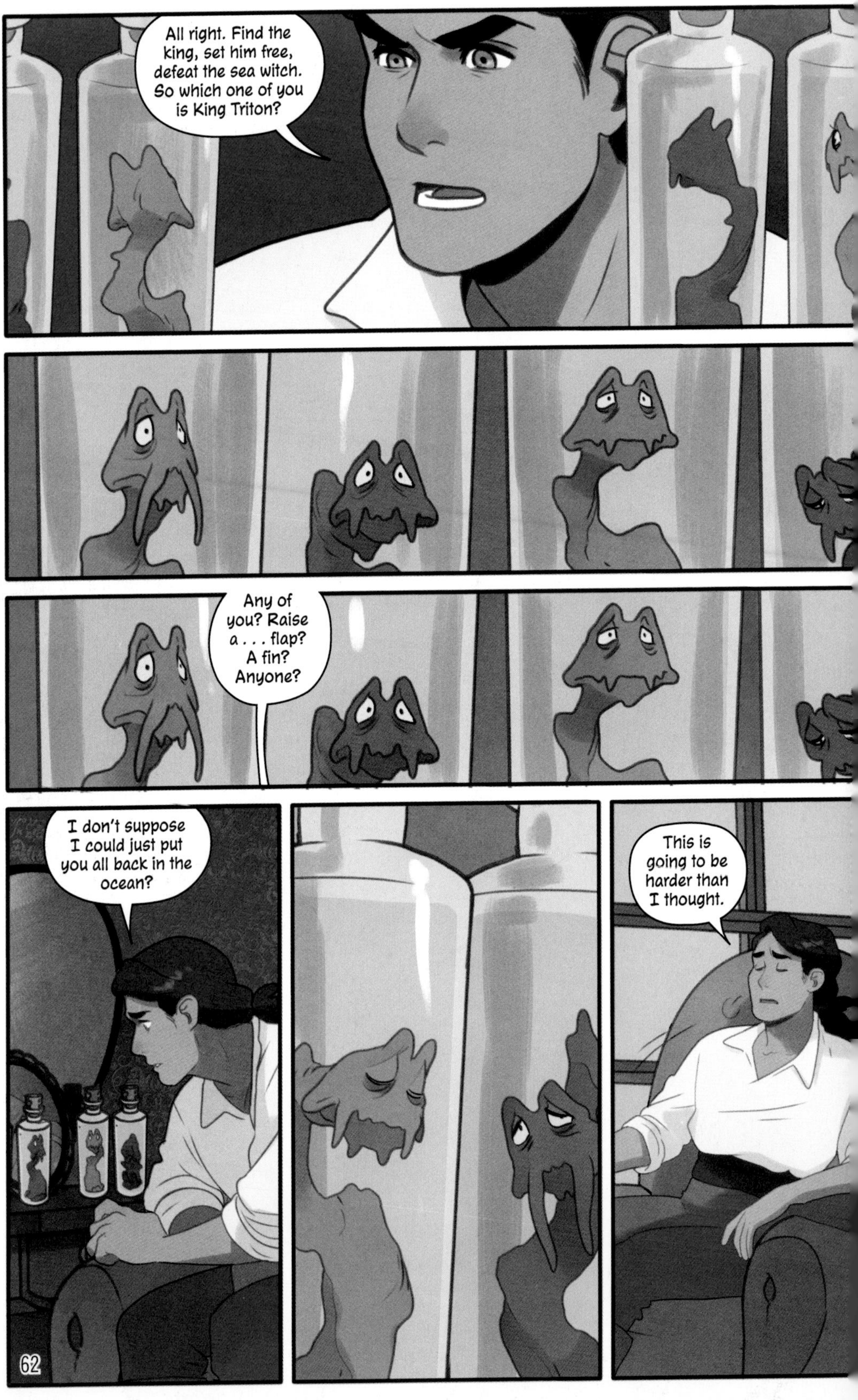
All right. Find the king, set him free, defeat the sea witch. So which one of you is King Triton?
Any of you? Raise a . . . flap? A fin? Anyone?
I don't suppose I could just put you all back in the ocean?
This is going to be harder than I thought.

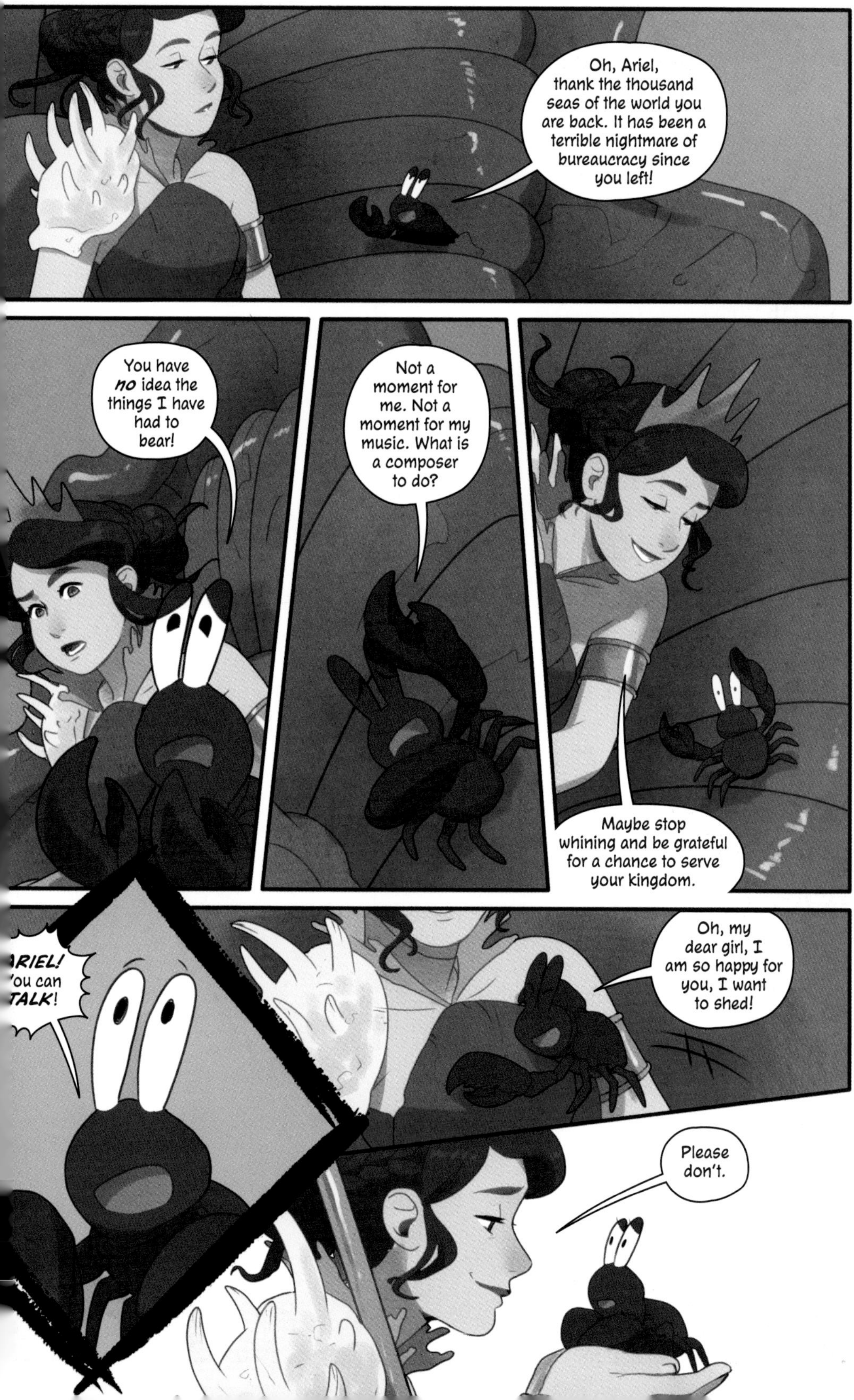
Oh, Ariel, thank the thousand seas of the world you are back. It has been a terrible nightmare of bureaucracy since you left!
You have *no* idea the things I have had to bear!
Not a moment for me. Not a moment for my music. What is a composer to do?
Maybe stop whining and be grateful for a chance to serve your kingdom.
ARIEL! You can TALK!
Oh, my dear girl, I am so happy for you, I want to shed!
Please don't.

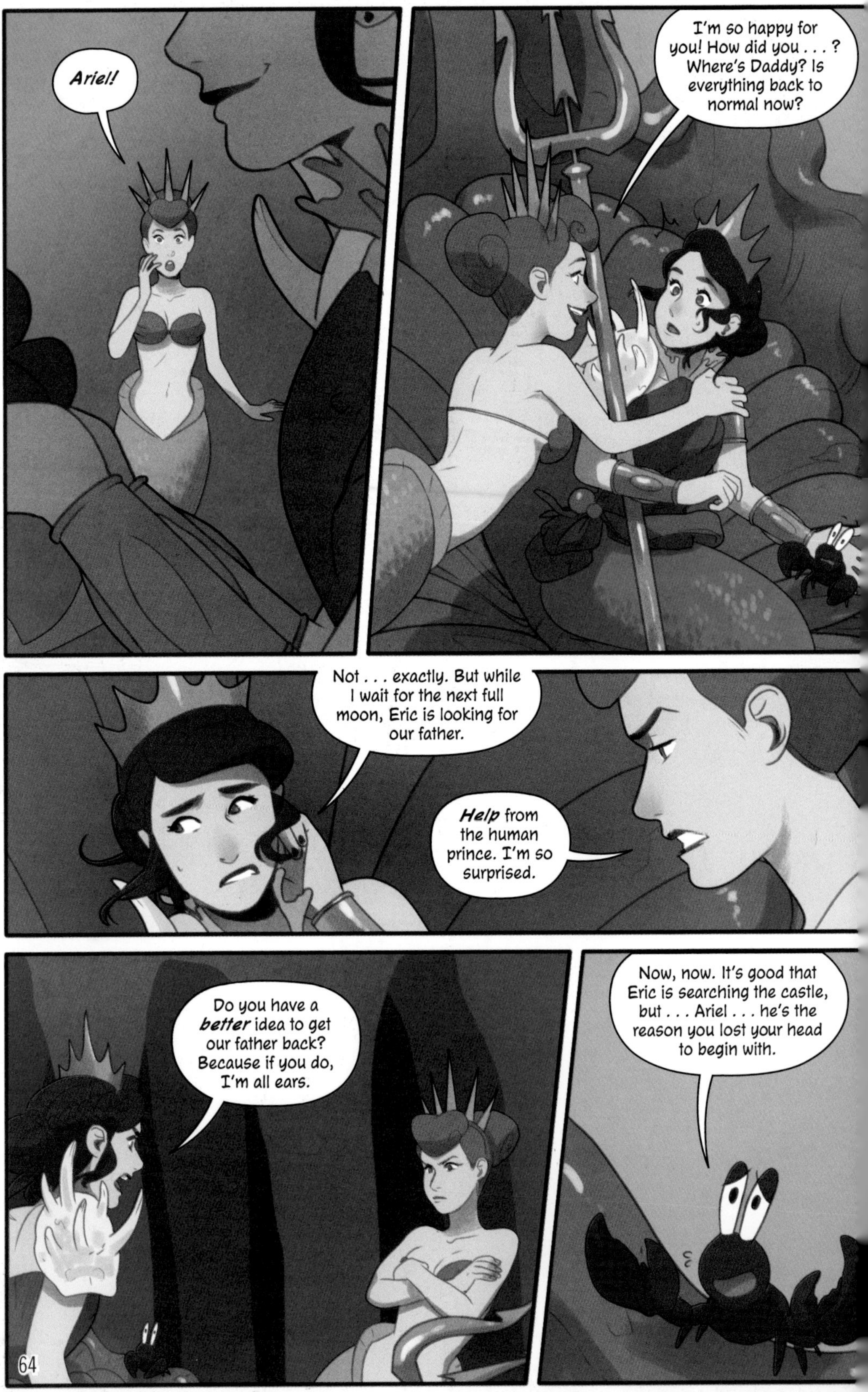
Ariel!
I'm so happy for you! How did you . . . ? Where's Daddy? Is everything back to normal now?
Not . . . exactly. But while I wait for the next full moon, Eric is looking for our father.
Help from the human prince. I'm so surprised.
Do you have a better idea to get our father back? Because if you do, I'm all ears.
Now, now. It's good that Eric is searching the castle, but . . . Ariel . . . he's the reason you lost your head to begin with.

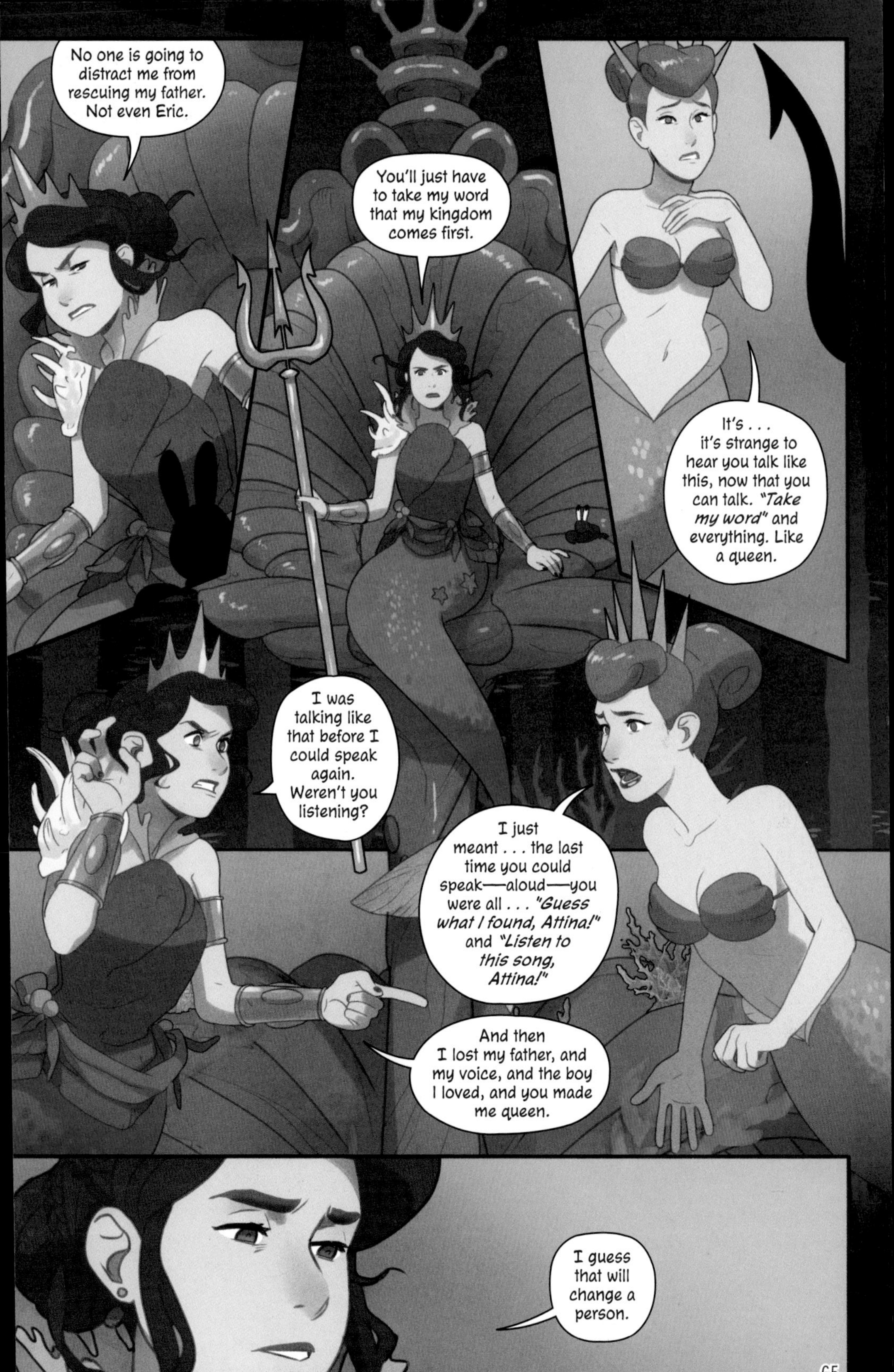
No one is going to distract me from rescuing my father. Not even Eric.
You'll just have to take my word that my kingdom comes first.
It's . . . it's strange to hear you talk like this, now that you can talk. *"Take my word"* and everything. Like a queen.
I was talking like that before I could speak again. Weren't you listening?
I just meant . . . the last time you could speak—aloud—you were all . . . *"Guess what I found, Attina!"* and *"Listen to this song, Attina!"*
And then I lost my father, and my voice, and the boy I loved, and you made me queen.
I guess that will change a person.

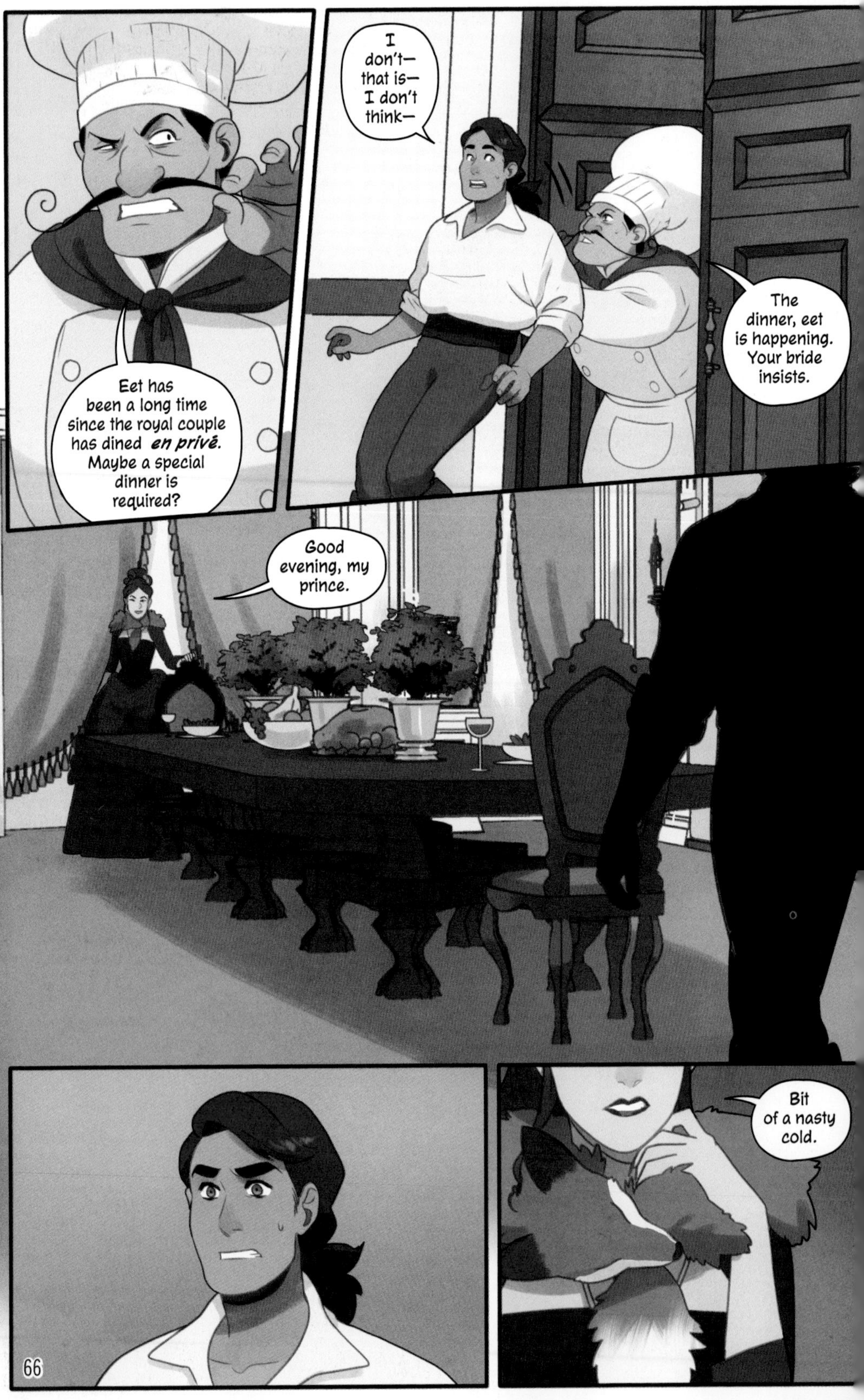
Eet has been a long time since the royal couple has dined *en privé.* Maybe a special dinner is required?
I don't— that is— I don't think—
The dinner, eet is happening. Your bride insists.
Good evening, my prince.
Bit of a nasty cold.

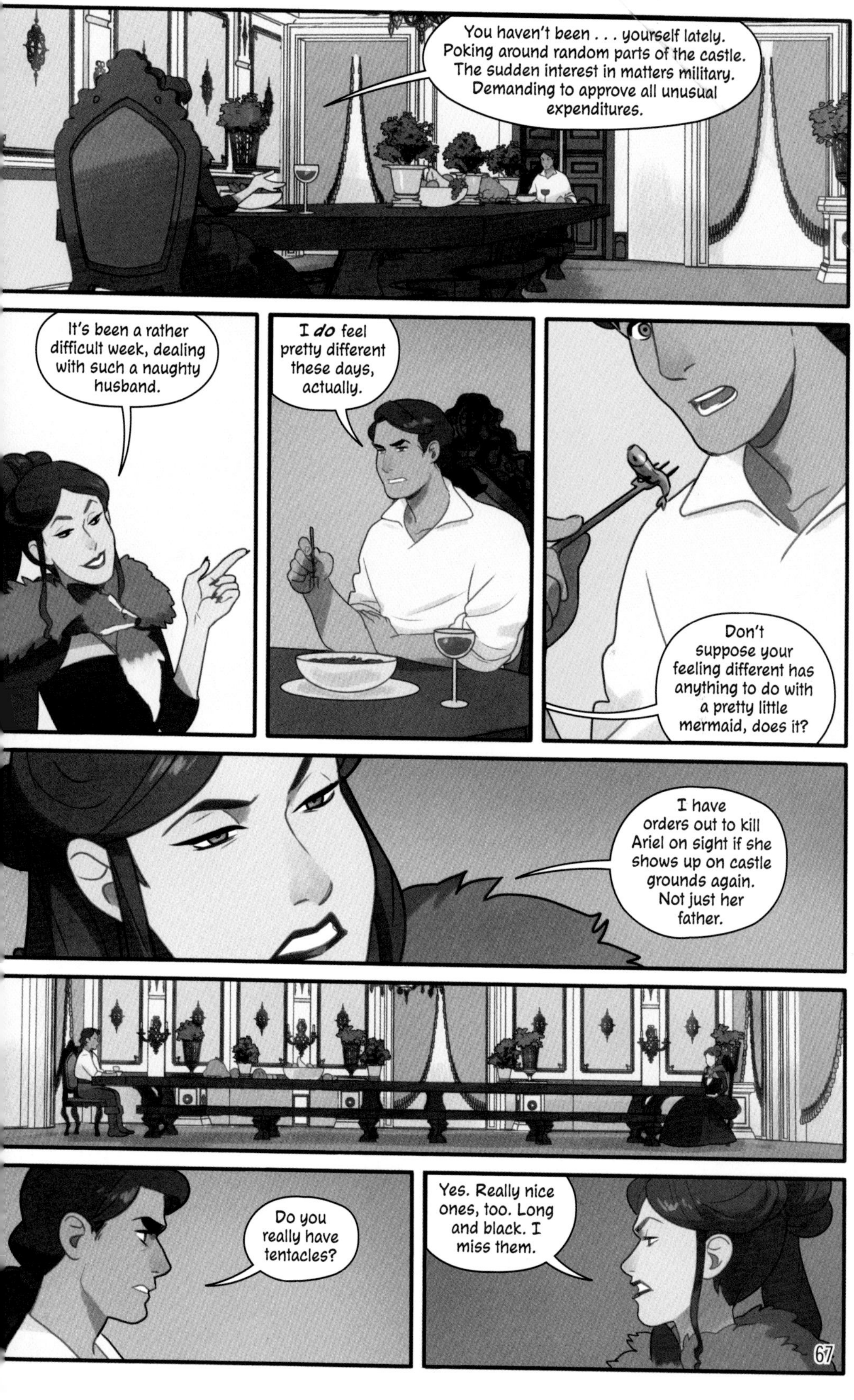
You haven't been . . . yourself lately. Poking around random parts of the castle. The sudden interest in matters military. Demanding to approve all unusual expenditures.
It's been a rather difficult week, dealing with such a naughty husband.
I *do* feel pretty different these days, actually.
Don't suppose your feeling different has anything to do with a pretty little mermaid, does it?
I have orders out to kill Ariel on sight if she shows up on castle grounds again. Not just her father.
Do you really have tentacles?
Yes. Really nice ones, too. Long and black. I miss them.

What do you want?

What?

What? Do you *want*? Why are you still here? If my . . . memory . . . and legend has it right, you really are a powerful witch under the sea. What do you want to be here for?

Here's the truth, then, if we are speaking plainly. I find I rather *like* you humans! You're so shortsighted and power-hungry . . . such a mess of wants and desires.

Such fun to play with . . .

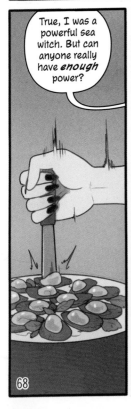

True, I was a powerful sea witch. But can anyone really have *enough* power?

Even with Triton gone, there are seven sisters defending his crown and a mer army. Here? I *am* running the show.

And once my warships are completed, who knows how far my empire will extend? One puny kingdom under the sea is nothing compared to an entire *continent*.

And all it took was a marriage.

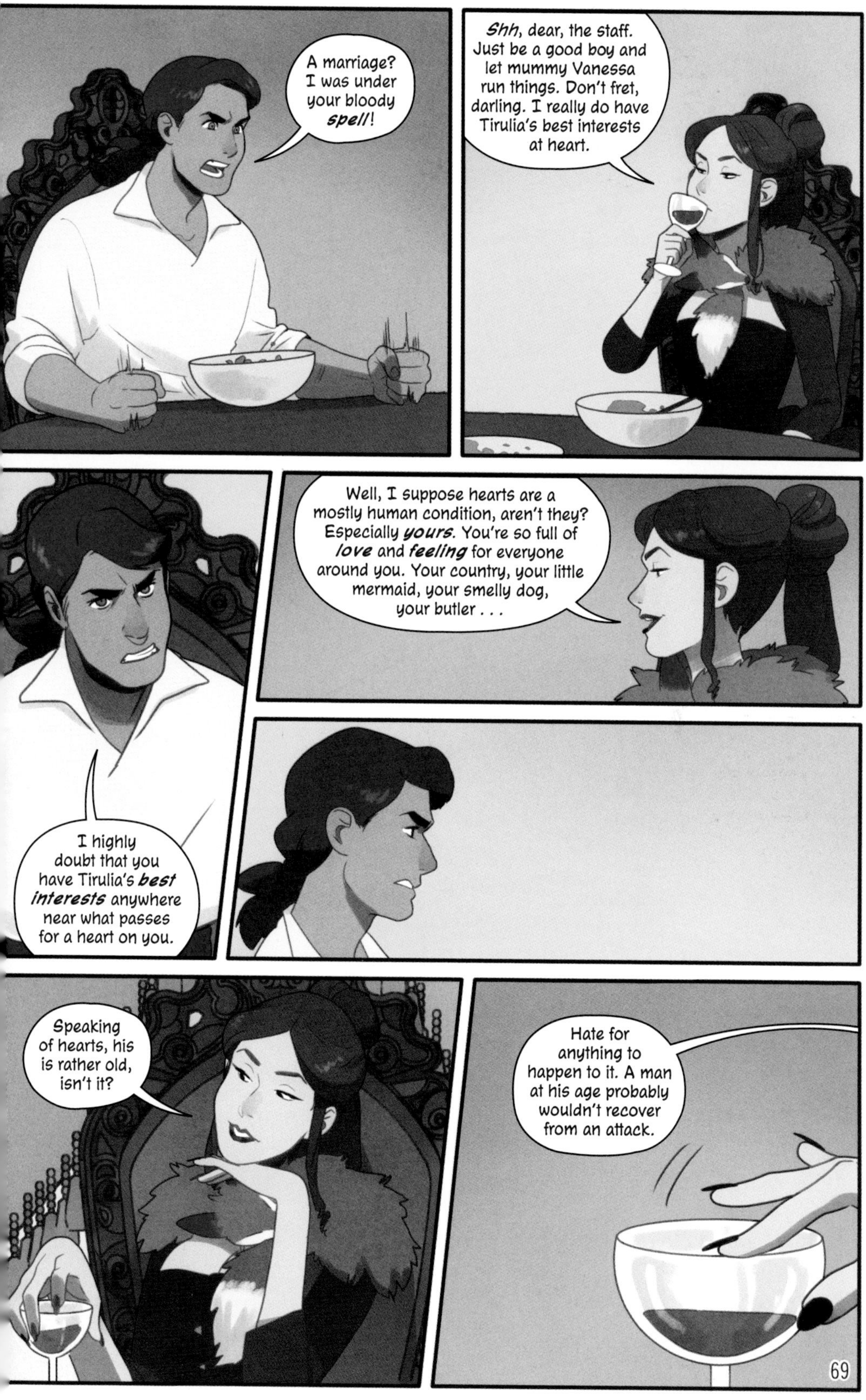

A marriage? I was under your bloody *spell*!
Shh, dear, the staff. Just be a good boy and let mummy Vanessa run things. Don't fret, darling. I really do have Tirulia's best interests at heart.
Well, I suppose hearts are a mostly human condition, aren't they? Especially ***yours***. You're so full of ***love*** and ***feeling*** for everyone around you. Your country, your little mermaid, your smelly dog, your butler . . .
I highly doubt that you have Tirulia's ***best interests*** anywhere near what passes for a heart on you.
Speaking of hearts, his is rather old, isn't it?
Hate for anything to happen to it. A man at his age probably wouldn't recover from an attack.

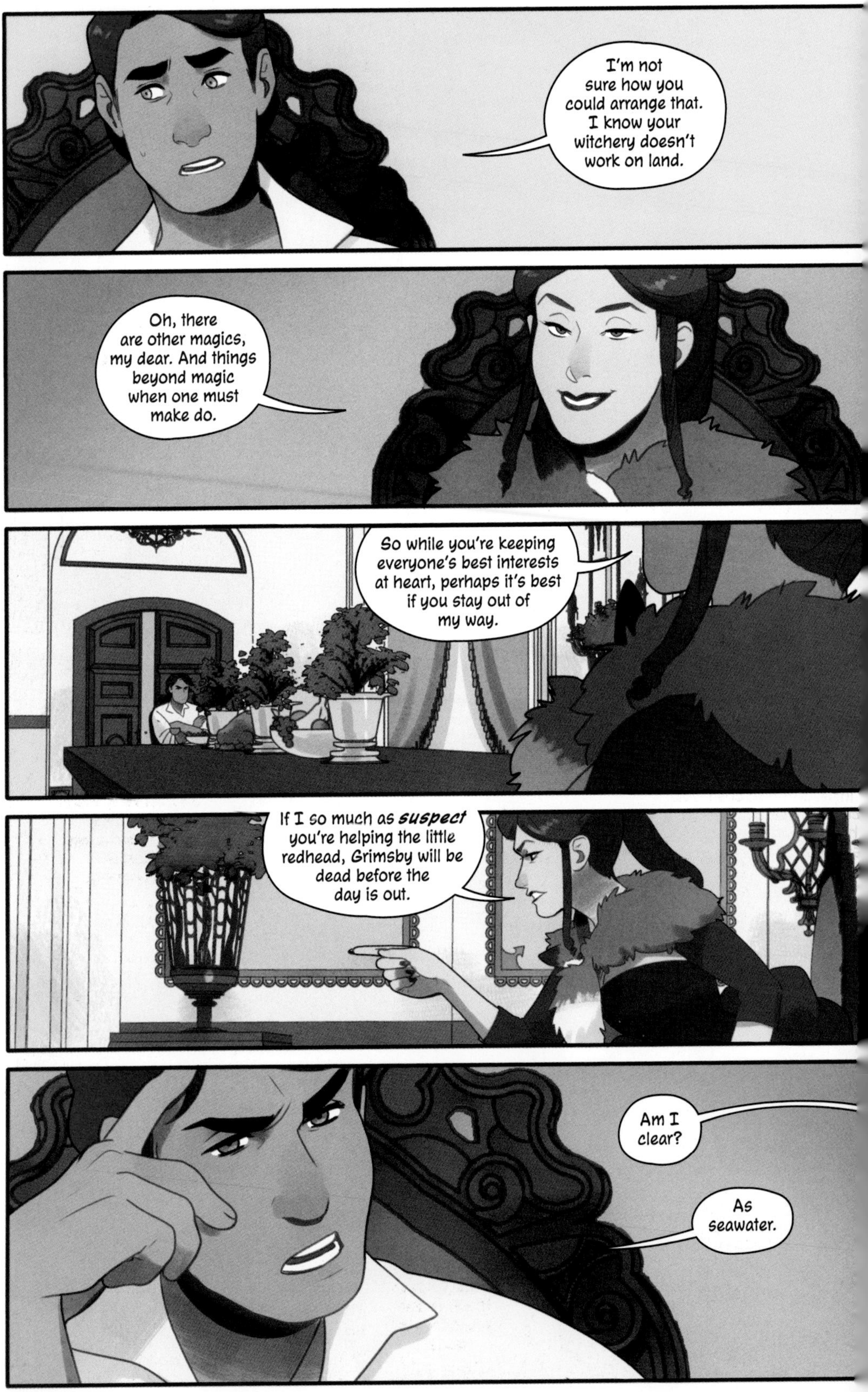
I'm not sure how you could arrange that. I know your witchery doesn't work on land.
Oh, there are other magics, my dear. And things beyond magic when one must make do.
So while you're keeping everyone's best interests at heart, perhaps it's best if you stay out of my way.
If I so much as *suspect* you're helping the little redhead, Grimsby will be dead before the day is out.
Am I clear?
As seawater.

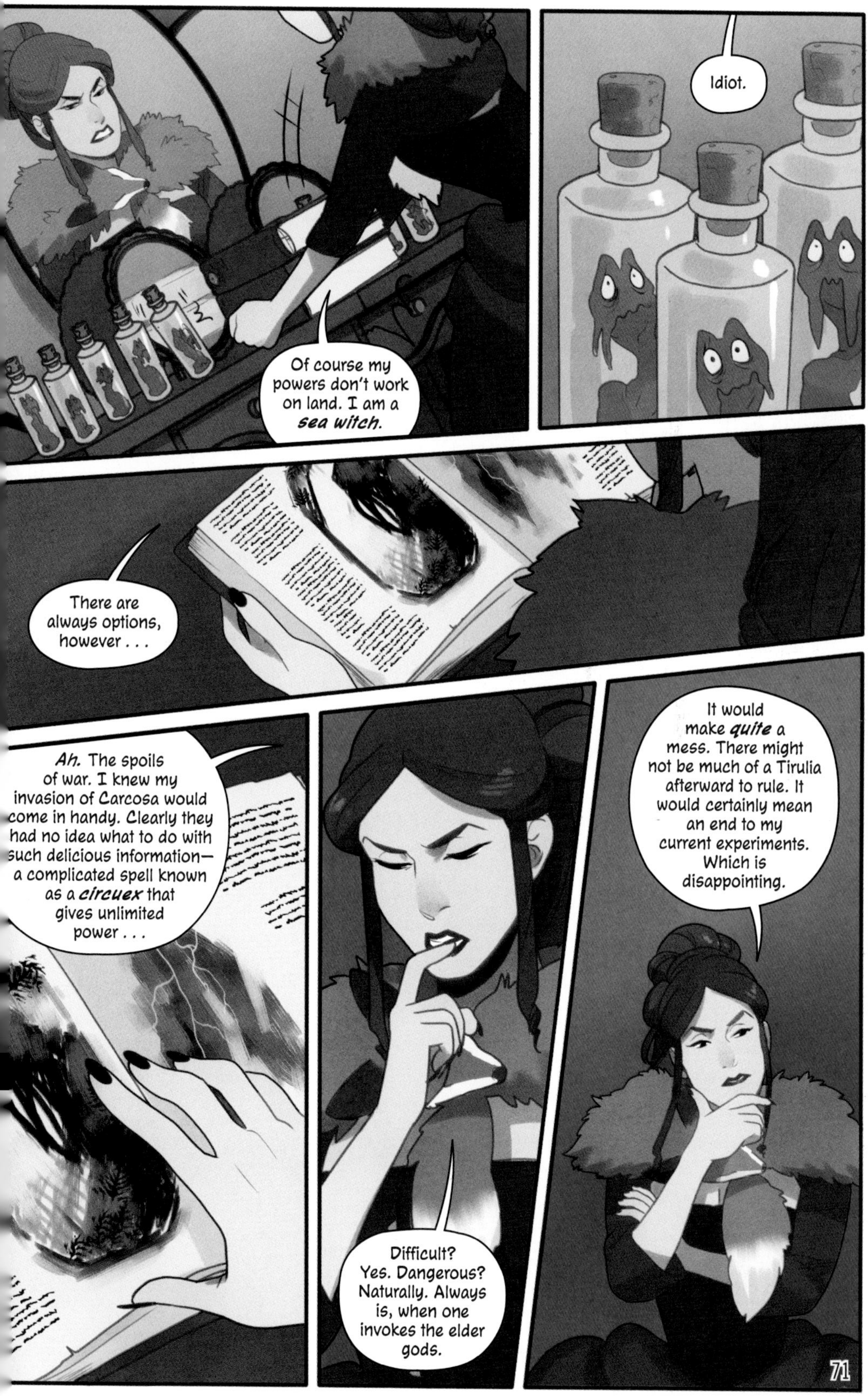
Of course my powers don't work on land. I am a *sea witch.*
Idiot.
There are always options, however . . .
Ah. The spoils of war. I knew my invasion of Carcosa would come in handy. Clearly they had no idea what to do with such delicious information—a complicated spell known as a *circuex* that gives unlimited power . . .
Difficult? Yes. Dangerous? Naturally. Always is, when one invokes the elder gods.
It would make *quite* a mess. There might not be much of a Tirulia afterward to rule. It would certainly mean an end to my current experiments. Which is disappointing.

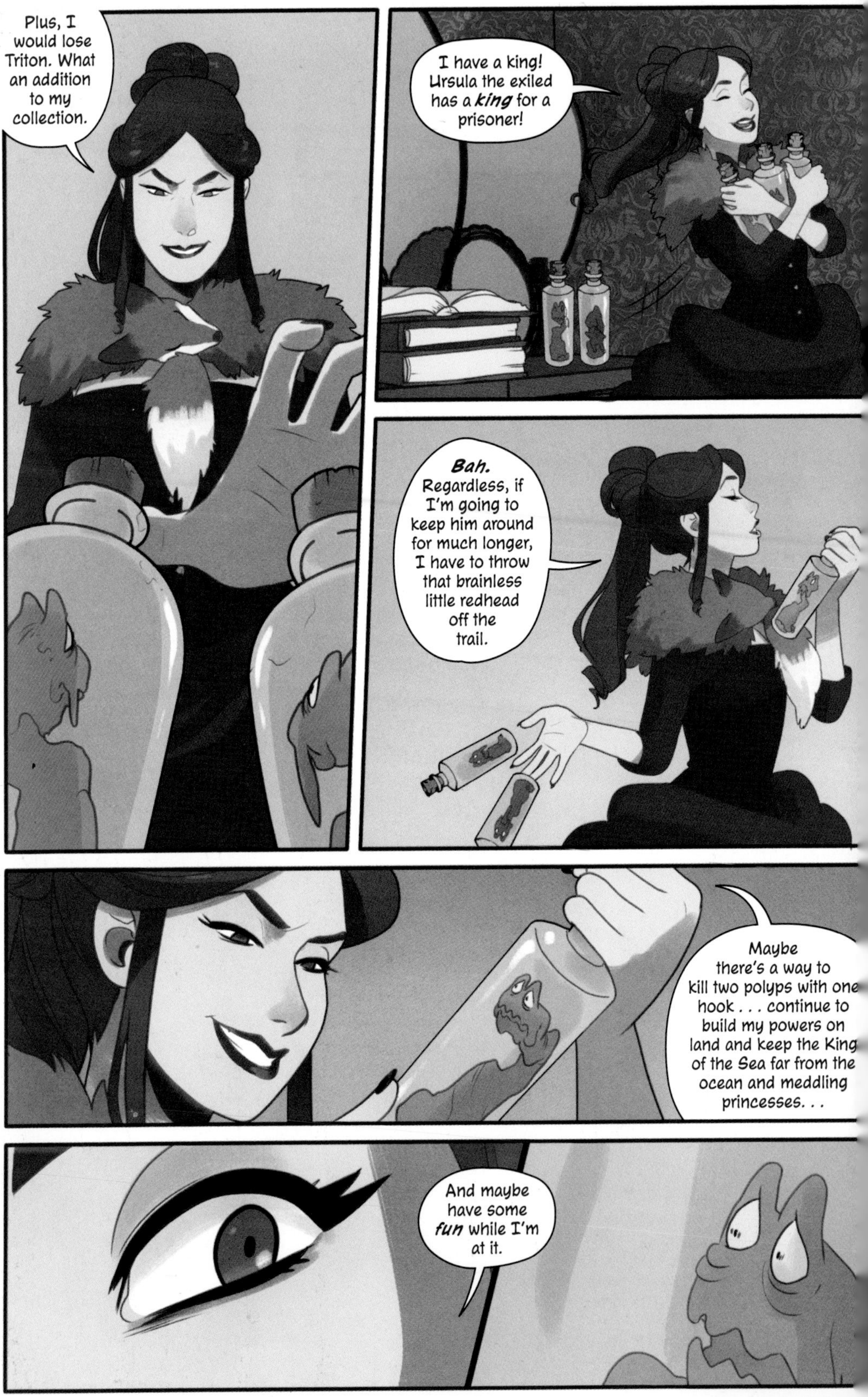
Plus, I would lose Triton. What an addition to my collection.
I have a king! Ursula the exiled has a *king* for a prisoner!
Bah. Regardless, if I'm going to keep him around for much longer, I have to throw that brainless little redhead off the trail.
Maybe there's a way to kill two polyps with one hook . . . continue to build my powers on land and keep the King of the Sea far from the ocean and meddling princesses. . .
And maybe have some *fun* while I'm at it.

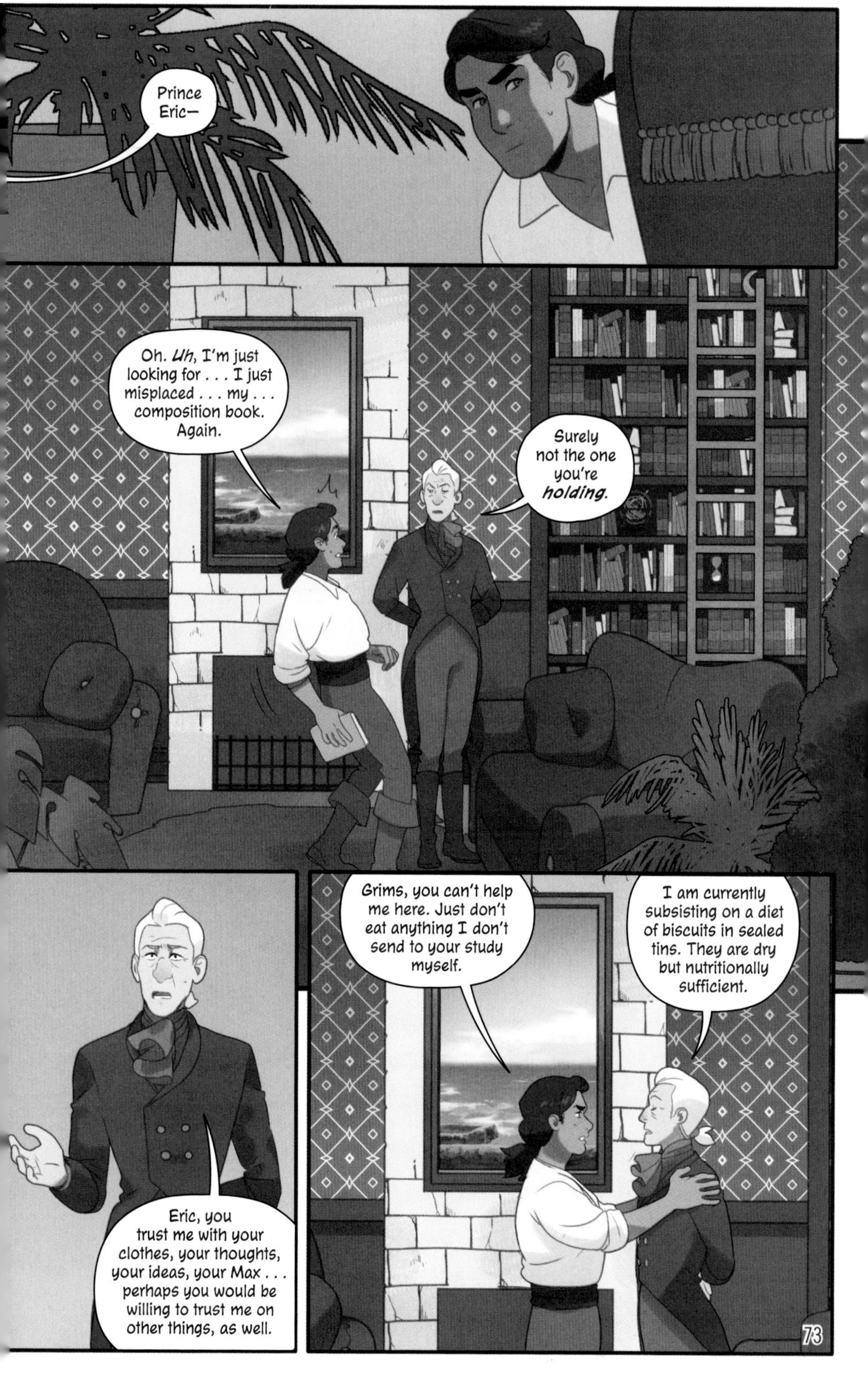
Prince Eric—
Oh. *Uh*, I'm just looking for . . . I just misplaced . . . my . . . composition book. Again.
Surely not the one you're *holding*.
Eric, you trust me with your clothes, your thoughts, your ideas, your Max . . . perhaps you would be willing to trust me on other things, as well.
Grims, you can't help me here. Just don't eat anything I don't send to your study myself.
I am currently subsisting on a diet of biscuits in sealed tins. They are dry but nutritionally sufficient.

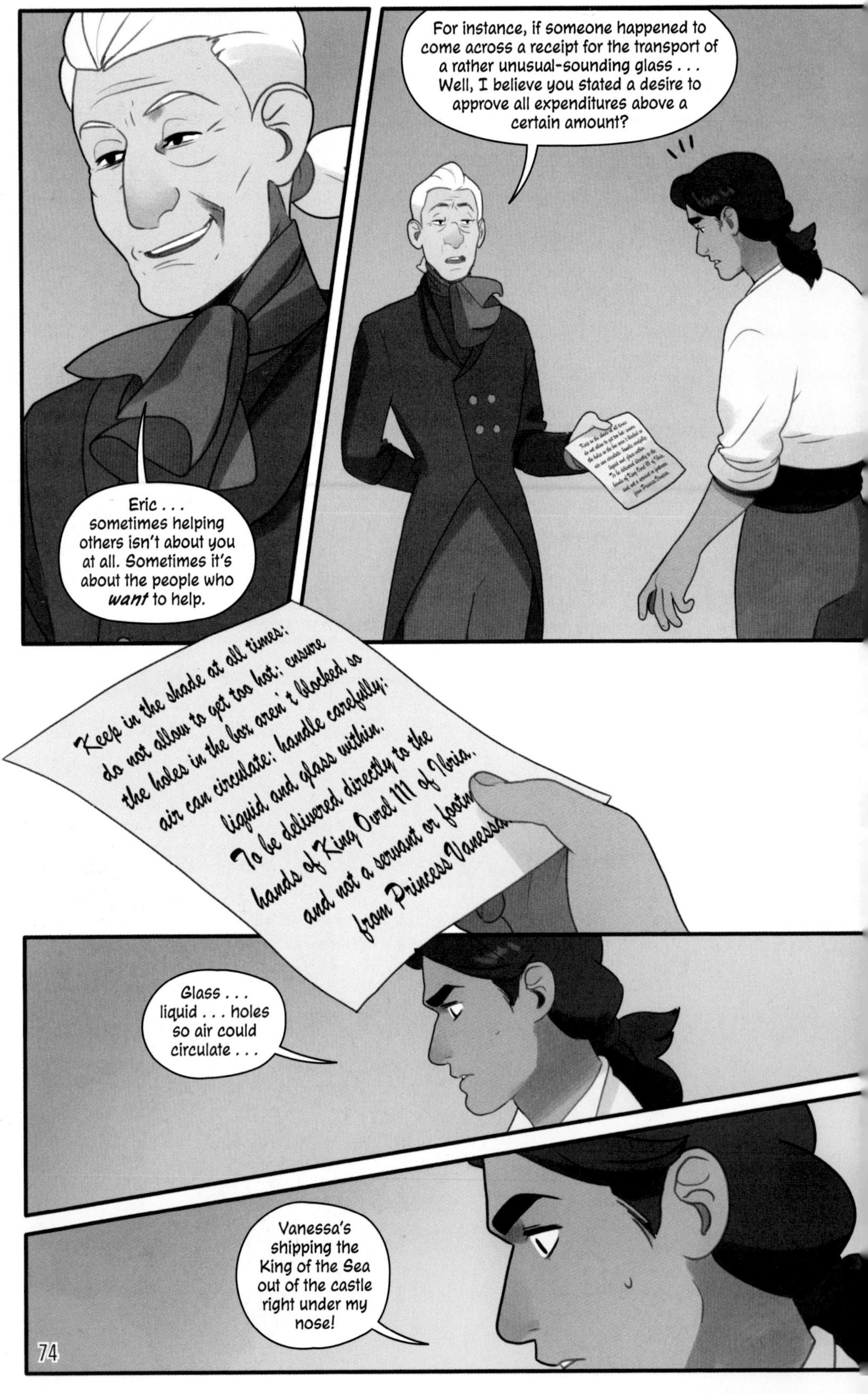
For instance, if someone happened to come across a receipt for the transport of a rather unusual-sounding glass . . . Well, I believe you stated a desire to approve all expenditures above a certain amount?
Eric . . . sometimes helping others isn't about you at all. Sometimes it's about the people who *want* to help.
Keep in the shade at all times; do not allow to get too hot; ensure the holes in the box aren't blocked so air can circulate; handle carefully; liquid and glass within. To be delivered directly to the hands of King Ovrel III of Ibria and not a servant or footm
from Princess Vanessa
Glass . . . liquid . . . holes so air could circulate . . .
Vanessa's shipping the King of the Sea out of the castle right under my nose!

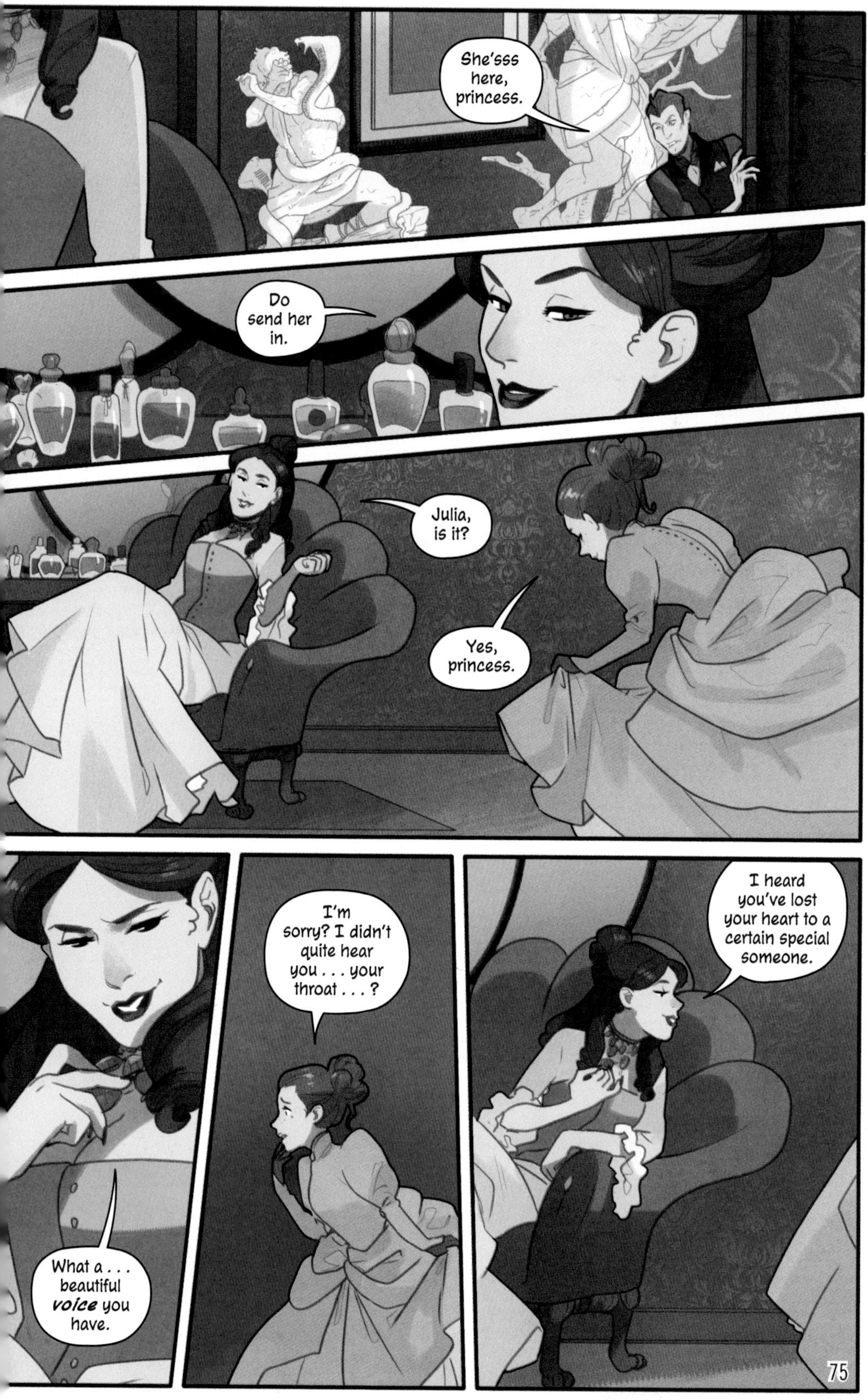
She'sss here, princess.
Do send her in.
Julia, is it?
Yes, princess.
What a . . . beautiful *voice* you have.
I'm sorry? I didn't quite hear you . . . your throat . . . ?
I heard you've lost your heart to a certain special someone.

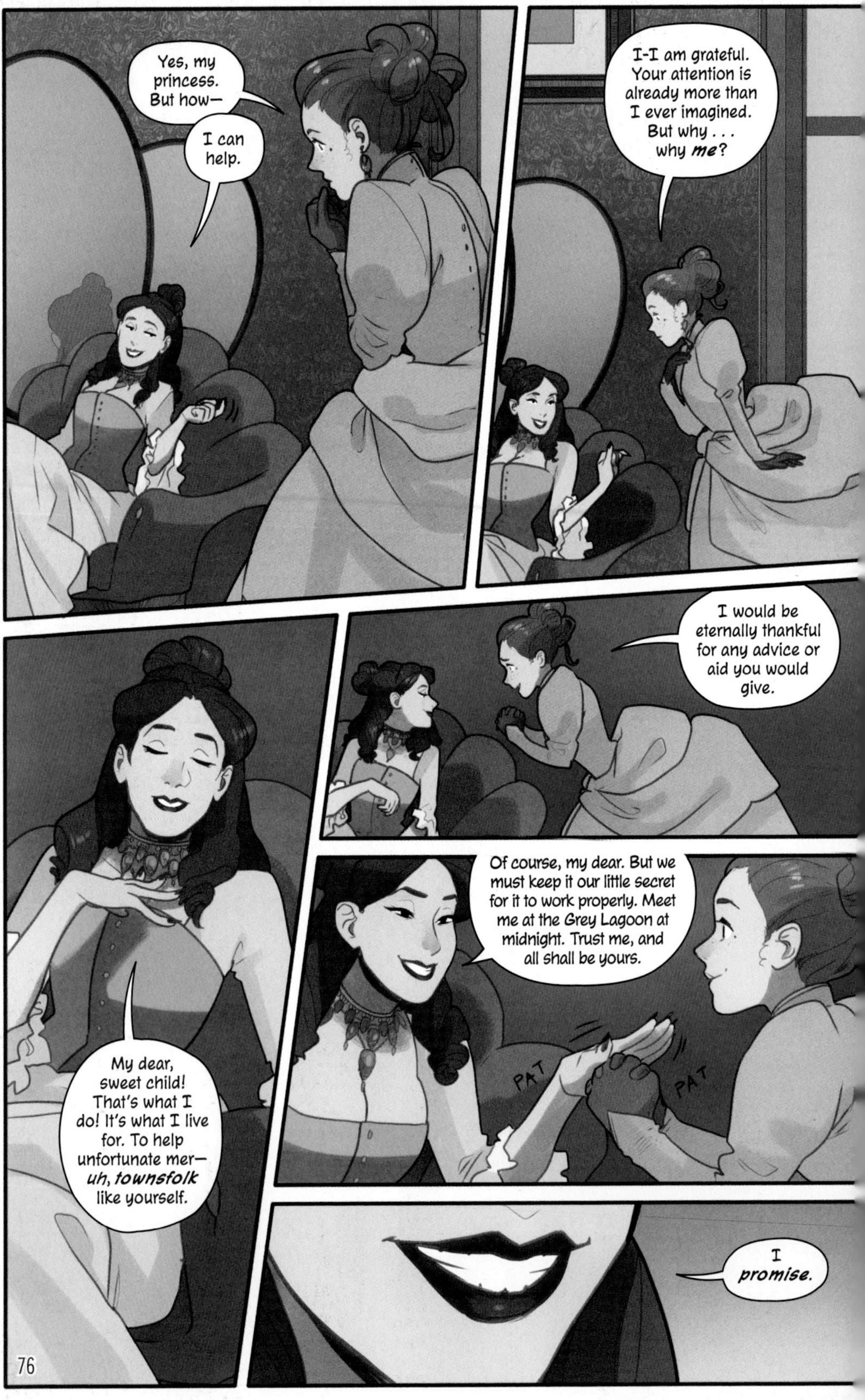
Yes, my princess. But how—
I can help.
I-I am grateful. Your attention is already more than I ever imagined. But why . . . why *me*?
My dear, sweet child! That's what I do! It's what I live for. To help unfortunate mer— *uh, townsfolk* like yourself.
I would be eternally thankful for any advice or aid you would give.
Of course, my dear. But we must keep it our little secret for it to work properly. Meet me at the Grey Lagoon at midnight. Trust me, and all shall be yours.
PAT
PAT
I *promise.*

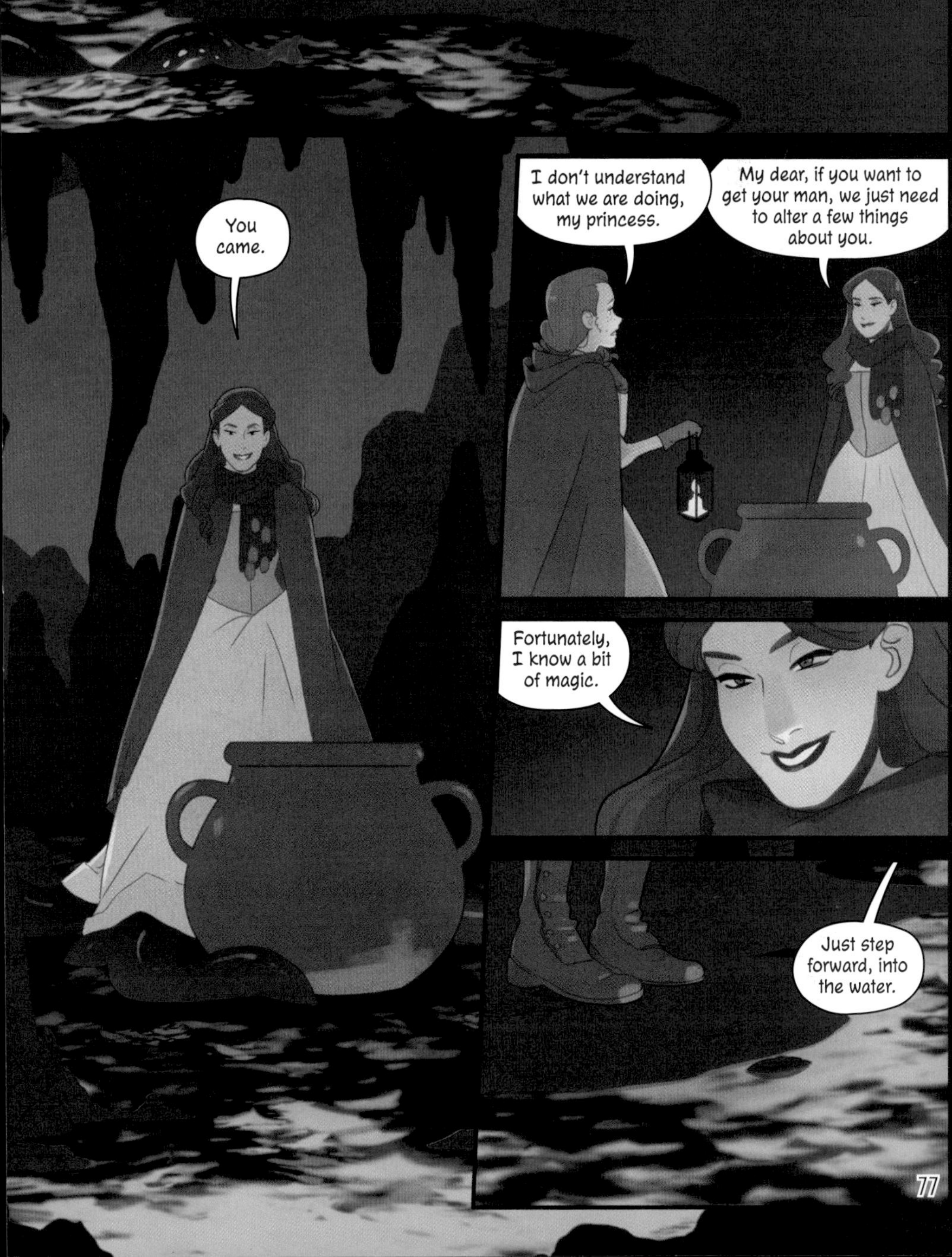
You came.
I don't understand what we are doing, my princess.
My dear, if you want to get your man, we just need to alter a few things about you.
Fortunately, I know a bit of magic.
Just step forward, into the water.

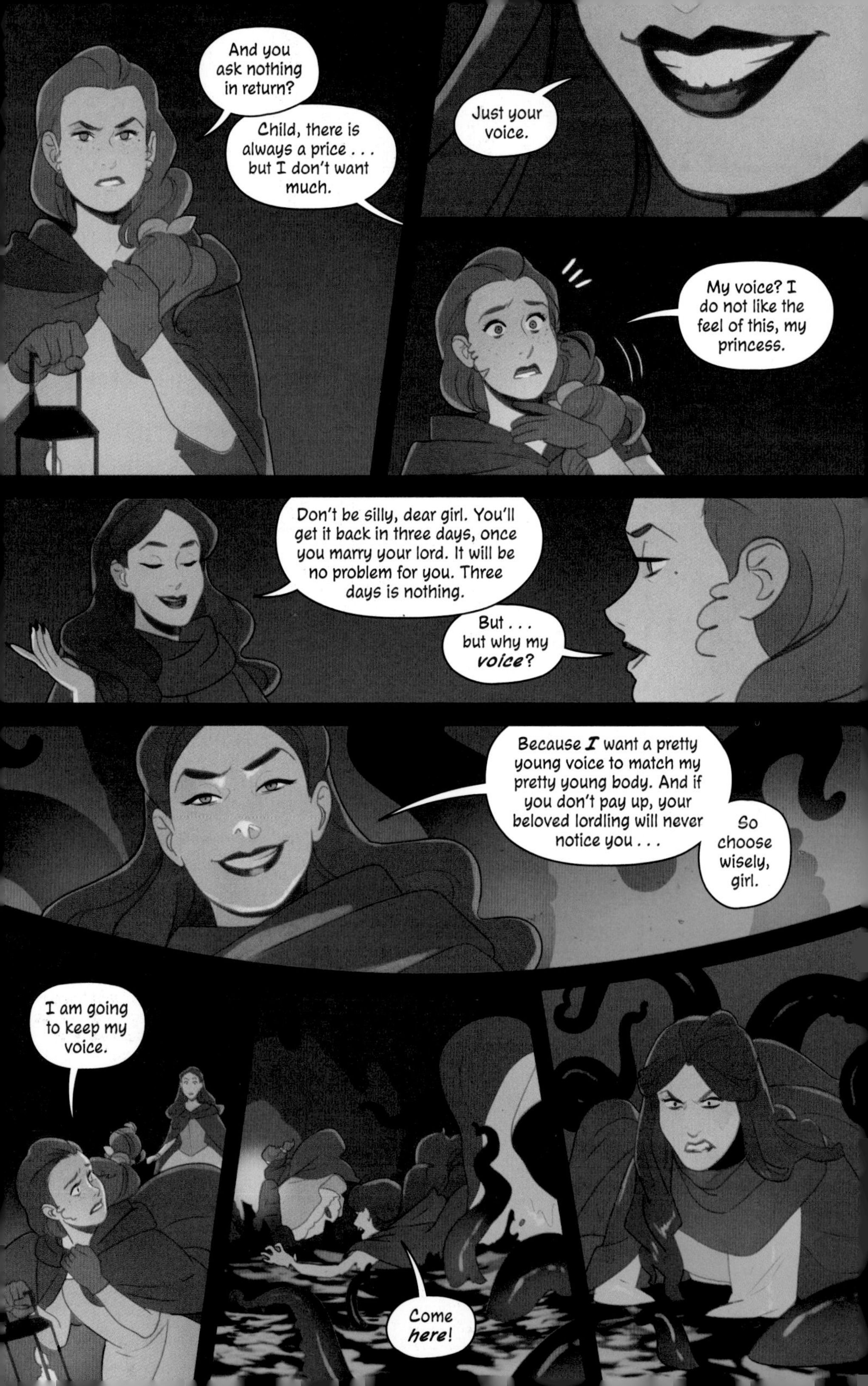
And you ask nothing in return?
Child, there is always a price . . . but I don't want much.
Just your voice.
My voice? I do not like the feel of this, my princess.
Don't be silly, dear girl. You'll get it back in three days, once you marry your lord. It will be no problem for you. Three days is nothing.
But . . . but why my *voice*?
Because *I* want a pretty young voice to match my pretty young body. And if you don't pay up, your beloved lordling will never notice you . . .
So choose wisely, girl.
I am going to keep my voice.
Come *here*!

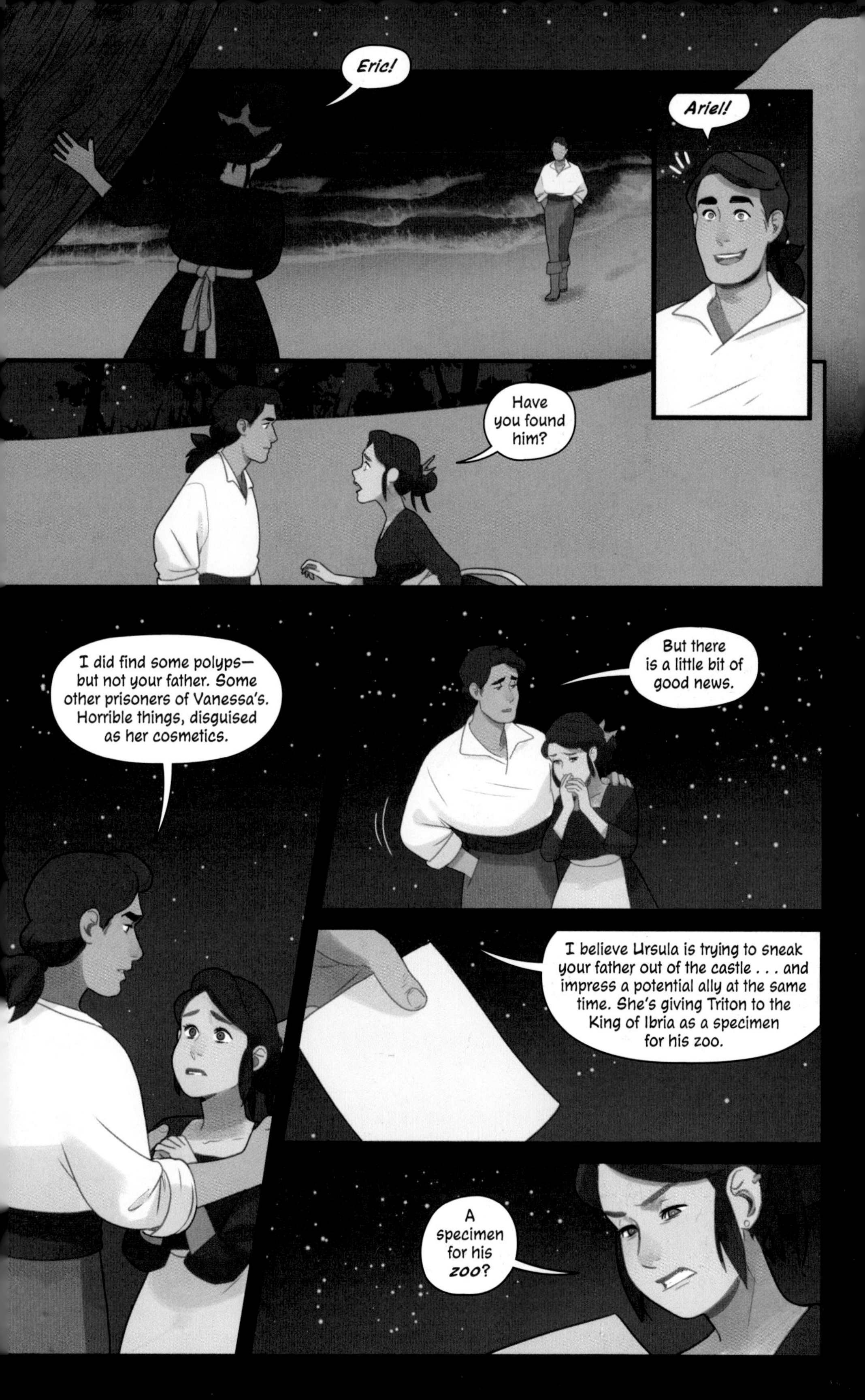
Eric!
Ariel!
Have you found him?
I did find some polyps—but not your father. Some other prisoners of Vanessa's. Horrible things, disguised as her cosmetics.
But there is a little bit of good news.
I believe Ursula is trying to sneak your father out of the castle . . . and impress a potential ally at the same time. She's giving Triton to the King of Ibria as a specimen for his zoo.
A specimen for his zoo?

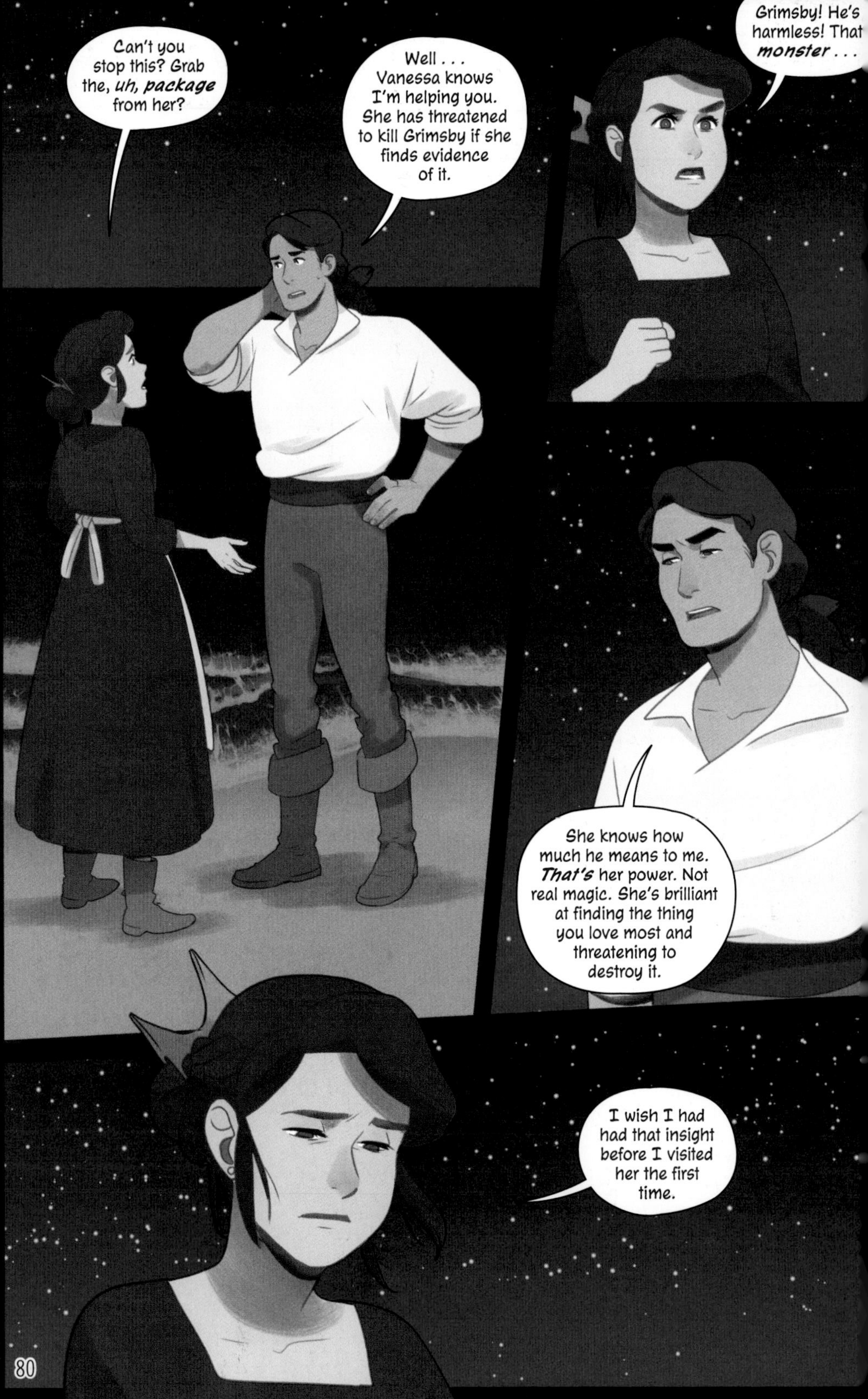
Can't you stop this? Grab the, *uh, package* from her?
Well . . . Vanessa knows I'm helping you. She has threatened to kill Grimsby if she finds evidence of it.
Grimsby! He's harmless! That *monster* . . .
She knows how much he means to me. *That's* her power. Not real magic. She's brilliant at finding the thing you love most and threatening to destroy it.
I wish I had had that insight before I visited her the first time.

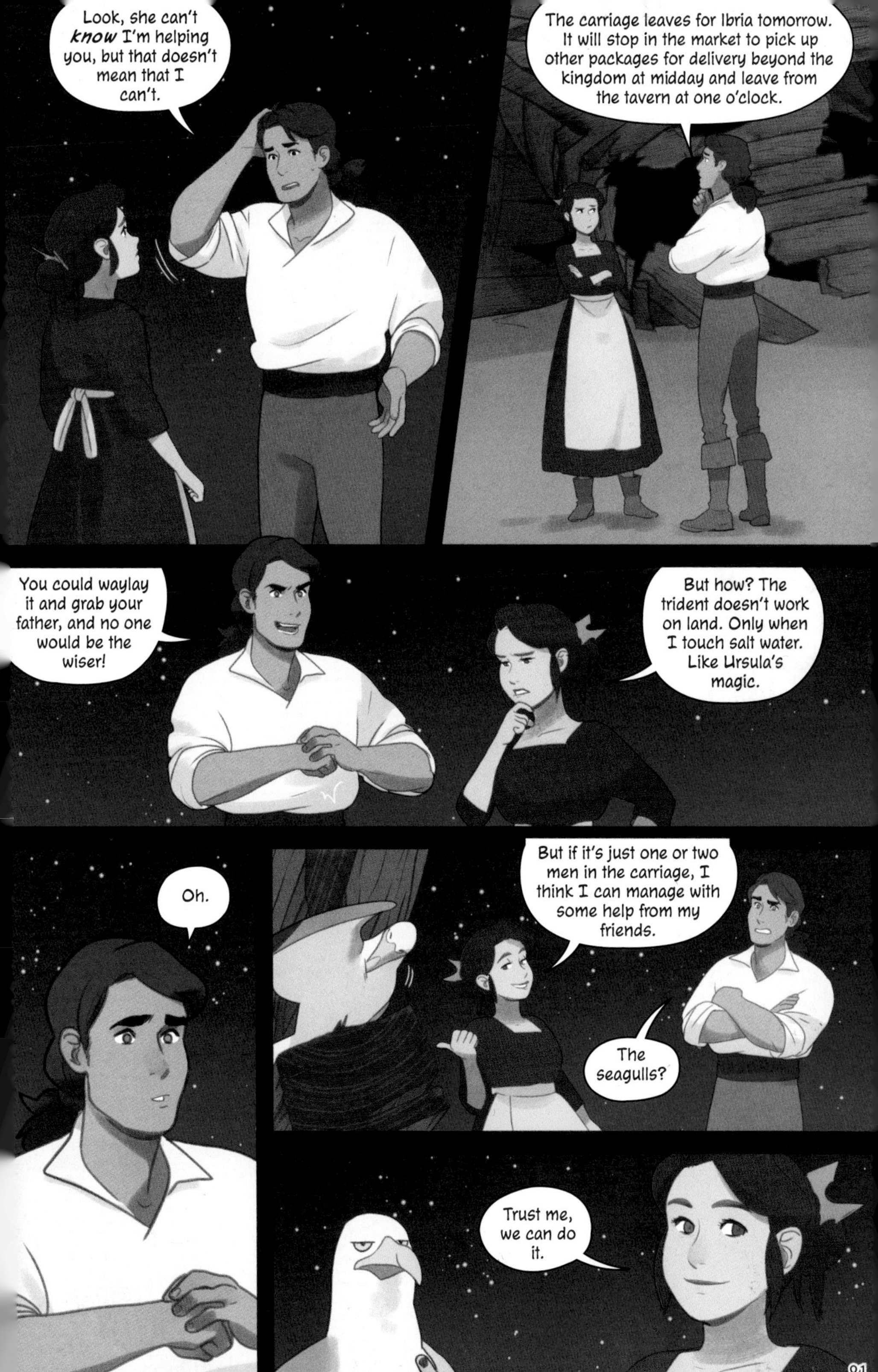
Look, she can't *know* I'm helping you, but that doesn't mean that I can't.
The carriage leaves for Ibria tomorrow. It will stop in the market to pick up other packages for delivery beyond the kingdom at midday and leave from the tavern at one o'clock.
You could waylay it and grab your father, and no one would be the wiser!
But how? The trident doesn't work on land. Only when I touch salt water. Like Ursula's magic.
Oh.
But if it's just one or two men in the carriage, I think I can manage with some help from my friends.
The seagulls?
Trust me, we can do it.

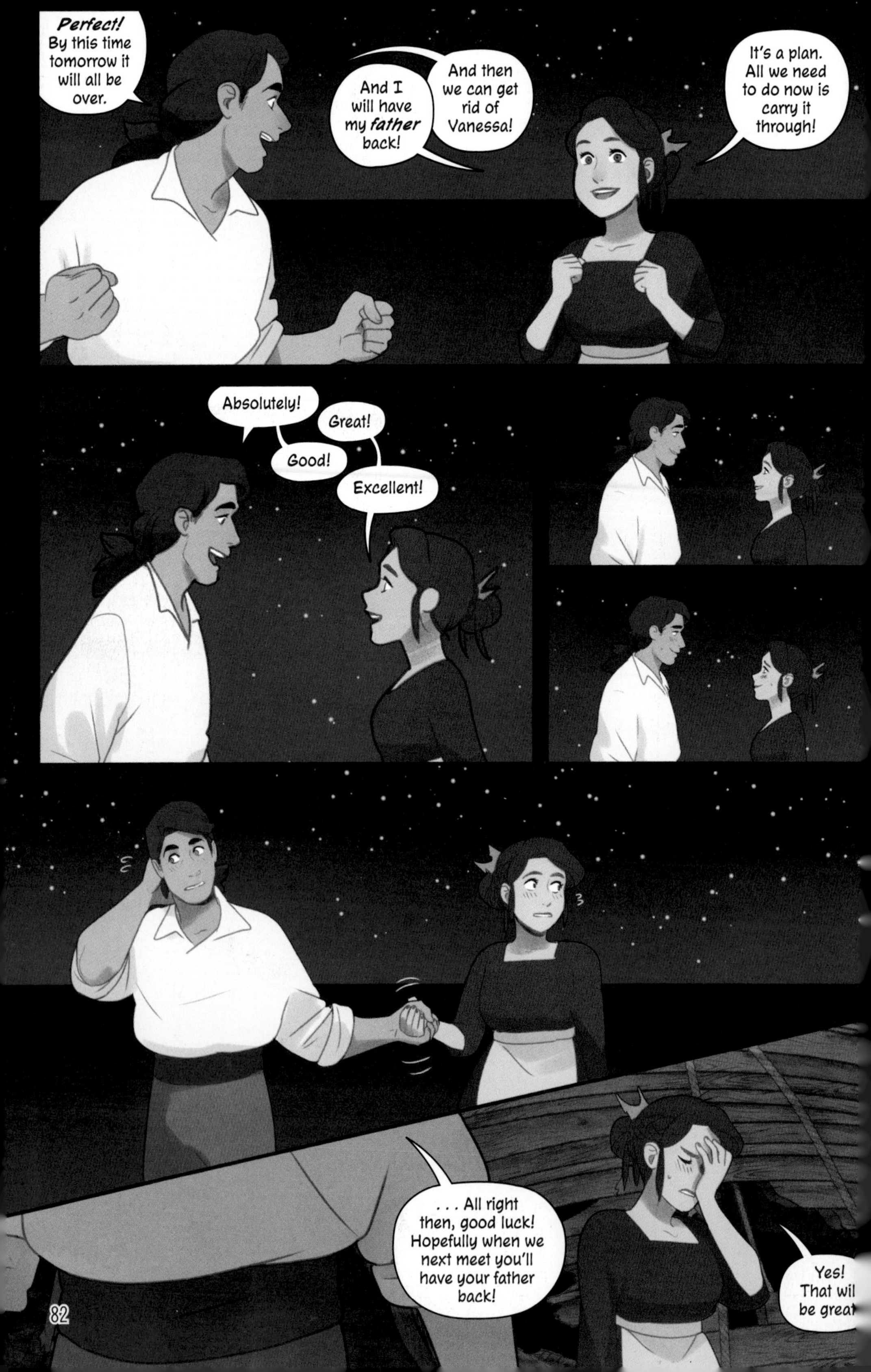

Perfect! By this time tomorrow it will all be over.
And I will have my *father* back!
And then we can get rid of Vanessa!
It's a plan. All we need to do now is carry it through!
Absolutely!
Good!
Great!
Excellent!
. . . All right then, good luck! Hopefully when we next meet you'll have your father back!
Yes! That wil
be great

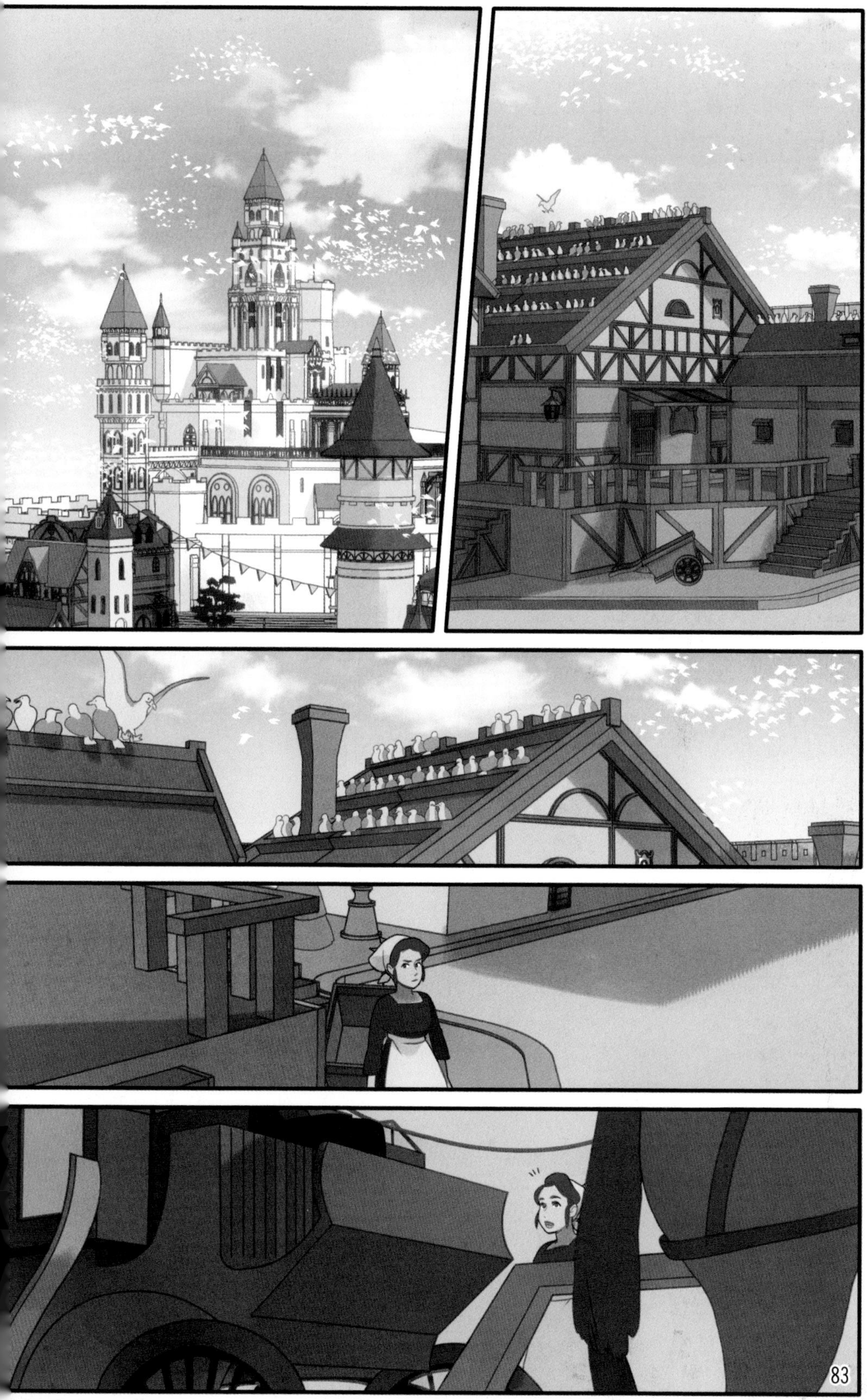

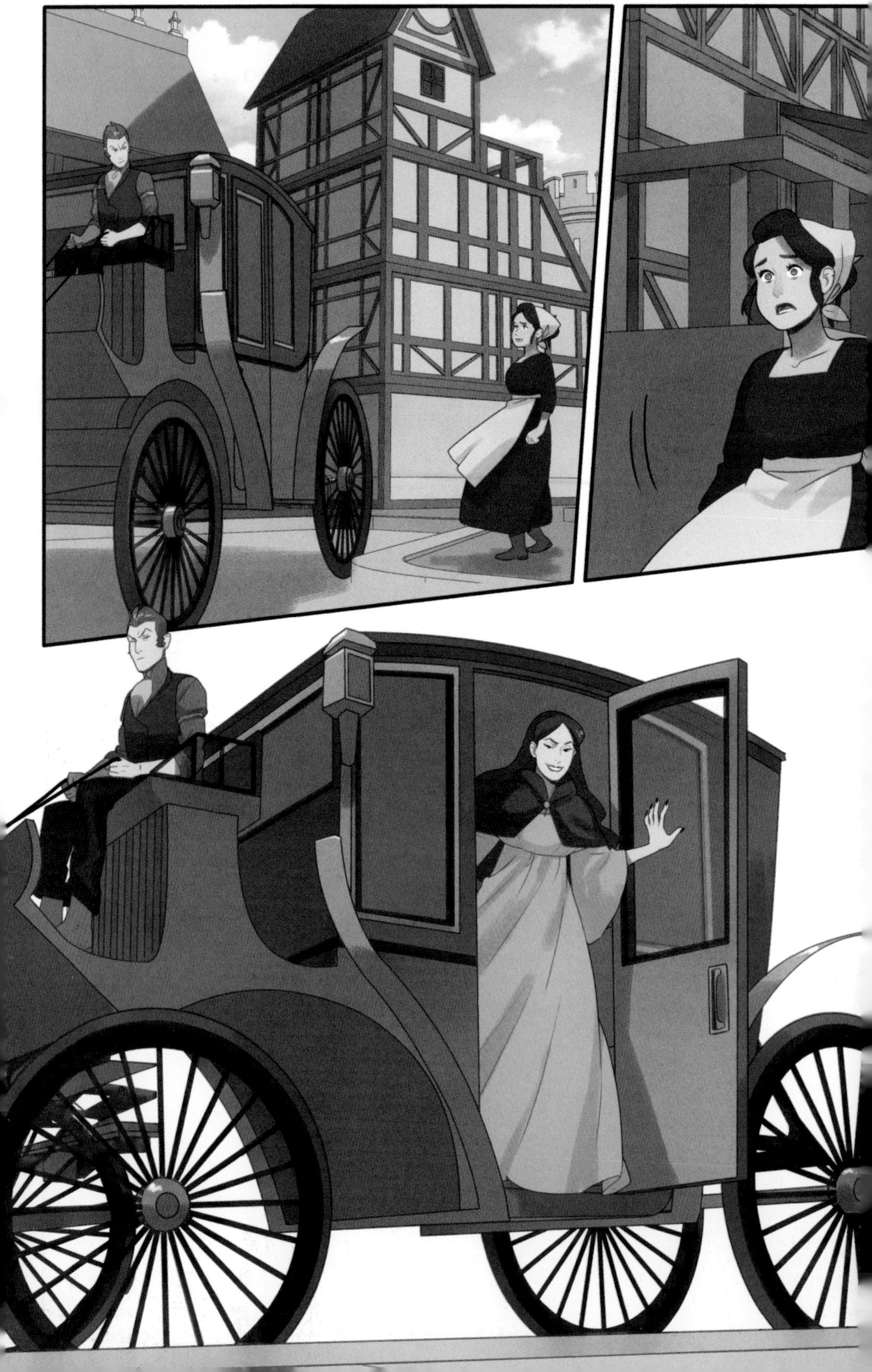

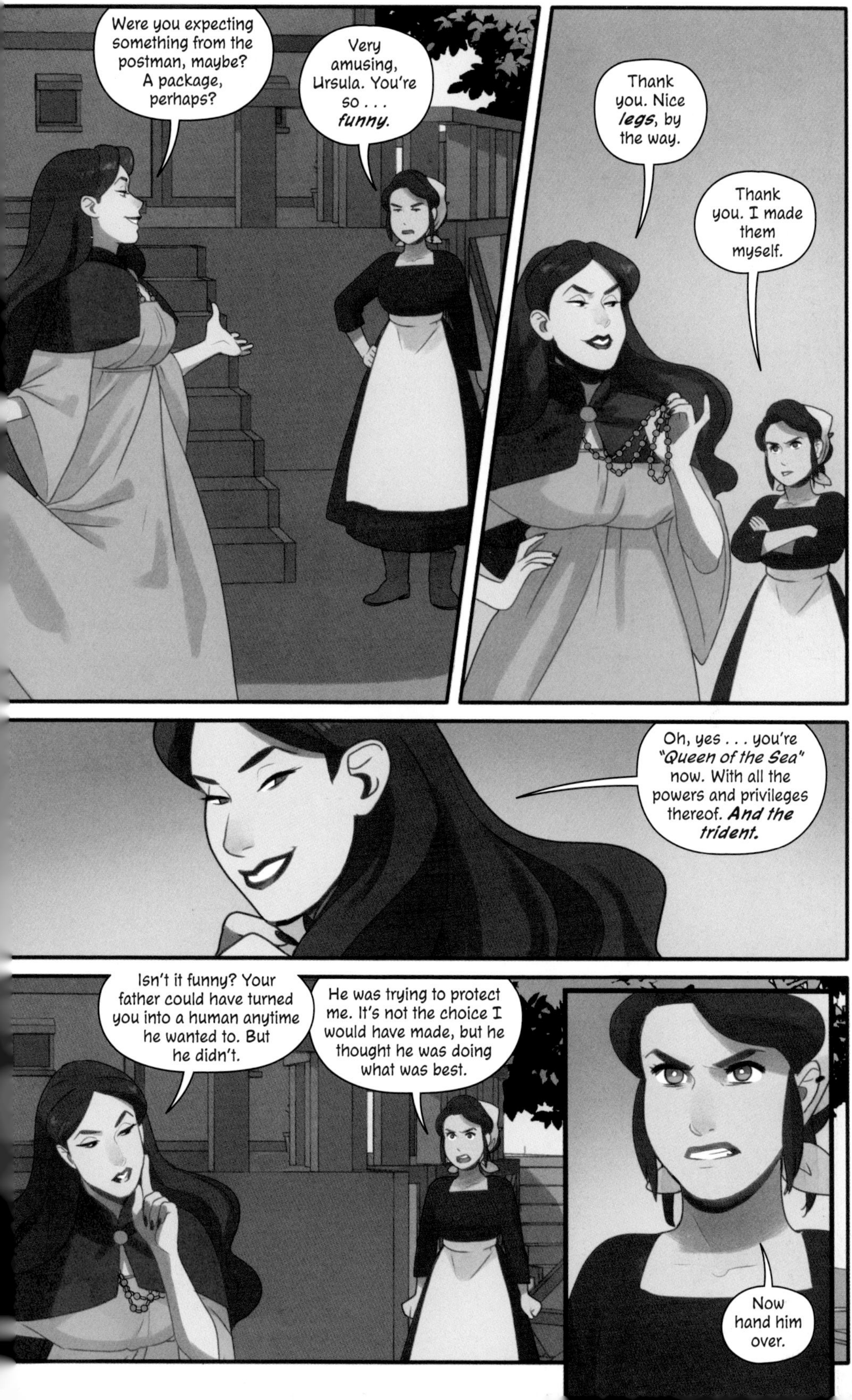
Were you expecting something from the postman, maybe? A package, perhaps?
Very amusing, Ursula. You're so . . . *funny.*
Thank you. Nice *legs*, by the way.
Thank you. I made them myself.
Oh, yes . . . you're *"Queen of the Sea"* now. With all the powers and privileges thereof. *And the trident.*
Isn't it funny? Your father could have turned you into a human anytime he wanted to. But he didn't.
He was trying to protect me. It's not the choice I would have made, but he thought he was doing what was best.
Now hand him over.

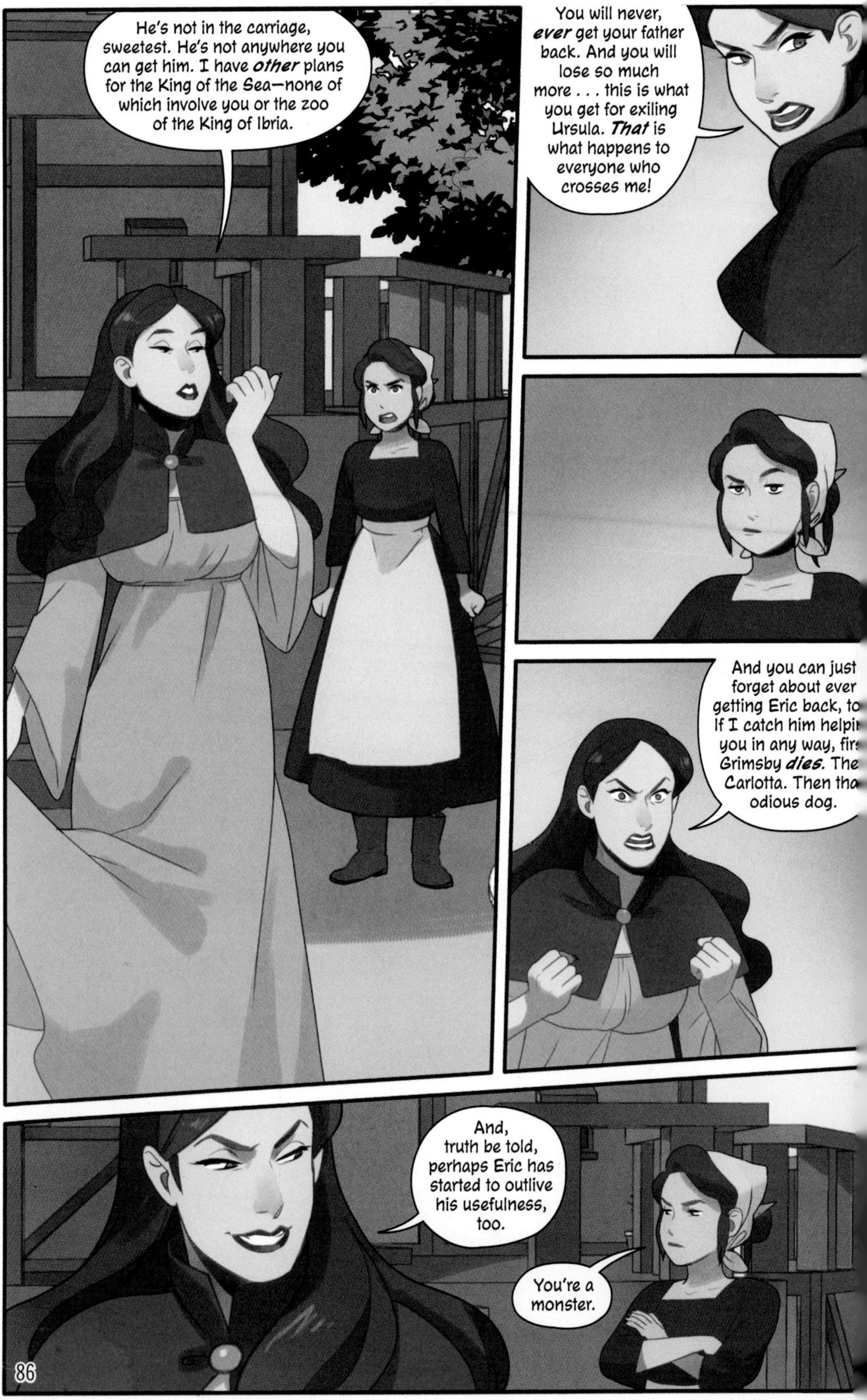
He's not in the carriage, sweetest. He's not anywhere you can get him. I have *other* plans for the King of the Sea—none of which involve you or the zoo of the King of Ibria.
You will never, *ever* get your father back. And you will lose so much more . . . this is what you get for exiling Ursula. *That* is what happens to everyone who crosses me!
And you can just forget about ever getting Eric back, to If I catch him helpi you in any way, fir Grimsby *dies*. The Carlotta. Then tha odious dog.
And, truth be told, perhaps Eric has started to outlive his usefulness, too.
You're a monster.

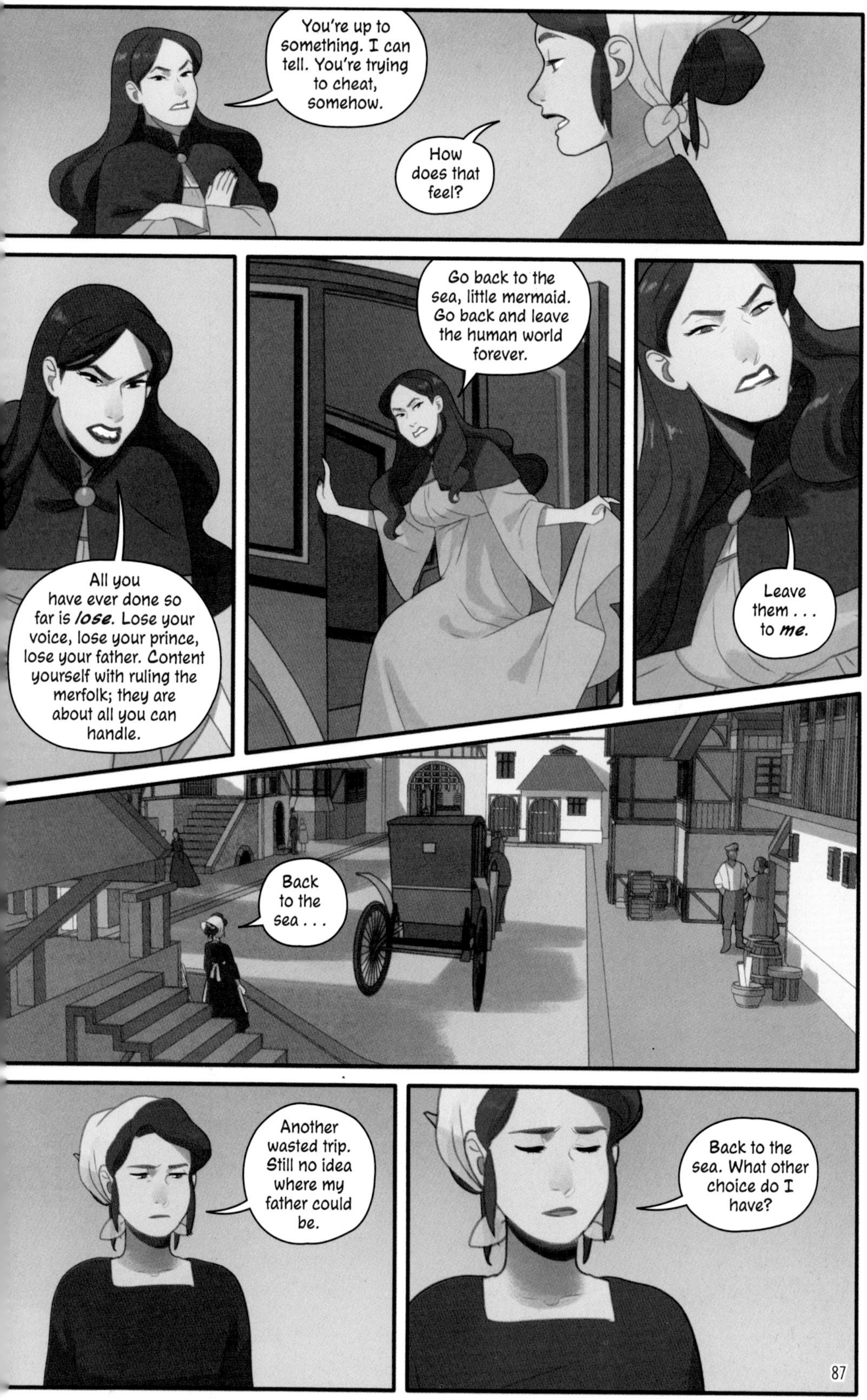
You're up to something. I can tell. You're trying to cheat, somehow.
How does that feel?
All you have ever done so far is *lose*. Lose your voice, lose your prince, lose your father. Content yourself with ruling the merfolk; they are about all you can handle.
Go back to the sea, little mermaid. Go back and leave the human world forever.
Leave them . . . to ***me***.
Back to the sea . . .
Another wasted trip. Still no idea where my father could be.
Back to the sea. What other choice do I have?

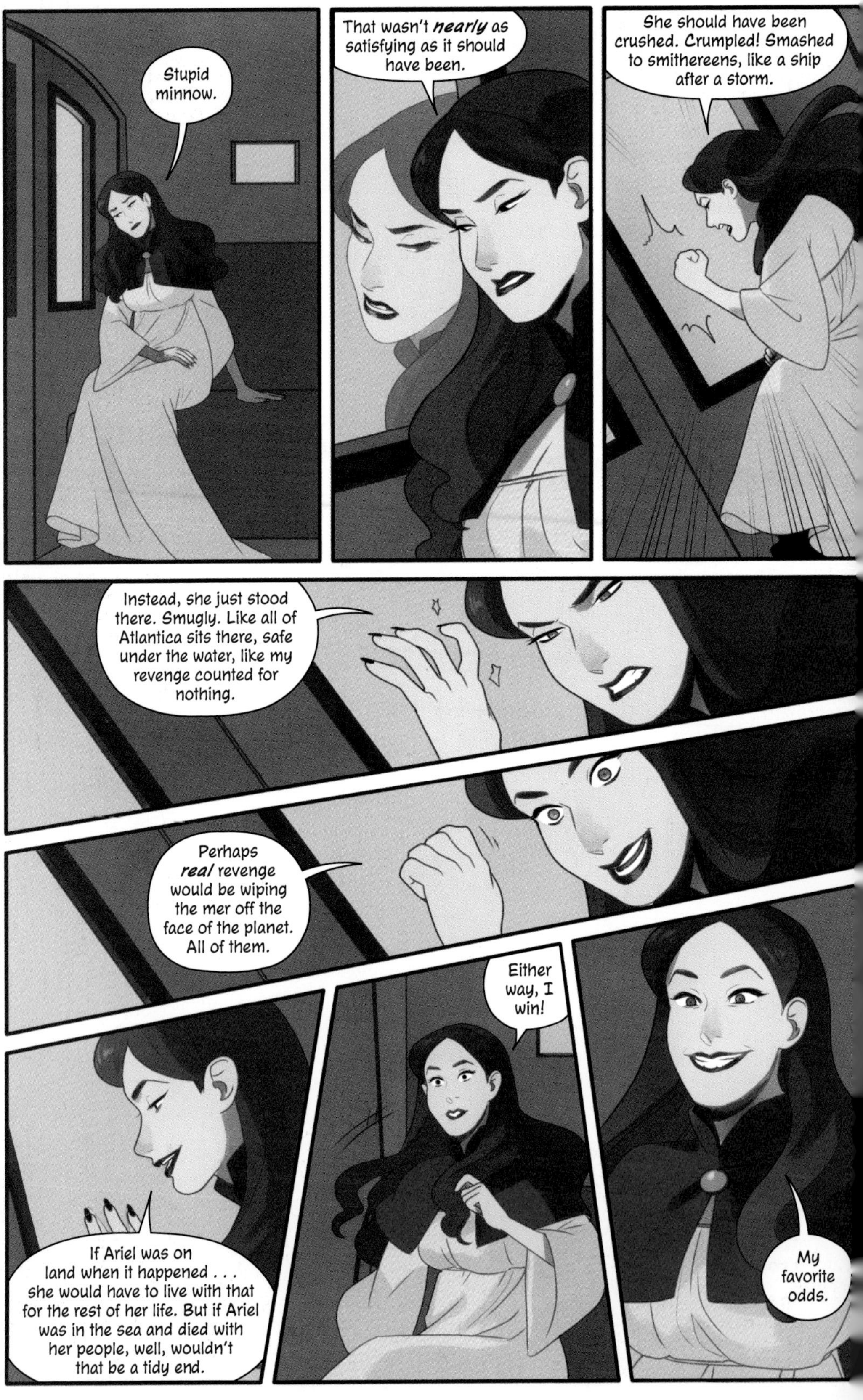
Stupid minnow.
That wasn't *nearly* as satisfying as it should have been.
She should have been crushed. Crumpled! Smashed to smithereens, like a ship after a storm.
Instead, she just stood there. Smugly. Like all of Atlantica sits there, safe under the water, like my revenge counted for nothing.
Perhaps *real* revenge would be wiping the mer off the face of the planet. All of them.
If Ariel was on land when it happened . . . she would have to live with that for the rest of her life. But if Ariel was in the sea and died with her people, well, wouldn't that be a tidy end.
Either way, I win!
My favorite odds.

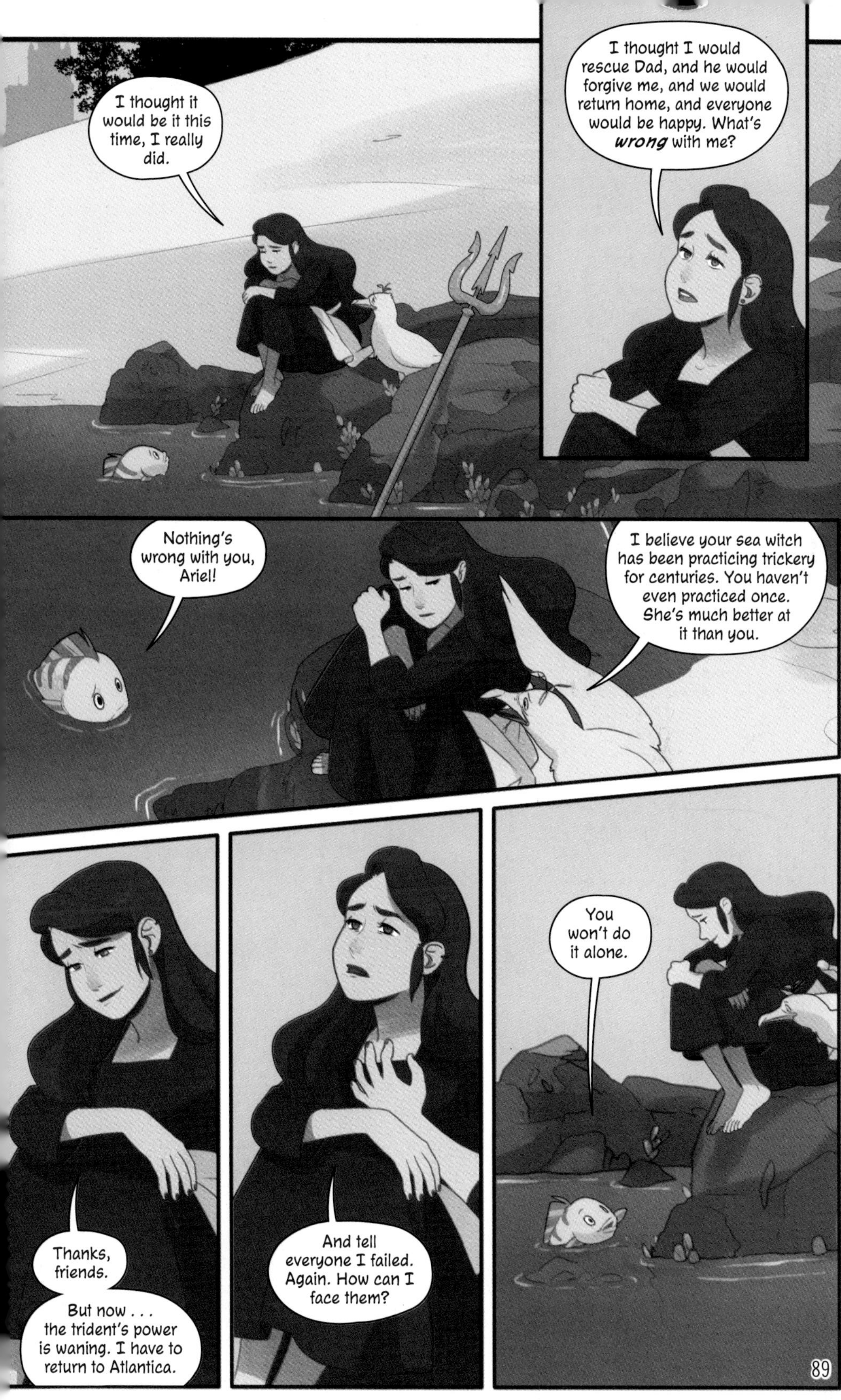
I thought it would be it this time, I really did.
I thought I would rescue Dad, and he would forgive me, and we would return home, and everyone would be happy. What's *wrong* with me?
Nothing's wrong with you, Ariel!
I believe your sea witch has been practicing trickery for centuries. You haven't even practiced once. She's much better at it than you.
Thanks, friends.
But now . . . the trident's power is waning. I have to return to Atlantica.
And tell everyone I failed. Again. How can I face them?
You won't do it alone.

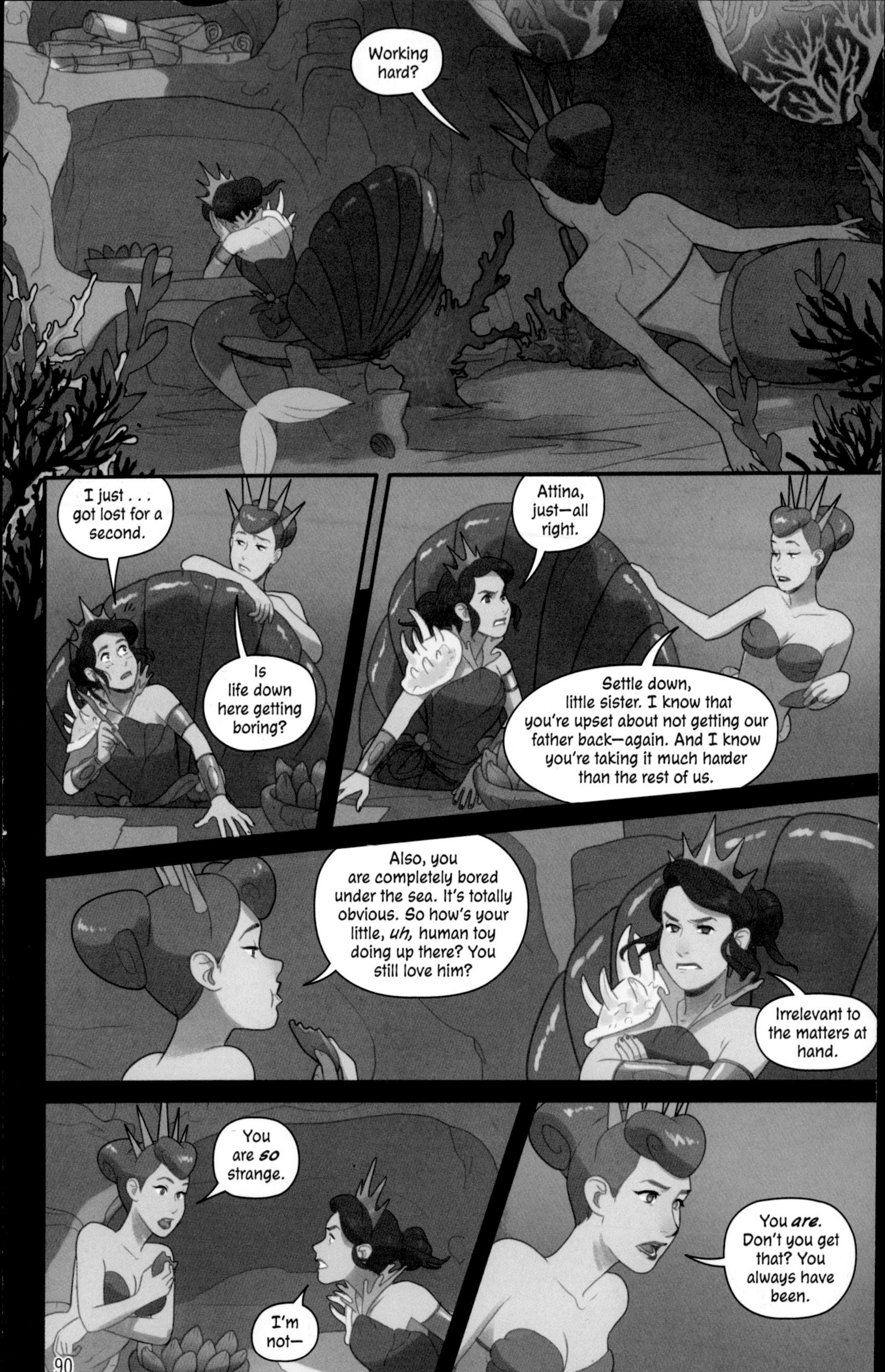
Working hard?
I just . . . got lost for a second.
Is life down here getting boring?
Attina, just—all right.
Settle down, little sister. I know that you're upset about not getting our father back—again. And I know you're taking it much harder than the rest of us.
Also, you are completely bored under the sea. It's totally obvious. So how's your little, *uh,* human toy doing up there? You still love him?
Irrelevant to the matters at hand.
You are ***so*** strange.
I'm not—
You ***are.*** Don't you get that? You always have been.

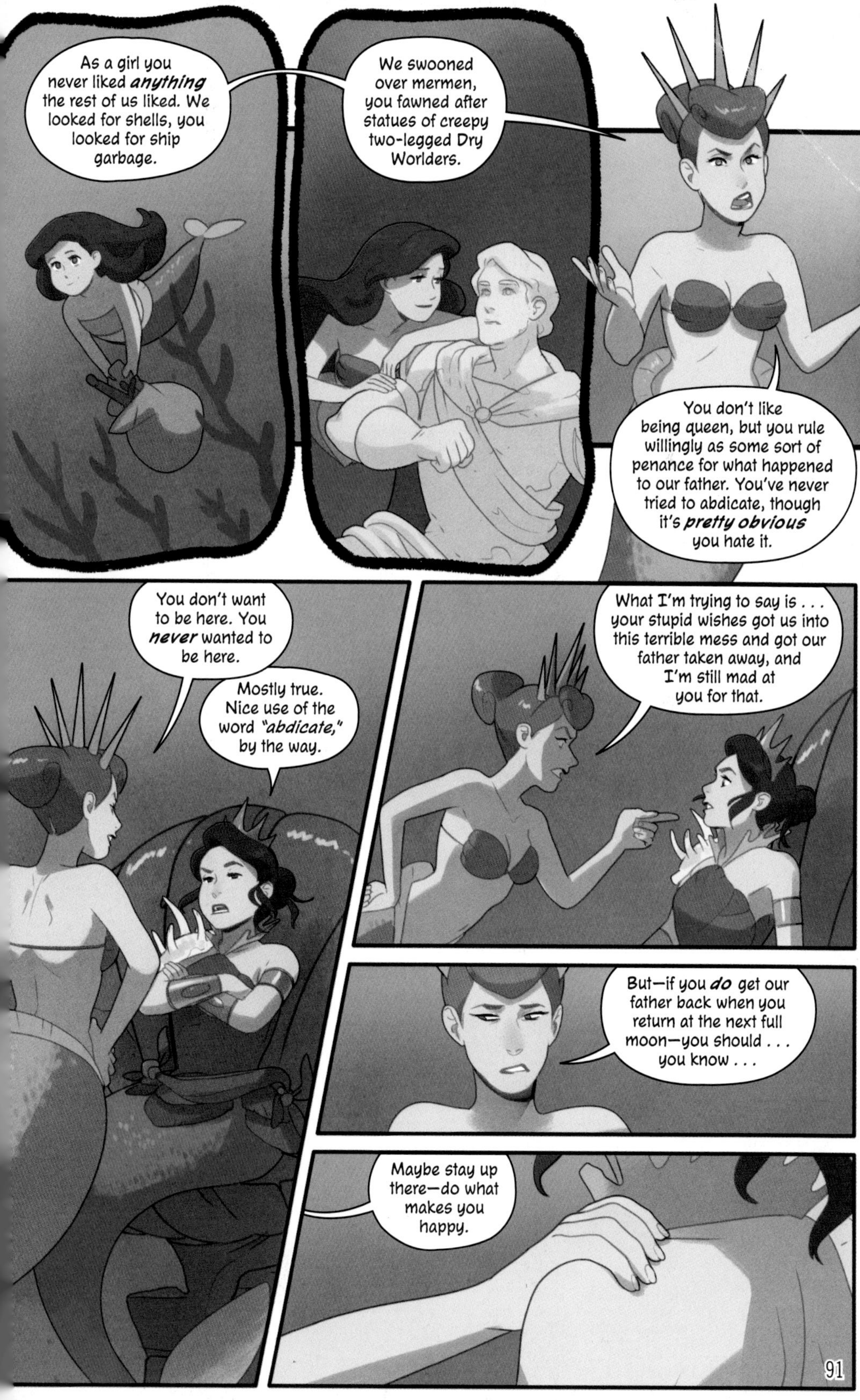
As a girl you never liked ***anything*** the rest of us liked. We looked for shells, you looked for ship garbage.
We swooned over mermen, you fawned after statues of creepy two-legged Dry Worlders.
You don't like being queen, but you rule willingly as some sort of penance for what happened to our father. You've never tried to abdicate, though it's ***pretty obvious*** you hate it.
You don't want to be here. You ***never*** wanted to be here.
Mostly true. Nice use of the word *"abdicate,"* by the way.
What I'm trying to say is . . . your stupid wishes got us into this terrible mess and got our father taken away, and I'm still mad at you for that.
But—if you ***do*** get our father back when you return at the next full moon—you should . . . you know . . .
Maybe stay up there—do what makes you happy.

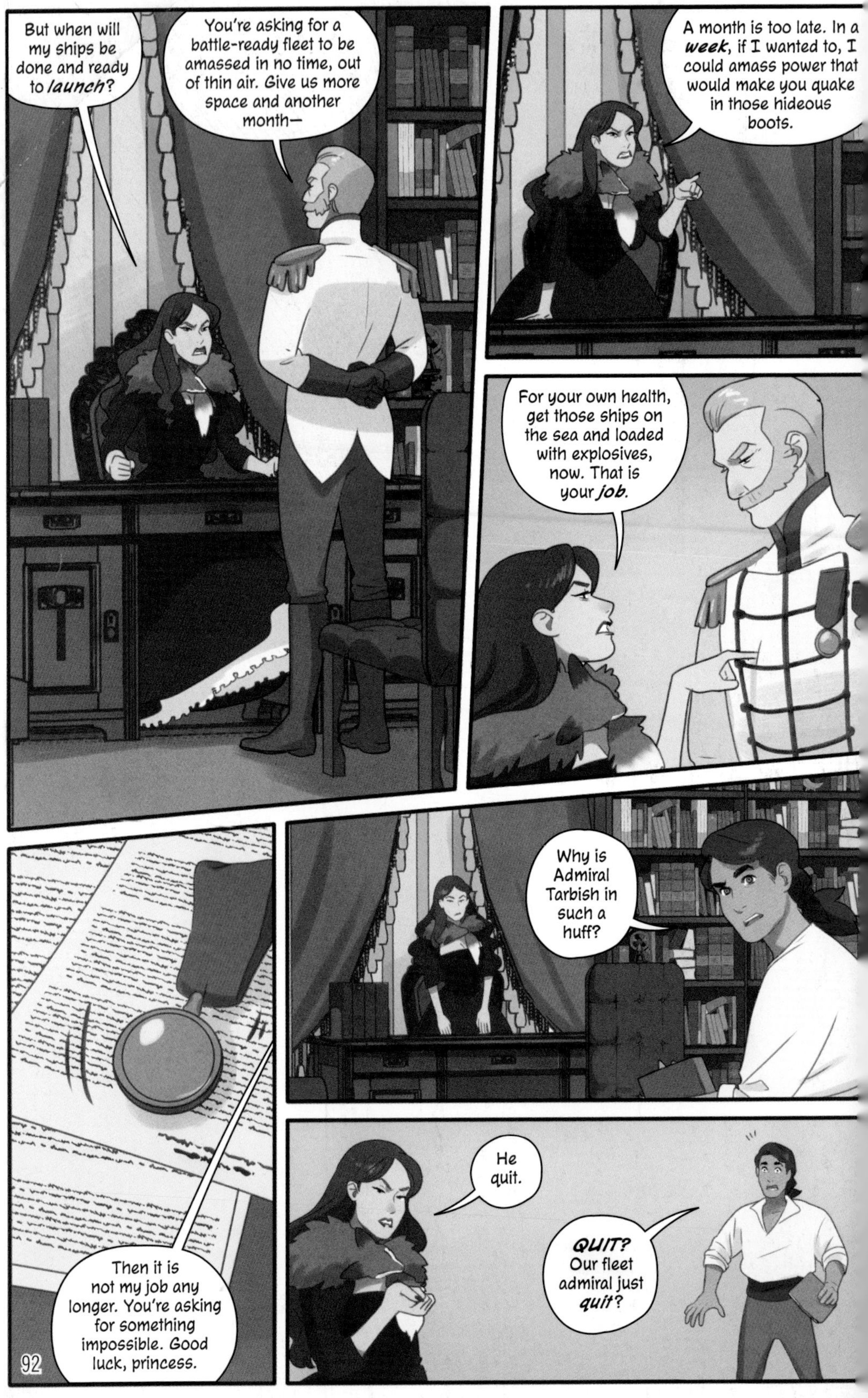
But when will my ships be done and ready to *launch*?
You're asking for a battle-ready fleet to be amassed in no time, out of thin air. Give us more space and another month—
A month is too late. In a *week*, if I wanted to, I could amass power that would make you quake in those hideous boots.
For your own health, get those ships on the sea and loaded with explosives, now. That is your *job*.
Then it is not my job any longer. You're asking for something impossible. Good luck, princess.
Why is Admiral Tarbish in such a huff?
He quit.
QUIT? Our fleet admiral just *quit*?

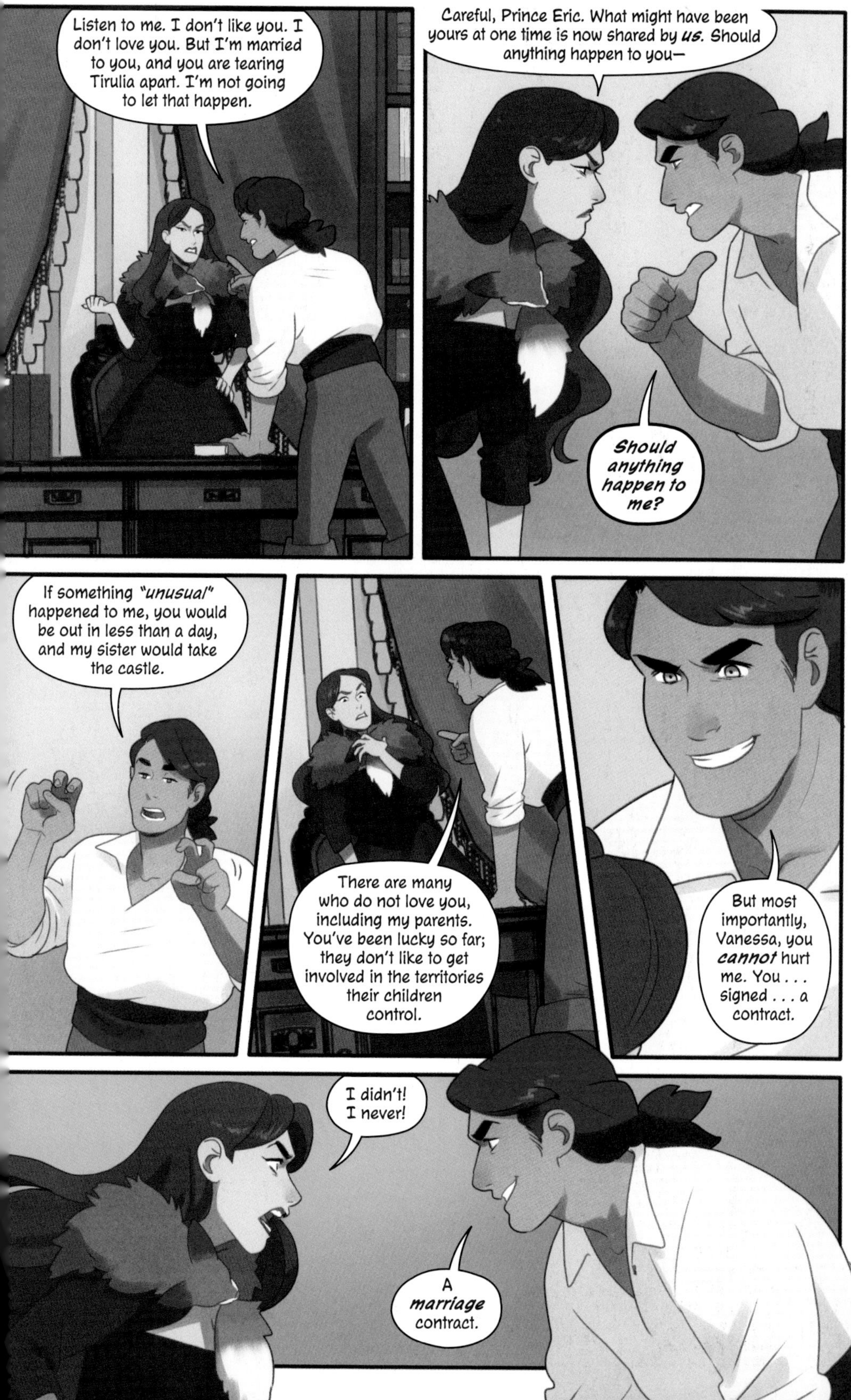
Listen to me. I don't like you. I don't love you. But I'm married to you, and you are tearing Tirulia apart. I'm not going to let that happen.
Careful, Prince Eric. What might have been yours at one time is now shared by *us*. Should anything happen to you—
Should anything happen to me?
If something *"unusual"* happened to me, you would be out in less than a day, and my sister would take the castle.
There are many who do not love you, including my parents. You've been lucky so far; they don't like to get involved in the territories their children control.
But most importantly, Vanessa, you *cannot* hurt me. You . . . signed . . . a contract.
I didn't! I never!
A *marriage* contract.

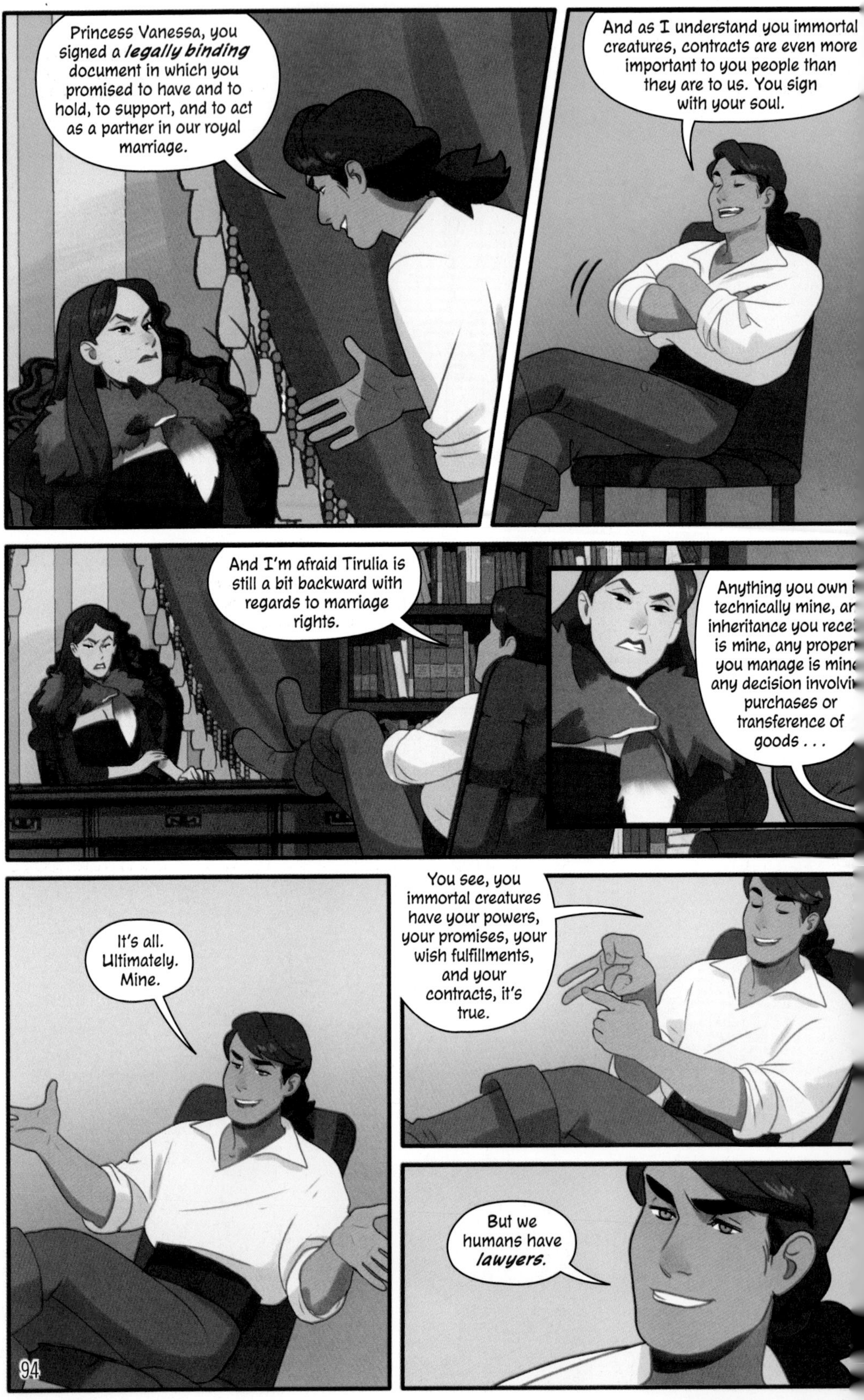
Princess Vanessa, you signed a ***legally binding*** document in which you promised to have and to hold, to support, and to act as a partner in our royal marriage.
And as I understand you immortal creatures, contracts are even more important to you people than they are to us. You sign with your soul.
And I'm afraid Tirulia is still a bit backward with regards to marriage rights.
Anything you own technically mine, a inheritance you rece is mine, any proper you manage is min any decision involvi purchases or transference of goods . . .
It's all. Ultimately. Mine.
You see, you immortal creatures have your powers, your promises, your wish fulfillments, and your contracts, it's true.
But we humans have ***lawyers***.

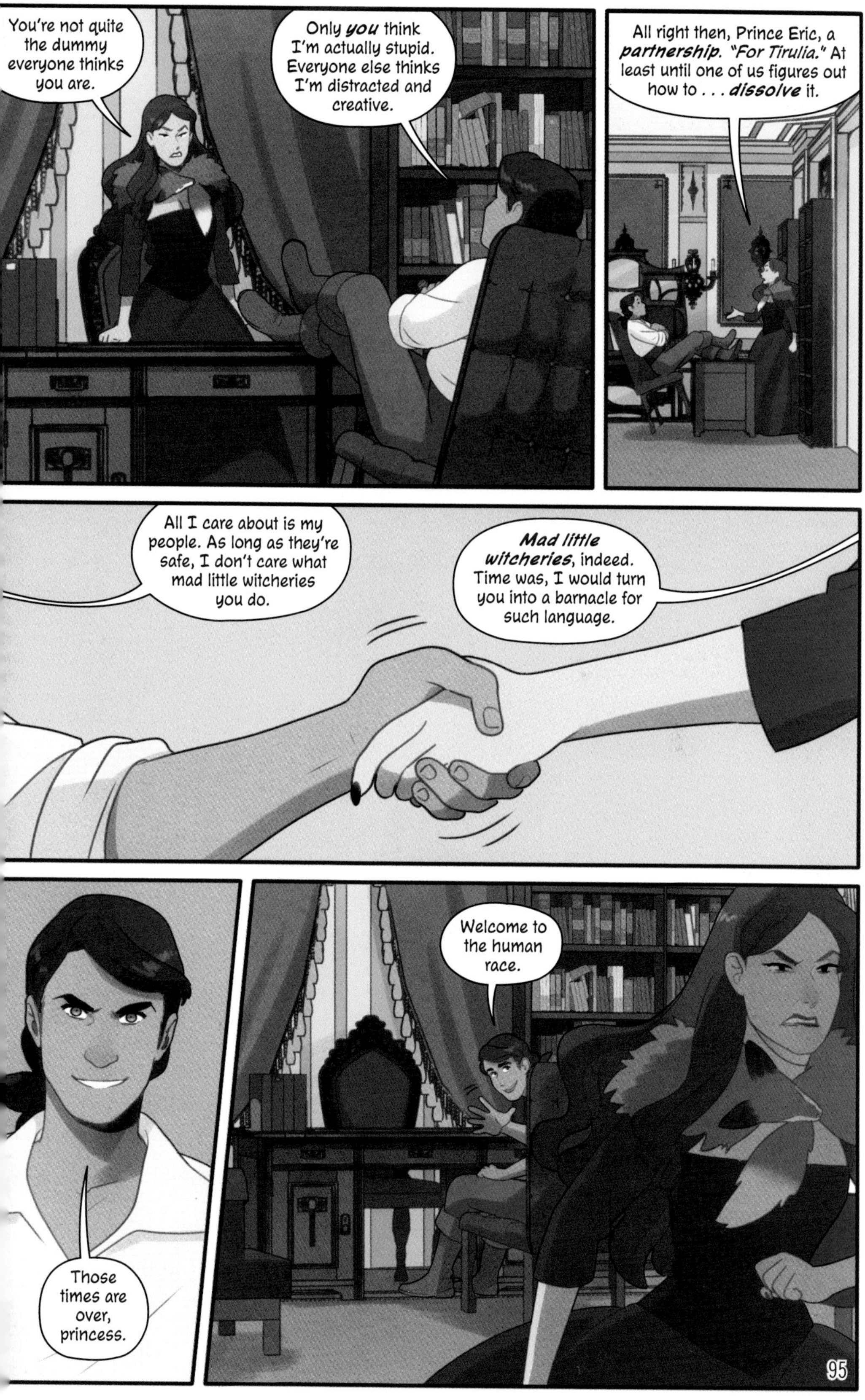
You're not quite the dummy everyone thinks you are.
Only *you* think I'm actually stupid. Everyone else thinks I'm distracted and creative.
All right then, Prince Eric, a ***partnership***. *"For Tirulia."* At least until one of us figures out how to . . . ***dissolve*** it.
All I care about is my people. As long as they're safe, I don't care what mad little witcheries you do.
Mad little witcheries, indeed. Time was, I would turn you into a barnacle for such language.
Those times are over, princess.
Welcome to the human race.

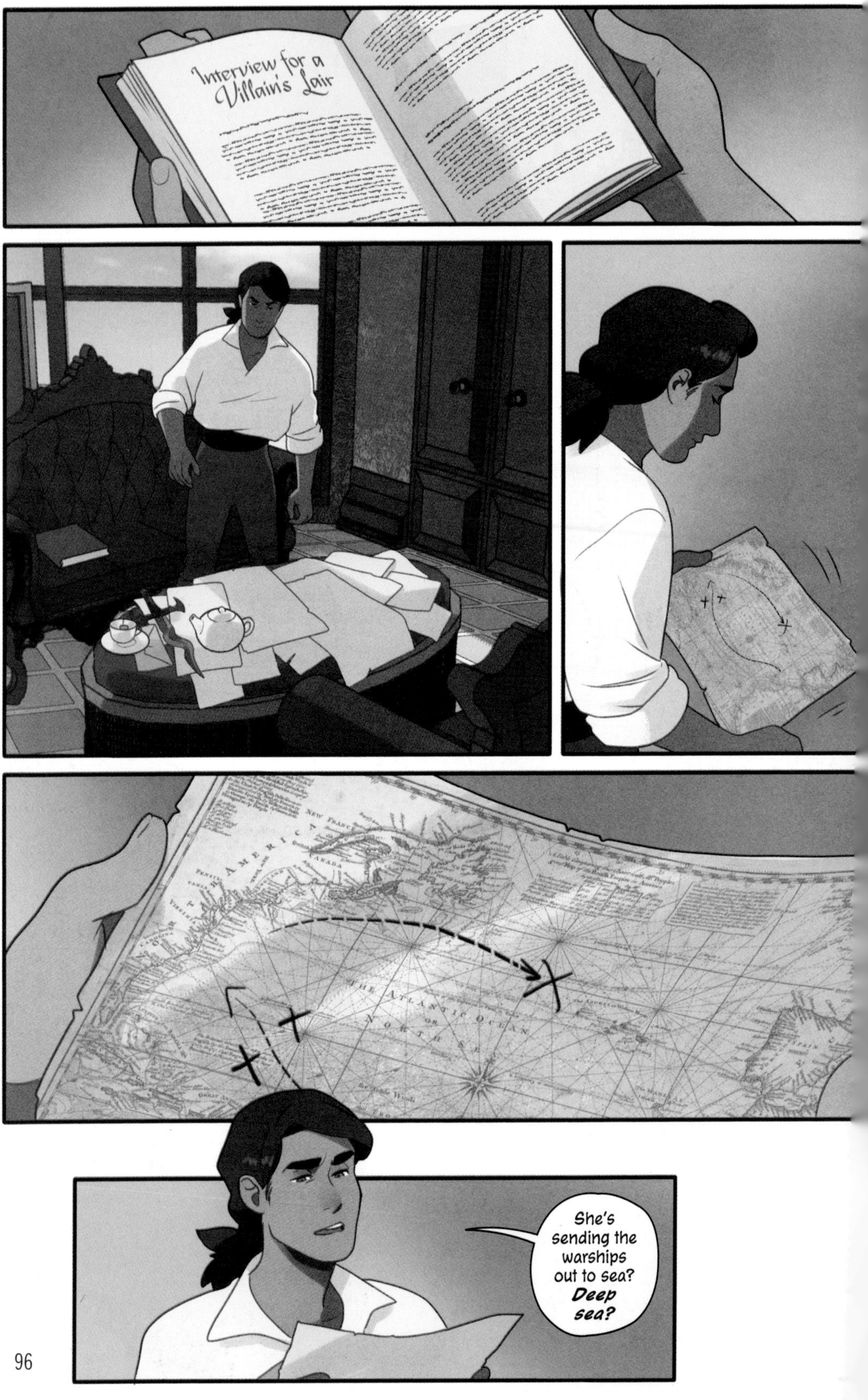
Interview for a Villain's Lair
She's sending the warships out to sea? ***Deep sea?***

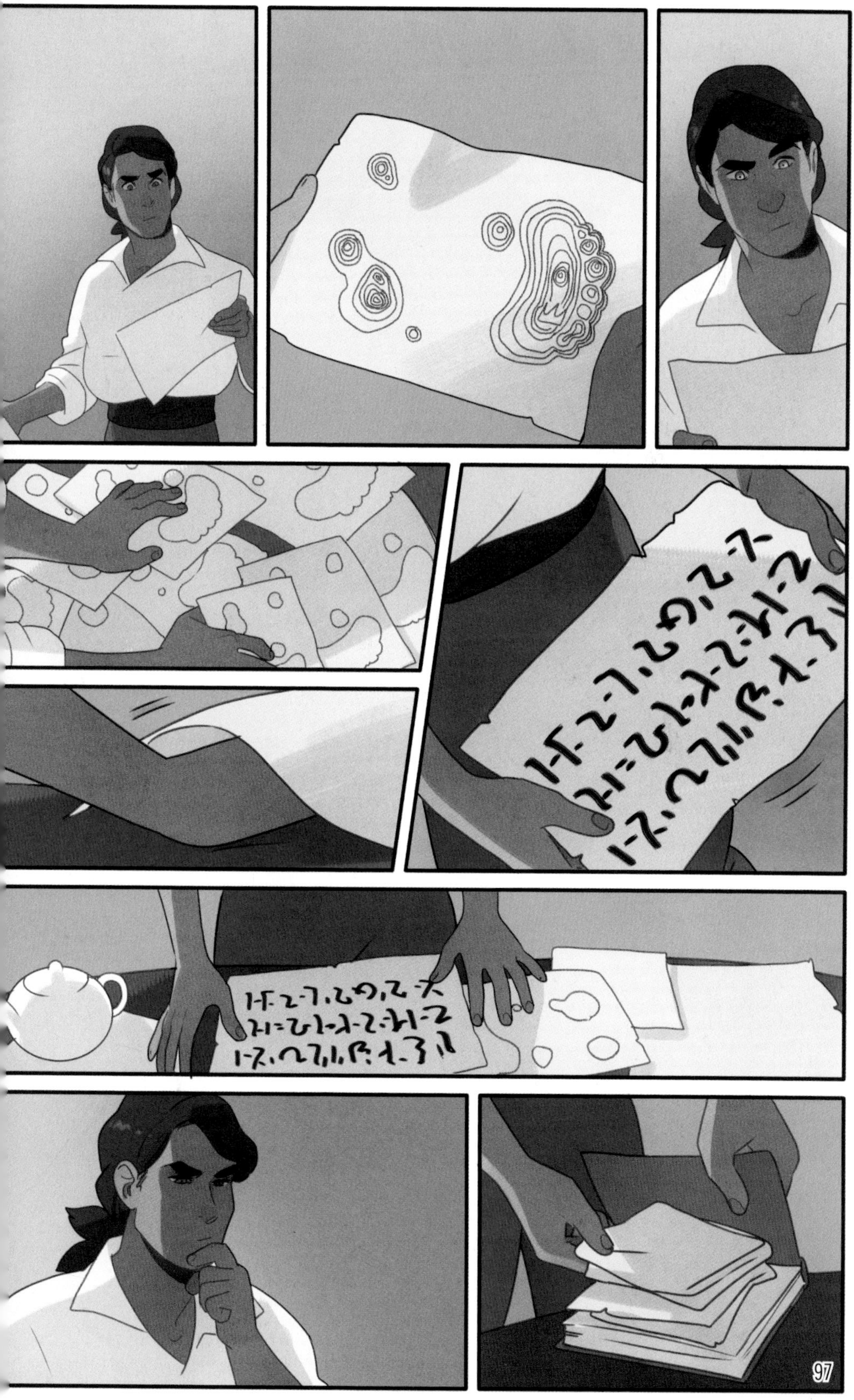

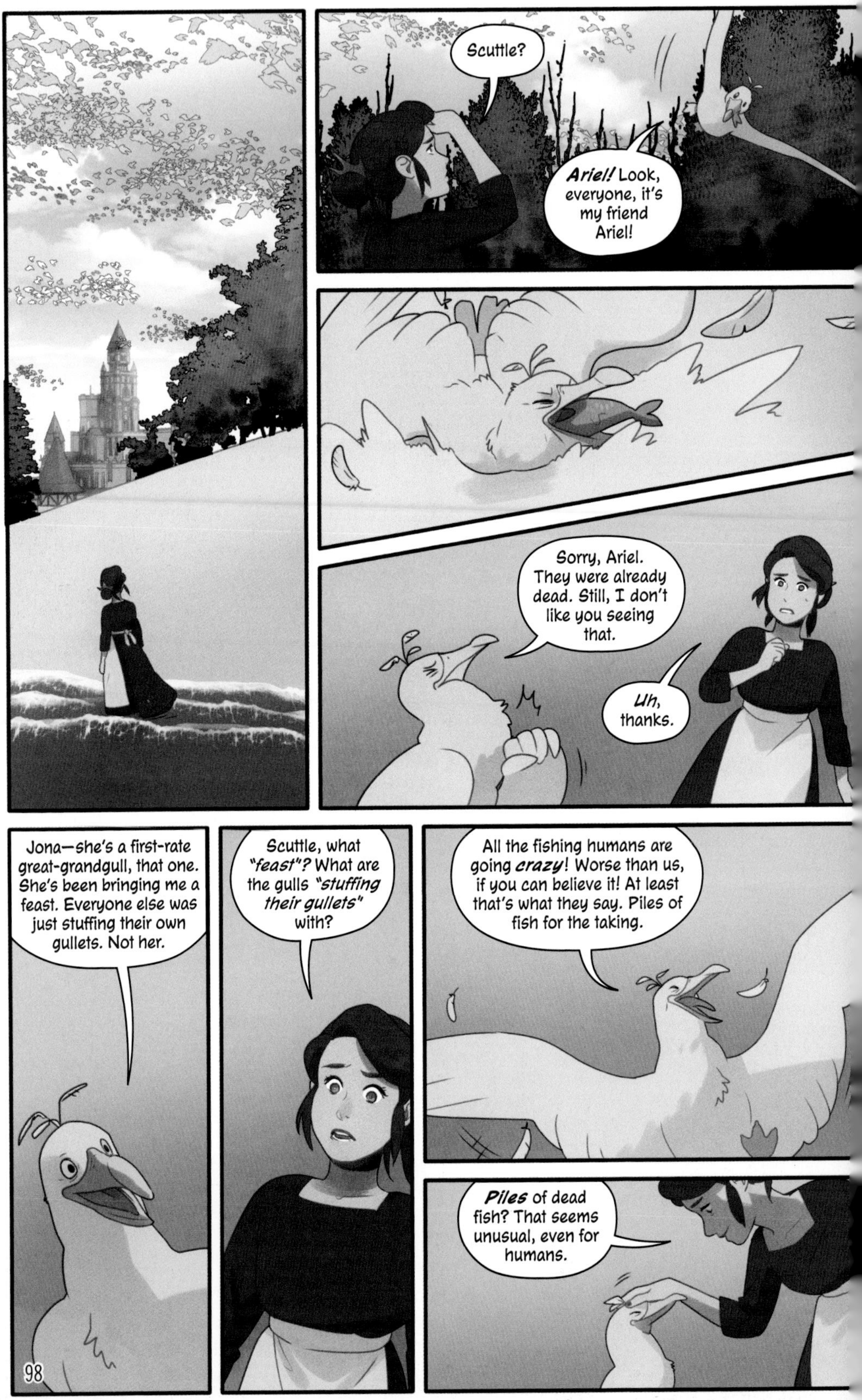
Scuttle?
Ariel! Look, everyone, it's my friend Ariel!
Sorry, Ariel. They were already dead. Still, I don't like you seeing that.
Uh, thanks.
Jona—she's a first-rate great-grandgull, that one. She's been bringing me a feast. Everyone else was just stuffing their own gullets. Not her.
Scuttle, what "feast"? What are the gulls "stuffing their gullets" with?
All the fishing humans are going crazy! Worse than us, if you can believe it! At least that's what they say. Piles of fish for the taking.
Piles of dead fish? That seems unusual, even for humans.

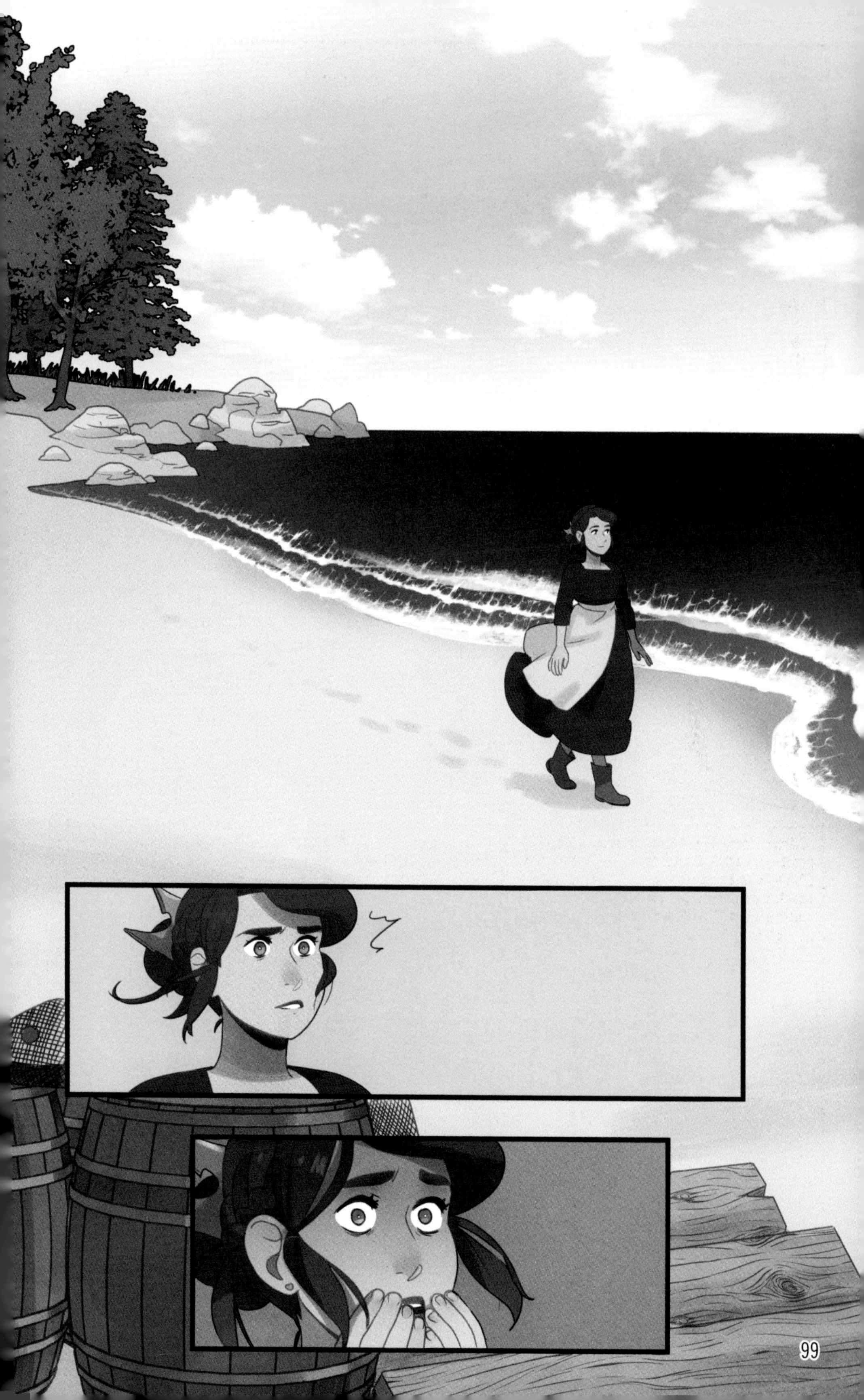

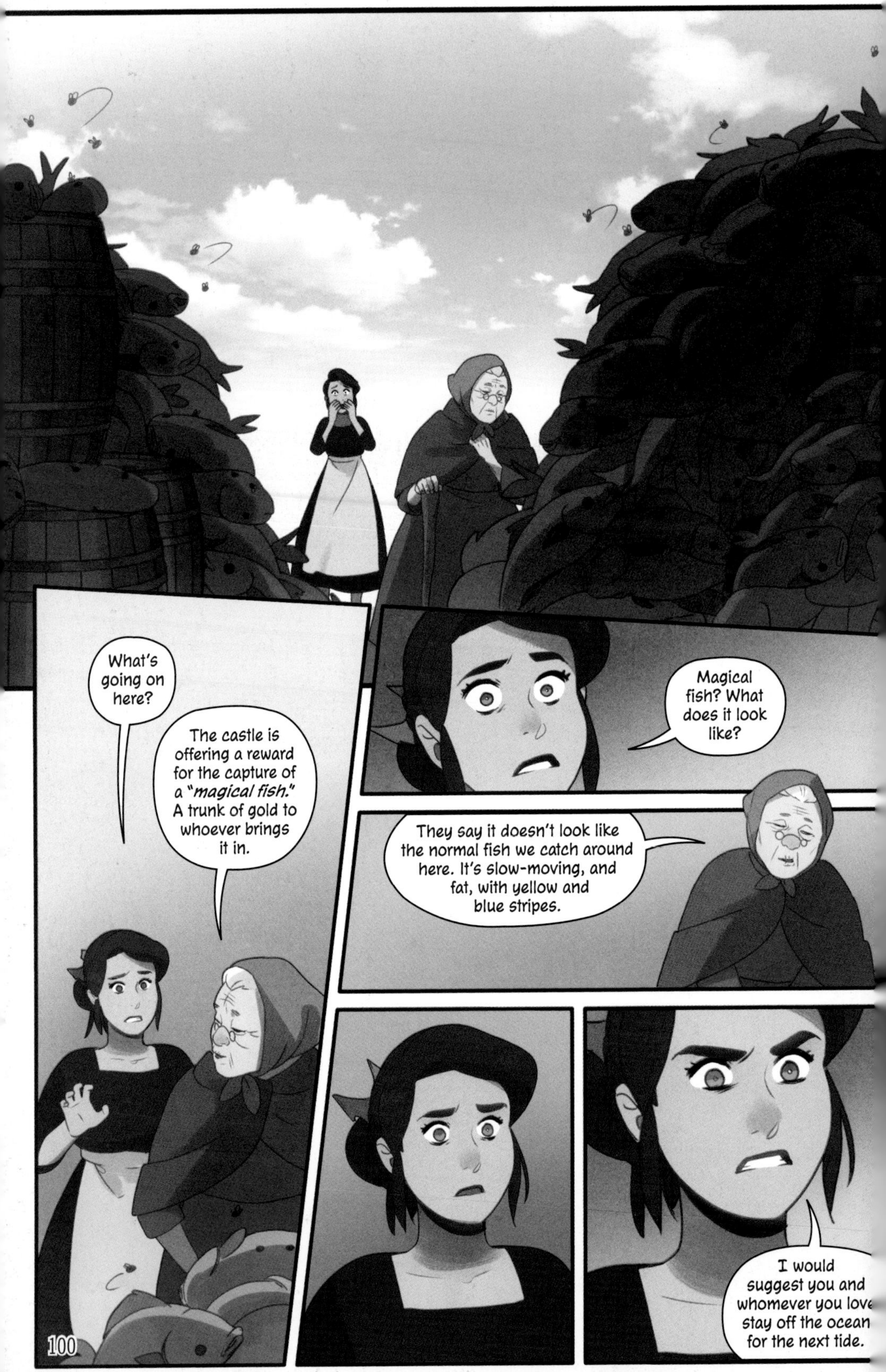

What's going on here?
The castle is offering a reward for the capture of a "*magical fish.*" A trunk of gold to whoever brings it in.
Magical fish? What does it look like?
They say it doesn't look like the normal fish we catch around here. It's slow-moving, and fat, with yellow and blue stripes.
I would suggest you and whomever you love stay off the ocean for the next tide.

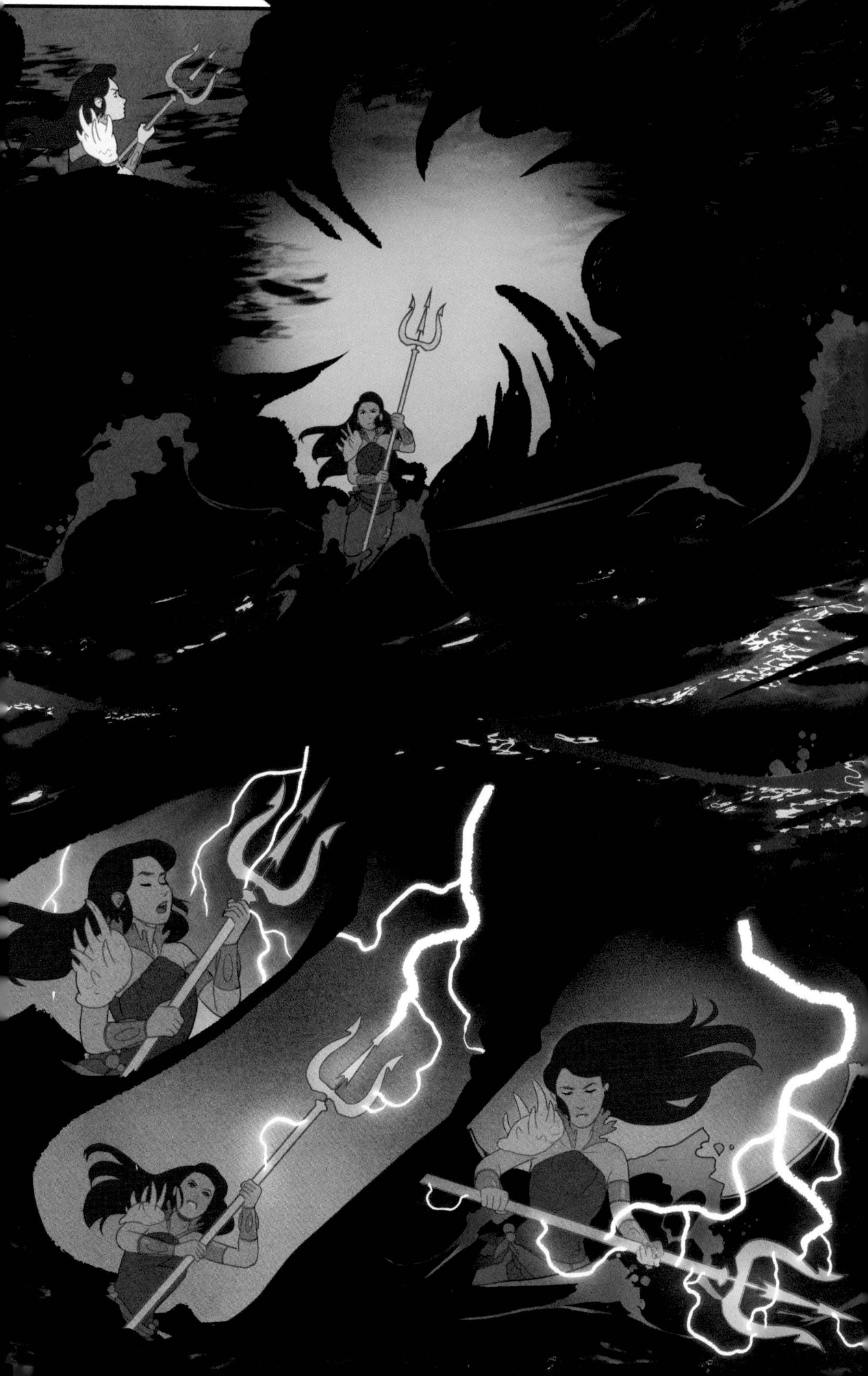

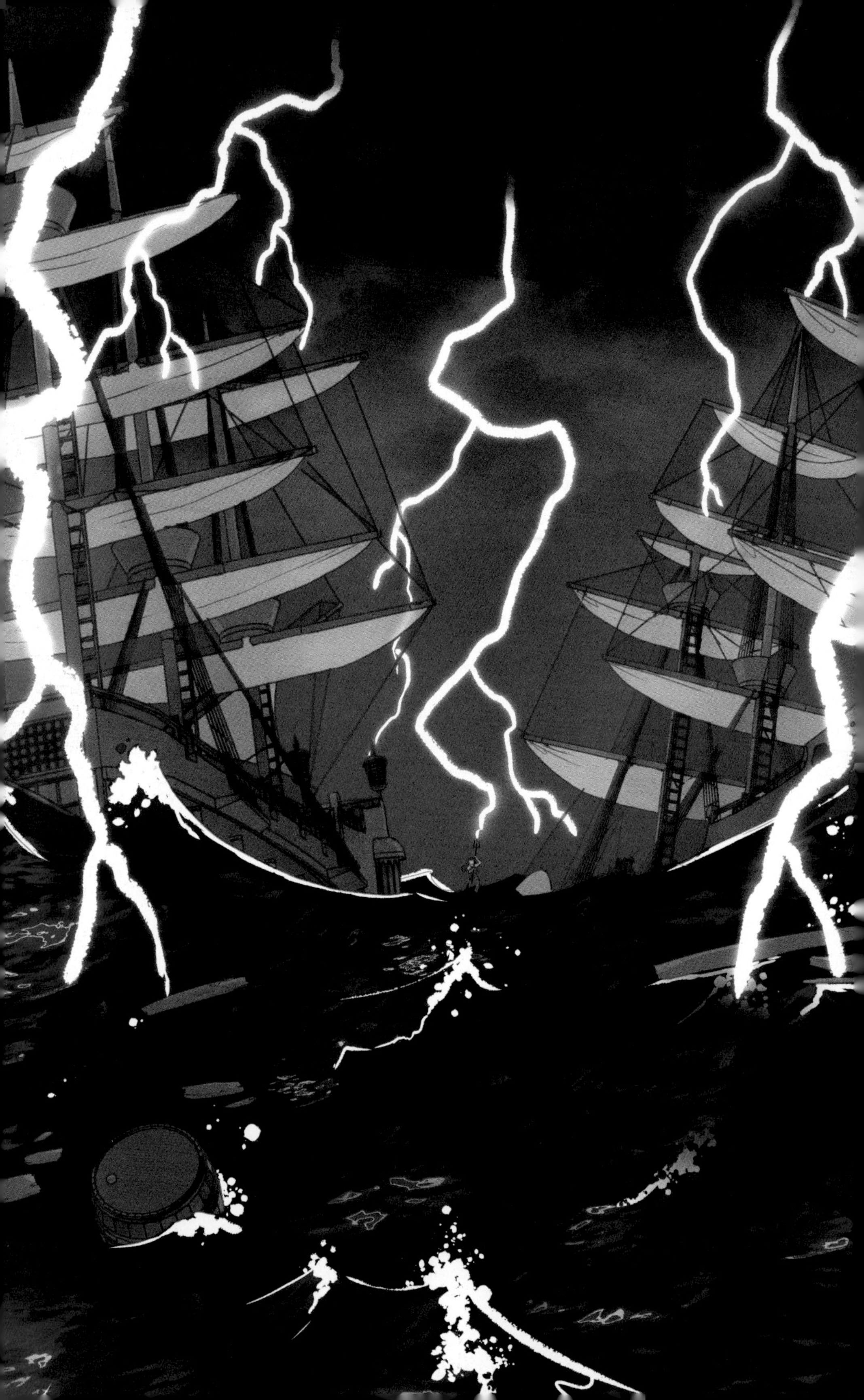

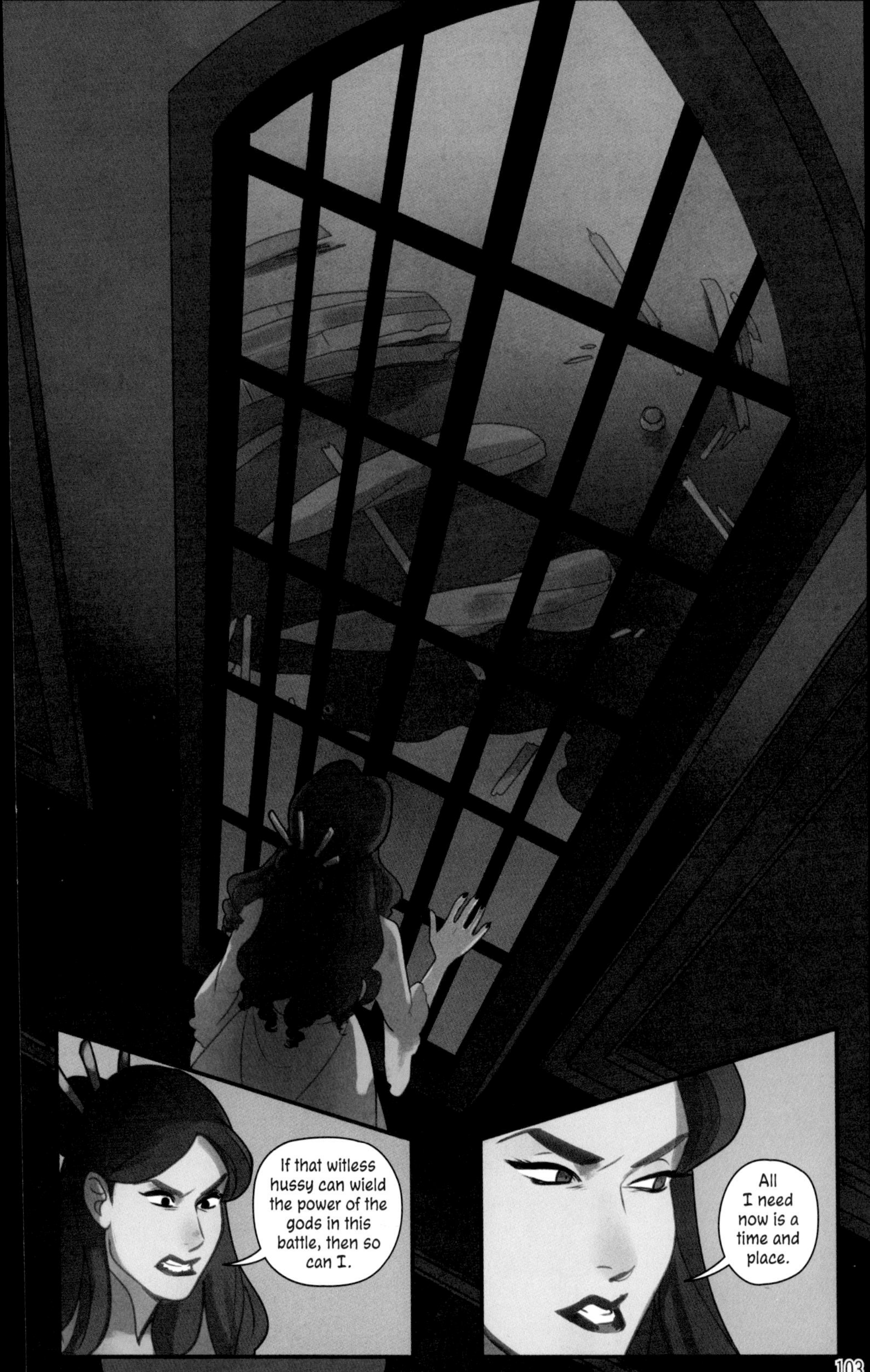
If that witless hussy can wield the power of the gods in this battle, then so can I.
All I need now is a time and place.

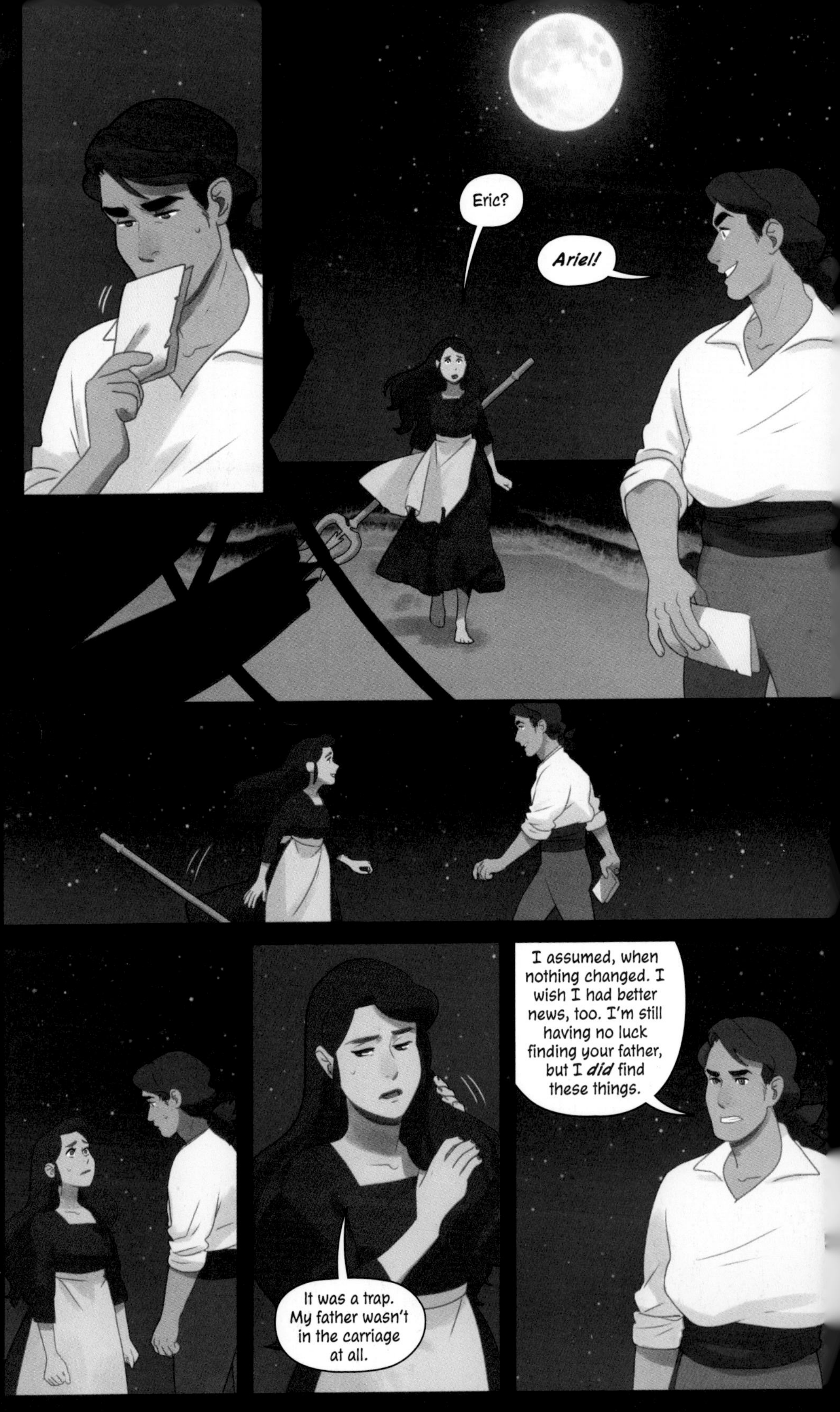
Eric?
Ariel!
I assumed, when nothing changed. I wish I had better news, too. I'm still having no luck finding your father, but I *did* find these things.
It was a trap. My father wasn't in the carriage at all.

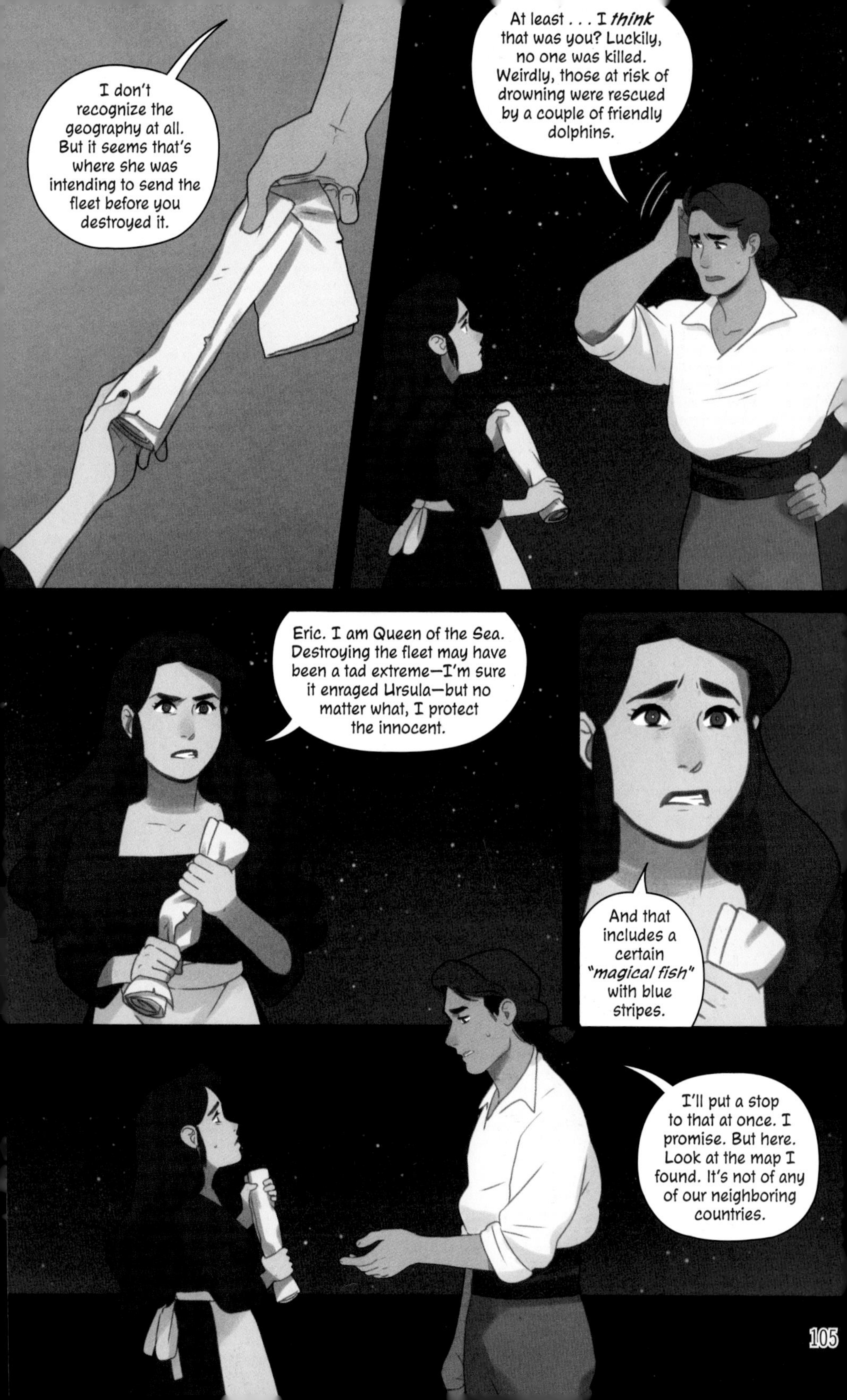

At least . . . I *think* that was you? Luckily, no one was killed. Weirdly, those at risk of drowning were rescued by a couple of friendly dolphins.
I'll put a stop to that at once. I promise. But here. Look at the map I found. It's not of any of our neighboring countries.
I don't recognize the geography at all. But it seems that's where she was intending to send the fleet before you destroyed it.
Eric. I am Queen of the Sea. Destroying the fleet may have been a tad extreme—I'm sure it enraged Ursula—but no matter what, I protect the innocent.
And that includes a certain *"magical fish"* with blue stripes.

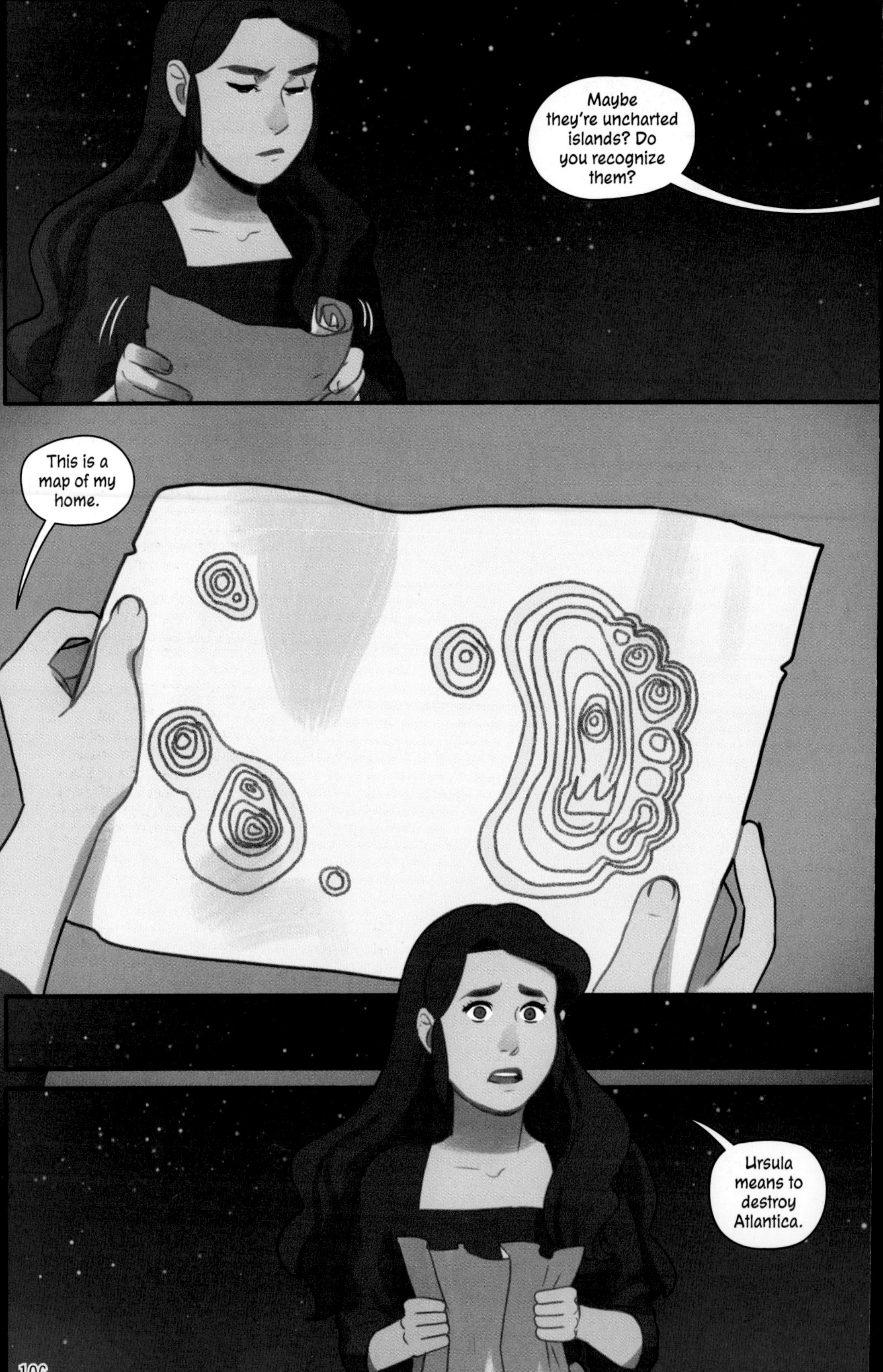

Maybe they're uncharted islands? Do you recognize them?
This is a map of my home.
Ursula means to destroy Atlantica.

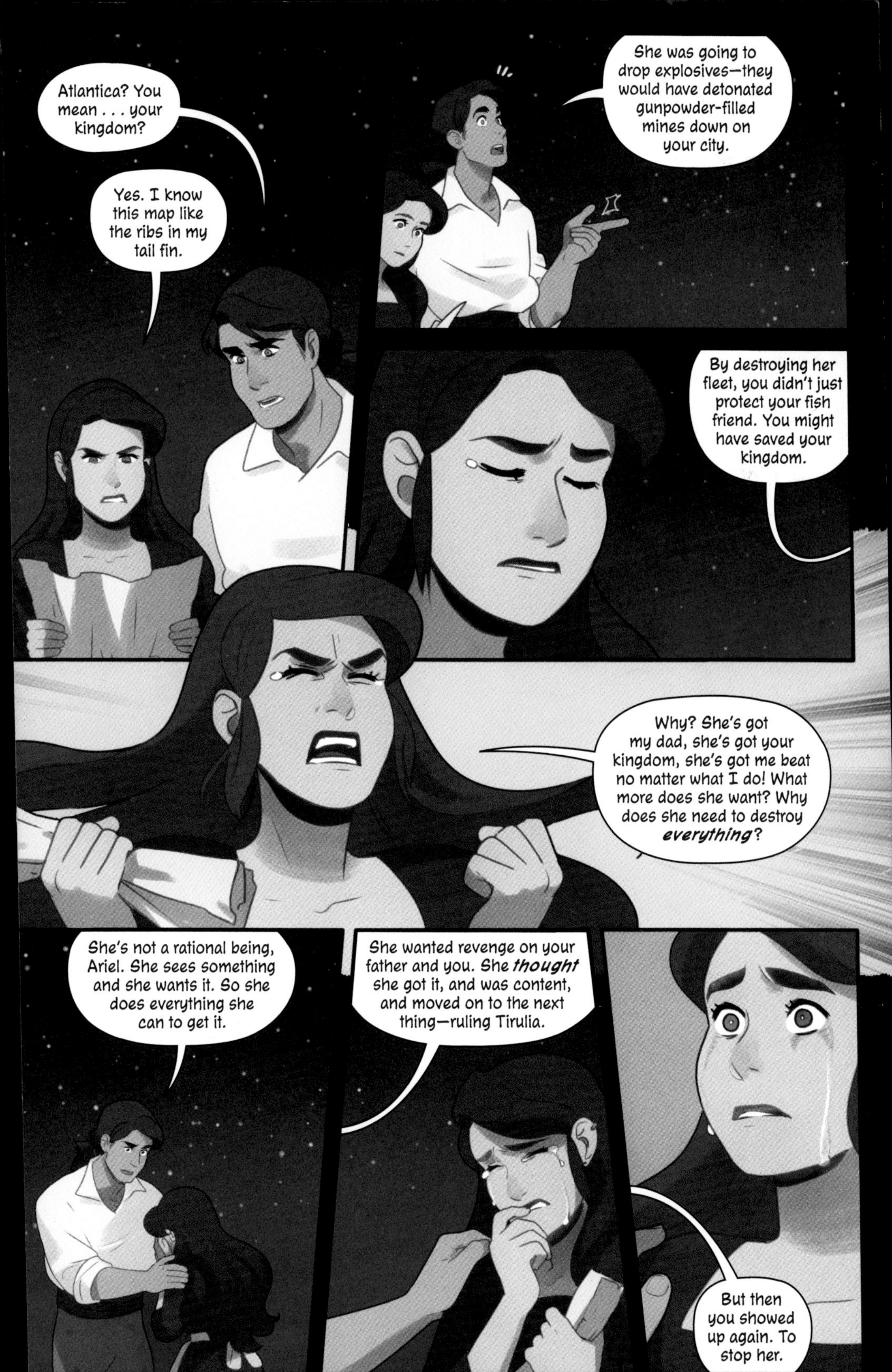
Atlantica? You mean . . . your kingdom?
Yes. I know this map like the ribs in my tail fin.
She was going to drop explosives—they would have detonated gunpowder-filled mines down on your city.
By destroying her fleet, you didn't just protect your fish friend. You might have saved your kingdom.
Why? She's got my dad, she's got your kingdom, she's got me beat no matter what I do! What more does she want? Why does she need to destroy *everything*?
She's not a rational being, Ariel. She sees something and she wants it. So she does everything she can to get it.
She wanted revenge on your father and you. She *thought* she got it, and was content, and moved on to the next thing—ruling Tirulia.
But then you showed up again. To stop her.

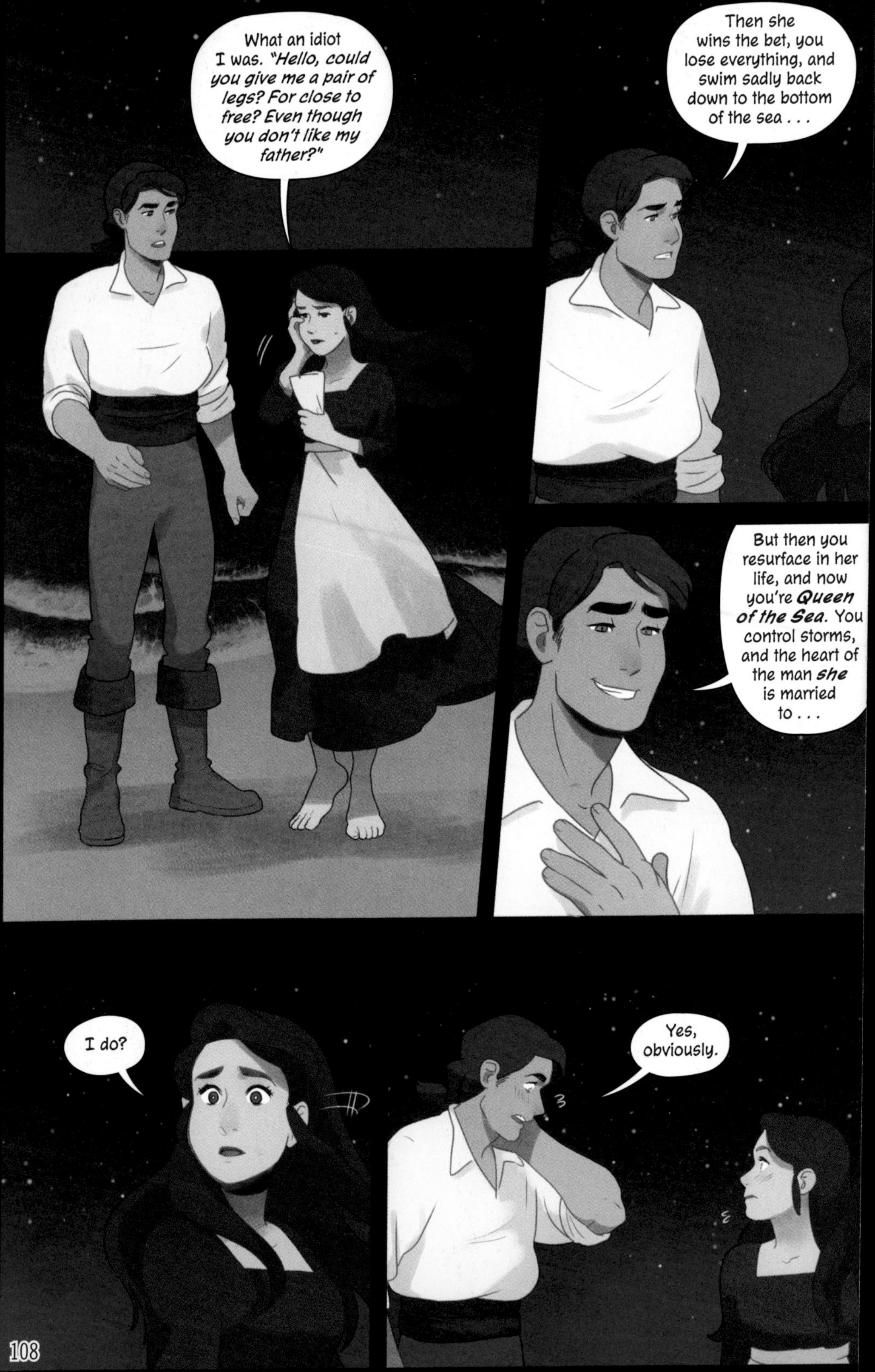
What an idiot I was. *"Hello, could you give me a pair of legs? For close to free? Even though you don't like my father?"*
Then she wins the bet, you lose everything, and swim sadly back down to the bottom of the sea . . .
But then you resurface in her life, and now you're ***Queen of the Sea***. You control storms, and the heart of the man ***she*** is married to . . .
I do?
Yes, obviously.

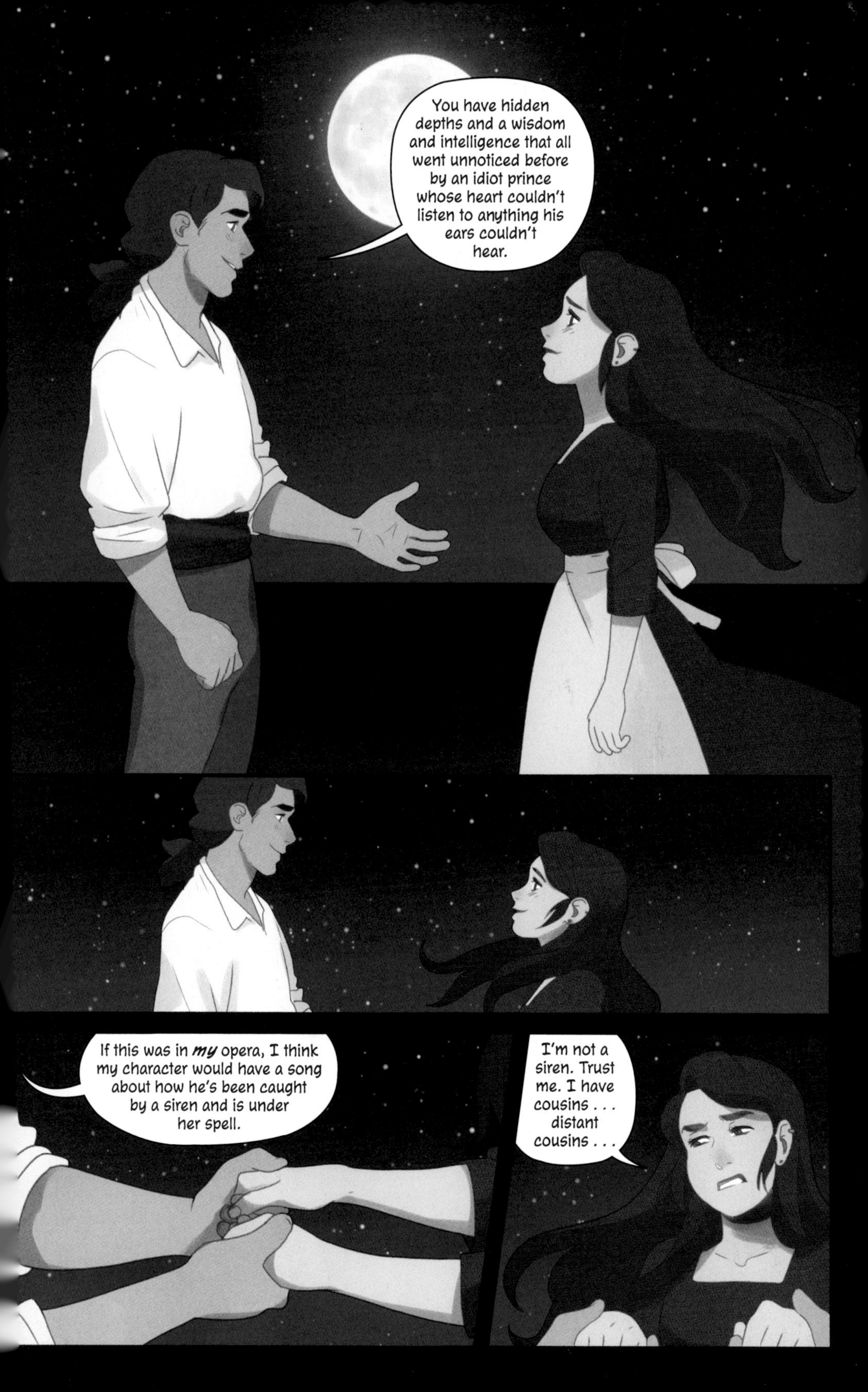
You have hidden depths and a wisdom and intelligence that all went unnoticed before by an idiot prince whose heart couldn't listen to anything his ears couldn't hear.
If this was in *my* opera, I think my character would have a song about how he's been caught by a siren and is under her spell.
I'm not a siren. Trust me. I have cousins . . . distant cousins . . .

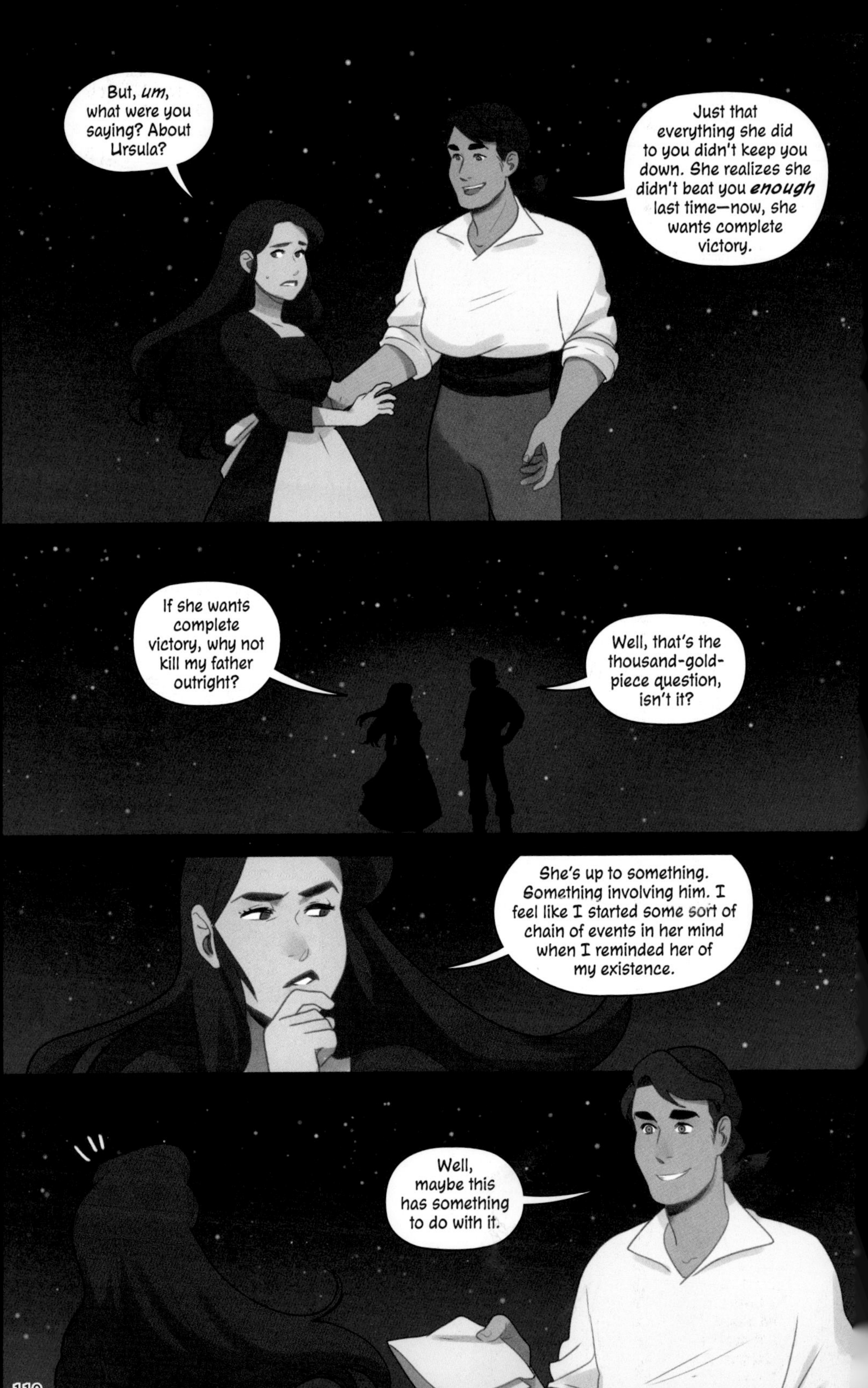
But, *um*, what were you saying? About Ursula?
Just that everything she did to you didn't keep you down. She realizes she didn't beat you ***enough*** last time—now, she wants complete victory.
If she wants complete victory, why not kill my father outright?
Well, that's the thousand-gold-piece question, isn't it?
She's up to something. Something involving him. I feel like I started some sort of chain of events in her mind when I reminded her of my existence.
Well, maybe this has something to do with it.

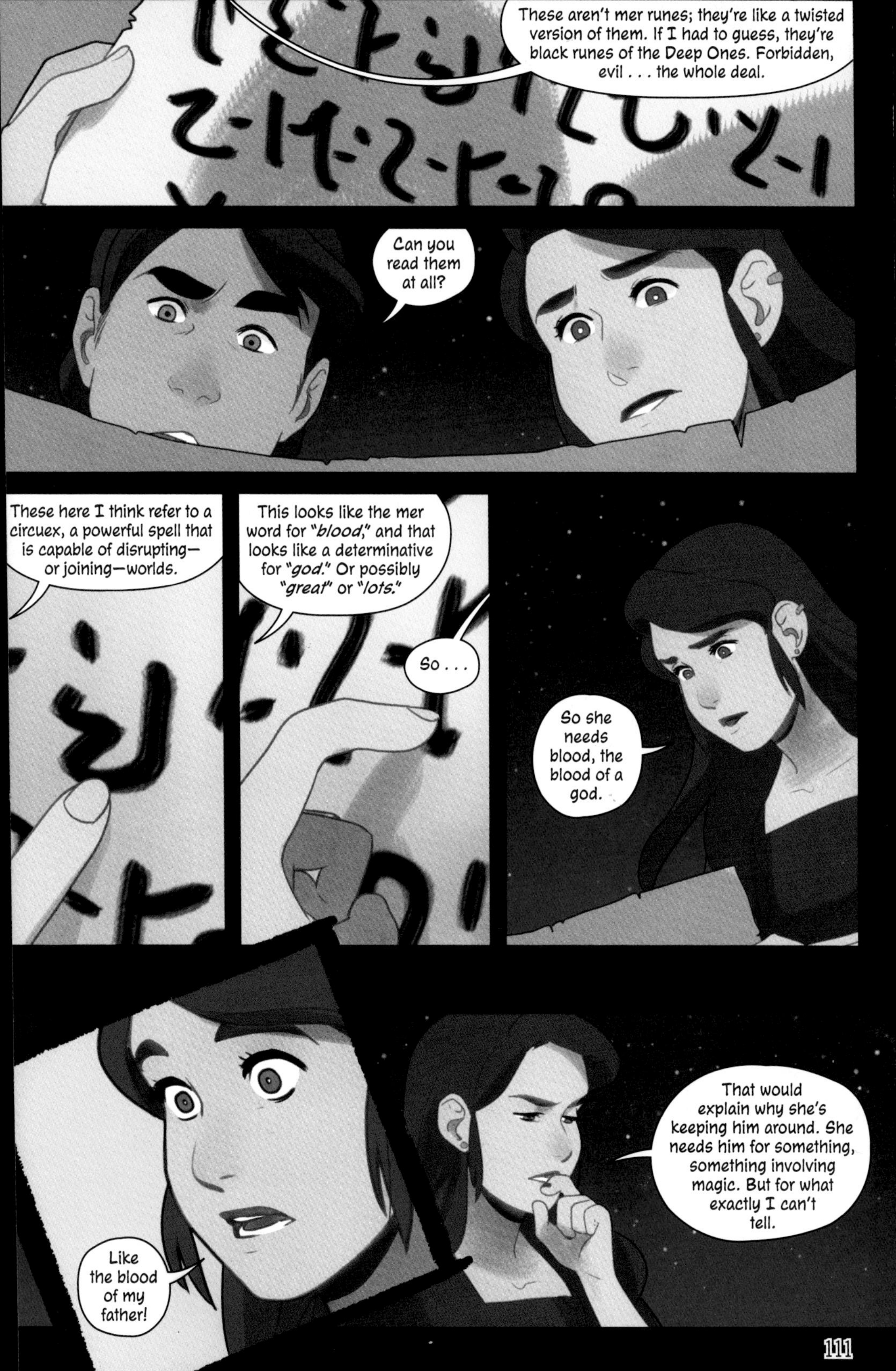
These aren't mer runes; they're like a twisted version of them. If I had to guess, they're black runes of the Deep Ones. Forbidden, evil . . . the whole deal.
Can you read them at all?
These here I think refer to a circuex, a powerful spell that is capable of disrupting—or joining—worlds.
This looks like the mer word for "*blood*," and that looks like a determinative for "*god*." Or possibly "*great*" or "*lots*."
So . . .
So she needs blood, the blood of a god.
Like the blood of my father!
That would explain why she's keeping him around. She needs him for something, something involving magic. But for what exactly I can't tell.

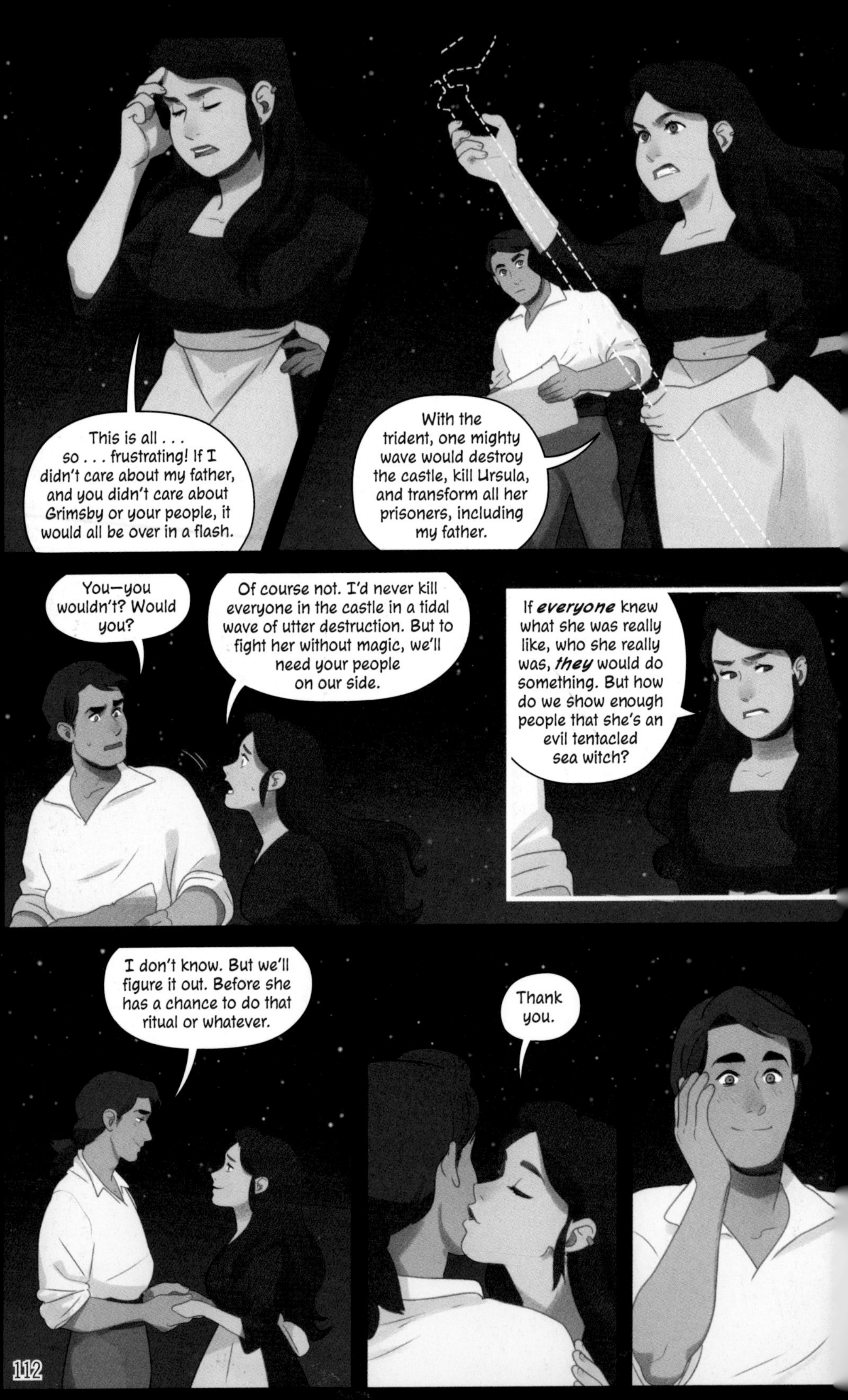
This is all . . . so . . . frustrating! If I didn't care about my father, and you didn't care about Grimsby or your people, it would all be over in a flash.
With the trident, one mighty wave would destroy the castle, kill Ursula, and transform all her prisoners, including my father.
You—you wouldn't? Would you?
Of course not. I'd never kill everyone in the castle in a tidal wave of utter destruction. But to fight her without magic, we'll need your people on our side.
If *everyone* knew what she was really like, who she really was, *they* would do something. But how do we show enough people that she's an evil tentacled sea witch?
I don't know. But we'll figure it out. Before she has a chance to do that ritual or whatever.
Thank you.

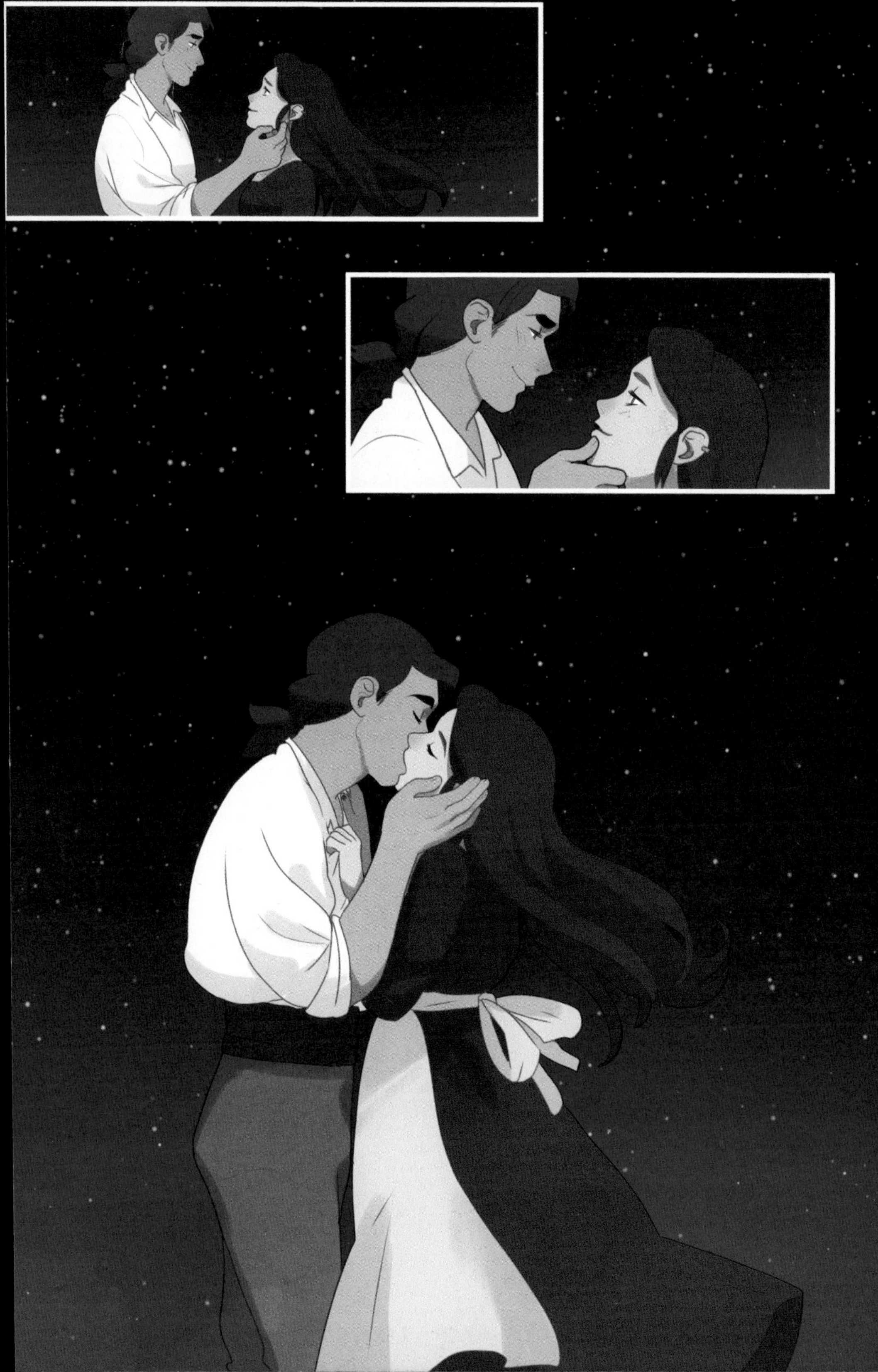

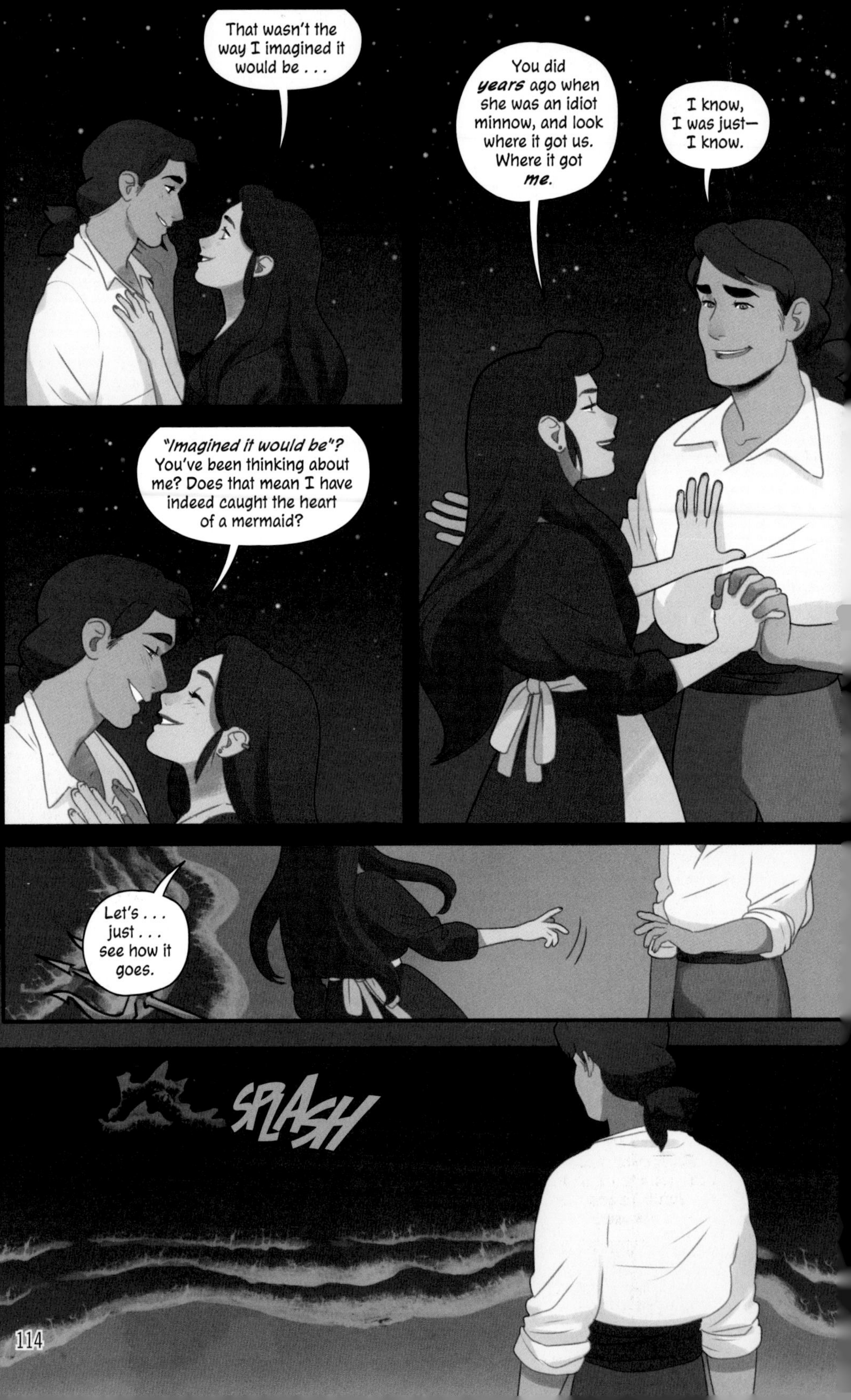
That wasn't the way I imagined it would be . . .
"*Imagined it would be*"? You've been thinking about me? Does that mean I have indeed caught the heart of a mermaid?
You did ***years*** ago when she was an idiot minnow, and look where it got us. Where it got ***me.***
I know, I was just— I know.
Let's . . . just . . . see how it goes.
SPLASH

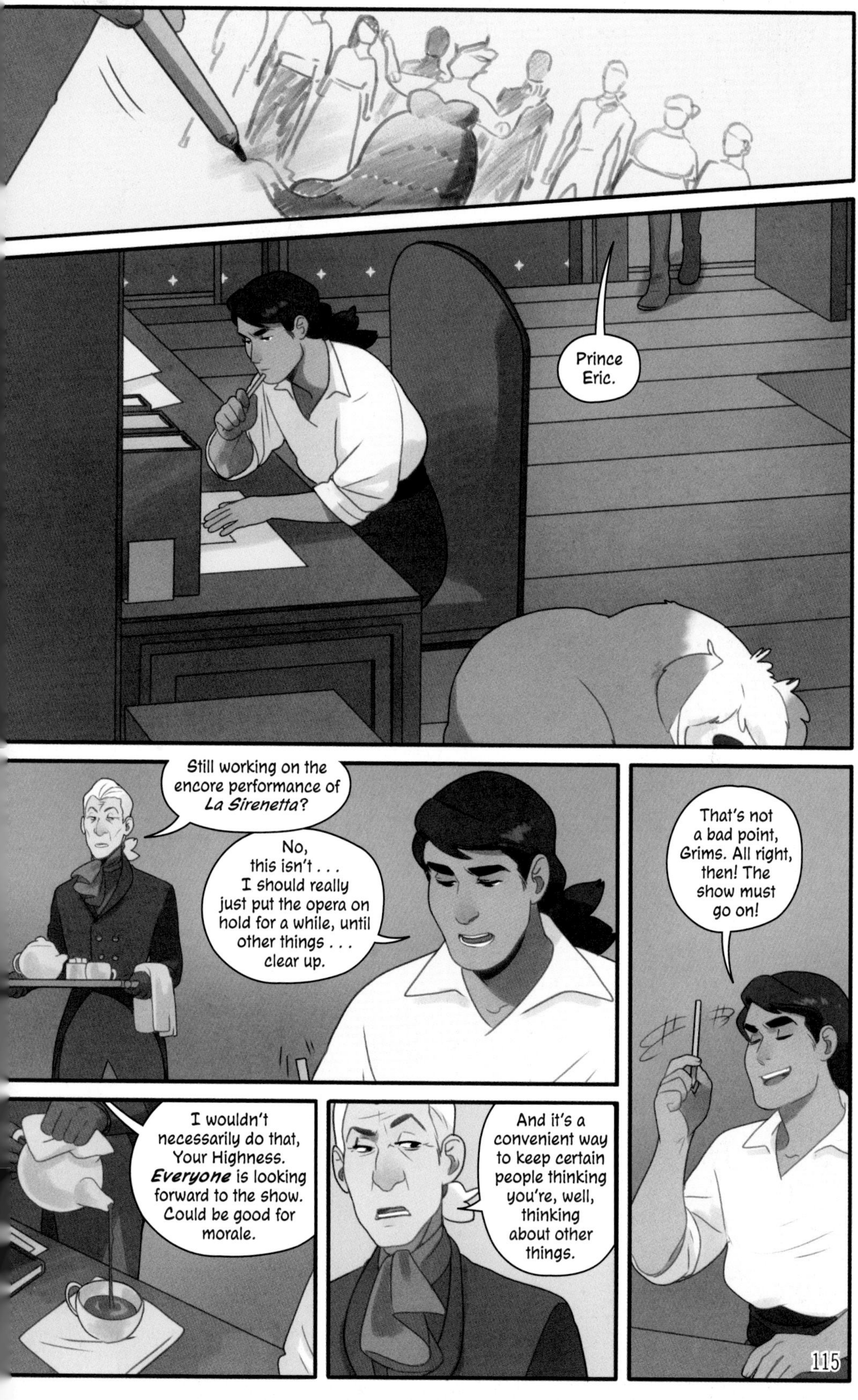
Prince Eric.
Still working on the encore performance of *La Sirenetta*?
No, this isn't . . . I should really just put the opera on hold for a while, until other things . . . clear up.
I wouldn't necessarily do that, Your Highness. ***Everyone*** is looking forward to the show. Could be good for morale.
And it's a convenient way to keep certain people thinking you're, well, thinking about other things.
That's not a bad point, Grims. All right, then! The show must go on!

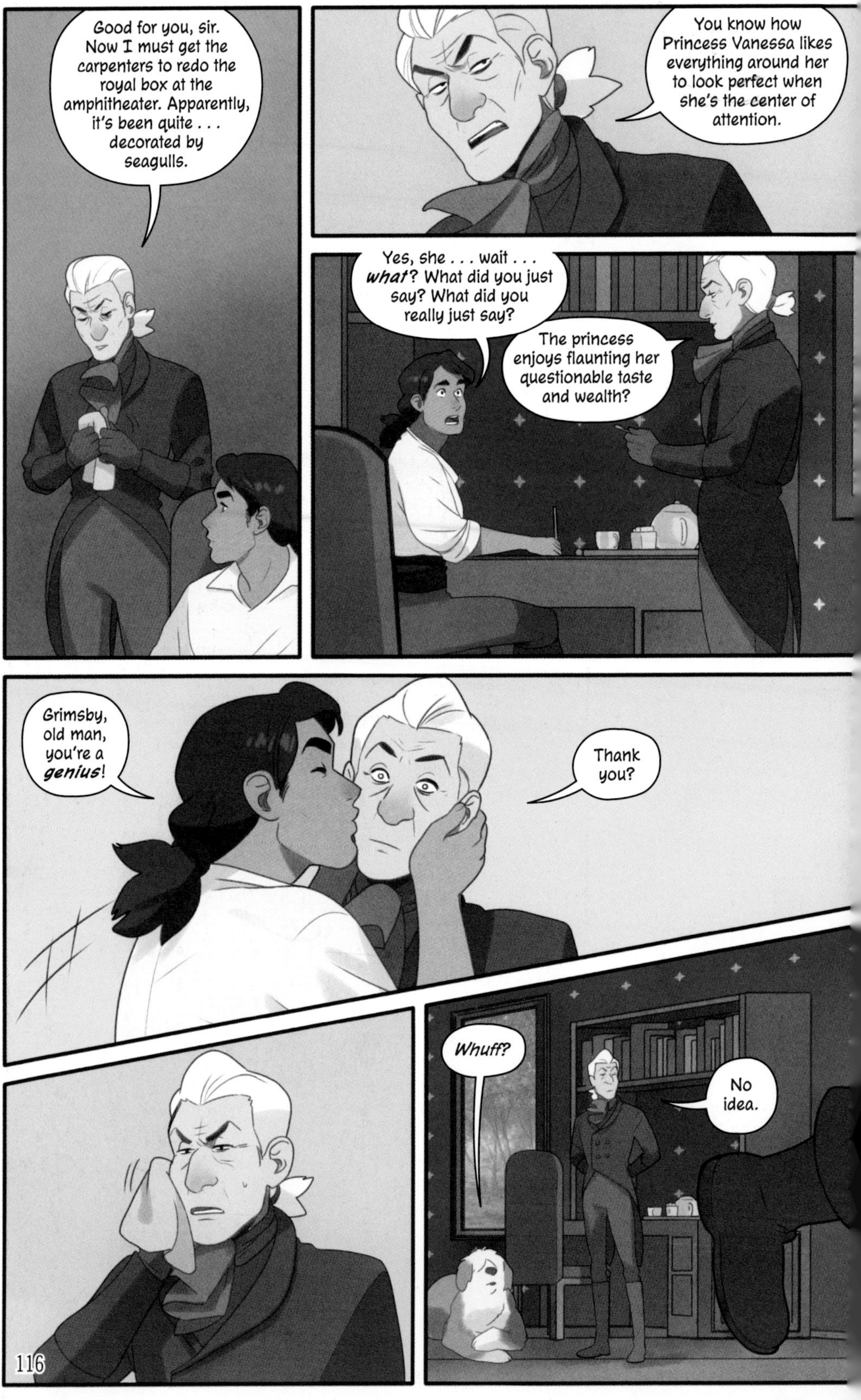
Good for you, sir. Now I must get the carpenters to redo the royal box at the amphitheater. Apparently, it's been quite . . . decorated by seagulls.
You know how Princess Vanessa likes everything around her to look perfect when she's the center of attention.
Yes, she . . . wait . . . *what*? What did you just say? What did you really just say?
The princess enjoys flaunting her questionable taste and wealth?
Grimsby, old man, you're a *genius*!
Thank you?
Whuff?
No idea.

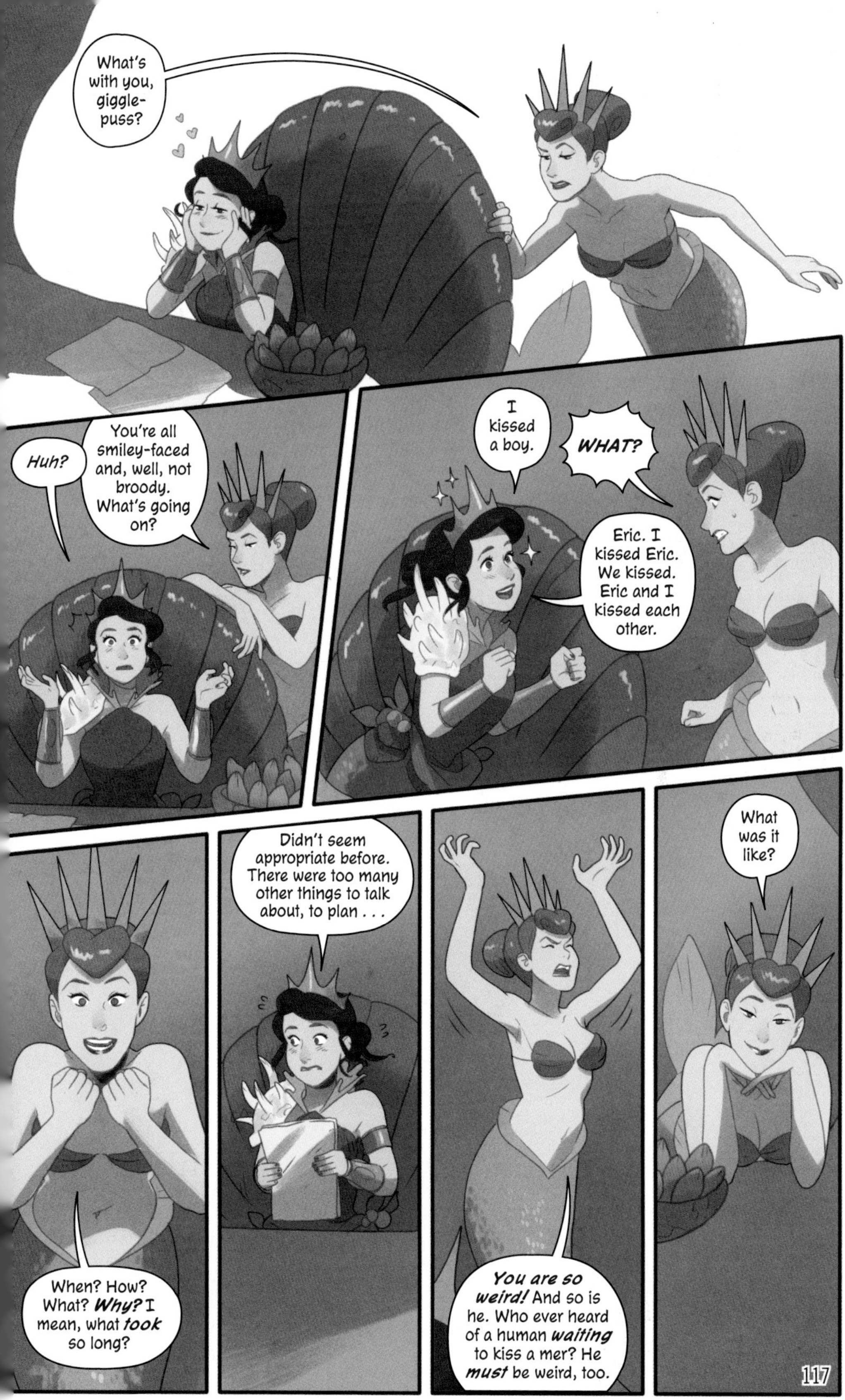
What's with you, giggle-puss?
Huh?
You're all smiley-faced and, well, not broody. What's going on?
I kissed a boy.
WHAT?
Eric. I kissed Eric. We kissed. Eric and I kissed each other.
When? How? What? Why? I mean, what took so long?
Didn't seem appropriate before. There were too many other things to talk about, to plan . . .
You are so weird! And so is he. Who ever heard of a human waiting to kiss a mer? He must be weird, too.
What was it like?

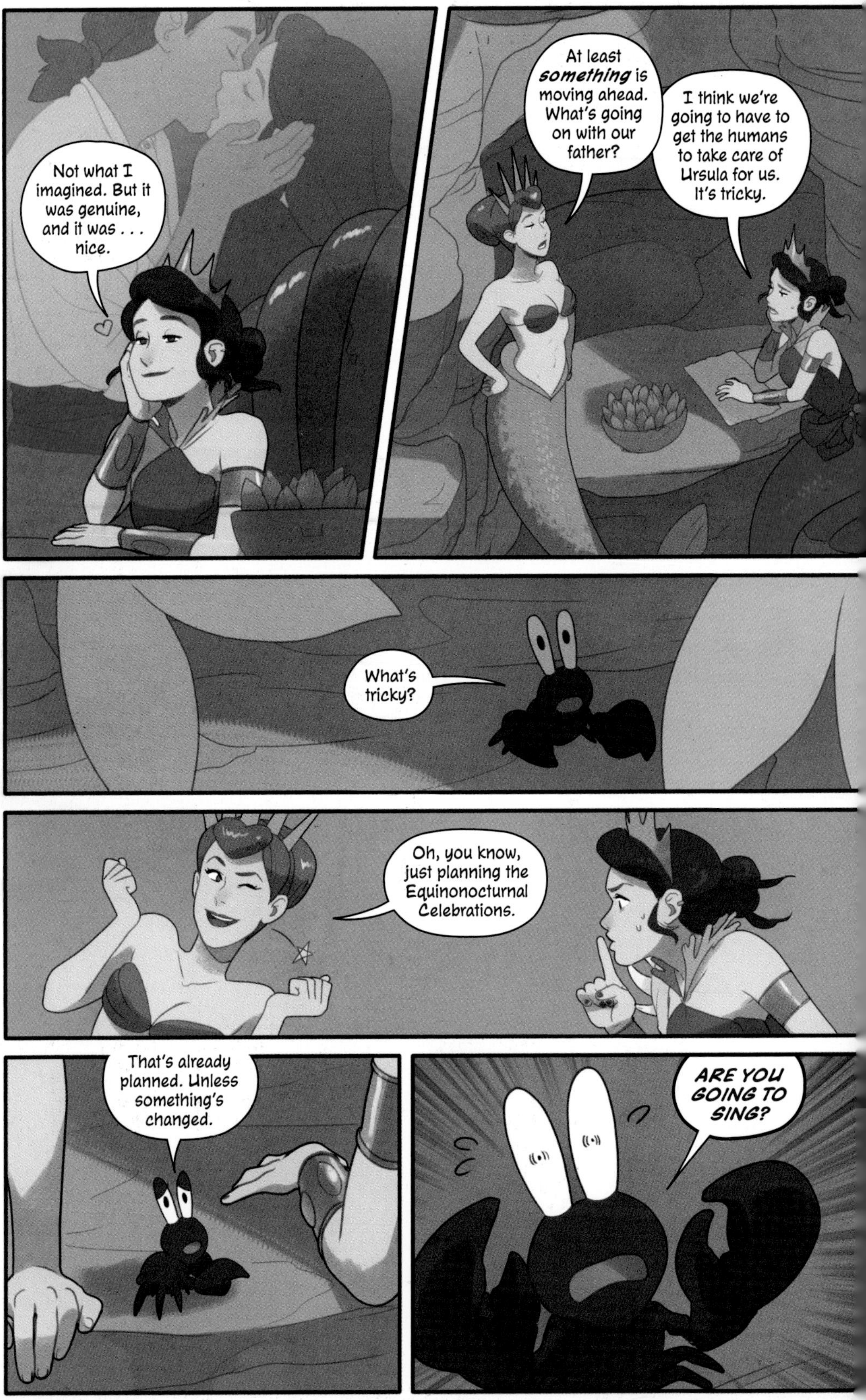
Not what I imagined. But it was genuine, and it was . . . nice.
At least *something* is moving ahead. What's going on with our father?
I think we're going to have to get the humans to take care of Ursula for us. It's tricky.
What's tricky?
Oh, you know, just planning the Equinonocturnal Celebrations.
That's already planned. Unless something's changed.
ARE YOU GOING TO SING?

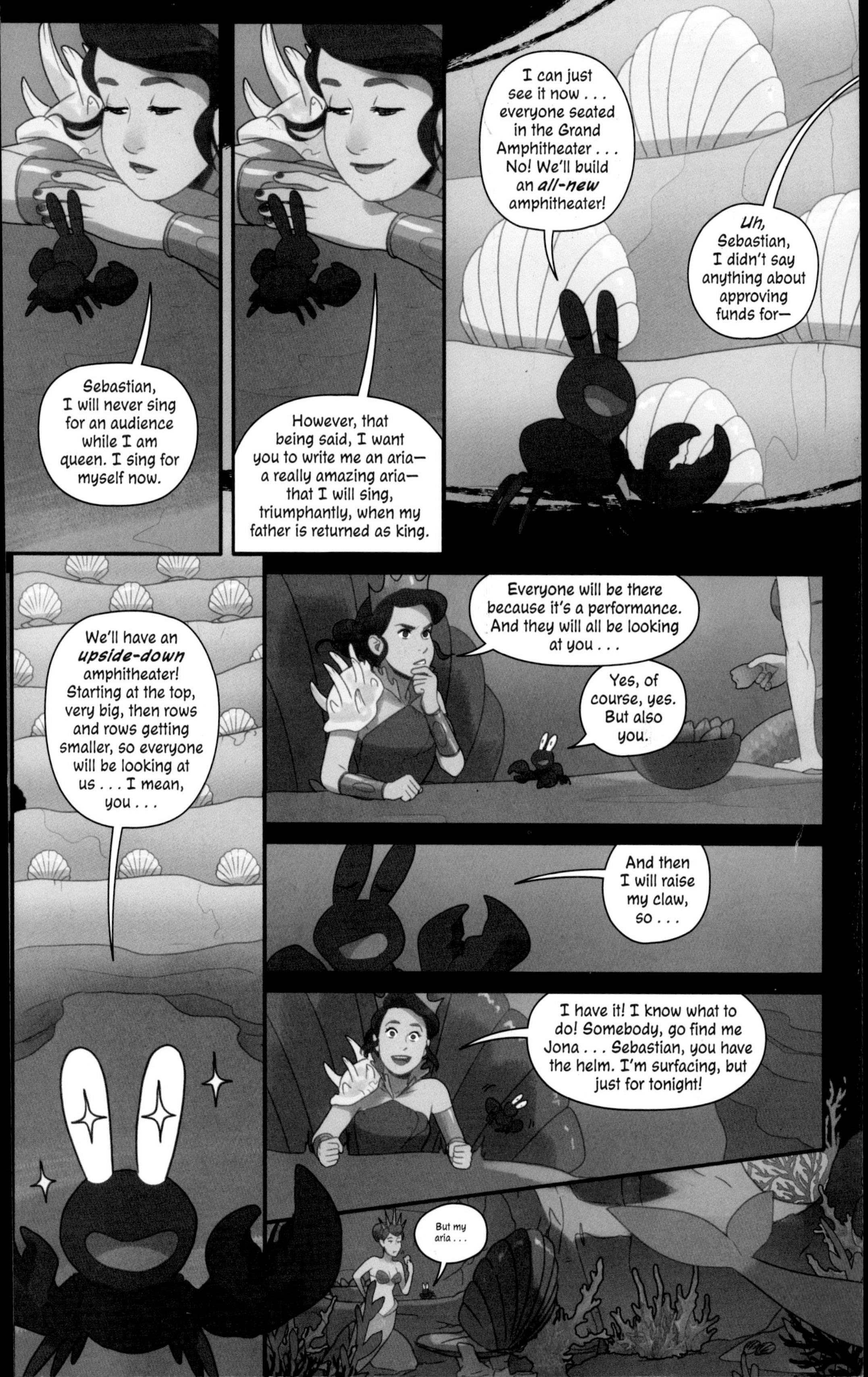

Sebastian, I will never sing for an audience while I am queen. I sing for myself now.
However, that being said, I want you to write me an aria— a really amazing aria— that I will sing, triumphantly, when my father is returned as king.
I can just see it now . . . everyone seated in the Grand Amphitheater . . . No! We'll build an *all-new* amphitheater!
Uh, Sebastian, I didn't say anything about approving funds for—
We'll have an ***upside-down*** amphitheater! Starting at the top, very big, then rows and rows getting smaller, so everyone will be looking at us . . . I mean, you . . .
Everyone will be there because it's a performance. And they will all be looking at you . . .
Yes, of course, yes. But also you.
And then I will raise my claw, so . . .
I have it! I know what to do! Somebody, go find me Jona . . . Sebastian, you have the helm. I'm surfacing, but just for tonight!
But my aria . . .

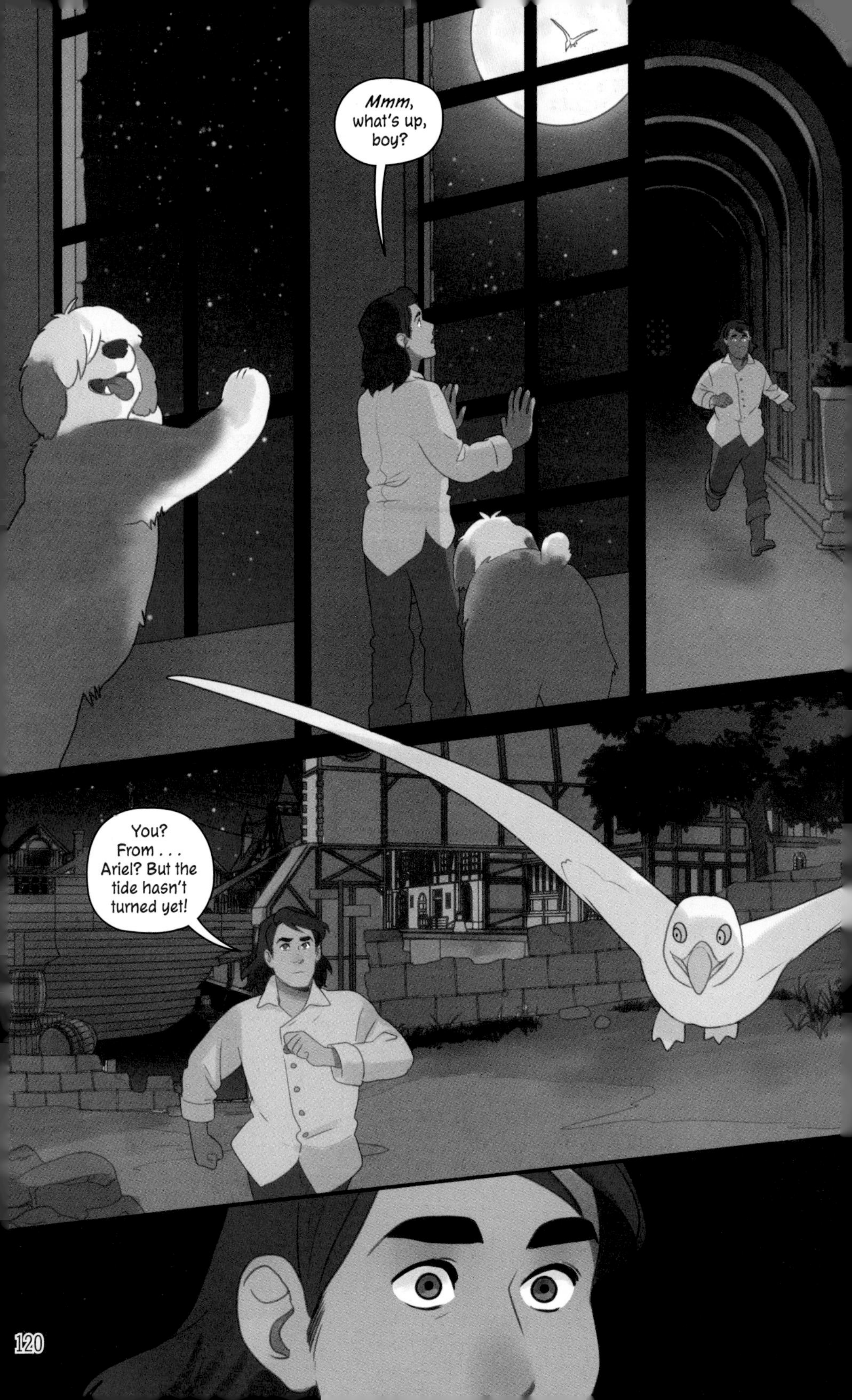
Mmm, what's up, boy?
You? From . . . Ariel? But the tide hasn't turned yet!

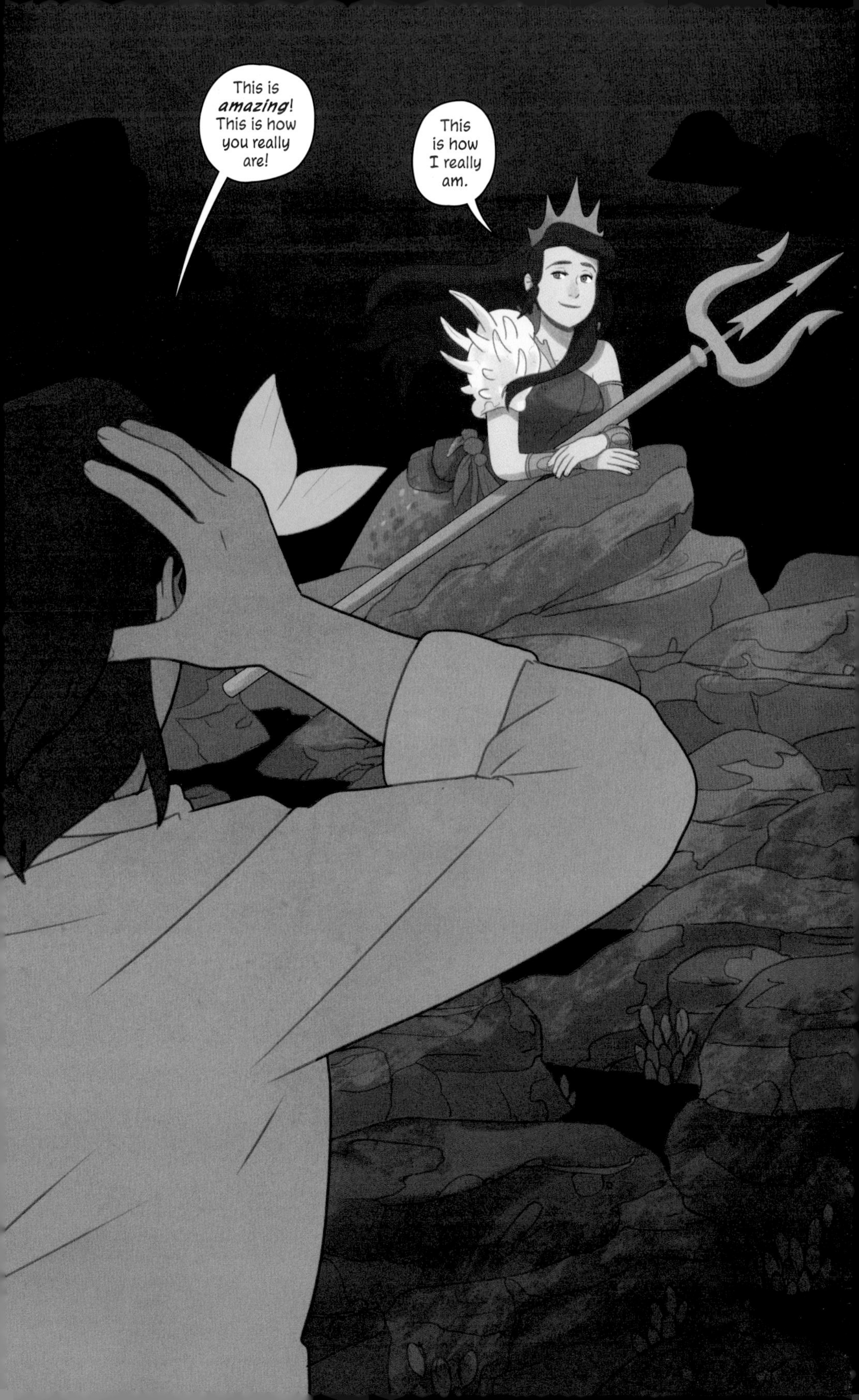
This is *amazing*! This is how you really are!
This is how I really am.

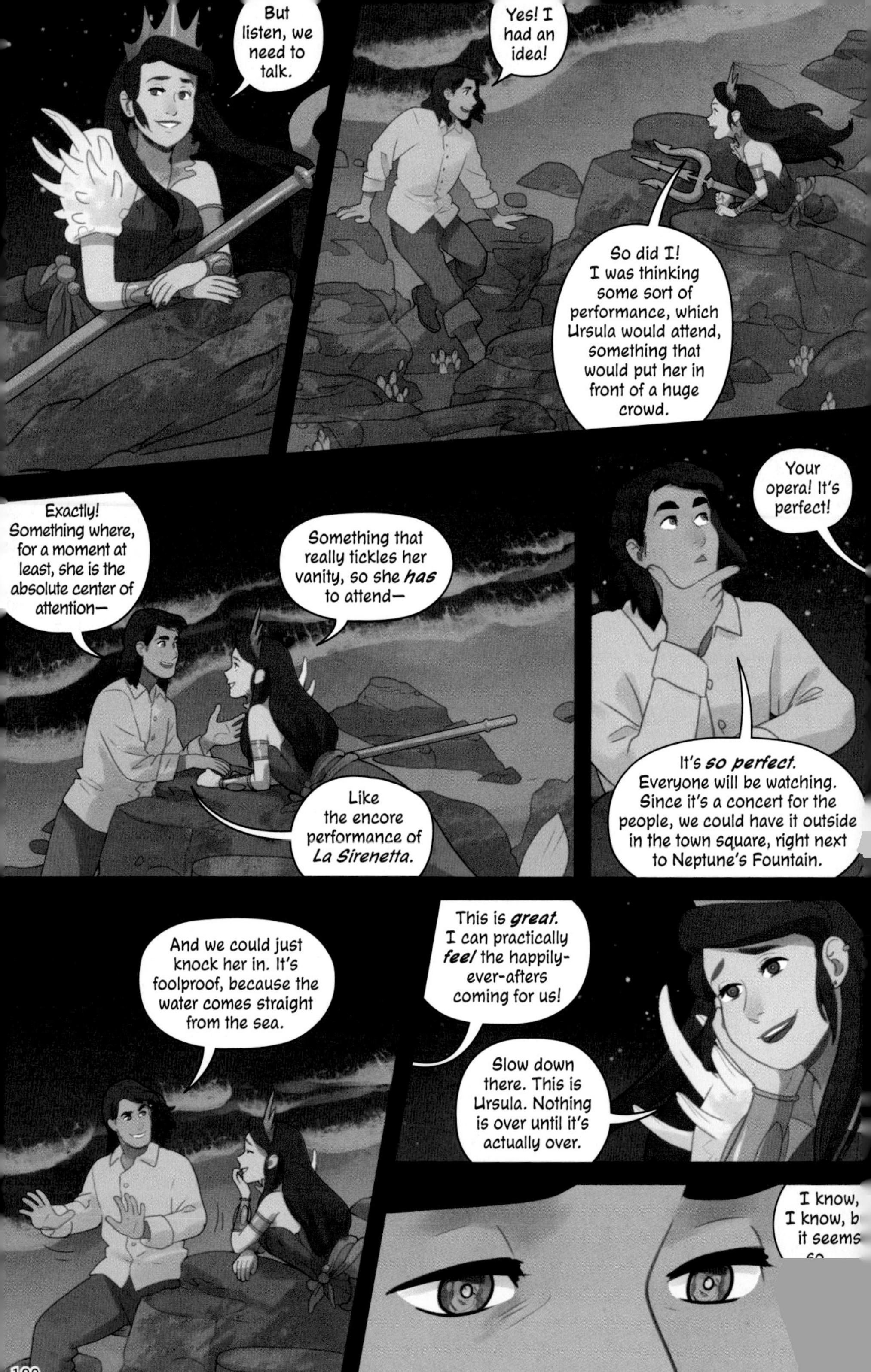
But listen, we need to talk.
Yes! I had an idea!
So did I! I was thinking some sort of performance, which Ursula would attend, something that would put her in front of a huge crowd.
Exactly! Something where, for a moment at least, she is the absolute center of attention—
Something that really tickles her vanity, so she *has* to attend—
Like the encore performance of *La Sirenetta*.
Your opera! It's perfect!
It's *so perfect*. Everyone will be watching. Since it's a concert for the people, we could have it outside in the town square, right next to Neptune's Fountain.
And we could just knock her in. It's foolproof, because the water comes straight from the sea.
This is *great*. I can practically *feel* the happily-ever-afters coming for us!
Slow down there. This is Ursula. Nothing is over until it's actually over.

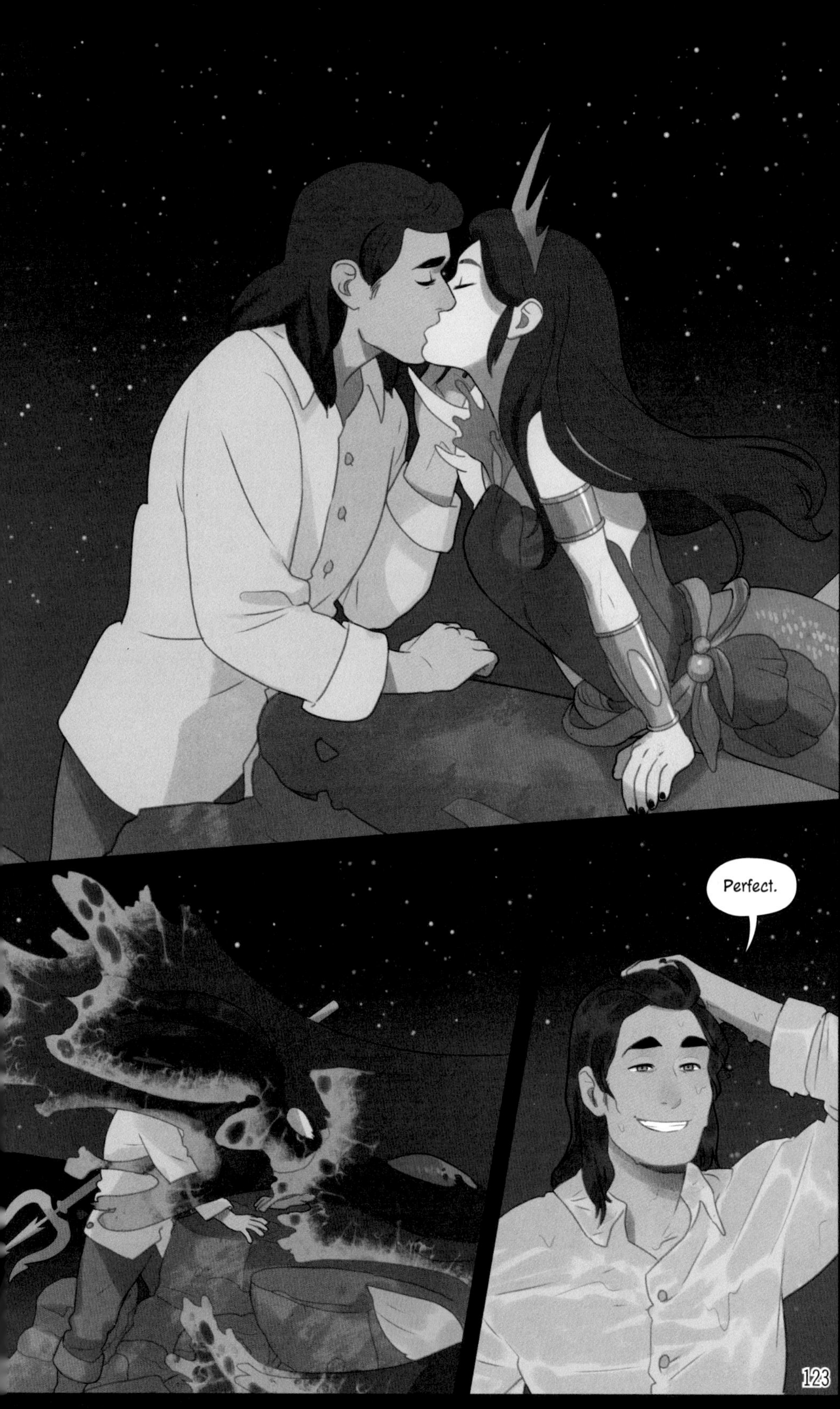
Perfect.

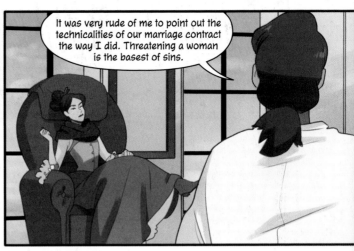

It was very rude of me to point out the technicalities of our marriage contract the way I did. Threatening a woman is the basest of sins.

I am here to offer a détente, and a bit of an apology for our . . . argument in your study.

Please leave gender out of this. Apology formally accepted—although I don't believe it for a moment.

Here is part one of my peace offering.

Part two is that the encore—and farewell—performance of *La Sirenetta*, I am dedicating to you.

Why?

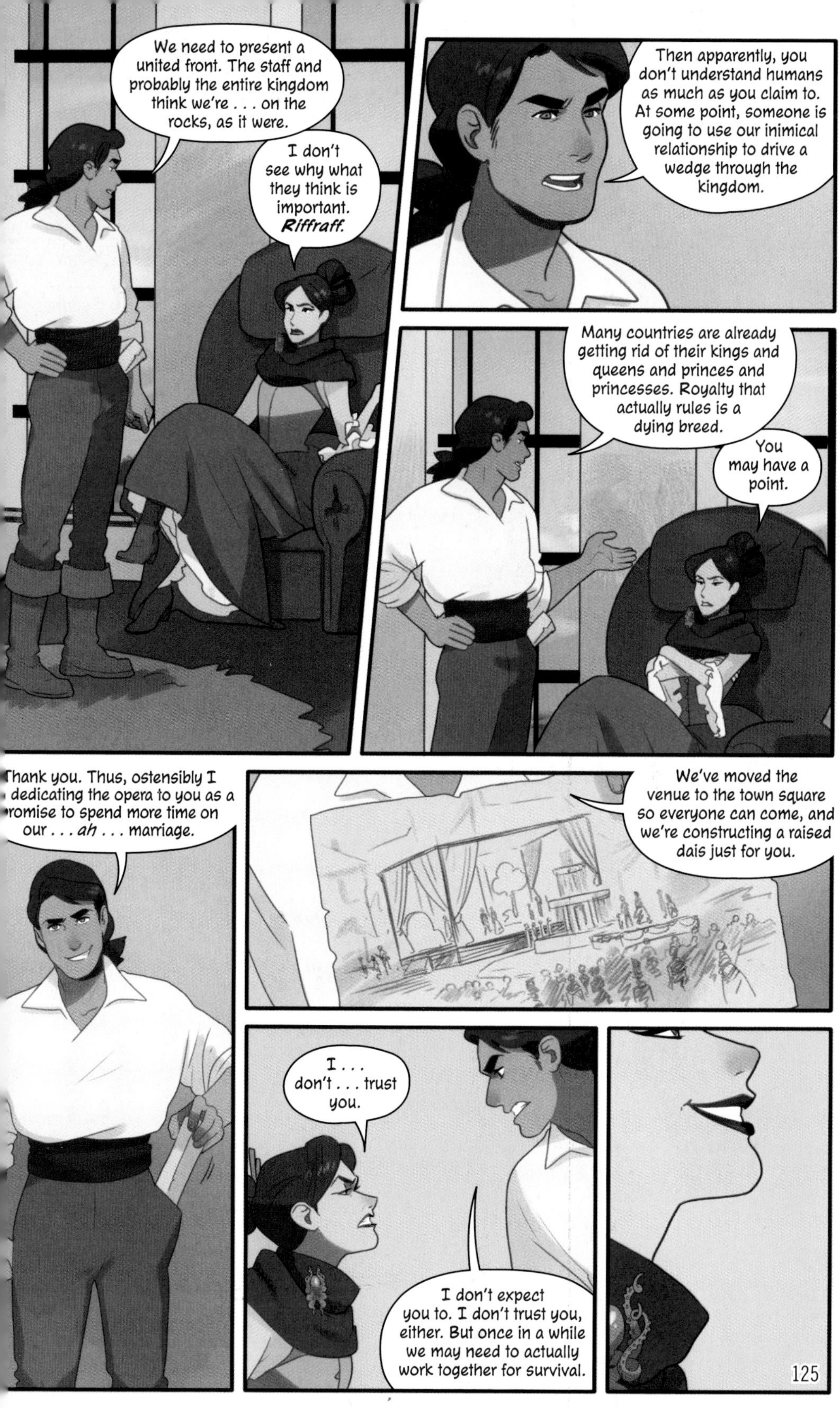
We need to present a united front. The staff and probably the entire kingdom think we're . . . on the rocks, as it were.
I don't see why what they think is important. *Riffraff.*
Then apparently, you don't understand humans as much as you claim to. At some point, someone is going to use our inimical relationship to drive a wedge through the kingdom.
Many countries are already getting rid of their kings and queens and princes and princesses. Royalty that actually rules is a dying breed.
You may have a point.
Thank you. Thus, ostensibly I dedicating the opera to you as a promise to spend more time on our . . . *ah* . . . marriage.
We've moved the venue to the town square so everyone can come, and we're constructing a raised dais just for you.
I . . . don't . . . trust you.
I don't expect you to. I don't trust you, either. But once in a while we may need to actually work together for survival.

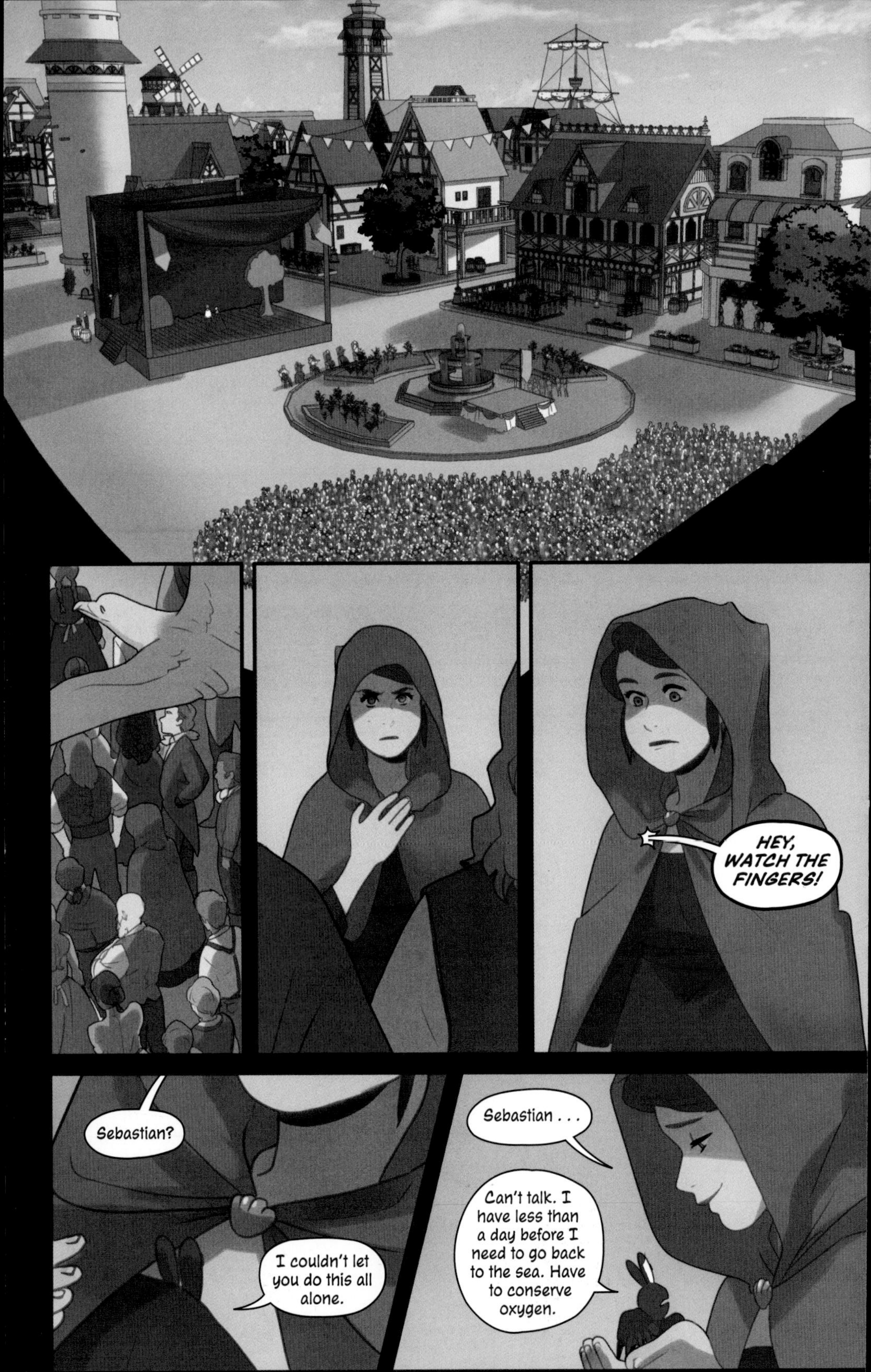
HEY, WATCH THE FINGERS!
Sebastian?
I couldn't let you do this all alone.
Sebastian . . .
Can't talk. I have less than a day before I need to go back to the sea. Have to conserve oxygen.

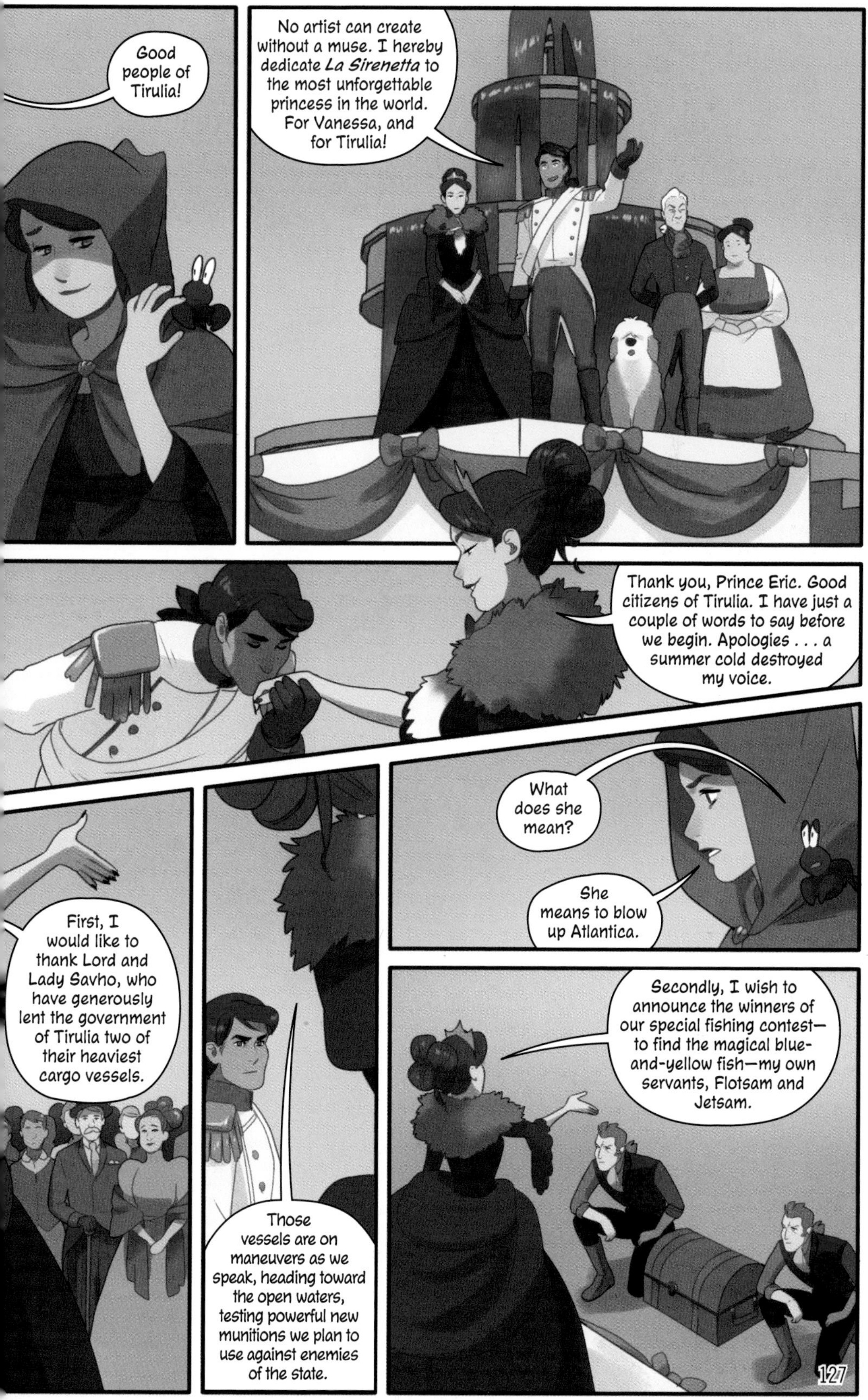

Good people of Tirulia!
No artist can create without a muse. I hereby dedicate *La Sirenetta* to the most unforgettable princess in the world. For Vanessa, and for Tirulia!
Thank you, Prince Eric. Good citizens of Tirulia. I have just a couple of words to say before we begin. Apologies . . . a summer cold destroyed my voice.
First, I would like to thank Lord and Lady Savho, who have generously lent the government of Tirulia two of their heaviest cargo vessels.
Those vessels are on maneuvers as we speak, heading toward the open waters, testing powerful new munitions we plan to use against enemies of the state.
What does she mean?
She means to blow up Atlantica.
Secondly, I wish to announce the winners of our special fishing contest—to find the magical blue-and-yellow fish—my own servants, Flotsam and Jetsam.

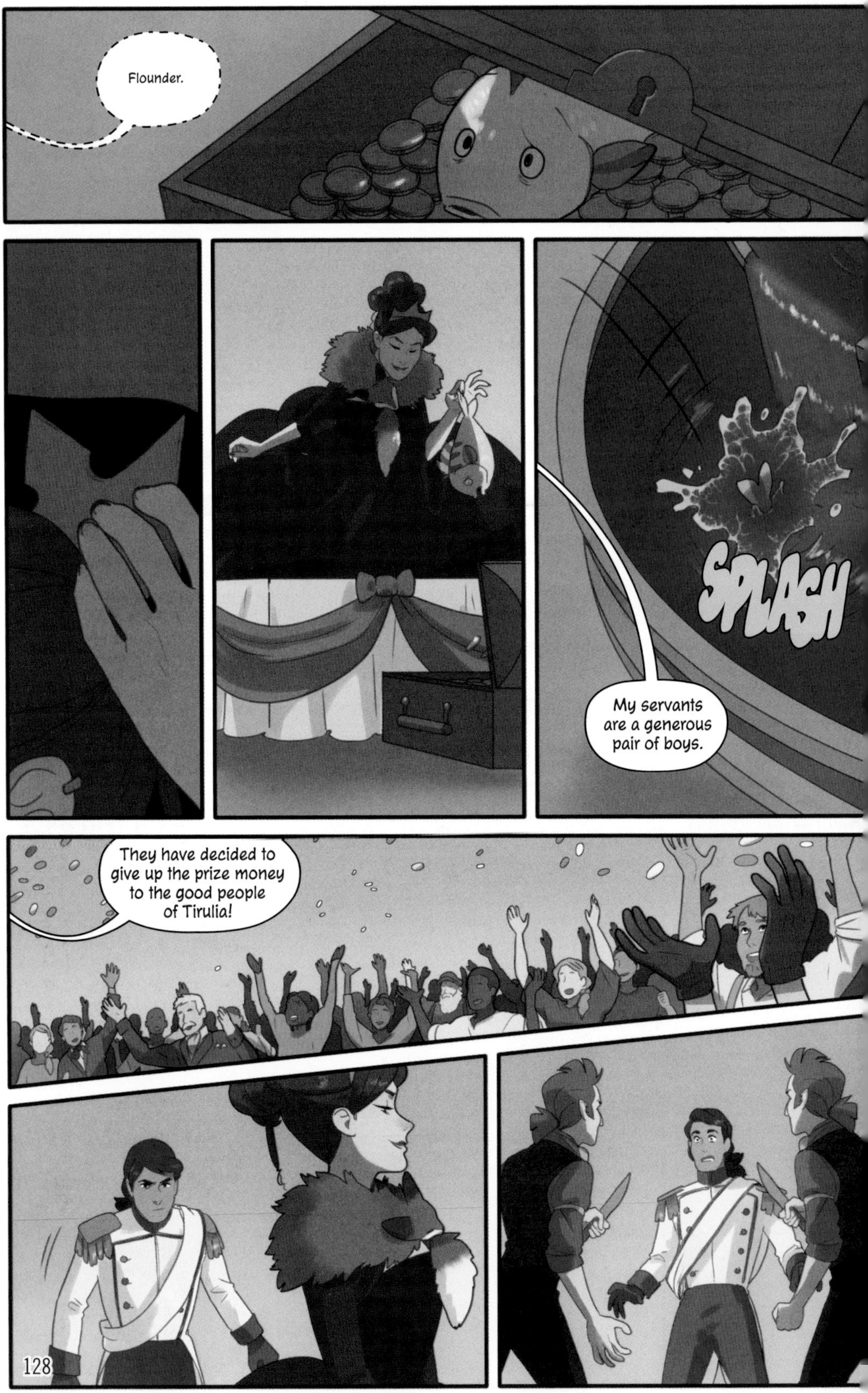
Flounder.
SPLASH
My servants are a generous pair of boys.
They have decided to give up the prize money to the good people of Tirulia!

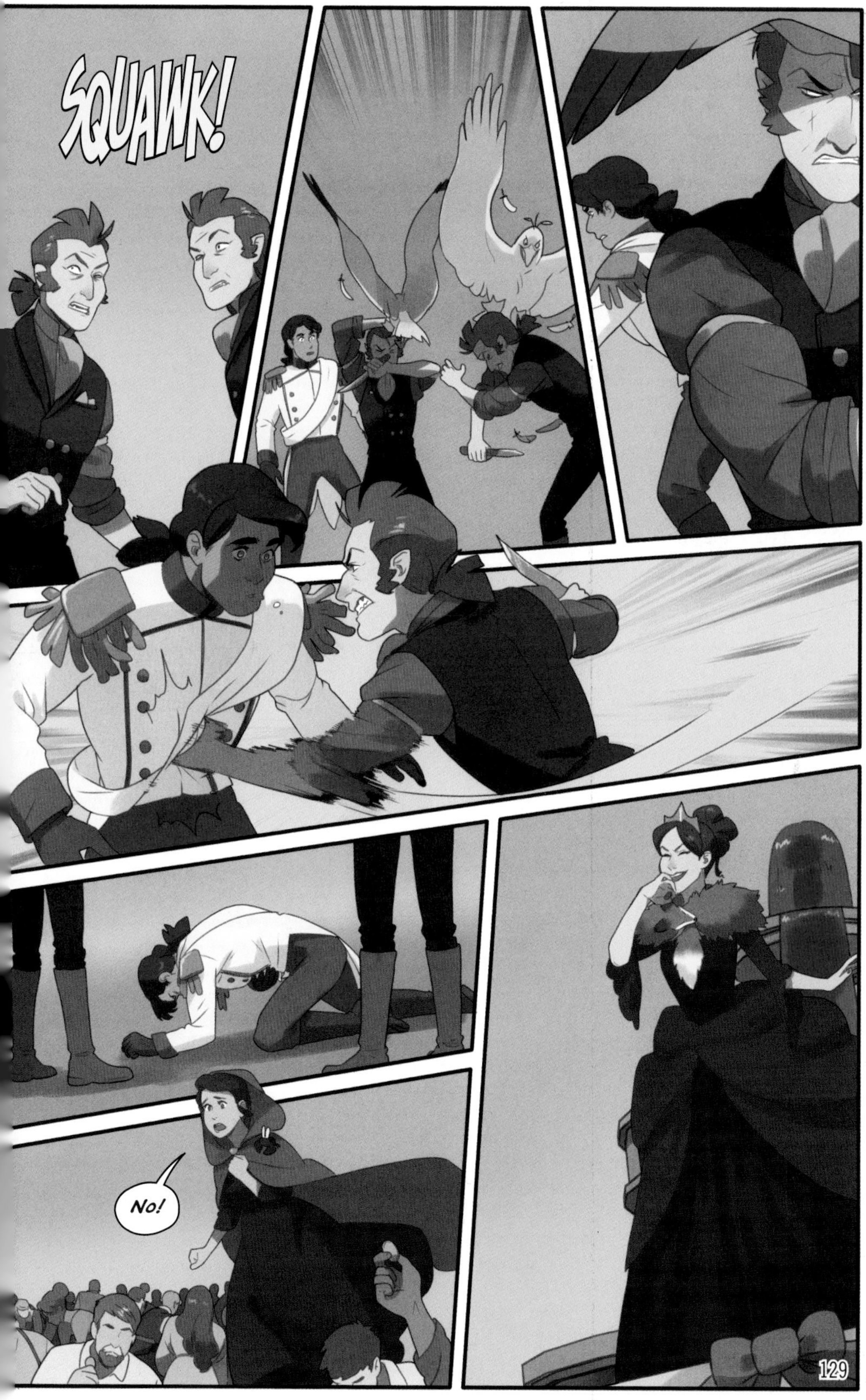

SQUAWK!
No!

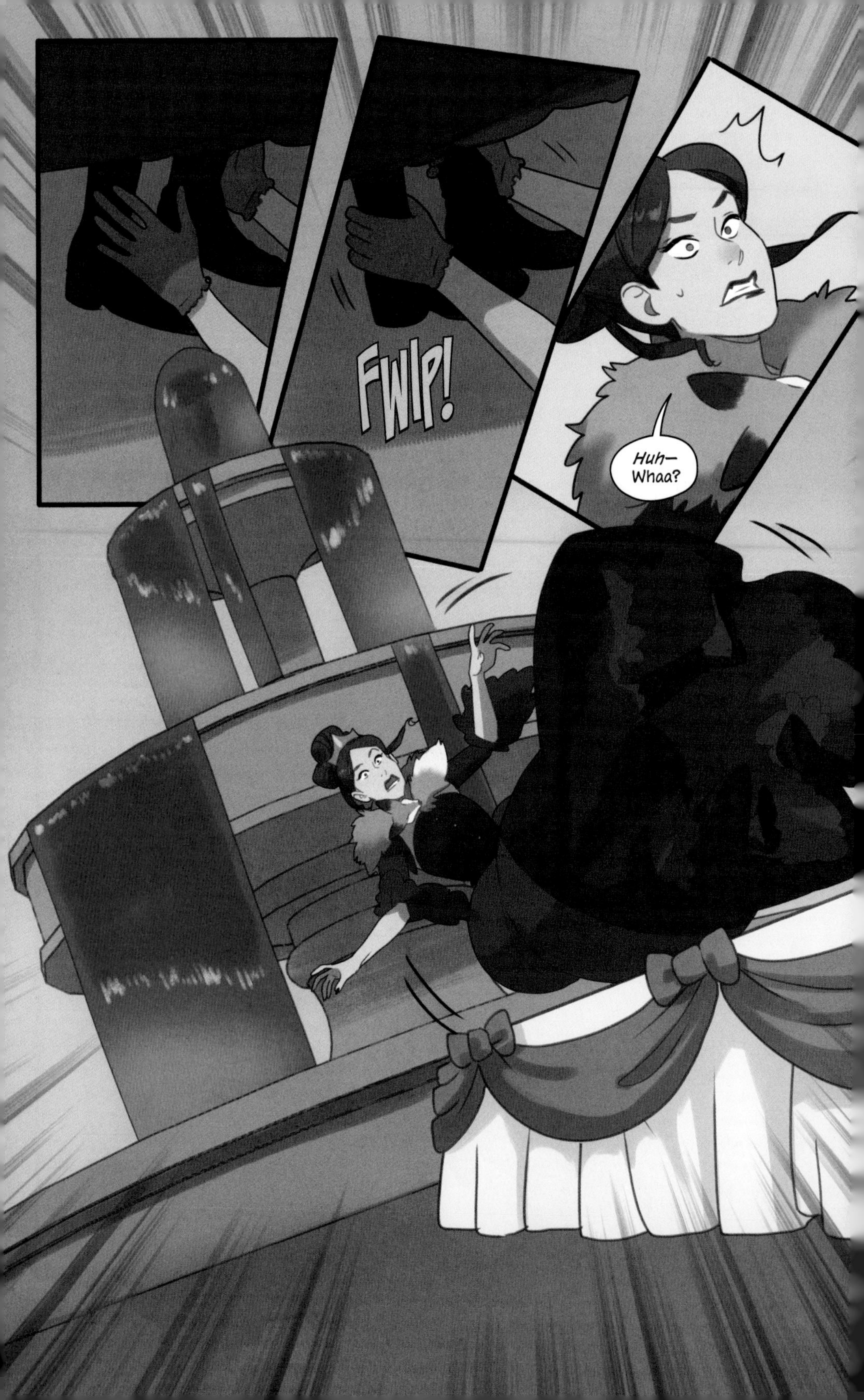
FWIP!
Huh—
Whaa?

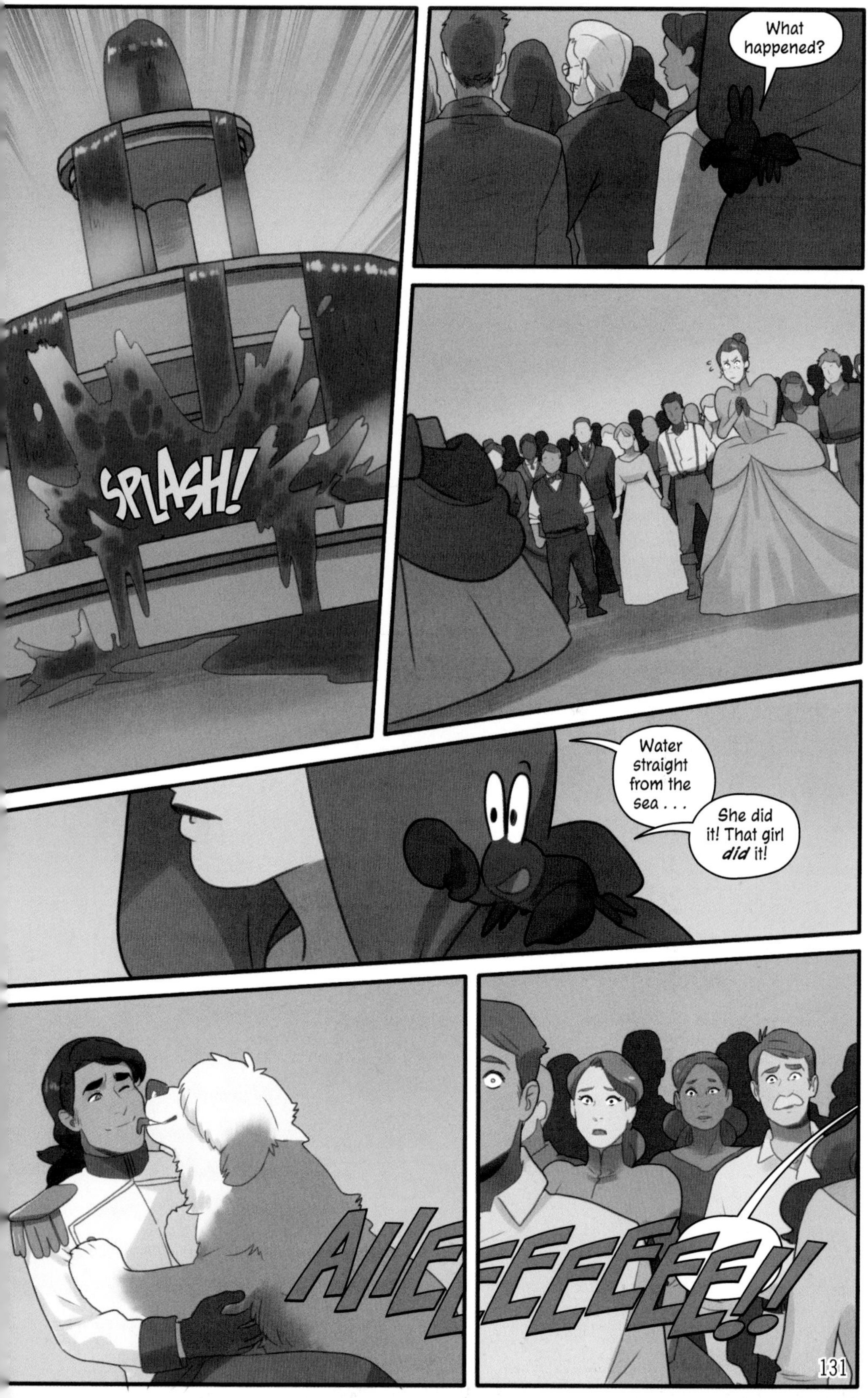
SPLASH!
What happened?
Water straight from the sea . . .
She did it! That girl *did* it!
AIIEEEEEEE!!

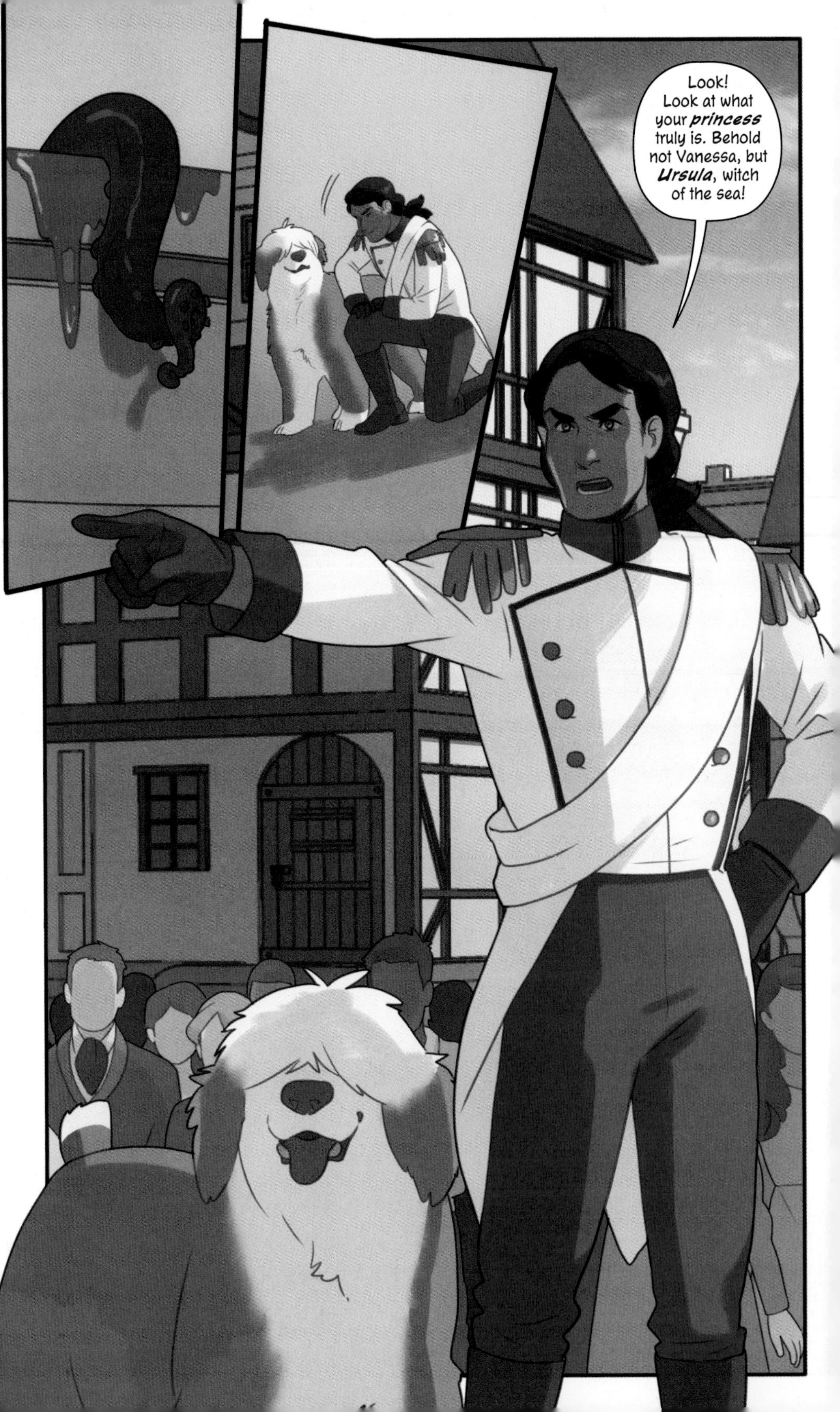
Look!
Look at what your ***princess*** truly is. Behold not Vanessa, but ***Ursula***, witch of the sea!

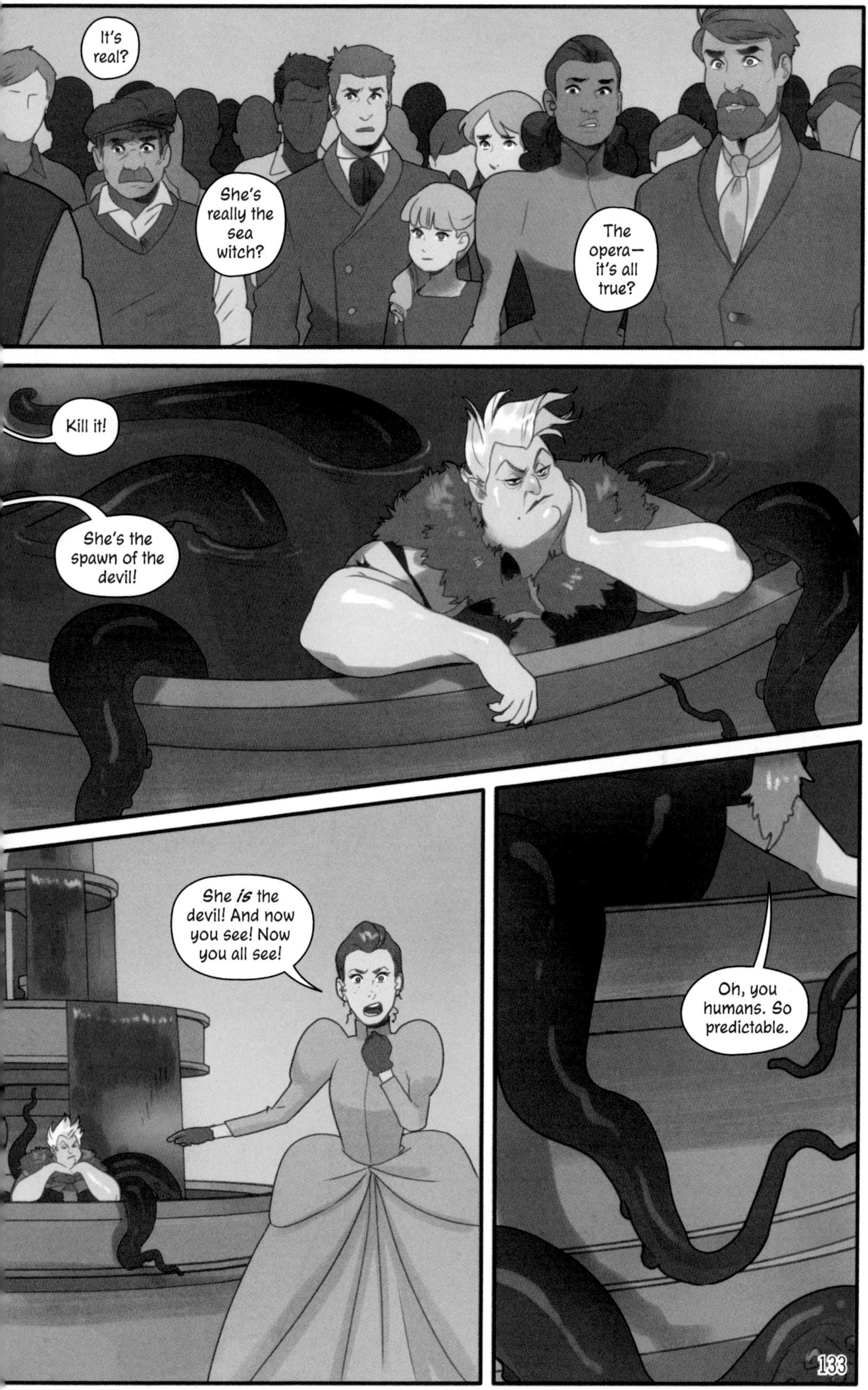
It's real?
She's really the sea witch?
The opera— it's all true?
Kill it!
She's the spawn of the devil!
She *is* the devil! And now you see! Now you all see!
Oh, you humans. So predictable.

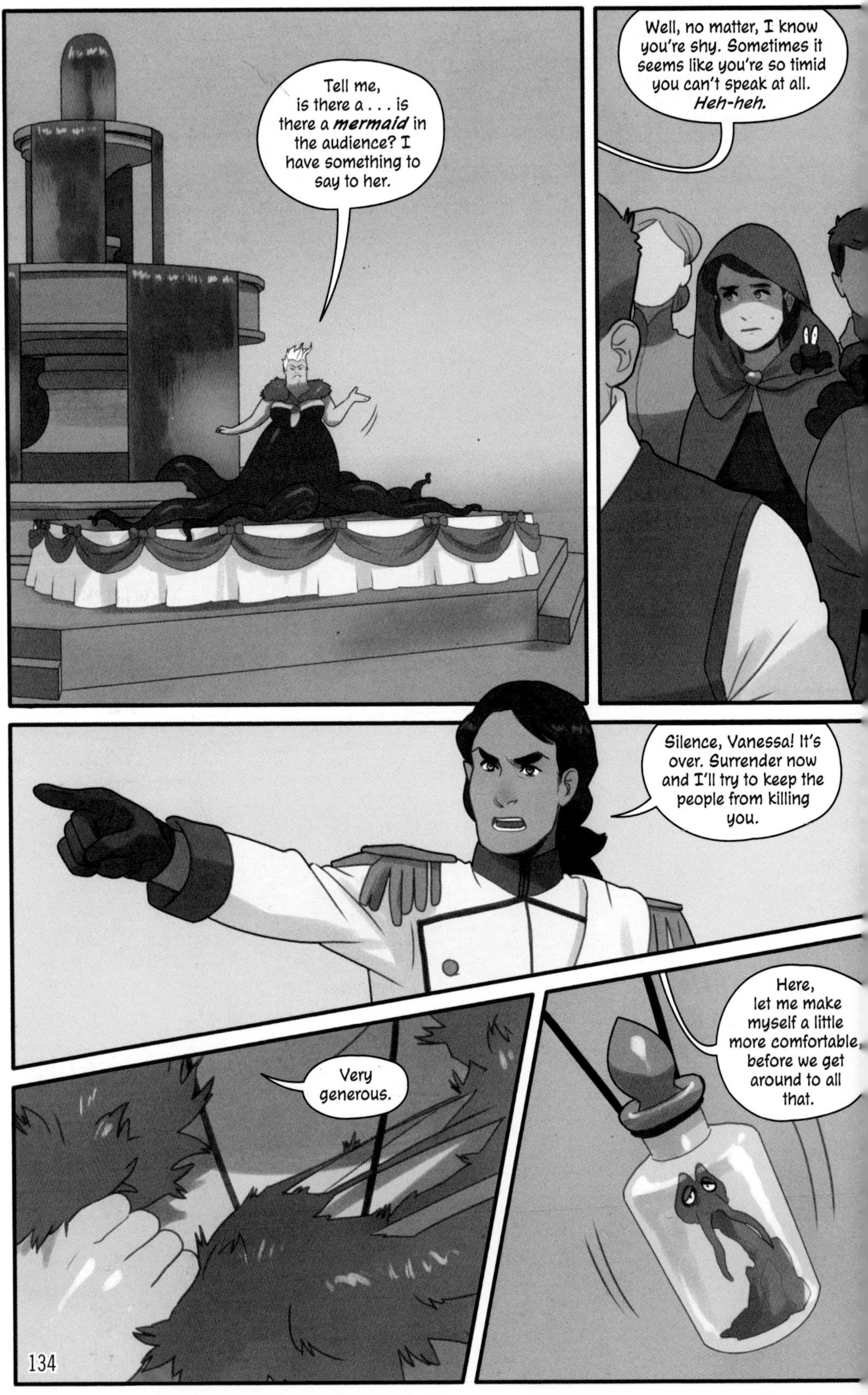
Tell me, is there a . . . is there a *mermaid* in the audience? I have something to say to her.
Well, no matter, I know you're shy. Sometimes it seems like you're so timid you can't speak at all. *Heh-heh.*
Silence, Vanessa! It's over. Surrender now and I'll try to keep the people from killing you.
Very generous.
Here, let me make myself a little more comfortable, before we get around to all that.

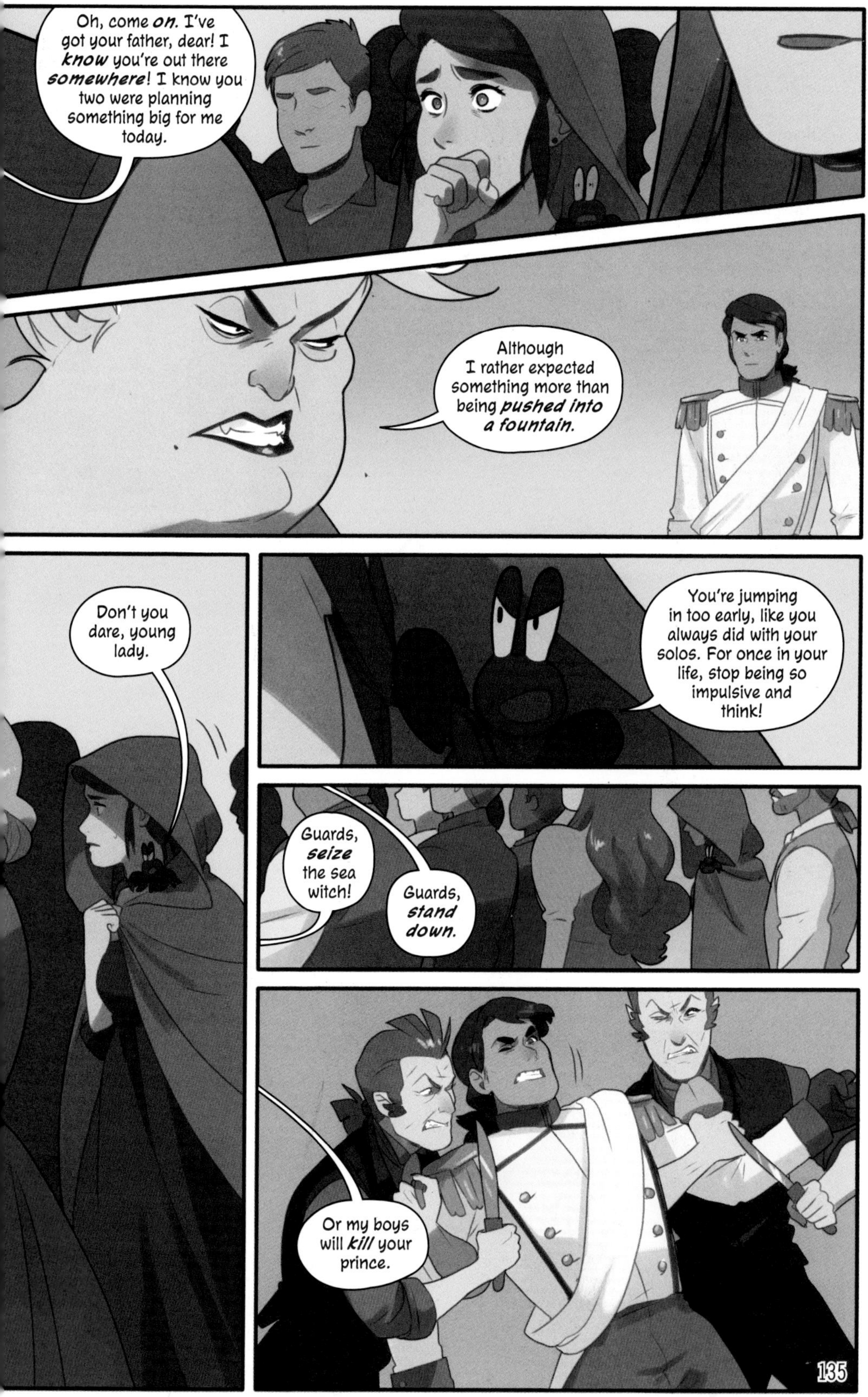
Oh, come on. I've got your father, dear! I know you're out there somewhere! I know you two were planning something big for me today.
Although I rather expected something more than being pushed into a fountain.
Don't you dare, young lady.
You're jumping in too early, like you always did with your solos. For once in your life, stop being so impulsive and think!
Guards, seize the sea witch!
Guards, stand down.
Or my boys will kill your prince.

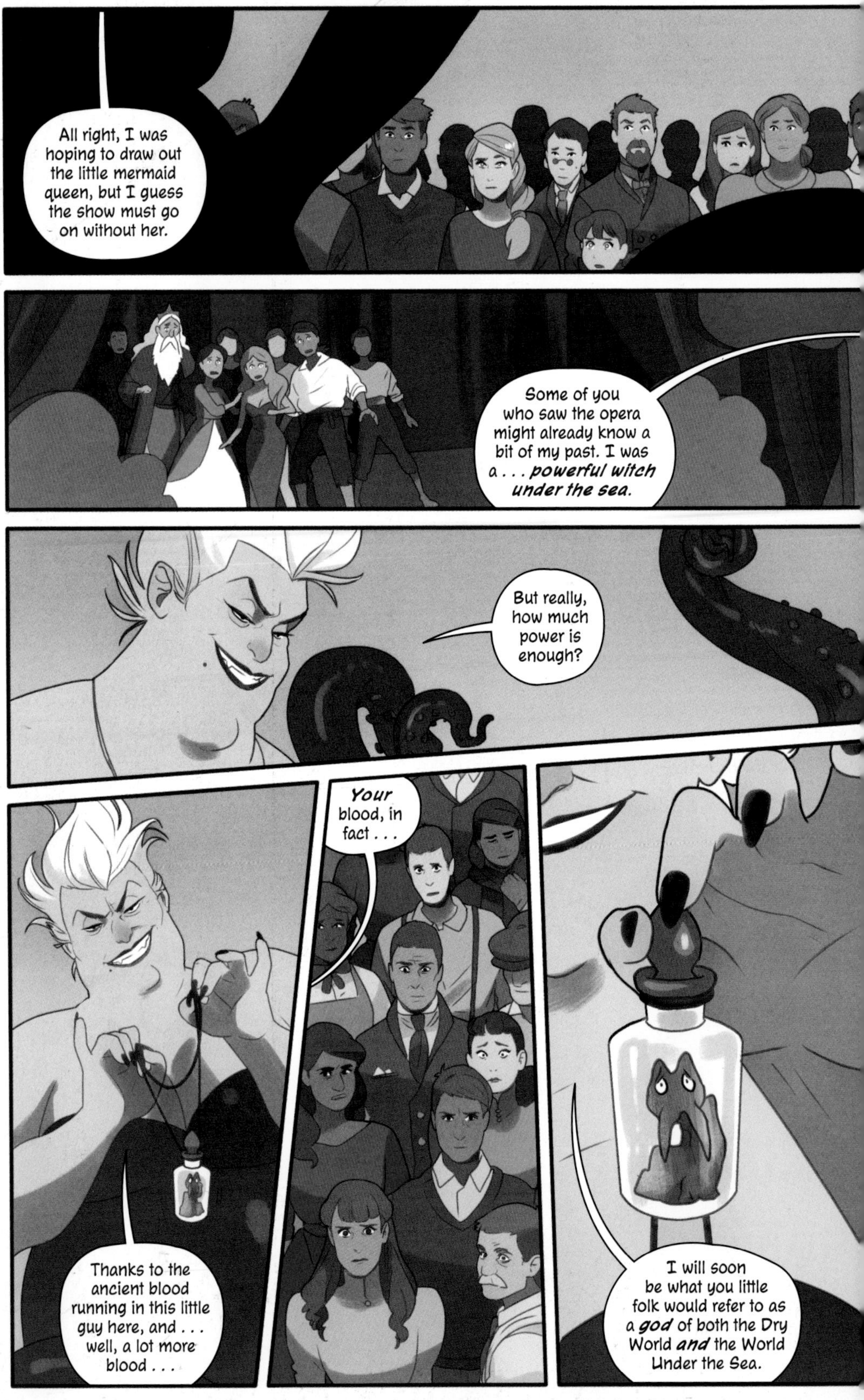
All right, I was hoping to draw out the little mermaid queen, but I guess the show must go on without her.
Some of you who saw the opera might already know a bit of my past. I was a . . . *powerful witch under the sea.*
But really, how much power is enough?
Thanks to the ancient blood running in this little guy here, and . . . well, a lot more blood . . .
Your blood, in fact . . .
I will soon be what you little folk would refer to as a *god* of both the Dry World *and* the World Under the Sea.

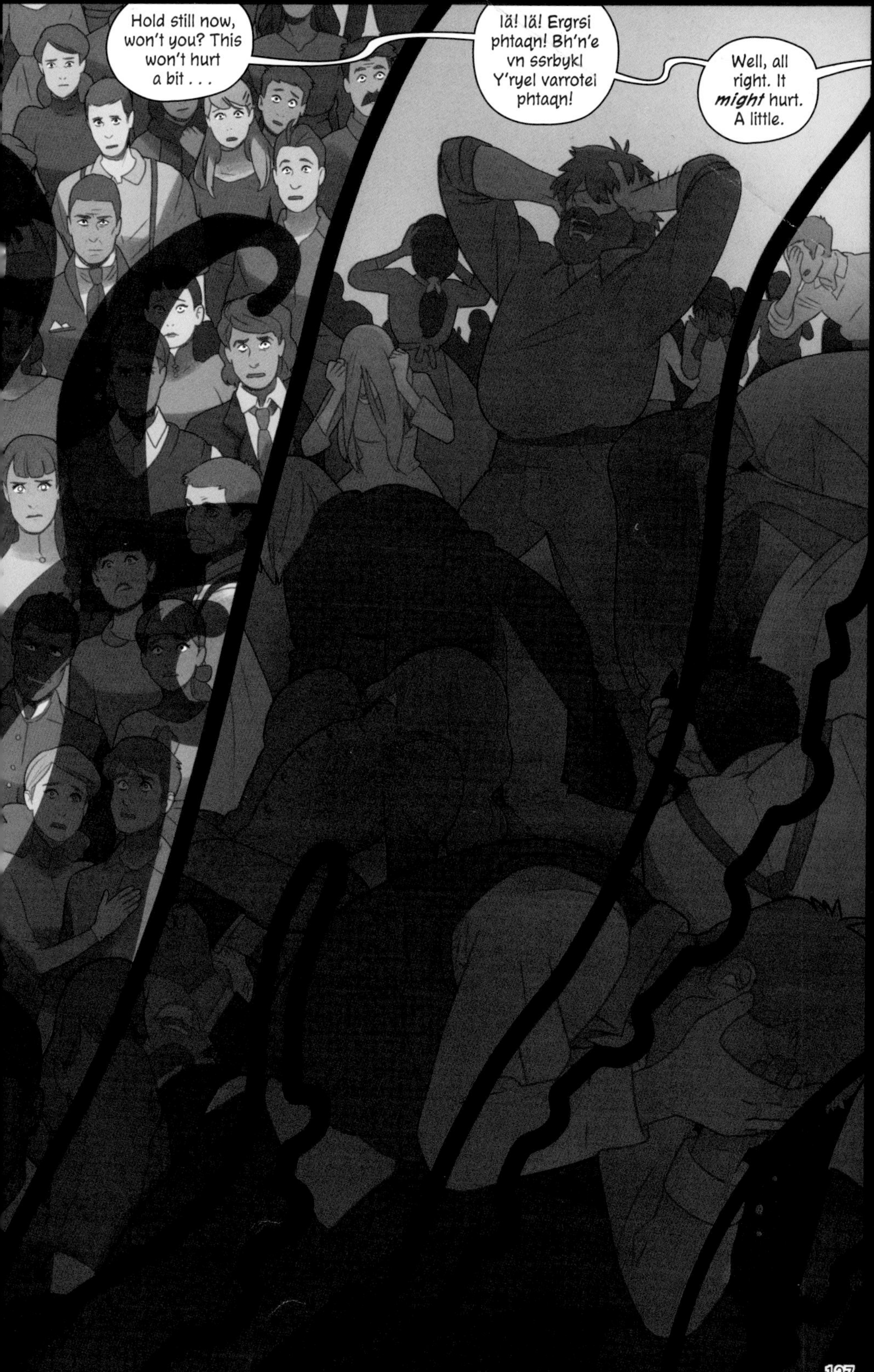
Hold still now, won't you? This won't hurt a bit . . .
Iä! Iä! Ergrsi phtaqn! Bh'n'e vn ssrbykl Y'ryel varrotei phtaqn!
Well, all right. It *might* hurt. A little.

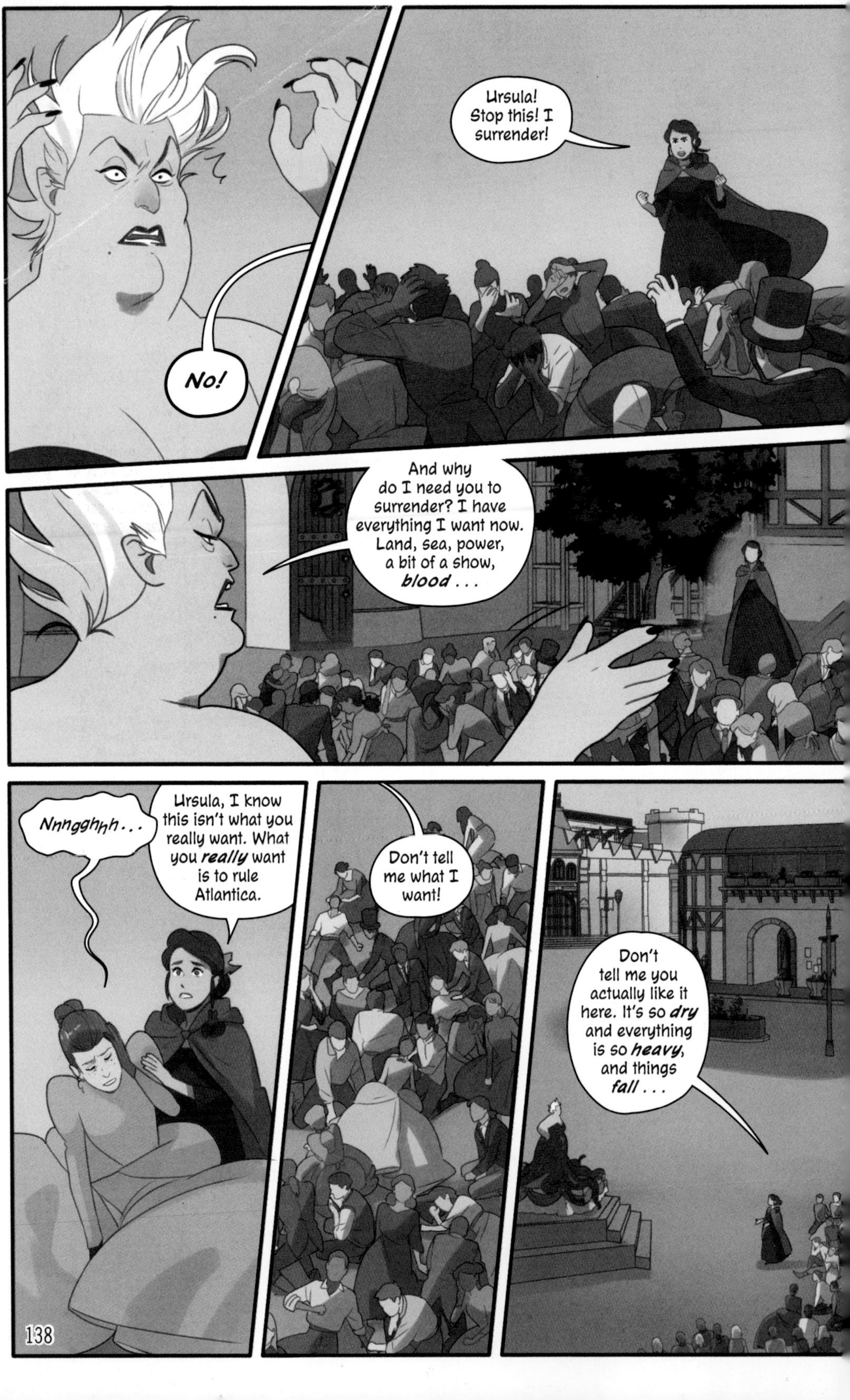
Ursula! Stop this! I surrender!
No!
And why do I need you to surrender? I have everything I want now. Land, sea, power, a bit of a show, *blood . . .*
Nnngghhh . . .
Ursula, I know this isn't what you really want. What you *really* want is to rule Atlantica.
Don't tell me what I want!
Don't tell me you actually like it here. It's so *dry* and everything is so *heavy*, and things *fall . . .*

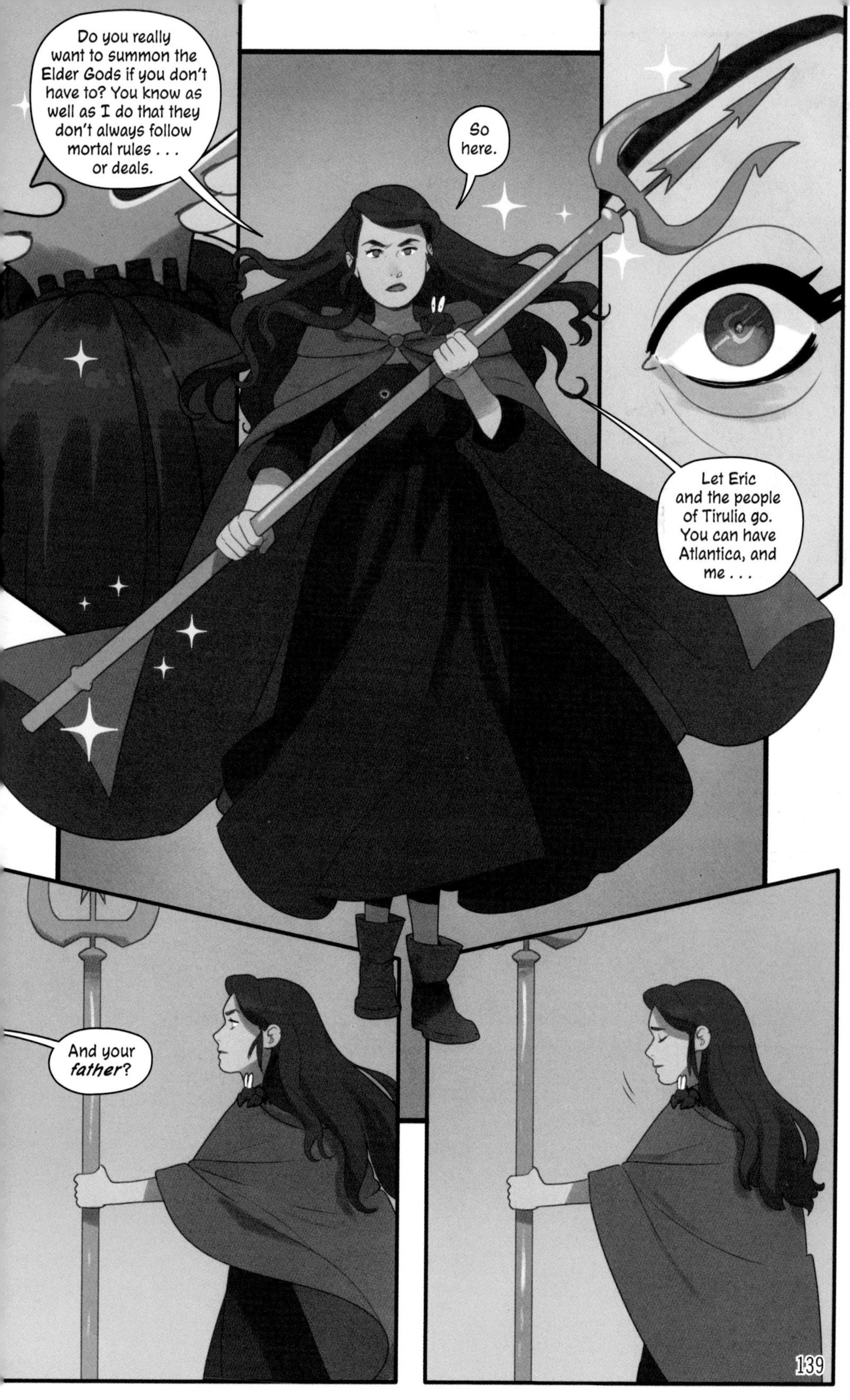
Do you really want to summon the Elder Gods if you don't have to? You know as well as I do that they don't always follow mortal rules . . . or deals.
So here.
Let Eric and the people of Tirulia go. You can have Atlantica, and me . . .
And your *father*?

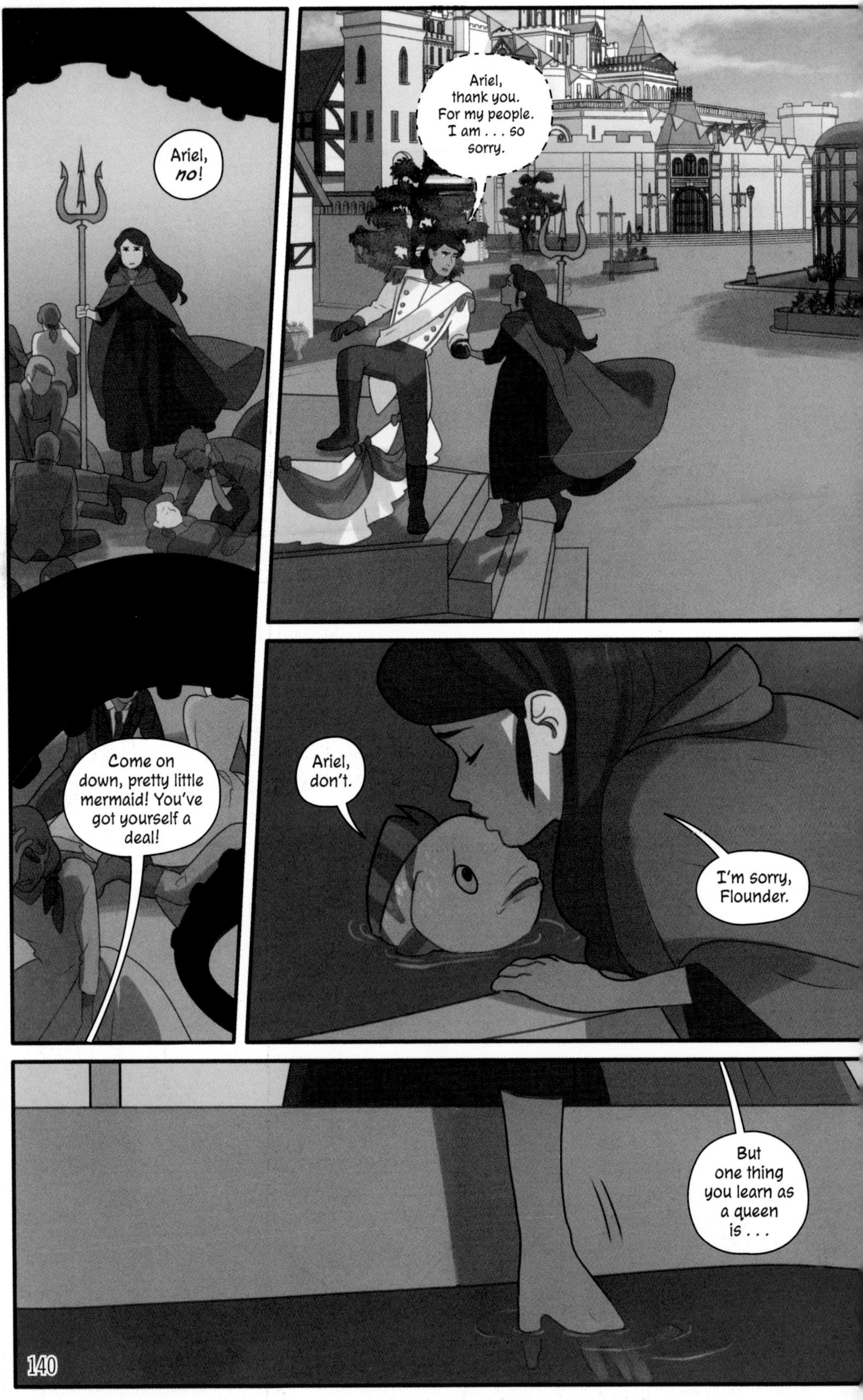
Ariel, *no*!
Ariel, thank you. For my people. I am . . . so sorry.
Come on down, pretty little mermaid! You've got yourself a deal!
Ariel, don't.
I'm sorry, Flounder.
But one thing you learn as a queen is . . .

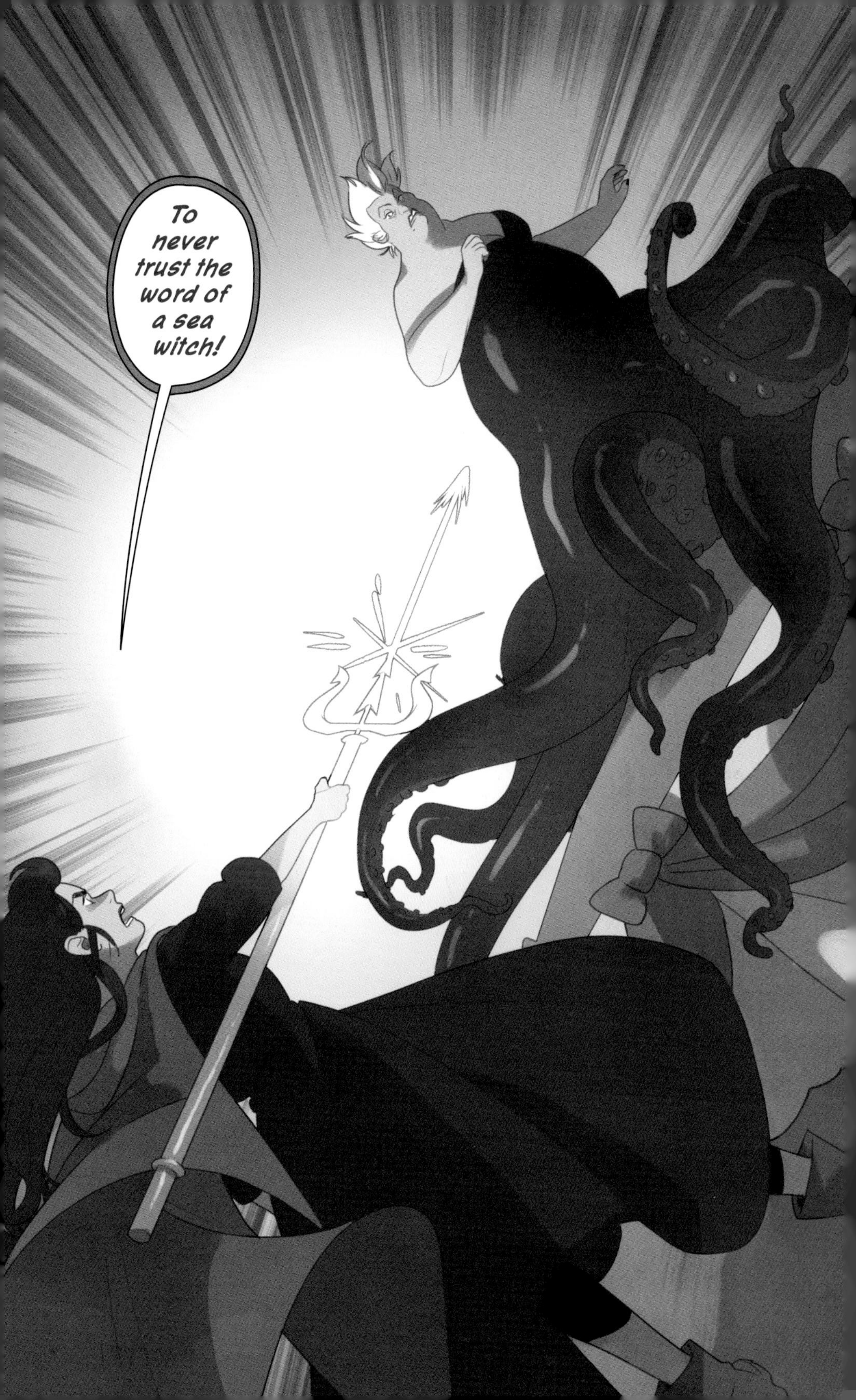
To never trust the word of a sea witch!

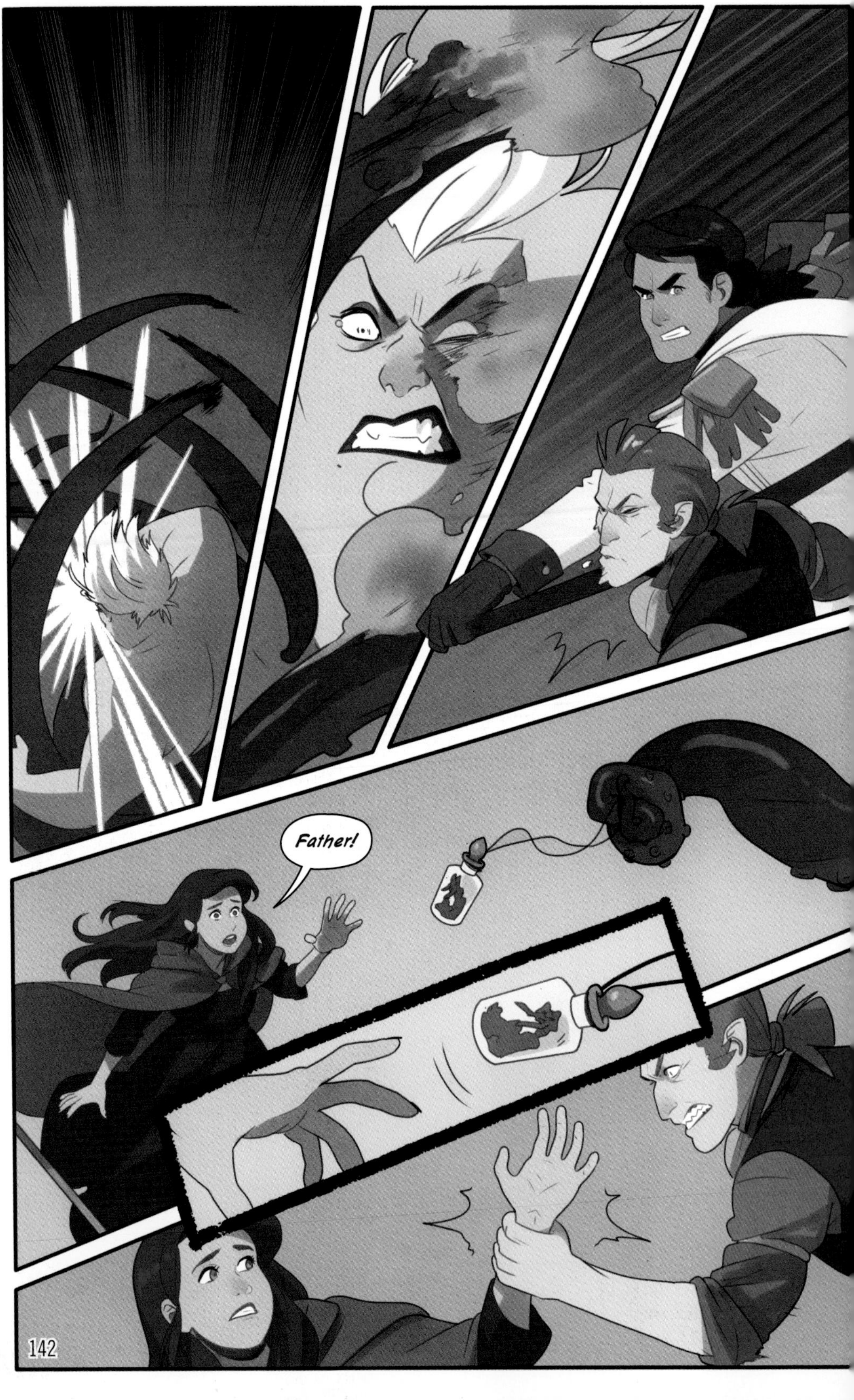
Father!

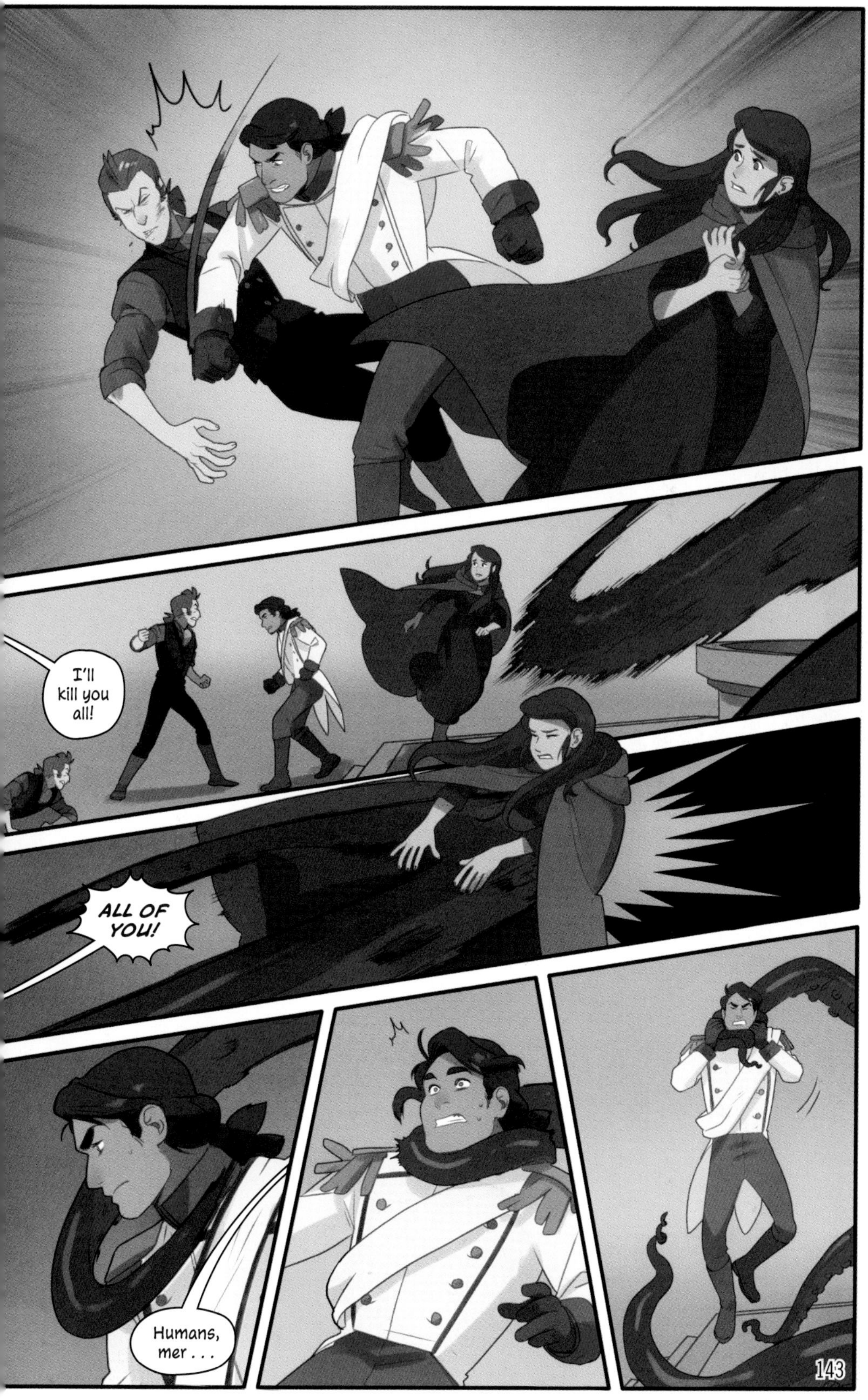
I'll kill you all!
ALL OF YOU!
Humans, mer . . .

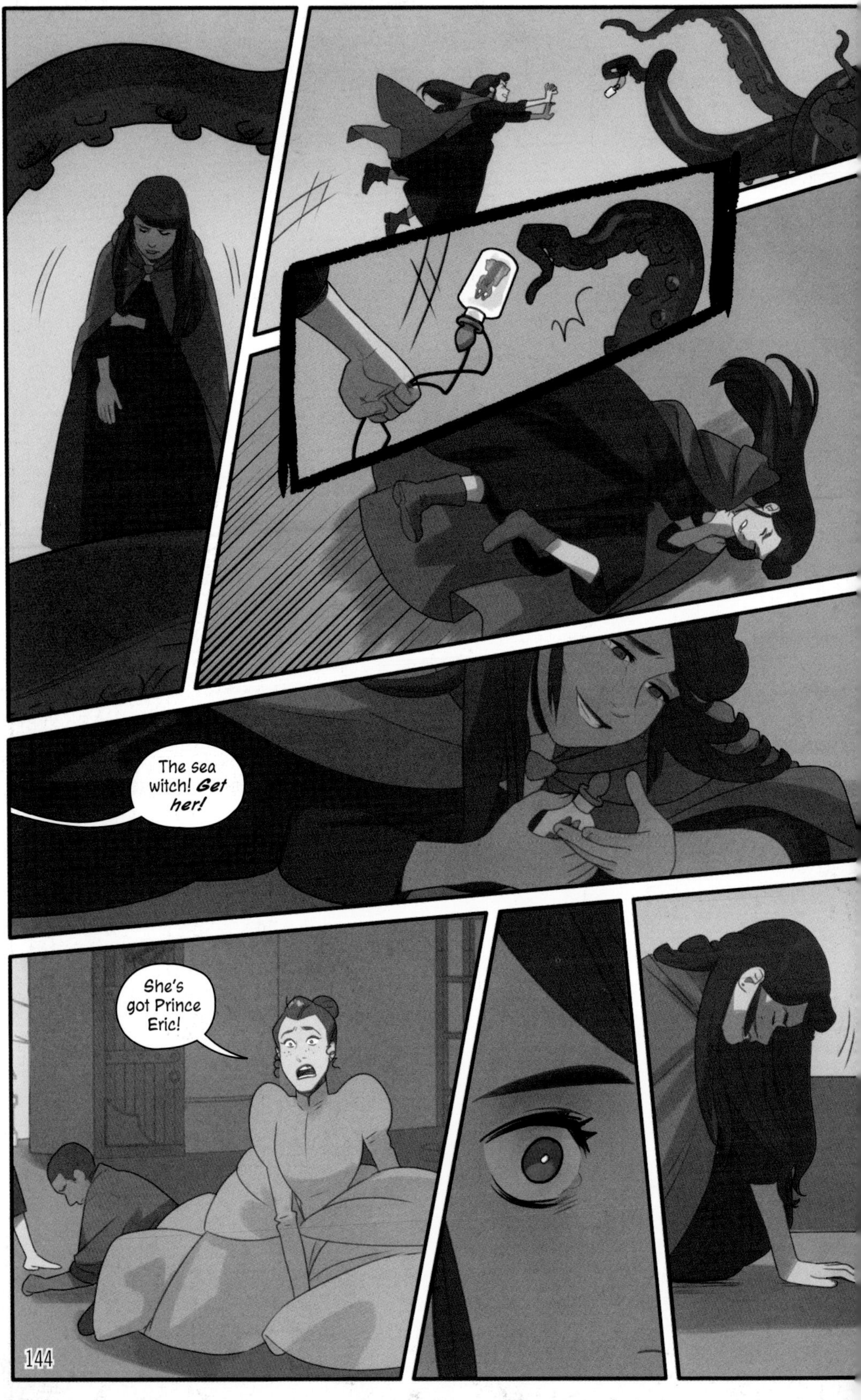
The sea witch! Get her!
She's got Prince Eric!

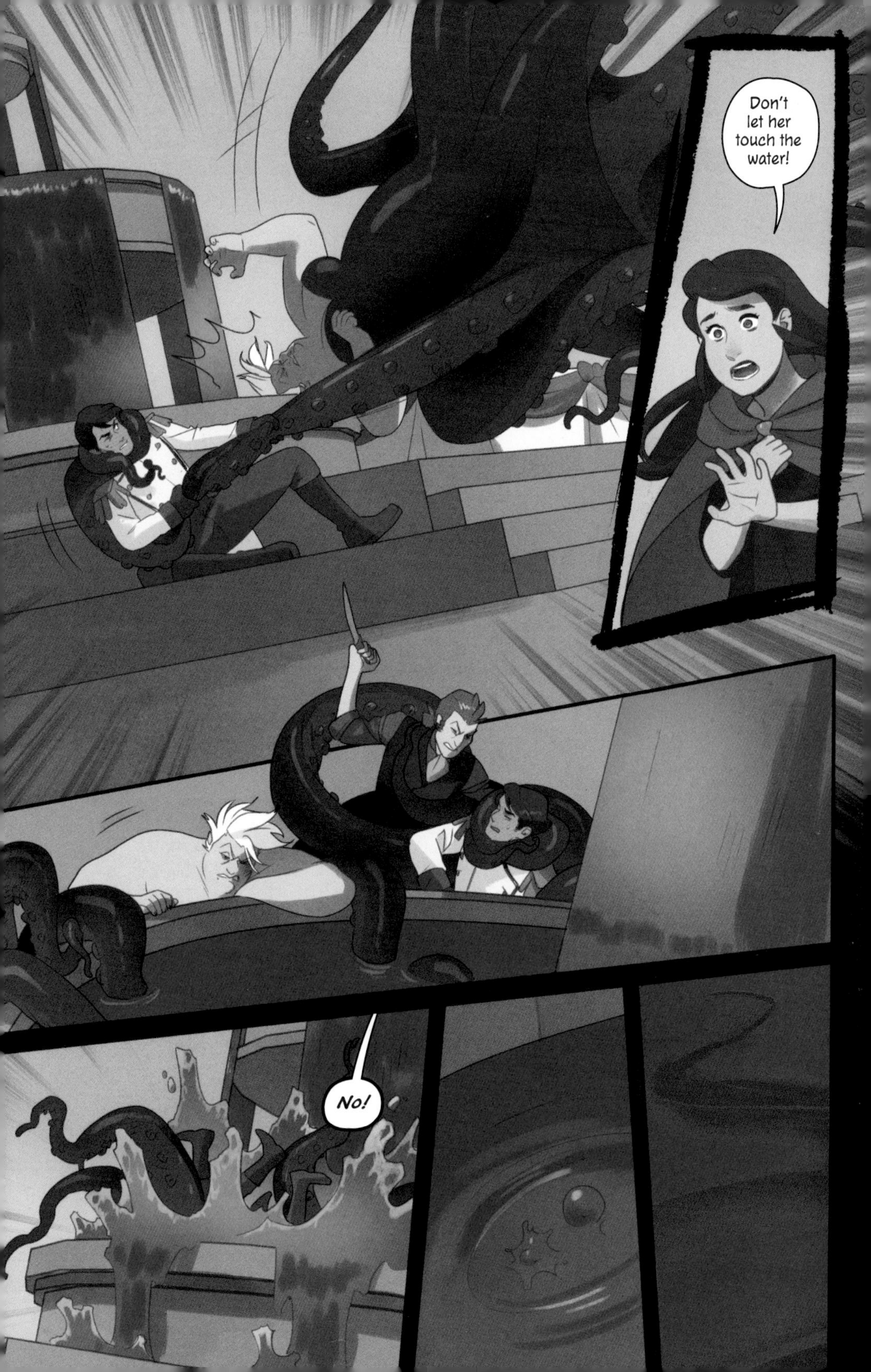
Don't let her touch the water!
No!

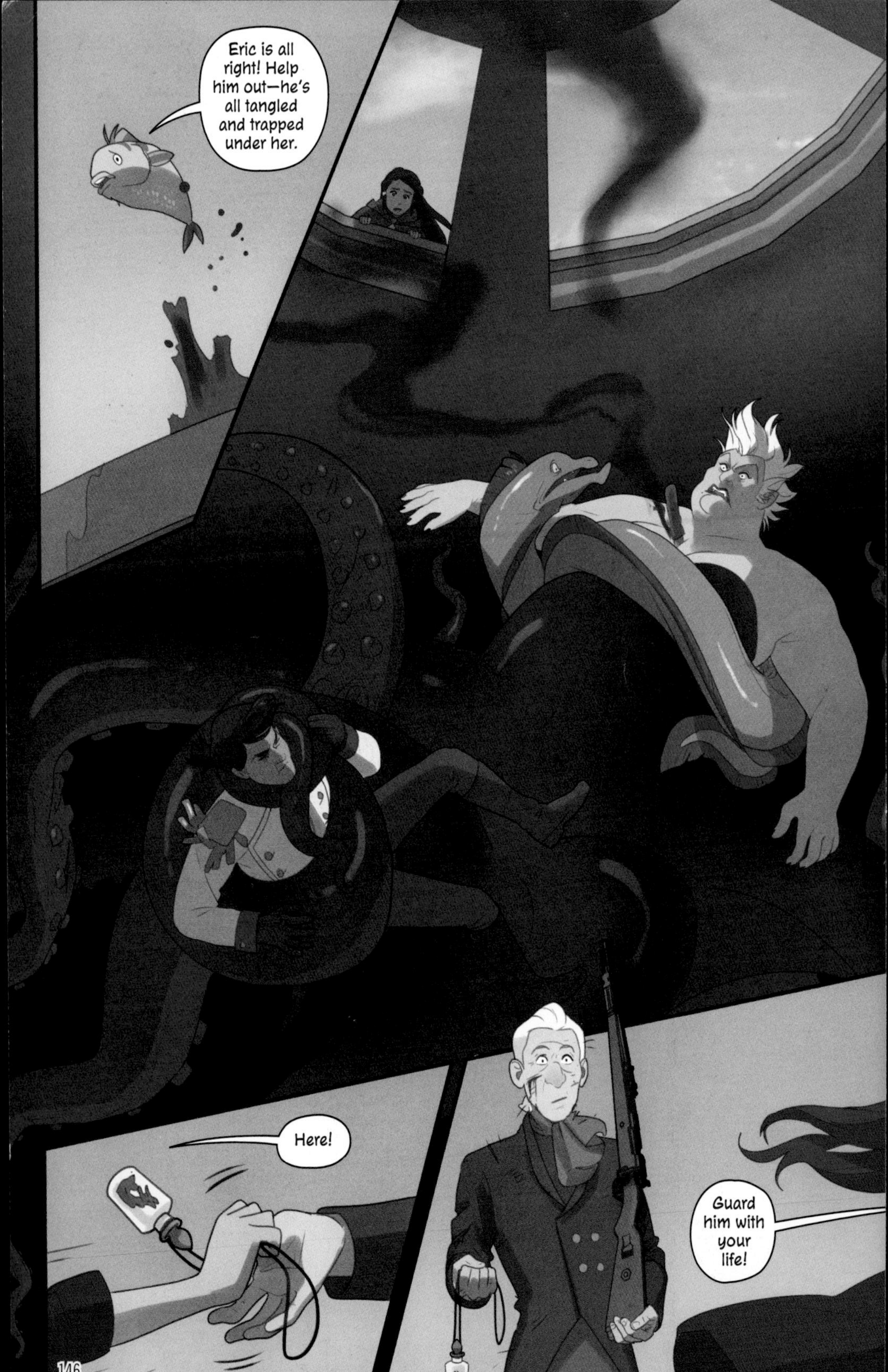

Eric is all right! Help him out—he's all tangled and trapped under her.
Here!
Guard him with your life!

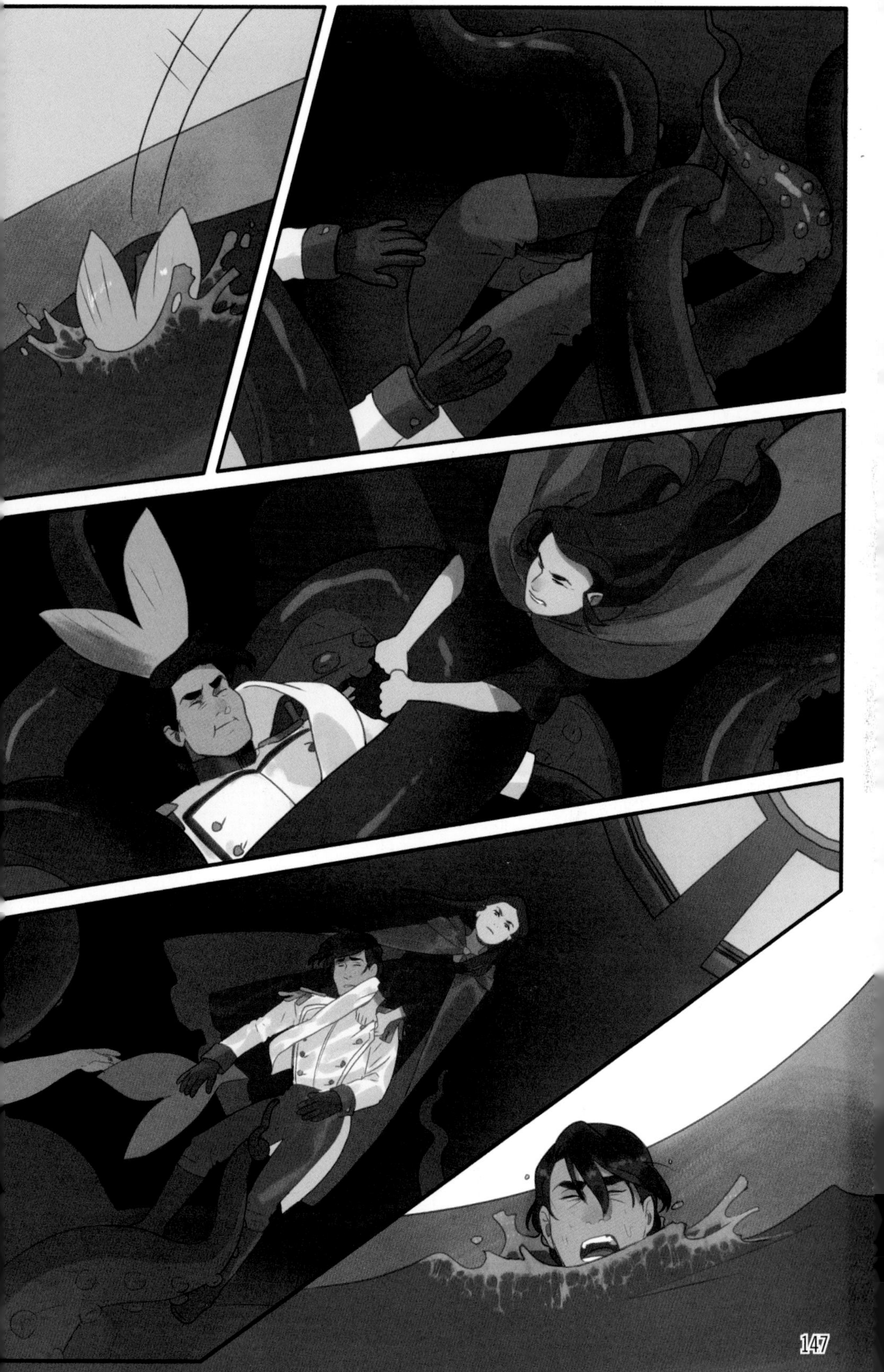

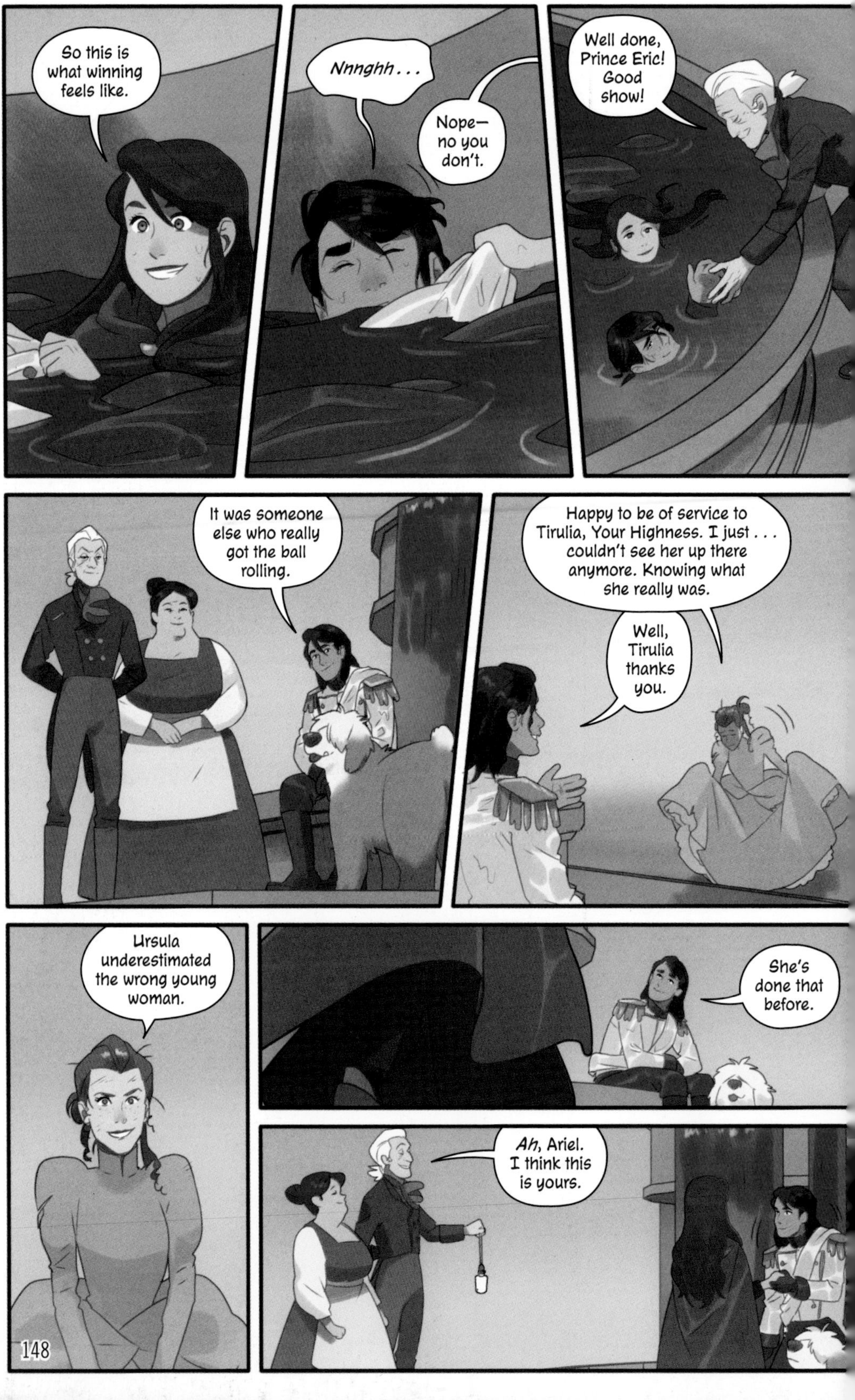

So this is what winning feels like.
Nnnghh . . .
Nope— no you don't.
Well done, Prince Eric! Good show!
It was someone else who really got the ball rolling.
Happy to be of service to Tirulia, Your Highness. I just . . . couldn't see her up there anymore. Knowing what she really was.
Well, Tirulia thanks you.
Ursula underestimated the wrong young woman.
She's done that before.
Ah, Ariel. I think this is yours.

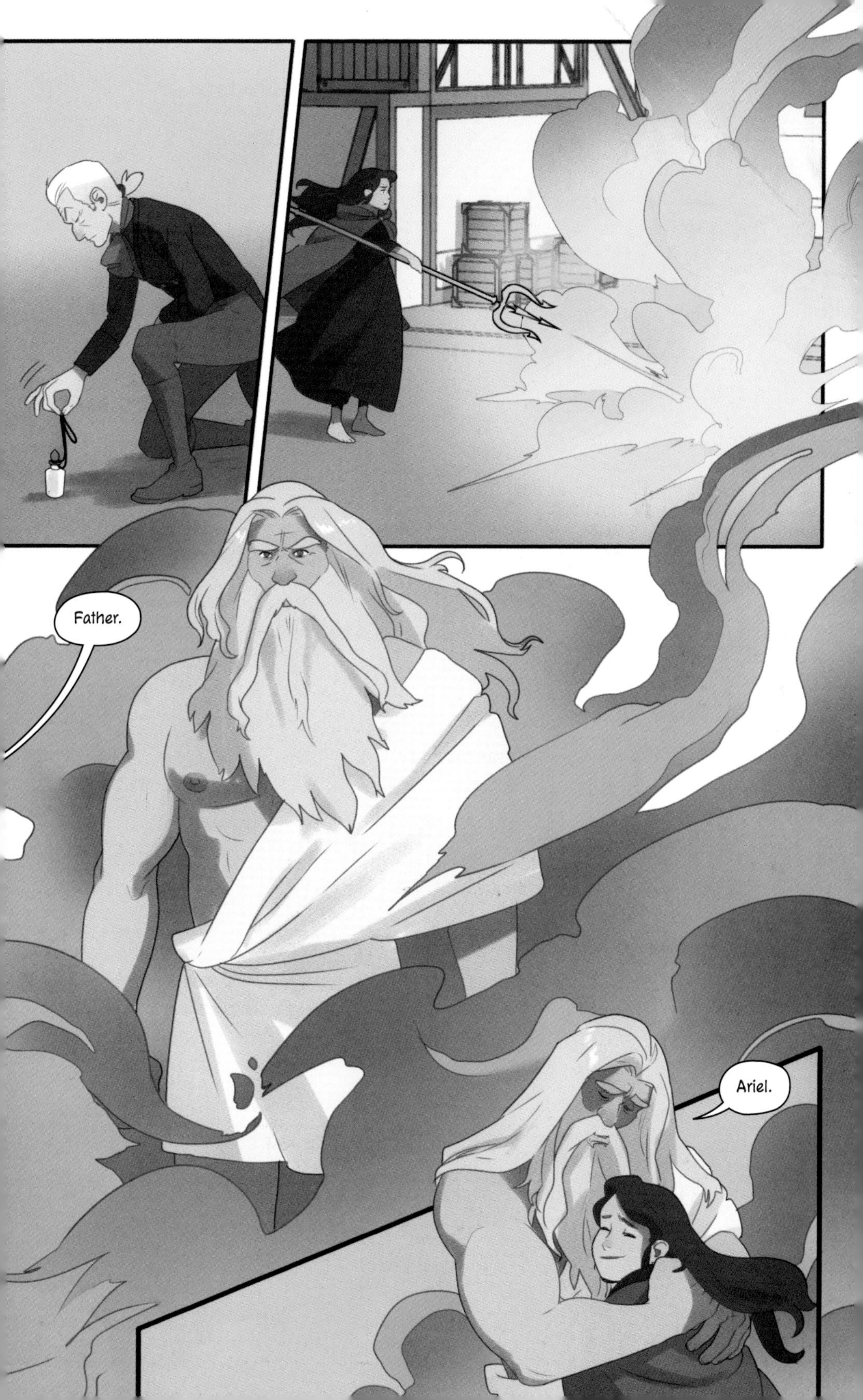
Father.
Ariel.

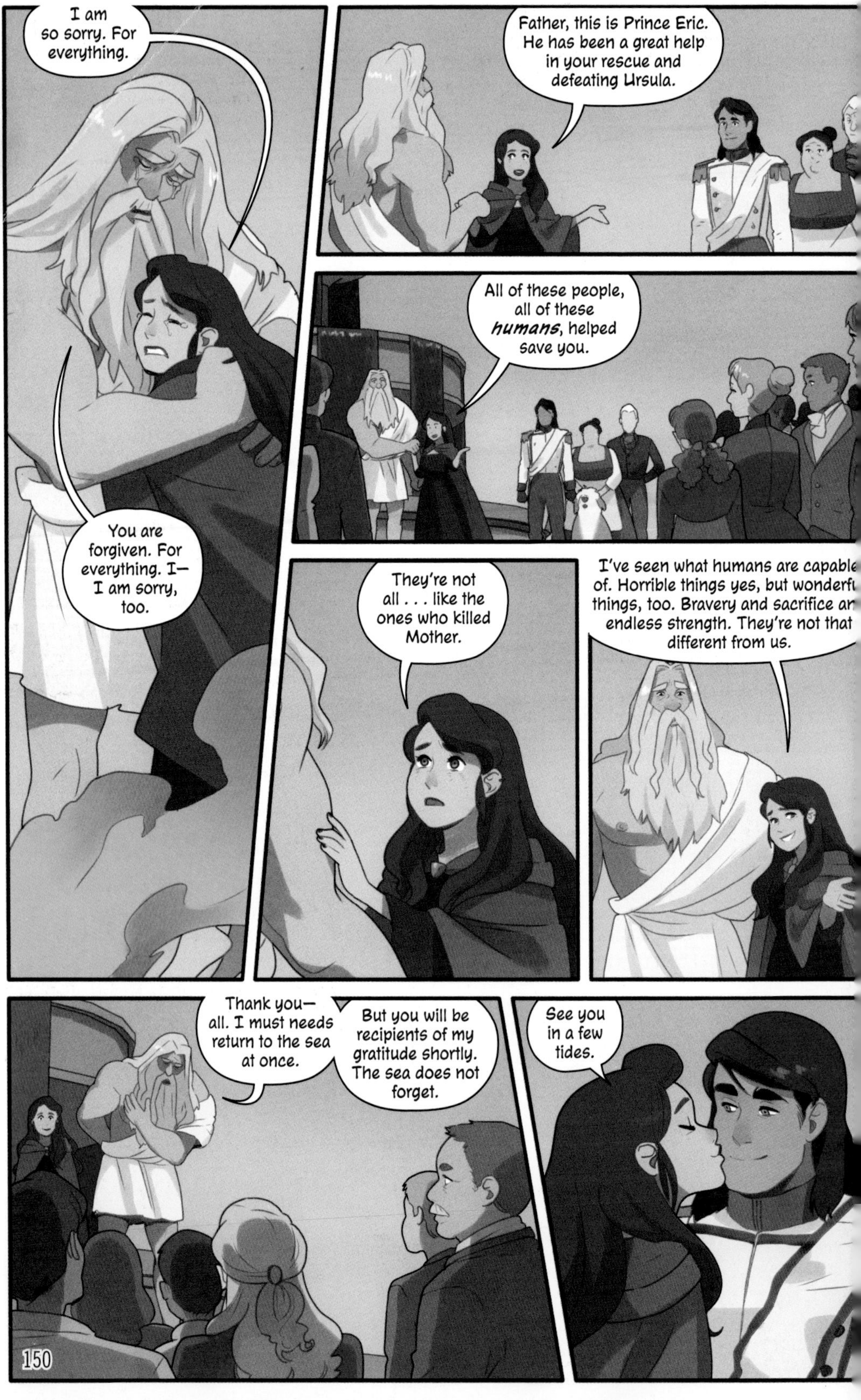
I am so sorry. For everything.
You are forgiven. For everything. I— I am sorry, too.
Father, this is Prince Eric. He has been a great help in your rescue and defeating Ursula.
All of these people, all of these *humans*, helped save you.
They're not all . . . like the ones who killed Mother.
I've seen what humans are capabl of. Horrible things yes, but wonderf things, too. Bravery and sacrifice ar endless strength. They're not that different from us.
Thank you— all. I must needs return to the sea at once.
But you will be recipients of my gratitude shortly. The sea does not forget.
See you in a few tides.

There were terrible, terrible messes to clean up afterward.

For the first and perhaps only time in history, a seagull was used to deliver a message to the ships sent out to sea—to prevent them from bombing Atlantica.

Troops from everywhere had to be recalled immediately, stopping the invasion of the north.

Prince Eric oversaw a careful scripting of the official record of the events of the day. It was endless and exhausting work.

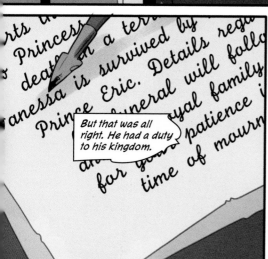

But that was all right. He had a duty to his kingdom.

Being prince wasn't just fun and games and operas.

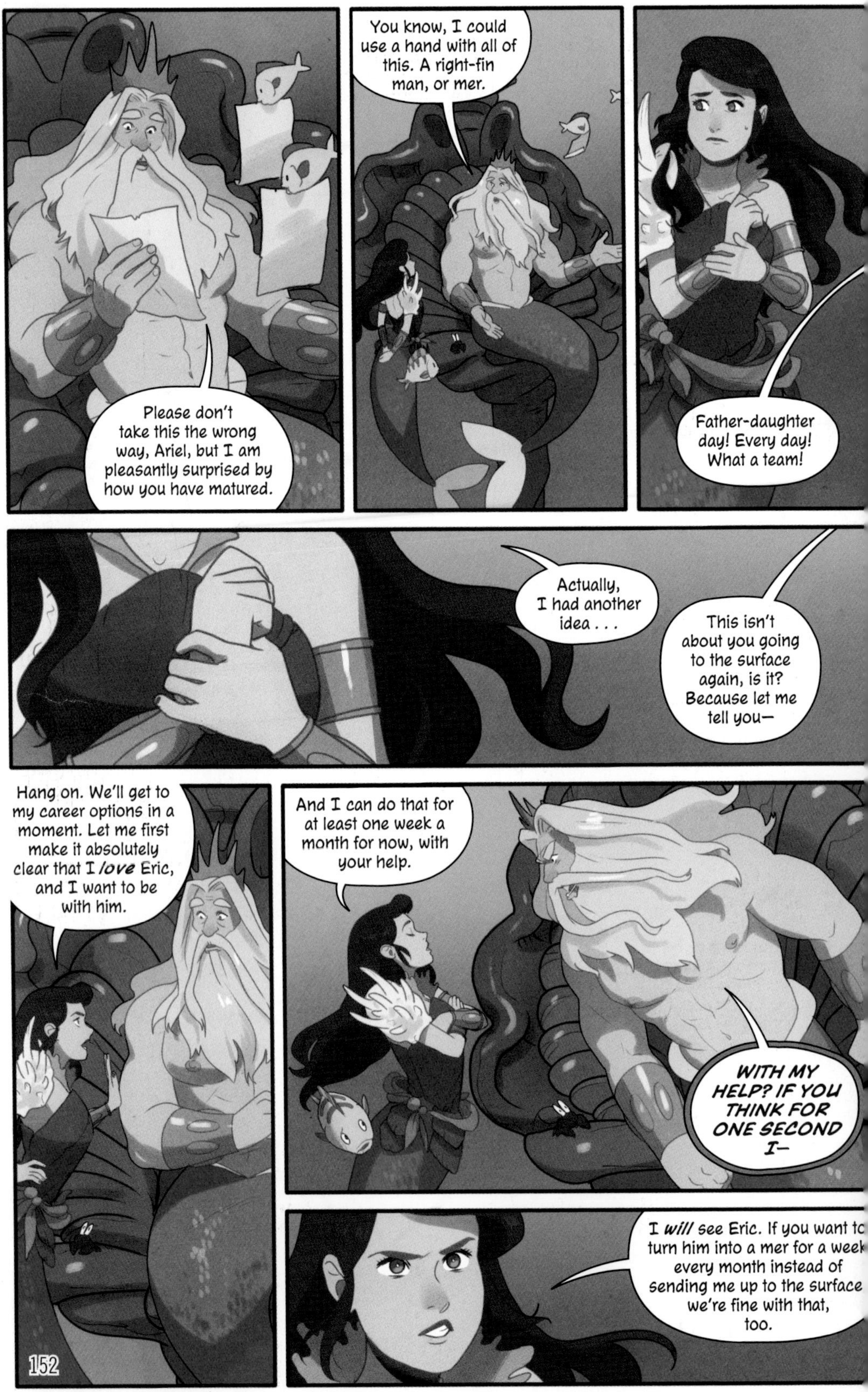

Please don't take this the wrong way, Ariel, but I am pleasantly surprised by how you have matured.
You know, I could use a hand with all of this. A right-fin man, or mer.
Father-daughter day! Every day! What a team!
Actually, I had another idea . . .
This isn't about you going to the surface again, is it? Because let me tell you—
Hang on. We'll get to my career options in a moment. Let me first make it absolutely clear that I *love* Eric, and I want to be with him.
And I can do that for at least one week a month for now, with your help.
WITH MY HELP? IF YOU THINK FOR ONE SECOND I—
I *will* see Eric. If you want to turn him into a mer for a week every month instead of sending me up to the surface, we're fine with that, too.

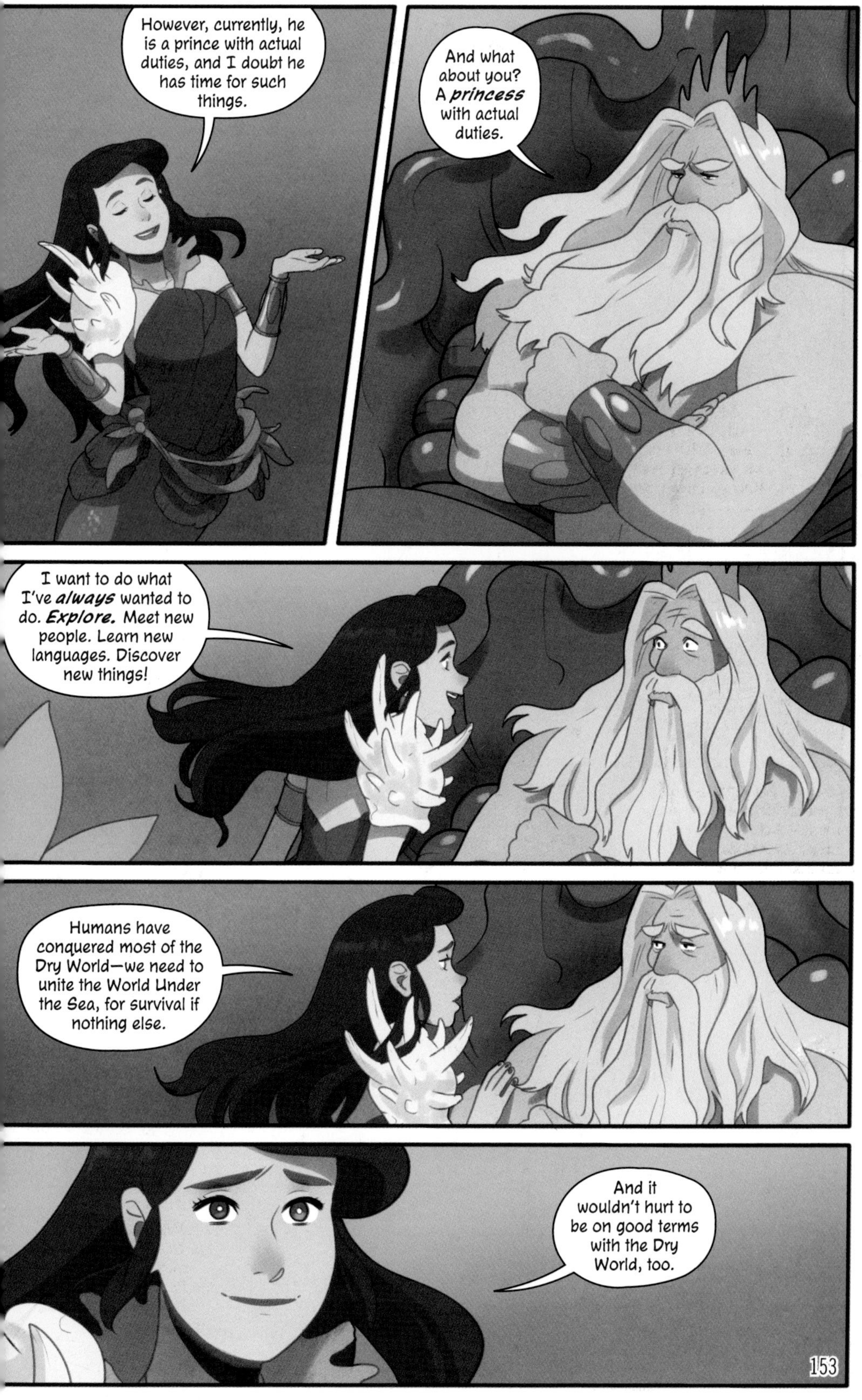
However, currently, he is a prince with actual duties, and I doubt he has time for such things.
And what about you? A *princess* with actual duties.
I want to do what I've *always* wanted to do. *Explore.* Meet new people. Learn new languages. Discover new things!
Humans have conquered most of the Dry World—we need to unite the World Under the Sea, for survival if nothing else.
And it wouldn't hurt to be on good terms with the Dry World, too.

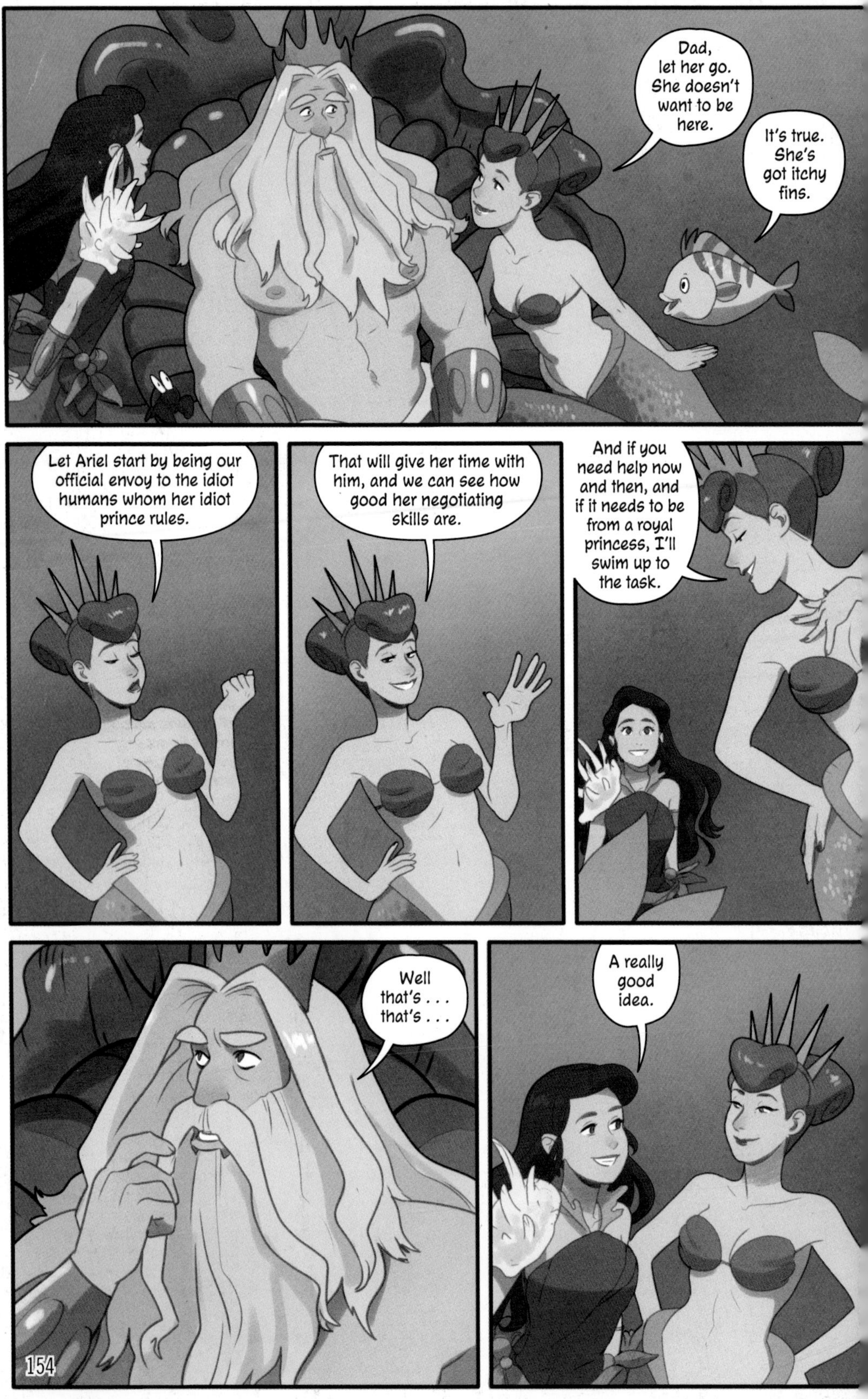
Dad, let her go. She doesn't want to be here.
It's true. She's got itchy fins.
Let Ariel start by being our official envoy to the idiot humans whom her idiot prince rules.
That will give her time with him, and we can see how good her negotiating skills are.
And if you need help now and then, and if it needs to be from a royal princess, I'll swim up to the task.
Well that's . . . that's . . .
A really good idea.

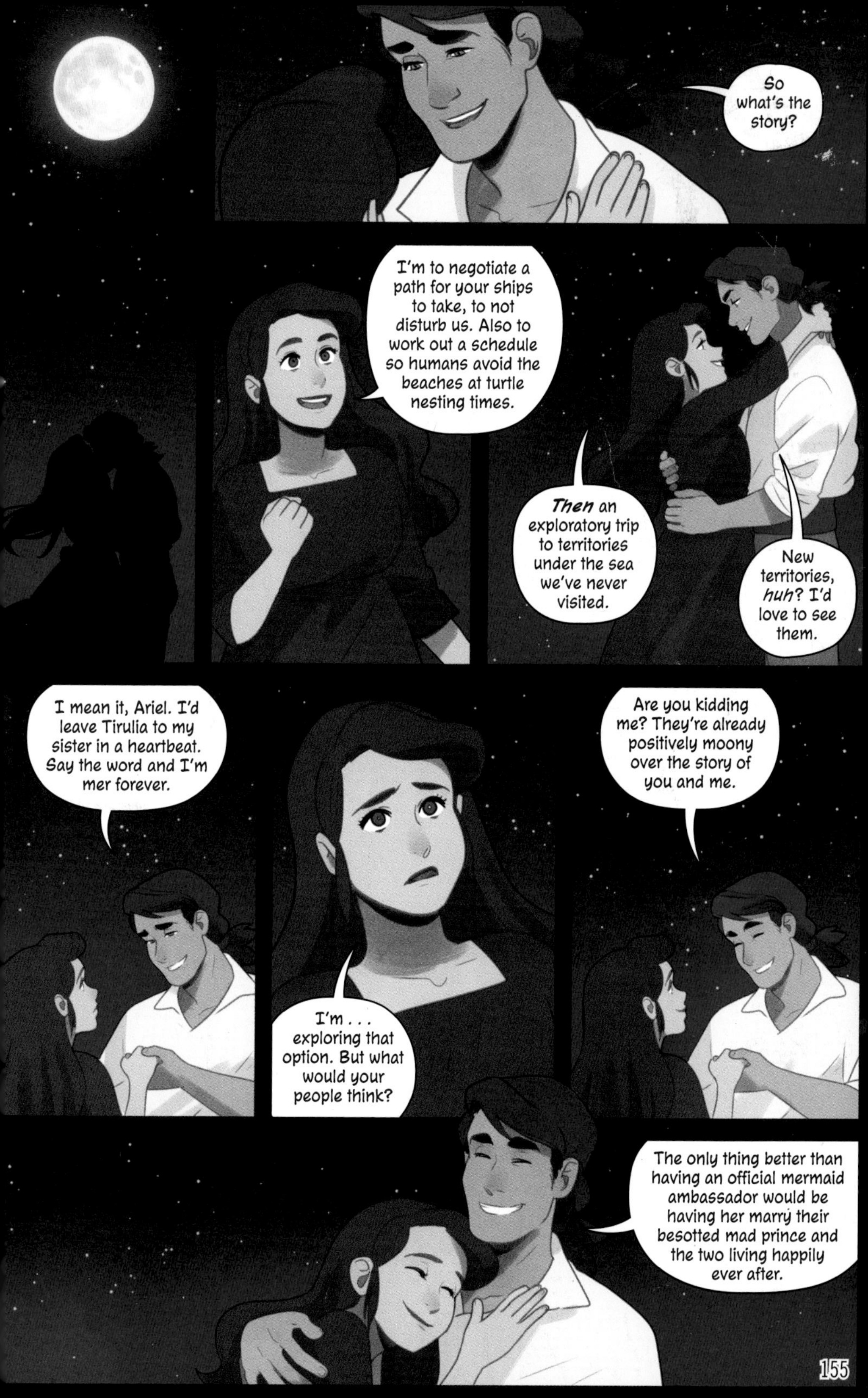
So what's the story?
I'm to negotiate a path for your ships to take, to not disturb us. Also to work out a schedule so humans avoid the beaches at turtle nesting times.
Then an exploratory trip to territories under the sea we've never visited.
New territories, *huh*? I'd love to see them.
I mean it, Ariel. I'd leave Tirulia to my sister in a heartbeat. Say the word and I'm mer forever.
I'm . . . exploring that option. But what would your people think?
Are you kidding me? They're already positively moony over the story of you and me.
The only thing better than having an official mermaid ambassador would be having her marry their besotted mad prince and the two living happily ever after.

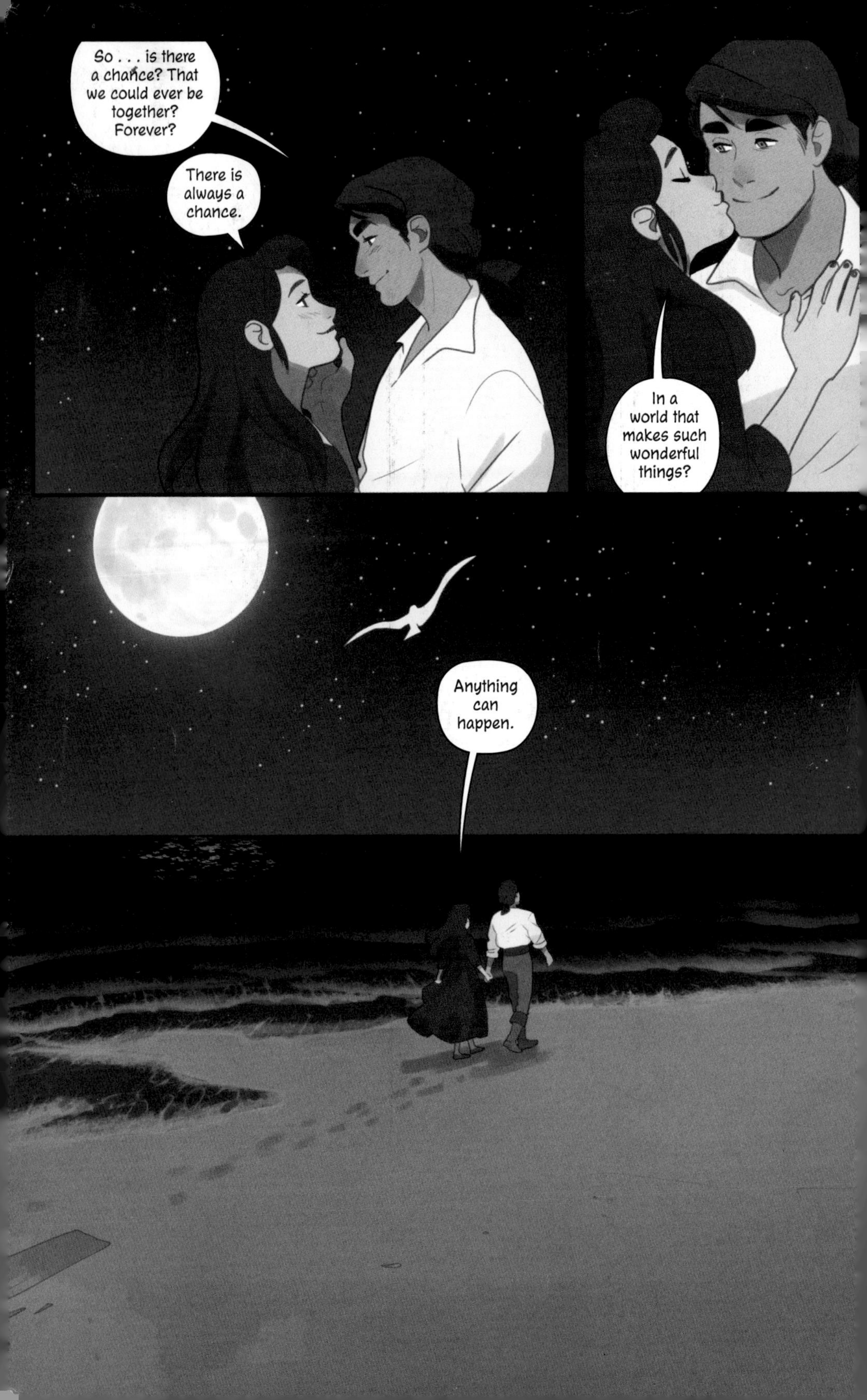
So . . . is there a chance? That we could ever be together? Forever?
There is always a chance.
In a world that makes such wonderful things?
Anything can happen.